Margaret Thornton was born in Blackpool and has lived there all her life. She is a qualified teacher but has retired in order to concentrate on her writing. She has two children and five grandchildren. Her previous Blackpool sagas, *It's a Lovely Day Tomorrow*, *A Pair of Sparkling Eyes*, *How Happy We Shall Be*, *There's a Silver Lining*, *Forgive Our Foolish Ways*, *A Stick of Blackpool Rock*, *Wish Upon a Star*, *The Sound of her Laughter*, *Looking at the Moon* and *Beyond the Sunset*, are also available from Headline and have been highly praised:

'A brilliant read'   *Woman's Realm*

'A gentle novel whose lack of noise is a strength'
                                                       The Sunday Times

'A delightful first novel'   Netta Martin, *Annabel*

All You Need Is Love

Margaret Thornton

HEADLINE

First published in 2001 by
HEADLINE BOOK PUBLISHING

First published in paperback in 2002
by HEADLINE BOOK PUBLISHING

10 9 8 7 6 5 4 3 2 1

ISBN 0 7472 6829 0

Typeset by
Letterpart Limited, Reigate, Surrey

Printed and bound in Great Britain by
Mackays of Chatham plc, Chatham, Kent

HEADLINE BOOK PUBLISHING
A division of Hodder Headline
338 Euston Road
LONDON NW1 3BH

www.headline.co.uk
www.hodderheadline.com

For all my family, with love

For Elaine and Steve;
David and Angela;
and my five lovely grandchildren,
Amy, Lucy and Sarah,
Robert and Christopher.
My love and thanks, as always, to my husband, John,
for his continuing encouragement and support.

Thanks, also, to my agent, Darley Anderson,
and to my new editor at Headline, Shona Sutherland.

Chapter 1

'I've told you, Mum, till I'm sick and tired of telling you. I don't want to go to Blackpool. I don't want to be dragged around looking at stupid old houses. Why do we have to move anyway? It's a stupid idea. I don't want to and neither does our Simon.'

Abbie Horsfall, as usual, bit her tongue. She would have liked to argue back at Sandra, above all to tell her exasperating daughter to remove that word from her vocabulary. Everything was 'stupid' at the moment – and how many more times could Abbie hear the words 'I don't want to' without retaliating? But Abbie hated arguing with anyone. She preferred, always, to be reasonable and try to see the other person's point of view, even when it was a fourteen-year-old girl who should, some might say, be put firmly in her place.

As I was at her age, thought Abbie, remembering her own mother and the way she had been dominated in her formative years. She knew this was the reason she was lenient with Sandra; she did not want her daughter to be repressed and to suffer, as a result, the same lack of confidence and self-esteem that she had done. Not that there was much chance of Sandie being subdued by anything or anybody, her mother thought with a wry smile. She was what one might call 'her own person' and Abbie guessed she always would be.

'Very well, dear,' Abbie answered now, quite calmly. 'I get

the message. You don't want to come house-hunting. All right then – you can stay with your gran and grandad and I will go on my own. That is, if Simon chooses not to come as well. But we *will* be moving to Blackpool when I have found a suitable house. I have made up my mind about that and—'

'As a matter of fact, I've already asked Gran if I can stay with her next weekend,' answered Sandie in an indifferent tone, which Abbie's own mother would have considered downright insolent, 'and she said, yes, of course I can. Gran enjoys having me. She says I'm very good company and that she's glad I'm not going with you.'

Abbie doubted her mother-in-law had said any such thing. Lily Horsfall was too diplomatic to make inflammatory statements, but it was true that Sandie got on very well with her grandmother, and Abbie was sure the girl did not behave in her grandparents' house in the same rebellious way that she did at home.

'And our Simon's not going to Blackpool neither,' her daughter added. 'Honestly, Mum, did you really expect him to when Norwich City's playing at home?'

'No, I daresay that's reasonable enough,' agreed Abbie, smiling a little. 'I'd forgotten his team were at home. So . . . you've got it all planned between you then, you and Simon. You're not coming?'

'Dead right, Mum. You've got it in one. Go to the top of the class.'

Again, Abbie refused to rise to the bait. 'Very well, dear,' she said again. 'I just thought you might enjoy a trip to Blackpool, especially at this time of the year. The Illuminations are on, you know.'

'How thrilling! I can't wait.' Sandie uttered the words under her breath, but not so softly that her mother could fail to hear.

'And I know you always like seeing Veronica,' Abbie continued, ignoring her remark. 'You get on well together, don't you, with you being about the same age?'

Sandie shrugged. 'She's all right, I suppose.'

'Grandad Winters'll be sorry you're not with me, you and Simon. He looks forward to seeing you.'

'For heaven's sake, Mum, can't you shut up about it? I've told you we're not going, and that's that. Anyway, if we go and live there, Grandad'll be seeing a lot of us, won't he? Are you going to stay with him this weekend, or are you staying with Aunty Doreen?' For the first time since they started this fruitless conversation Abbie noticed a slight flicker of interest in her daughter's eyes. Could it be regret that she might, after all, be missing something? But Abbie knew Sandra too well to hope she would climb down from the high stand she had taken. Besides, Abbie was already thinking that it would be far more peaceful for her to go to Blackpool on her own.

'I'm staying with your grandad and Aunty Faith,' she answered now. 'Doreen's place will be full up with visitors, with the Illuminations and it being half-term as well; but she says she'd like to go house-hunting with me. I've always fancied living in Bispham myself, or North Shore. Somewhere not too far from the sea. There's not much point in living at the seaside if you don't go and look at the sea now and again.' Although she did not want an out and out argument with her daughter, Abbie was determined that Sandra should be in no doubt as to her intentions. They would definitely be moving to Blackpool.

The girl was looking at her mother in a way that could only be called calculating. Her long legs, clad in tight-fitting jeans, were stretched out in front of her as she sprawled on the settee. Looking back at her, Abbie was reminded of her late husband, Peter. Sandie was so much like him it was uncanny. She had the same fairish hair which refused to curl. She wore it short with a wispy fringe and, so far, had not pestered to have a home perm as some of her friends had done. Her longish nose, too, and her wide mouth and slightly hooded eyes – brown, though, not blue as her father's had been – were exactly like Peter's. But whereas

3

Peter could never have been called handsome, Sandie was more than usually attractive. Not pretty, for her features were too large for a conventional prettiness, but Abbie guessed her daughter would grow into a stunning-looking young women.

If only she would smile a little more. It made all the difference to her face when she smiled. She was a volatile girl, her moods shifting suddenly like sunshine after rain. Abbie remembered how her daddy had used to tease her, when she was only a toddler, that she was like the little girl in the nursery rhyme. She could hear him now, in her memory, reciting the verse to Sandie:

> 'There was a little girl and she had a little curl,
> Right in the middle of her forehead;
> When she was good she was very, very good,
> But when she was bad, she was HORRID!'

They would shout out the last word together and laugh.

Yes, Sandra had always been very much her daddy's girl, far closer to him than Simon, two years younger, although Peter had tried not to show any favouritism. His death, six years ago, when Sandra was eight years old, had had a devastating effect on the little girl. This was another reason why Abbie tended to be more indulgent with her sometimes wilful daughter.

'I'll tell you something else Gran said.' Sandie stared at her mother with a guileless expression. 'She said she's surprised at you taking me away from school when I'm in the middle of my education. I'll be doing my O-levels in less than two years, you know. It would serve you right if I failed them all.'

Abbie drew in her breath and this time, when she replied, her tone was a good deal sharper. 'We'll have no talk of failure, young lady. That's nonsense as you well know. You're always up near the top of the class, so there's no chance you're going to fail, no matter which school you attend. I happen to know there are some very good grammar schools in Blackpool. It will be quite easy to arrange a transfer for you and Simon. And I'm sure we'll be able to find you a good music teacher as well.'

'D'you really think you will, Mum? Be able to find somebody as good as Mrs Halliday?' The girl sounded quite genuinely concerned now and the scornful look had gone from her eyes. She swung her long legs down from the settee and leaned forward, her elbows on her knees. Abbie, sensing a change in her mood, sat down at the side of her. She squeezed her arm briefly in an affectionate manner.

'Of course I will. I'll make it a number one priority, you can be sure of that.' Sandra had taken to piano lessons like a duck to water, as Peter had said, starting to learn when she was seven years old. His death, just over a year later, had made the little girl more keen than ever to succeed, and when she had recovered from the initial shock of losing him, she had said she wanted to 'play as good as Daddy'. She had now passed her Grade 6 exam with a Distinction and it seemed as though she would go from strength to strength. Her music was the main interest in her life although she worked well at school, too, and was nearly always, as her mother had reminded her, near the top of her class. She was in no way big-headed, for which Abbie was thankful. Her daughter did have her good points as well as the . . . not so good.

'I'm sure there must be any number of good music teachers in Blackpool,' said Abbie now. 'They take it very seriously up there. You've heard of the Blackpool Musical Festival, haven't you? Well, you'll be able to enter for that now. I'm surprised Mrs Halliday hasn't entered you before.'

'She said she wanted me to concentrate on my exams,' replied Sandie, 'because they were more important. D'you really think I'd be able to go in for the festival, Mum?' Blackpool Musical Festival was one of the largest and most famous of its kind. It was held at the Winter Gardens complex every autumn and attracted singers, instrumentalists and choirs not only from its own town, but from as far afield as Scotland, Cornwall and the Isle of Man.

'Of course you could,' replied Abbie. 'You'd knock spots off them all.'

'Oh, I don't know so much about that, Mum. There'd be fierce competition.'

'Yes, so there would, but I'm sure you'd do very well. It's something to look forward to, isn't it?' she added tentatively.

'Mmm.' When Sandie looked at her mother again her expression, and her tone of voice, were quite different. 'P'raps I might not mind it too much after all, moving to Blackpool. Look, you don't care about me not coming this weekend, do you? I've said I'll go out on Saturday night with Melanie and Susan.'

'No, I honestly don't mind.' Abbie breathed a thankful sigh. What a chameleon her daughter was, to be sure. 'Where are you thinking of going – to the pictures?'

'No, there's a disco at the Youth Club. We thought we might go there. There's ever so many going from our form, Mum,' Sandie added, as though sensing her mother might object. 'And I've told Gran. She say's it's all right for me to go. It's over at eleven anyway, so I shan't be late.'

Abbie nodded. 'Yes, very well. Go straight back to Gran's though, won't you?' she ventured, as her daughter seemed now to be in a more receptive mood.

''Course I will, Mum. Stop fussing.' The girl frowned slightly, hitching her legs up on to the settee again, this time curling them beneath her and returning to her *Bunty* magazine.

Eleven o'clock would have been considered very late in my day, thought Abbie. She well remembered what trouble she had been in, even at nineteen years of age, when she had returned home just a few minutes after ten o'clock, and not dead on the hour as her mother had insisted. Nor did the excuse of a lost cloakroom ticket or a missed tram carry any weight with an irate parent. It had been wartime, of course. There had been the black-out to contend with and the dance halls all closed at ten o'clock. Nevertheless, Abbie had been in hot water and had been confined to the house as a punishment, forcing her to miss a date with Peter, the RAF lad she had met in the Palace ballroom.

But that was all long, long ago. Light years away, it seemed now, although it was, in reality, just about twenty years. How times had changed. 'Discos', they were calling the dances now, usually at the Youth Club or the church hall. Abbie doubted that her daughter could get into much trouble there. Sandra did not appear, as yet, to be taking an interest in boys. Her friends were all girls, as she went to a single-sex grammar school. As for the sort of dancing they did these days, well, there seemed to be very little harm in that. Rock and roll consisted of jigging about on your own. It was certainly not the smoochy sort of dancing that had been all the rage in Abbie's youth, hands wandering all over the place as you drifted around the dance floor with some fellow or other. Not that she and Peter had behaved like that – not in public, at any rate – even after they had been engaged. But it was wartime, after all. Some girls had danced the night away in a young man's arms, only to hear, maybe the very next night, that he had been shot down in a bombing raid over Germany. As Peter had been . . .

Abbie found her thoughts returning to the past as she left her daughter to her magazine and went into the kitchen to prepare their tea. A mixed grill tonight; she took the bacon, sausages, mushrooms and tomatoes from the fridge, thinking that Simon would be hungry when he came in, as he always was. Perhaps she should do some fried bread as well, in the pan with the eggs? He was kicking a football around on the nearby field with his mates, but he would be home shortly as it was dropping dark. Sandra already seemed to be less antagonistic to the idea of Blackpool, she thought, as she snipped the rind from the bacon. But as for Simon . . . She was not too sure about her son. She had hoped he might be won round by the prospect of watching Stanley Matthews playing every fortnight at Bloomfield Road, then she had heard that the 'wizard of the dribble', as they called him, had recently been transferred. But maybe the prospect of watching First Division football instead of Third would be sufficient to persuade her football-mad son that a move would be no bad thing?

Abbie had lived here in the Norfolk market town of Wymondham for more than sixteen years, and she had been promising herself, ever since Peter's death, that one day she would return home. She still thought of the seaside town as home, as did all 'sand grown 'uns' – those who were born in and around the Fylde Coast. Lily and Frank Horsfall had been ideal parents-in-law, two in a million, Abbie often declared. Even now, when the news that their daughter-in-law wished to return to her home town must have come as something of a shock to them, they were trying hard to understand. Peter had been their only son. Consequently they were very close to and protective of their grand-children. To part from them would be a wrench, but Abbie was determined they would all keep in touch and visit one another as often as possible. Blackpool was not all that far away, especially in these days of motorway travel and faster trains. Abbie did not drive a car. She and Peter had never owned one as he had lived within walking distance of his place of employment, the Midland Bank. But that was something else Abbie had promised herself she would do after the move; learn to drive a car.

She had to admit that Peter had not been overly ambi-tious and, following his serious war injuries, he had lost much of his former 'get up and go'. He had returned to his previous occupation as a bank clerk, but although he worked hard and seemed contented enough he had never been given, or had even sought, promotion. Abbie had not cared about this. She had been only too thankful to have had him returned to her in what had seemed like a near miracle.

Abbie had been informed, in 1943, that Peter had been killed in a bombing raid over Germany. They had been engaged then and the wedding date had already been fixed. For more than a year she had believed he was dead, and it had been the biggest shock of her life when the news had come that he was, in fact, alive, though badly injured and suffering from the after-effects of concussion and loss of memory. For a time he had not been expected to live. Abbie had guessed that that was the reason he had been sent home from Germany on the exchange of prisoners scheme organised by the Red Cross movement, because they had believed he would not recover. The war had been drawing to a close when he returned to England in the spring of 1945. Lily Horsfall, such a generous-spirited woman, had always maintained that it was being reunited with his beloved Abbie that had given Peter the incentive to get well again, to pull himself out of the doldrums where he had lingered for a while after his return home.

They had married in the autumn of 1945 in Wymondham, not in Blackpool as they originally planned to do before Peter's near-fatal crash. And it was in Wymondham that they had settled down to married life; a very happy but, regrettably, short spell of only ten years. Sandra was born in the January of 1947, followed by Simon, a little more than two years later. Abbie had always had the presentiment, however, that she would not have her husband with her for very long. In the winter of 1955 he had died following an attack of pneumonia. His weakened constitution, due to the internal injuries from which he had never entirely recovered, had been unable to withstand the severity of the illness.

Abbie had been desolate for a time, missing his cheerfulness and his devoted love for her almost more than she could bear. She had hardly ever known her husband to be miserable or moody, except during those first dreadful few weeks after his return home when he had been in hospital and it had been 'touch and go'. She had the good sense, however, after her initial period of mourning, to be thankful for the ten contented years they had enjoyed together after she had believed he was gone from her for ever.

But it was now six years since his death and Abbie knew it was time for her to make some changes in her life. Her own father was in rather poor health, a couple of minor strokes having incapacitated him much more than he had believed was possible. Cedric Winters had been a well-respected and most competent doctor, and now, being well aware of what was happening to him, he was not taking kindly to the enforced strictures upon his formerly active life. His second wife, Faith, who had at one time been the nurse in his clinic, was extremely patient and loving. But Abbie felt she owed it to him, as his only daughter, to spend the last part of his life as near to him as possible. Who could tell anyway? He might live for years and years.

Besides, she knew she was ready for a change of scene, possibly a change of occupation as well. She had been working as a dentist's receptionist in Wymondham since 1954, when Simon was old enough to start school. She was confident that she would be able to find similar employment in Blackpool; on the other hand, she might branch out and try something completely different.

The sound of the back door opening then closing with a bang brought Abbie back from her wandering thoughts.

'Hi, Mum. What's for tea?' Simon dashed in. He peered beneath the eye-level grill, at the same time taking off his duffel-coat and unwinding his blue and white football scarf from around his neck. 'Sausages and bacon – smashing! Do lots of fried bread, will you, Mum? I'm starving!'

'So what's new?' Abbie smiled back at him, heartened as always by his cheery grin, but her smile dwindled a little when she saw the state of his boots. 'For goodness' sake, Simon, how many times do I have to tell you to leave your

10

boots outside? Just look at them. You've brought half the field in with you. Go on – out – this minute!'

'Oh, I forgot. Sorry.' He grinned again, beguilingly, before disappearing outside. There was the thump of heavy boots being dropped on the paved area outside the back door. Abbie knew he would clean them himself later. Simon was good like that, and with other jobs like carrying in the coal and making his own bed, and even occasionally washing or drying the pots. Recently he had seemed to be growing into the role of the man in the household.

Simon was a well-adjusted lad who had not experienced the same trauma as Sandra had over the death of their father. He had been younger, of course, and it had helped that he was more sanguine in temperament than his mercurial sister. Like Peter, in fact, easygoing and uncomplicated; but in looks he resembled his mother. His hair was dark and his deep brown eyes glowed with enthusiasm in a round rosy-cheeked face. There was a look of Peter, too, inevitably, but the face that smiled so disarmingly at Abbie was, she knew, very much like her own, except for the air of confidence. Never, as a child, had Abbie possessed such a self-assured manner as did both her son and her daughter.

Simon was back in a tick, sniffing the air appreciatively. 'Tea'll be ready that much faster if you set the table for me,' his mother informed him. 'Go and drag your sister away from her magazine and she can help you.'

'OK, Mum – will do.' His reply was cheerful. Not so Sandie's, as her brother told her, quite pleasantly but emphatically, to get off her bum and help with the tea.

'Aw, shurrup you! Don't have to, just 'cause you say so.' All the same, she did come, though wearing a martyred expression as she banged the cups and saucers on the table with more force than was necessary. Abbie knew her aggrieved air was largely assumed, and she had learned to take no notice of it.

On the whole they were not bad kids, she pondered as she

11

served out the mixed grill, not compared with some that she had heard about. And there were only two of them. Abbie, an only child, had never been used to the rough and tumble of life in a large family and could not imagine herself coping with more than two – unlike her friend, Doreen, whom she would be seeing that weekend. Doreen had five children – the eldest was fifteen and the youngest was nine – and she seemed to manage them all with good-humoured efficiency at the same time as running a boarding house. Abbie had never ceased to admire her and her commonsensical approach to life's ups and downs. Very little seemed to faze Doreen. Thinking about her now, Abbie realised afresh how much she had missed her. At one time, in the early war years, the two of them had been inseparable. Abbie was looking forward, on her return to Blackpool, to picking up the threads of their friendship. Every time they met it was as though they had never been apart.

Chapter 2

'I say, kid, just look at you! And to think you used to envy me because I was slim and dainty. At least, that was what you used to tell me.' Doreen was staring at her friend in wide-eyed admiration.

Abbie, smiling back at her, could see that their roles had indeed been reversed. Doreen, now, was positively plump – there was no other word for it – whereas she, Abbie, was certainly much slimmer than her friend.

'Well, remember that I'm a lot taller than you. I've never been able to do anything about that, have I? Yes, I did used to wish I was a dainty little thing like you. I always felt like a clod-hopping elephant when I was a girl. D'you remember that first time we went to the Palace together? You were all sweet and pretty in a pink and white frock, but goodness knows what I looked like! And I thought I was the bees' knees, honestly, in that dress from Sally Mae's.' Abbie's tone was wistful. That was the night she had first met Peter.

'You were elegant, though,' replied Doreen loyally. 'A bit old-fashioned, p'raps – but that was yer mam's doing – but you were real elegant, especially when you started choosing your own clothes, and that was something I never could be. 'Specially now. Not that I'm bothered.' She shrugged cheerfully. 'I've put on a bit of weight. So what?'

'I would've thought all the dashing about you do would help to keep your figure trim,' Abbie said. 'You lead a very busy life, don't you? I shouldn't imagine you have much time for yourself.'

'I sample all the dishes I cook, that's my downfall,' Doreen revealed. 'Pies, puddings, pastries – the lot. But I do make time for myself, believe me.' She nodded, winking slyly at her friend. 'You know what they say – all work and no play, et cetera. And this Jill certainly doesn't intend to be a dull girl. No . . . I've started going to night school two nights a week.'

'Oh, that sounds interesting. What subjects are you doing?'

'Cookery – well, Advanced Cookery it is really, 'cause I'm all right with the ordinary stuff. This is more your Cordon Bleu – you know, fancy pastries and foreign dishes an' all that. And on the other night I do Flower Arranging. That was one of my efforts on the little table in the hall. Did you notice it?'

'Yes, I did. Very impressive.' Abbie had been struck by the colourful arrangement of chrysanthemums and dahlias, interspersed with autumn foliage, which had caught her eye as soon as she came through the door. A bright and cheerful welcome, she had thought, for the visitors who crossed the threshold of *Dorabella*. That was the somewhat fanciful name Doreen had given to her boarding house, or private hotel, as they were now starting to be called, on Hornby Road, quite near to the town centre of Blackpool.

'It's all to do with your work, though, isn't it,' asked Abbie, 'cookery and arranging flowers? From what you were saying, I thought you might be doing something completely different – learning a language, perhaps, or painting, or Keep Fit.'

'Are you suggesting I need to keep fit?' Doreen laughed, patting at her waistline. 'And as for learning a language, well, you know I'm not much of a brain-box, not like you. No . . . it's the company you meet there that makes it interesting.' She leaned forward in her chair, lowering her voice, although there was no one but Abbie to hear. She winked again. 'I've met this ra-ather dishy fellow, you see.'

Abbie blinked rapidly, gaping open-mouthed at her friend for a moment before replying. 'What? You're seeing another man? But what about Norman?'

'What about him?' Doreen giggled. 'Oh, don't be so stuffy, Abbie. I'm not doing anything wrong. There's nothing like *that*. It's just that we get on well together, me and this fellow, that's all. I haven't even been out with him . . . yet. I just see him at night school; he goes the same two nights as I do, and we have a cup of coffee together and a chat. That's all,' she said, for the second time.

'You mean he goes to Advanced Cookery and Flower Arranging?' said Abbie, bemused.

'No, silly, of course not.' Doreen laughed again, and Abbie could see that the fair-haired, blue-eyed, petite girl that she had first met more than twenty years ago had not changed very much, at least not in her features. She was still pert and pretty and vivacious; Abbie could well imagine how any fellow might take a fancy to her. 'He's doing Car Maintenance and Conversational Italian, as a matter of fact. But they're on the same two nights as my classes and we met at the break. There's a snack bar in the main hall, and they serve tea and coffee and biscuits. We happened to be sitting at the same table and we got talking . . . and that was that.'

'Oh, I see. What's he called?' asked Abbie.

'His name's Ken. Not that it matters what he's called. I've told you, I'm not doing anything wrong.'

'Be careful, Doreen.' Abbie looked at her in some concern. 'I suppose there's no harm in it if you're just having a chat. But I thought you and Norman were happy. You must be. You've had five children, haven't you?'

'What's that got to do with it? Yes, of course we're happy. Or at least, we *used* to be happy. We still are, I suppose. I'd never really thought about it. We just jog along.'

15

'You were keen enough to marry him,' retorted Abbie. 'I remember when you first met him, you were tickled pink about getting friendly with the farmer's son.'

Abbie and Doreen had joined the Women's Land Army together in 1941, but after spending their initial training and their first farm placement together they had been separated. It was at her farm near Northallerton, in the North Riding of Yorkshire, that Doreen had met Norman Jarvis, some nine years older than herself. A studious young man, he had been to college to learn about the scientific approach to farming and was all set, one day, to take over his father's farm. And so he had done; then, three years ago, they had decided to sell up and move to Blackpool where several of Doreen's family still lived. Doreen had started the boarding house and Norman had gone to work as a gardener with the Parks Department. Abbie had thought, from the start, that the couple might be mis-matched, but she could tell that Norman thought the world of Doreen, as she seemed to do of him. And the fact that they were both Roman Catholics had made all the difference. It was this – recalling how uncompromising Doreen had used to be about her faith – that made Abbie wonder about her friend now. What on earth was she getting herself into? Had she really changed so much?

'We're all keen enough at first, aren't we?' sighed Doreen. 'And then the gilt wears off the gingerbread. It's bound to, isn't it?'

'Mine never did,' replied Abbie, sounding, she knew, a little pious and disapproving.

'Oh . . . I say, kid, I'm sorry.' Doreen's big blue eyes looked distressed. 'I wasn't thinking. You and Peter, well, that was a real love match, wasn't it?'

'Yes, so it was.' Abbie smiled a little sadly. 'It's more than six years since he died. I thought I was getting over it, but I suppose I'm still a bit vulnerable. Let's change the subject, shall we? How are the kids?'

'They're all very well. You could see that for yourself, couldn't you?' The children, all five of them, had come in to say hello to Abbie when she arrived and then, at Doreen's demands to 'make yourselves scarce', because she wanted to have a good old chin-wag with her friend, they had all disappeared again. There was Veronica, aged fifteen; Paul, thirteen; Teresa and Michael, the eleven-year-old twins; and Bernadette, usually known as Bernie, aged nine. Norman, a bespectacled, slightly balding man who was ageing, it seemed, far more rapidly than his wife, had come in as well to have a few words with Abbie before going off to watch television in the lounge with a few of the visitors who had stayed in, though most of them were out, seeing the Lights. Abbie liked Norman very much. He was pleasant and easygoing, as her own husband had been, and Abbie would hate to see him hurt. Surely Doreen would have more sense?

'I tried to persuade Sandie to come to Blackpool with me,' Abbie said now. 'I thought she and Veronica might get together and have a natter, but she had other ideas. You know what they're like at that age.'

'Don't I just,' said Doreen. 'Our Veronica's got a will of her own, I can tell you. I'm not so sure that your Sandie would get on so well with her now,' she added, a trifle cagily.

'Why's that? Has she got a boyfriend?' asked Abbie. 'She's a bit older than Sandie, of course. I suppose that'll be the next thing with her.'

'No, it's not that,' said Doreen. 'Sometimes I wish it was. No, she's gone all religious. Mass every Sunday – that goes without saying – and during the week an' all, and she never misses going to Confession. What's more, she's got this altar in the corner of the bedroom; fresh flowers every week in front of the statue of Our Lady. Our Teresa and Bernie aren't so keen on the idea, but she takes no notice of 'em.'

'But I thought you were all very keen,' said Abbie. 'I know you used to be. You put the rest of us to shame, the way you were so zealous about church attendance.' Abbie was C of E,

17

and she did attend morning service more often than not, but she was by no means fanatical.

'Well, we are and we're not,' replied Doreen, 'if you know what I mean. It's not as easy for me to go since I got the hotel, although Norman still goes quite regularly. And of course I made sure the kids were all confirmed. Veronica's the only one that's taken it really seriously, though, ever since her First Communion. Me, I hardly ever go to Confession now.' Doreen shrugged. 'I can't remember the last time I went. Veronica's always on at me to go.' She paused. 'She'd be on at me even more if she knew about what I've just been telling you.'

Abbie had often wondered at the way Catholics could seemingly square their consciences simply by going to Confession. Doreen, though, was not going at all; maybe she thought she had nothing to confess? Or too much. 'I thought we were changing the subject,' she said now with a wry glance at her friend. 'You don't think Veronica's got ideas about going into the Church, do you?'

'Good heavens, I hope not!' said Doreen. 'She's still at the Convent school, and the teachers there are all nuns, of course, so they do have quite an influence over the girls, but I'm hoping it's just a phase she's going through.'

'She could do worse,' Abbie pointed out.

'Oh yes, I agree. She's the brainiest of the bunch. Our Paul passed his Eleven Plus exam an' all – he's at St Joseph's – but the twins are at the Secondary Modern and I reckon that's where Bernie'll go as well. Anyroad, time'll tell . . . How's yer dad, Abbie? I expect he's glad you're moving back up here, isn't he?'

Abbie told her that she had found her father in pretty good health, and she learned that Doreen's father, too, was keeping quite well. He lived with his second daughter, Vera – Doreen was the eldest of the family – who had settled in Blackpool after her marriage. Vera came in each day to help Doreen in the hotel. Their brother Billy still lived in the town, but the younger girls, Peggy and Janey, had moved away.

'I expect your daughters help you as well, don't they?' asked Abbie. 'It can't be easy running a place this size and doing all your own cooking.' The hotel had twelve bedrooms, three of them occupied by the family themselves. Doreen had told her that twenty guests was a reasonable number to accommodate; more than that was pushing things a little, but even in the low season she usually had ten or twelve.

'The boys as well as the girls,' replied Doreen. 'They all have to pull their weight. The boys peel the spuds for me – they don't seem to mind doing that – and Veronica waits at table at weekends. I don't expect too much of her during the week as she's got her homework, and I've a regular waitress as well, of course – Sheila, she comes in every day. Our Vera does the bedrooms and helps with the change-over on a Saturday. As for the younger girls, our Teresa and Bernie, so long as they keep their belongings tidy and make their own beds, that suits me. They're all good kids. I've a lot to be thankful for.'

You have a good husband as well, thought Abbie, just as Doreen went on to say, 'And Norman helps with the suppers. We put on a hot drink at night for those that want it – tea or coffee, hot chocolate or Horlicks, and a biscuit – and Norman sees to that, asking 'em what they want, then making it and serving it out. Not that I expect him to – he's working hard all day, bless him – but he likes to spend some time with the guests, watching telly and chatting. We've had to put a big telly in the lounge; it's a must these days or the visitors don't want to come. There's been some changes since the war, I can tell you. Not that I knew much about the boarding-house trade before the war, but I gather it's changed quite a lot.'

'I see you've got central heating as well,' observed Abbie. 'It's lovely and warm in here.' They were sitting in the family's private lounge at the rear of the hotel, a smallish room, comfortably furnished, though overcrowded with a three-piece suite, a desk, a small TV set and a massive sideboard overflowing with papers, books, magazines, half-finished Airfix models, gloves and rolled-up socks – all the paraphernalia of daily living – in between the vases, family photographs and fruit bowl. Doreen had explained that the family dined in the large kitchen, fitting their mealtimes around those of the guests, and when the hotel was empty of visitors they sometimes took their meals in a corner of the dining room.

'Central heating? Yes, that's another "must" these days,' Doreen told her. 'It's more important now than it used to be because the season's longer. We get nearly as many people coming for the Lights in September and October as we do in the summer. Only one more weekend, thank God, then there'll be a bit of a respite till Christmas. We've decided to do a four-day break this year, Christmas Eve till the day after Boxing Day.'

'Goodness, you're a glutton for punishment!' Abbie wondered how on earth Doreen managed to fit in everything she did and still have time to go to night school.

'It's a case of needs must,' her friend explained. 'It's cost us a packet keeping up with all the modern trends. Wash basins in all the rooms and more lavs – two on each floor now; fitted carpets, bedside lights, sprung interior mattresses. Visitors are more demanding these days, and if they don't get all the mod cons they won't come. So we're trying to earn back some of the money we've spent.'

'Yes, I can see that,' said Abbie. 'You've got to keep your profit margin up, haven't you? On the other hand, you don't want to get too pricey or the ordinary visitors won't come. I expect they still come mainly from the Lancashire inland towns, don't they – Blackburn, Burnley, Oldham and all those places?'

'Mainly from there,' Doreen nodded. 'They still have their

Wakes Weeks.' This was a tradition that had started when all the cotton mills had closed down for a week during the summer – 'wake' being the old word for holiday. Many of the mills, alas, were no longer operative, at least not for the production of cotton, but the term was still used. 'They come from further afield as well – Wales and the Isle of Man, and we've even had a few from down south. Blackpool's becoming much more of a national resort, especially when the Lights are on. They get better each year, or so they tell me. I never have time to see 'em meself. We're up against it, though, with the pirate landladies. That's what we call 'em in the trade. Damn nuisance, they are.'

'Pirate landladies?' queried Abbie.

'Aye, them as take visitors in private homes – ordinary semis and the like – without being registered as proper catering establishments.' Doreen looked and sounded indignant. 'It needs putting a stop to, but it seems there's no way round it. They just say they're entertaining friends, you see, and you can't prove otherwise. Then there's the holiday camps, any amount of 'em springing up, and self-catering flats – there's all the competition from them. A lot of folk prefer to go to Devon or Cornwall. The sea's warmer down there and they happen get a bit more sunshine. But I don't think, meself, that Blackpool'll ever be beaten. It's on the up and up and I can't see it ever losing its popularity.'

'Spoken like a true landlady,' laughed Abbie. 'You're really heart and soul into all this, aren't you? You deserve to do well, Doreen. I can see you work very hard, and I'm sure there's no hotel in the whole of Blackpool that's more comfortable than this one.'

'It's nice of you to say so.' Doreen was smiling proudly and Abbie could tell she was pleased at her friend's comments. 'Home from home, this place. That's what I like to think. We're still doing three meals a day. Cooked breakfast, midday dinner and high tea – that's just cold meat and salad, or sometimes fish and chips. And supper as well, like I was

21

telling you. And here comes the man himself, to see what we want,' she added as her husband, right on cue, entered the room.

'Now, girls, what are you having?' Norman beamed at them. 'Tea, coffee, chocolate, Horlicks, Ovaltine?' They both opted for Ovaltine, Abbie feeling that tea or coffee would keep her awake. She knew she would find it hard to settle in a strange bed, especially after an evening spent in endless chatter.

'You've got a gem of a husband there,' she could not help reminding her friend, after Norman had brought their drinks and departed again, though he promised to come and have a chat with Abbie before she left.

'You don't have to tell me – I know,' replied Doreen, a trifle huffily. 'Yes, Norman is worth his weight in gold an' all that. Dull gold, though – there's not much sparkle to him these days.'

'So who wants sparkle?' said Abbie. 'Often it's superficial, and that's something Norman certainly is not. He's loyal and kind and trustworthy.' She could see that he might be the teeniest bit boring, but she wasn't going to admit that to her friend. 'And I don't suppose he feels very sparkling when he's done a day's work. It's quite hard manual labour, isn't it, working for the Parks Department, all that digging and planting?'

'Backbreaking, certainly,' agreed Doreen. 'Not as hard as farming was, though. We know that for ourselves, don't we?'

'Too true.' Abbie smiled ruefully, remembering her days as a Land Girl. That work had been gruelling at times, but looking back she wouldn't have wanted to miss a day of it. 'We had some good times, didn't we, Doreen? D'you remember old man Rawnsley?'

'Could I ever forget him?' Doreen hooted with laughter. Mr Rawnsley had been the curmudgeonly farmer at their first placement, before the two girls went their separate ways. They found themselves, inevitably, reminiscing.

'And how time flies,' observed Doreen, when they had spent several moments down Memory Lane. 'It's twenty years since we joined up, and now we're pushing forty. I can hardly believe where the years have gone.'

'I turned forty last January,' Abbie admitted, 'and you'll be forty next March, won't you?'

'Don't remind me!' Doreen gave a mock shudder. 'But that's when life begins, isn't it? Or so they say. P'raps that's what I'm waiting for – something exciting to happen. You just jog along, year after year, in the same old routine, and then, before you know it, it's too late.'

'Too late for what?'

'Oh, I don't know. Excitement, romance . . . It seems a long time since I had any of that.'

'Don't you and Norman ever go away on holiday?' asked Abbie. 'That's a time when you can enjoy one another's company. Peter and I always used to love our holidays.'

'We only go up to Richmond to see Norman's parents.' Doreen sounded somewhat disgruntled. 'It's a nice little place, I admit, but not very exciting.' That word again; Doreen seemed to be craving excitement. 'We can't go in the summer because of this place. We usually go in March or April when the kids have their Easter break, and it's blooming cold up in North Yorkshire at that time of the year.'

'Perhaps you could go somewhere down south instead,' suggested Abbie. 'Just the two of you . . . that is, if you could leave the children? There's Torquay or Bournemouth, or you could even go abroad. It's very nice in Brittany. Peter and I went there once. Or what about Paris? That would be exciting, wouldn't it, and very romantic.' Doreen obviously needed to re-kindle the spark in her marriage before it went out completely; Abbie was worried about the restlessness that was apparent in her friend. The Jarvises could not be all that short of money; they should be able to afford a good holiday.

'Paris in the springtime, eh? Ooh, la la! That would be

quite something, wouldn't it?' said Doreen musingly. 'With the right person, of course. Take no notice of me, I'm just being daft,' she added as Abbie looked at her reprovingly. 'Yes, happen I'll suggest it to Norman. We could do with a change, that's for sure, but I don't know about leaving the kids. I'd have to think about that. Now, when do you want to go house-hunting?'

Abbie noticed that Doreen abruptly changed the subject as Norman re-entered the room. It was obvious she was not going to suggest to him now that they should take a holiday on their own. Would she ever? Abbie wondered.

'I've promised to go with you, remember,' Doreen went on. 'Just tell me when. You'll be starting on Monday, I suppose?'

'Yes, that's what I thought,' replied Abbie, 'but I'm wondering how on earth you'll manage it, you're so busy,'

'Oh, I can spare a few afternoons, can't I, Norman? Mornings are the busiest times, but our Vera'll work extra hours if I ask her nicely, and teas are quite easy to prepare. Happen you could sort out a few properties in the mornings, eh, then we could go and see them in the afternoons.'

'I'm glad Doreen's going with you, Abbie,' said Norman. 'It'll do her good to get away from this place for a few hours. I'm always telling her she works too hard, although I suppose there's nothing she can do about that. A boarding house is blooming hard work. That's why I'm pleased she's going to night school. At least it's a change of scenery, isn't it?'

'Er, yes,' Abbie said. 'She's been telling me about it.'

'And what about this house you're looking for,' asked Norman. 'Where do you fancy living? The Stanley Park area, near where your father lives?'

'No, I don't think so,' replied Abbie. 'Sometimes you can be too near. He's happy enough that we'll be living in the same town; we don't need to be on top of one another. The bus service is very good here, and I'm thinking of learning

24

to drive when we get settled. I rather fancied Bispham – North Shore, at any rate; somewhere not too far from the sea.'

'Houses are pricier up there,' Doreen pointed out. 'It's where the posh folk live.' She grinned. 'But I suppose money's no object, eh, Abbie? You're a woman of means now.'

'Oh, I wouldn't say that,' Abbie told her, 'but I'm hoping I can manage to buy a house without having to get a mortgage. I doubt if I'd get one anyway, being a widow. They're very cagey about lending money to women on their own. Our house is already sold, provisionally; people told me that was the best way to do it – to get a sale first and then start looking. But it means I can't waste much time. I'll have to find something fairly quickly.'

She knew there was no malice or envy in Doreen's remark about the money. There might have been at one time, when they first met. Abbie had been the strictly brought-up daughter of wealthy parents – wealthy by Doreen's standards, at any rate – living in a large house on Whitegate Drive, whereas Doreen had been one of six children from a small terraced house in the Central Drive area, known as Revoe. They had met when Abbie, at her father the doctor's request, had taken some clothes round to this much poorer family. Against all the odds, the two girls, so different in background and temperament, had become friends. Now, twenty years later, money, or the lack of it, was no longer an issue between them. Both women had done quite well for themselves.

Abbie had been left a legacy by her mother, who had died towards the end of the war, and another by her beloved Aunt Bertha who had died only a couple of years ago. This money, together with the proceeds of the sale of the house in Wymondham, should be able to buy what the estate agents would call a 'desirable residence' for Abbie and her two children.

'Will you be going out to work when you come to live in Blackpool?' asked Doreen. 'Or are you going to be a lady of leisure?'

'No chance of that,' laughed Abbie. 'I shall be finding a job, don't you worry. School uniforms and music lessons and bicycles don't pay for themselves. I've got my widow's pension, and I suppose I'm not too badly off, but I shall certainly get a job.'

'That'll be no problem for you,' said Doreen. 'You'll easily get a job. You're real brainy.'

'So you keep saying, but I'm not, you know.' Abbie shook her head. 'Well, I did get my School Certificate, way back in the Dark Ages, but I've no qualifications, have I, and that's what they seem to want more of these days.' She had left school at sixteen, at the insistence of her domineering mother who had wanted her tied to her apron strings. She had worked as a receptionist, then as an unqualified nursing assistant at her father's surgery. Joining the Land Army in 1941 had given her her first, long-overdue taste of freedom.

'Neither have I, but I've managed all right,' said Doreen airily.

'It's a pity not to make use of your School Certificate, though, Abbie,' said Norman, in his usual serious tone. 'I know you say it was ages ago, but it's still valid. You could train for something – get those qualifications you were talking about.'

'What? At my age?'

'Why not? It's never too late.' He shook his head solemnly.

'That's what I've been telling her; it's never too late,' added Doreen brightly. 'We weren't talking about exams though, were we? Didn't I say, Abbie, that life begins at forty?' She giggled and Abbie smiled back at her in a conspiratorial way. She didn't want to encourage her. Her friend's disclosures about the man at night school, although she might be making more of it than it really was, had surprised Abbie,

26

even shocked her a little – but Doreen's high spirits were infectious.

'What would I train for?' said Abbie. 'All the skills I had, if I ever had any in the first place, are rusty by now.'

'Don't sell yourself short,' said Norman. 'You worked for your father, didn't you, as a nursing assistant? And you've been a dental receptionist. Why don't you go and train to be a nurse?'

'Because I hated it, that's why,' Abbie admitted. 'I wasn't a proper nurse and I never wanted to be. Some of the things I had to help my father with made me squirm. Ugh!' She shuddered slightly. 'I hadn't the courage to tell him, not till later. No, that's definitely out.'

'You could go to training college and become a teacher,' Norman suggested. 'I know of quite a few people who have done that. Mature students, they call them. There's a Training College at Chelford, which isn't very far away – only forty minutes or so on the train. You'd be sure to get a grant, Abbie. They're crying out for teachers, so I've heard.'

'You've got it all cut and dried, haven't you?' said Abbie, smiling at him. 'It's something I might have considered, if I were younger. I've never had a lot to do with children, though, apart from my own.'

'You'd soon learn. You'd make a marvellous teacher, Abbie.'

'Oh, for heaven's sake, Norman, leave her alone!' Doreen said irritably. 'P'raps she doesn't want to be a boring old teacher. I say, Abbie, did you know they're pulling the Palace down? I meant to tell you earlier when you were talking about us going there, then we got side-tracked.'

'No!' exclaimed Abbie. 'Why on earth are they doing that? It was such a popular place, with the ballroom and the cinema and the variety theatre. Oh dear, what a shame.'

'Seems as though it's not as popular as it used to be,' said Doreen. 'Happen they think they've enough ballrooms, what with the Winter Gardens and the Tower. Apparently it's going to be a big department store. The site's been bought by the Lewis's group.'

The end of an era, thought Abbie. No doubt she would see many more changes when she moved back to Blackpool; things never stayed the same. But that was life; you had to move on, look towards the future. She said as much to Norman when he ran her back to her father's home at the end of the evening.

'I'll think about what you said, Norman, about the training college. It might be an idea. I feel as though I'm in a rut, not really getting anywhere, and I know I've to think about the future, not the past.'

Norman stopped the car – a brand new Ford it had been when they moved to Blackpool five years ago, and it was still his pride and joy – outside the bungalow where Cedric and Faith Winters lived, placing his hand fleetingly over Abbie's. 'You still miss Peter, don't you?' he said, his voice warm with understanding. 'I can tell.'

'Yes, I do.' She sighed a little. 'It's when I see couples together, and their families. Happy couples . . . I feel as though there's something missing in my life, which there is, of course. Yes, I miss him, but life has to go on. It's a cliché, I know, but very true.'

'I doubt if Doreen would miss *me*,' said Norman, not sadly or mawkishly, just as though he were stating a fact.

'Of course she would!' Abbie turned to stare at him. 'What a thing to say! Besides, you're not . . . going anywhere, are you?'

'I hope not. Not yet awhile.' He gave a chuckle. 'It's just that she's so busy with a thousand and one things, I sometimes wonder if I matter to her at all. She's so restless, too. You must have noticed it?'

'A little,' said Abbie evasively. 'I don't think it's anything to worry about, Norman. And of course you matter to her. The children are all growing up, aren't they? Perhaps she feels her role in life is changing.'

'She's getting broody, you mean?' Norman grinned. 'That's an idea.'

'No, I don't think so,' said Abbie quickly. 'That's not what I meant. Look, maybe you could try to spend a little more time together, just the two of you. Oh dear, that's awfully cheeky of me, isn't it? I'm not criticising, really I'm not, but she's so wrapped up in the hotel, and now . . . now there's this night-school thing,' she added daringly. 'Don't let yourself get pushed aside, Norman.' More than that she must not say.

'No. I don't suppose it's Doreen's fault that we don't spend as much time together as we used to,' said Norman, sighing a little. 'A boarding house is a hard taskmaster. But it was what she wanted. I was thinking perhaps we could have a little holiday together, though, just Doreen and me, perhaps next spring, before the season starts.'

'What a good idea,' said Abbie. All the better if the suggestion was to come from Norman. 'Just what you need. Don't worry.' She patted his hand affectionately. 'Doreen thinks the world of you; I know she does. She's rushed off her feet, that's the top and bottom of it. I must go, Norman – they'll be waiting up for me. Thanks for the lift.' She leaned across and kissed his cheek. 'I'll see you again before I go back to Norfolk.'

'I'm glad you're coming back here,' said Norman, returning her kiss, holding on to her arm momentarily as though for moral support. 'She takes notice of you; she always did. Goodnight, Abbie love. God bless.'

Chapter 3

Doreen did not mention the man she had met at night school when Abbie saw her two days later; in fact, she made no reference to him all week, all the time they were house-hunting. Nor did she complain again about Norman. Not that she had found fault with him unduly; she had just given the impression that she found him rather boring and set in his ways. On reflection Abbie realised it was Norman, more so than Doreen, who had bemoaned the fact that his wife no longer seemed to have much time for him. Abbie knew that Doreen had sensed her disapproval, hence her silence. Abbie was relieved at this. She did not want to be the recipient of any more confidences, from either of them, although she would do anything she could to help if she thought their marriage was in serious trouble.

But she did not think it was. They were probably going through a period of, not exactly boredom, but complacency, when living with the same person for umpteen years – sixteen, Abbie thought it was – started to pall a little. Maybe that was what happened to all couples at that crucial time in their marriage. Whenever a thought like that occurred to Abbie she was aware, at the same time, of a feeling of smugness because she was convinced it could never have happened to her and Peter. She would nod to herself a little self-righteously. Doreen and Norman – especially Doreen – should count their blessings and be thankful they still had a partner to complain about.

Times were changing, though. The ordinary folk, the men or women in the street, could not fail to be influenced to some degree by the radical changes that were taking place in their country and even further afield. There was a spirit of restlessness abroad. Earlier that year the building of the Berlin Wall had followed a serious deterioration in the relationship between the Communist and Western powers. Last year the Prime Minister, Harold Macmillan, had spoken about the 'wind of change', declaring that, 'Whether we like it or not, this growth of national consciousness is a political fact.' Opposition to the wind of change had led to a dreadful massacre in Sharpeville, South Africa, of seventy black protestors, demonstrating against the carrying of identity cards. Later in that year of 1960, on a much happier note, the United States of America had elected a new President, John F. Kennedy. He had been an unlikely candidate for the Democratic nomination, being young and a Catholic, but he had won and the White House was rapidly coming to be regarded as a glamorous and fashionable place.

In Britain, strait-laced morality was starting to go out of fashion. It was about a year ago, Abbie recalled, that Penguin Books had been prosecuted by the Crown for the publication of D.H. Lawrence's notorious novel *Lady Chatterley's Lover*. The prosecution failed and the book, written in the 1920s, became an immediate best-seller. The message seemed to be that people were now free to read whatever they chose without the interference of a moralising government. Abbie had still not read the book. She did not consider herself a prude, but it was hard to throw off the shackles of her childhood. Twenty, thirty years later, the dictates of an overbearing mother were still difficult to ignore.

Her father, though, seemed much freer and more relaxed these days, much happier – although Abbie felt this was a dreadful thing to say or even think – since her mother had died. Especially so since he had married Faith, not long after the end of the war. She had noticed a physical change in

31

him, however, since the last time she saw him. He was thinner and greyer and his features were more gaunt. One side of his face had been affected, though only imperceptibly and only discernible to those who knew about it, by his last stroke, and his speech was a little blurred, again, not so much that you would notice. Abbie noticed, however, and she was glad she had made the decision to come back to Blackpool.

'You must get out and about while you're here,' her father told her. 'You and Faith could go and see a show, or a film. You used to like going to the pictures, you and Doreen Miller. I remember a time when you went twice a week.'

'That's going back a bit, Dad.' She usually called him Dad now, not Father. It had always sounded so stiff and starchy, a product of her upbringing, but he had not commented on the new form of address. She laughed. 'It was before we joined the Land Army, twenty years ago. And she's Doreen Jarvis now, has been for years.'

'Yes, yes, I know; of course she is.' He sounded a little impatient. 'Nice girl – I'd like to see her again. Why don't you bring her round while you're here this week?'

'Yes, perhaps I will. We're going to look at some more houses tomorrow afternoon, so we'll pop in when we've finished, if Doreen has time. She's very busy with the hotel. She may have to dash back to see to the teas.'

'Busy, busy . . . everybody's busy these days.' Cedric Winters drummed his fingers impatiently on the arm of his chair. 'Sign of the times; nobody can keep still.'

Abbie knew his enforced curtailment of strenuous activity was sitting heavily on him. He read, he did the crossword in the newspaper, he pottered in the garden, he went for short walks in nearby Stanley Park and sometimes Faith drove him down to the promenade and they took a stroll, enjoying the sea air. He also watched a good deal of television. But Abbie well remembered a time when her father could never keep still; when he was the only doctor in a busy practice and he had, of his own volition, started a free clinic for his not-so-well-off patients. She exchanged a knowing and sympathetic glance now with Faith. Faith was small, slender and dark and looked much younger than her years. She was in her late fifties, some fifteen years younger than Cedric. Abbie knew she was an excellent wife and helpmate for him; loving, understanding and competent, but able, also, to stop him from feeling too sorry for himself.

'I think it's a good idea for us to go to a show,' said Faith, 'or a film, if you prefer, Abbie. You could come with us, Cedric,' she added brightly. 'There's nothing to stop you, is there? It would do you good to have a change. I think we watch a great deal too much television.'

'So you're always telling me,' replied Cedric, 'but you know you enjoy it just as much as I do . . . especially a certain programme.' There was a decided twinkle in his eye, and Abbie knew to which programme he was referring. It had surprised her that her father and Faith enjoyed *Coronation Street* so much; she could well imagine what her mother's reaction would have been to the goings-on of such 'common' people.

It was less than a year ago that the story of life in a northern street had first appeared on the television screen; and now the characters of Ken Barlow, Elsie Tanner, Jack and Annie Walker, Leonard Swindley, not to mention that indomitable trio, Ena, Martha and Minnie, were as well known to many folk as were their own family members. And often a good deal more interesting. Abbie's father had always taken an interest in ordinary folk and what made them 'tick'. She had thought he might have preferred *Emergency Ward Ten*, but both he and Faith declared it was not true to life; nurses and doctors were never so glamorous and they could not relate to these dazzling characters. Cedric also watched documentaries, the nightly news, and sports programmes, especially football. At one time he had followed this sport keenly, being a regular supporter of the 'Seasiders' at Bloomfield Road, something which was now denied to him as he would not be able to stand the pressure of the crowds. So, all in all, television had been a very good thing for her father since he became ill, though he and Faith might not like to admit to the hours they spent watching it.

'I tell you what I wouldn't mind doing,' Cedric continued. 'I don't care for the cinema very much, Faith, not now – you know that – but I wouldn't mind having a look at the Lights. Ena Sharples switched them on this year, Abbie, did you know?' He sounded quite elated. 'Miss Violet Carson, I ought to say. A local lady she is – lives up at Bispham. I believe the crowds loved her. It was all reported in the *Evening Gazette*, wasn't it, Faith?'

'Yes, apparently she was very elegant, dressed in grey satin and silver lamé, then she did a quick change into her old coat and hairnet.' Faith laughed. 'The crowds in Talbot Square went wild, so it said. Yes, we'll go and see the Illuminations, Cedric. What a good idea! I'll drive us round, of course. Perhaps if we go tonight it won't be so busy; the weekenders have mostly gone back by Monday. We'll have a look at the *Gazette* as well, Abbie, and see what's on in town. I know *West Side Story* is on at the Opera House, the stage production from London. Or you might prefer the cinema. Here, have a look for yourself.'

Abbie had almost forgotten, while living in the quiet Norfolk market town, what a variety of entertainment there was to be found in Blackpool. A dozen or more cinemas, several live theatres, two magnificent ballrooms, a circus, ice-skating, swimming, or wrestling for those so inclined. She ran her finger across the cinema adverts. *Breakfast at Tiffany's* at the Hippodrome, *A Taste of Honey* at the Odeon. Somehow, she thought Sheelagh Delaney's portrayal of life in a squalid bedsit would not appeal to Faith, probably not to herself, either. *Singin' in the Rain* was on at the ABC. Finally she decided on that one and Faith agreed it was a nice happy choice. They would go on Wednesday night. Sheer escapism, but what did that matter? You went to the pictures to enjoy yourself, not to be made miserable. That was Faith's point of view, more so these days since her dear husband's illness, and Abbie agreed with her.

'I only wish he'd come with us,' Faith whispered to her. 'He would enjoy it if he did, but he hates crowds these days, and there's no getting away from them in Blackpool. Also he says the cinema seats are too small for his long legs. Anyway, we'll make sure he enjoys the Illuminations tonight.'

When he retired Cedric had sold his large Hillman car, much to his disappointment, but he could see it made sense to own a smaller vehicle. He had changed it for a Morris Minor, which was more economical to run and easier to drive and to park. Faith now did the driving; that was something else he was having to come to terms with, but he was sensible enough to know his limitations. He could not resist a tiny grumble, however, as he lowered his tall frame into the front passenger seat. His slight tetchiness was a part of him now; his wife had come to expect it and he was sometimes guilty of putting it on for effect.

'These cars were built for dwarfs, not six-footers like me,' he said. 'It's like those confounded cinema seats. And these new toy cars are even worse. Did you ever see the like?' He turned to his daughter in the back seat. 'Whatever you do, Abigail, don't go buying one of those newfangled things. You'd have to cut a hole in the roof for your head to poke through.'

'He means those Mini-Minors,' said Faith smiling. 'He thinks they look like kiddies' pedal cars.'

'So they do, rather.' Abbie was amused. 'No, I won't be getting one of those, Dad. I'd thought of something like this one; I'm not quite as tall as you. But that's all in the future. I've to settle on a house first.'

'Are you sitting comfortably?' Faith asked her husband, a roguish gleam in her eye. 'Very well then. Off we go!'

It was a few years since Abbie had seen the Illuminations, the 'Lights' as they were fondly referred to by both residents and visitors. Not that the residents, by and large, bothered to go and see them, though they boasted about them to others. Sometimes they caught a glimpse of a section of them when making their way to a meeting or a place of entertainment in the town, or, feeling guilty at their lack of enthusiasm, they might take a hurried trip round on the last night before they were switched off for another year. Abbie's memories of the Lights stretched back to her childhood when her Aunt Bertha had, occasionally, taken her on a tram ride the length of the promenade. During the war years they had not shone, and since that time Abbie had seen them only twice, when she and Peter had brought the children on a visit to Blackpool. It was the same with Cedric and Faith; with the typical nonchalance of Blackpudlians they had simply 'not bothered'.

Faith drove along Whitegate Drive and Hawes Side Lane so they could start at the southern end, which was the customary way of doing things. All three of them were impressed, even more than they expected to be, by the colourful and dazzling spectacle which was opening up before them now, stretching all the way from Squire's Gate to the cliffs at Bispham. There was a fairy glen at South Shore, and an Alice in Wonderland scene with all the familiar characters Abbie remembered from childhood. Something about the Lights brought out the child in everyone. From the Central station area to Talbot Square you drove through a Toytown scene, with dolls, soldiers, teddy bears and golliwogs peering down on you, then on to the birds and bees fluttering and flickering between the lamp standards on the North Promenade. Abbie loved the illuminated tram, shaped like a rocket and aptly named the 'Tramnik', to commemorate Yuri Gagarin's first manned space flight earlier that year.

'I wish Sandie and Simon were with me,' she commented. 'They'd have pretended it was all too childish for words, but

I know they'd have loved it all the same.'

'There's always next year,' said her father. 'You'll be well settled by then, won't you? We can't tell you how pleased we are that you're coming back home, Abbie.'

She had not wanted to look at the scene of destruction starting to take place on the block next to the Tower where, as Doreen had told her, the Palace building was being demolished to make way for Lewis's store. They had had such happy times there in the early years of the war. The hundreds and thousands of RAF lads who were billeted in the town must have happy memories of the place, too.

There were other changes as well, which Abbie noticed the next day when she walked through the streets of Blackpool on her way to the estate agents' offices. There was a whole new look, a very modern look, to the corner of Abingdon Street and Church Street where property dating from the 1860s – Galloway's Chemist's, McCallister's Shoe Shop, and the old-fashioned sweet shop 'The Sugar Bowl' – had been replaced by Paige's Ladies Fashions and the Boston Man's Shop, faced in a mosaic of black and pink tiles. Abbie was pleased to see that Burton's café was still there, however, next door to the modern development, and further along Abingdon Street the familiar life-size hunter on his horse was still leaping over the doorway of Hunter's Gents' Outfitters. The cream and red Woolworth building on the prom was still there; so was RHO Hill's, Blackpool's leading department store; the two Marks & Spencer stores; and British Home Stores, a comparatively new shop, had opened in 1957 on the site of the old market hall. The Co-operative Emporium with its elegant pilloried frontage on Coronation Street was still there, too: Abbie remembered it from her childhood. Aunt Bertha had loved to shop there, collecting her 'divi' stamps and sticking them in a little book. Abbie's mother, however, had not been a Co-opite; it would have been much too plebeian for *her*. Abbie found herself wallowing in memories as she wandered through the streets of the town.

'The Boys' Grammar School's moved an' all,' Doreen told her, when she was commenting on the various changes she had noticed. 'Well, the old building's still there, on Church Street, but there was never any room, was there, for playing fields an' all that, slap bang in the middle of town. So they've moved up to Highfurlong where there's plenty of space to build. Doesn't make no difference to me; our Paul's at the Catholic School and Michael's at the Secondary Modern, but it's where your Simon'll be going, isn't it? Something to think about when you're deciding where to live . . . Now, I think we've whittled it down to two houses, haven't we? The one at Layton and the one at North Shore.'

Abbie smiled to herself at Doreen's use of 'we'. You could almost believe she was going to share the house with her friend. Her help had truly been invaluable. Abbie knew that over the past week she might well have been intimidated by estate agents and house-owners, had it not been for Doreen's bolstering support. It was the first major undertaking she had embarked upon since Peter's death. She had taken over the running of their house in Wymondham – the bills and budgeting and maintenance – with comparative ease and because she knew it was what she had to do, although these were matters which Peter had always dealt with. Her parents-in-law had always been there, too, for her to turn to if she needed advice. But as for buying a house on her own, Abbie had not realised just what was involved. Naively, she had thought it might be quite an easy matter, but there were so many hidden snags. Each house they visited, it seemed, had several things wrong with it.

After the first three days Abbie was beginning to think she would never find the house of her dreams. In point of fact, she had realised she must forget her dreams and lofty aspirations and settle, instead, for something that would suffice. Her anxiety was increased because she knew she must find somewhere this week; she couldn't keep making trips up to Blackpool. It all had to be sorted out quickly, mainly because there was already a sale on her property in Wymondham and she did not want to end up homeless. She found herself wishing that Peter was with her. She was missing him, this week, more than she had since those first dreadful days of her widowhood. But she knew this was a decision she must make completely on her own. Her friend and her relatives could advise her, but the ultimate decision rested with her.

They had visited a score of houses, mainly semi-detached residences. There was no shortage of property for sale on the outskirts of Blackpool. The main snag, however, was that the houses Abbie fell in love with were the ones way out of her price range, whereas the ones she could quite easily afford all had something wrong with them; the kitchen was too small, the garden too large for a woman on her own, the third bedroom barely the size of a boxroom, and so on.

'You're never going to find a place with everything just the way you want it, Mrs Fuss-pot,' Doreen told her. By Thursday afternoon it was time to come to a decision and Abbie was deliberating between two properties, both of them, fortunately, in the hands of the same estate agent. The two friends were now resting their weary feet over a cup of tea at Lockhart's café before Doreen went home to supervise the visitors' teas. 'Now, how about that one at North Shore?' Doreen went on. 'I could tell you quite liked that one, and it's near enough to Bispham. I know you'd set your heart on Bispham, but they're a wee bit pricey up there. What do you think? The rooms are a good size, it's near the trams on the prom and the garden's a manageable size. OK, so one or two of the rooms need decorating. So what? A few rolls of paper and a lick of paint'll soon put 'em to rights. I'll come and help you. We've a slack time coming up at the hotel, apart from Christmas, so I can give you a hand.'

'Doreen, whatever are you saying? You can't do that!'

Abbie looked aghast at her. 'You're far too busy. No, I couldn't possibly let you—'

'Shut up! I like paper-hanging. I find it relaxing. I won't take no for an answer.'

Abbie smiled. 'We'll see then, but I still think it's asking too much of you. You really are kind, Doreen. You've been a terrific help all week. But I haven't quite made up my mind about that house. There's the one at Layton, you remember.'

'Isn't Layton too far from the sea?' said Doreen. 'You said you wanted to be near the sea.'

'It's on a better bus route, though. And it would be nearer to Simon's school – that's if I can get him transferred to the Grammar School. There's Sandra to consider as well. Layton's quite near to the Collegiate School.'

'Why are you worrying about buses?' asked Doreen. 'They've both got bikes, haven't they? And you're going to learn to drive.'

'All in good time,' Abbie smiled. 'I tell you what I'll do; I'll sleep on it, as they say. Then I'll ask my father and Faith to go with me in the morning to look at both houses again. I know he wants to feel included, and I can rely on Faith to give me good advice. Not that you haven't already done so, Doreen. I'm really grateful to you. I could never have managed on my own.'

'OK, OK, I know how blooming marvellous I am,' replied Doreen, grinning. 'Yes, Faith's a good sort, isn't she? Practical and sensible an' all that. Not a giddy kipper like me. I bet she's glad she's got you as a step-daughter and not me. I could see her giving me a few funny looks, all disapproving like, at some of the things I said.' Faith had already accompanied the two young women on one of their house-hunting trips when Doreen, in her usual forth-right manner, had not been afraid to air her views about antiquated lavatories or a kitchen that might well have been used by Mrs Noah in the Ark. Fortunately, she had not said too much in front of the house-owners.

'No, she wasn't disapproving at all,' said Abbie. 'Didn't you see her laughing? Faith likes you; so does my father. They're glad I'll have a friend here when I move back. That's one of my main reasons for wanting to come back, you know; to be near you again. I've missed you, Doreen.'

'And I've missed you an' all, kid.' Doreen's blue eyes met Abbie's dark brown ones across the tea table and they exchanged a look of deep affection which held a host of memories, both happy and sad. Abbie knew that the friends she had made since she went to live in Norfolk could not compare with Doreen. They were mainly work acquaintances or the mothers of Sandie and Simon's friends, not close confidantes. And until she had met Doreen at nineteen years of age Abbie had never had a real friend. She hoped nothing would ever happen to damage the deep regard they had for one another.

Doreen looked away, as though a little discomfited by the intensity of her friend's gaze. 'I bet Faith isn't a dab hand at paper-hanging like I am,' she said, speaking quickly. 'That house in Layton needs quite a bit of titivating as well, from what I remember. Wasn't that the one with the ghastly brown wallpaper in the hall? And the dining room was a bit grotty an' all. Ne'er mind, kid; we'll soon put it to rights.'

'So that's the one you want me to go for now, is it?' said Abbie, beginning to feel confused again. 'Oh dear. I thought you liked the other one.'

'Sleep on it,' said Doreen, 'like you said you would. It's got to be your decision in the end, you know. It's you that's got to live there. Come on now, sup up. The hungry hordes'll be wanting their tea.'

Abbie finally decided, with her father and Faith's advice, on the house at Layton. She knew she must not waver any longer. Time was running out and she was anxious, by now, to get back to Norfolk and her family. A phone call to her mother-in-law had assured her that the children were well

41

and happy and enjoying their half-term holiday. Abbie must not worry; she could stay as long as she wished, as long as it took to sort things out. Mrs Horsfall had not expected her back within the week, anyway.

As it happened, Abbie was able to sort out all the preliminary paperwork with the estate agent straight away since the house had the added advantage of vacant possession.

Situated in a quiet avenue off the main thoroughfare, the house was near to good bus routes, the shopping area, and not too far from the two schools she hoped the children would attend. Another point in its favour, which Abbie had not yet mentioned to anyone, was its proximity to the railway station.

Norman's suggestion about training to become a teacher had quietly taken root in Abbie's mind. The more she thought about it, the more she liked the idea. She would need to travel by train to Chelford, where the Training College was situated – provided, of course, she was offered a place. Fortunately, her new house was only a few minutes' walk from Layton station.

You must sort out your own two children first, she admonished herself as the train carried her back towards Norfolk. They must be your priority. Schools for Sandra and Simon, a good music teacher for her daughter, and the assurance for both of them that she would always be there for them. For she knew, when it came to the crunch, that they would both be resistant to the move to Blackpool. And once they got there, she would have to get a job. The next college year was ten months away and she would need some sort of income to enhance her widow's pension.

Abbie closed her eyes, trying to clear her mind of its jumbled thoughts and the headache brought on by nervous tension. It had been a relief to sign the contract for the house, but she was still anxious. There was no going back now, and she knew that making the move to another town was not going to be as simple as it had first appeared. Especially as a woman on her own. *Oh, Peter!* she found herself crying inside her head. *Why did you have to die and leave me on my own?* It was a long time since she had felt so alone.

Chapter 4

Half an hour from the end of her journey Abbie woke up to the fact that she would soon be seeing her two children again. The thought cheered her considerably, and she told herself sharply to 'Pick yourself up, dust yourself off, and start all over again.' That had been a familiar song in the days when she and Peter had danced together in the Palace ballroom. Whatever would he think of her now if he could see her wallowing in self-pity at the thought of moving to a new house on her own? Peter would have wanted her to tackle this new challenge boldly, and Abbie knew she had a hidden reserve of strength she could call upon to help her with the problems that lay ahead. There had been times in the past when she had needed this inner courage; when she believed that Peter had been killed; at the time of her mother's death, with all the trauma and shocks that had brought in its wake; and, more recently, at the death of her dear Aunt Bertha who had been more of a mother to her than her own parent. It had not failed her then. She had got through all these calamities and she knew she would do so again.

Her Aunt Bertha would have told her – and so would Lily Horsfall, her mother-in-law – to say a prayer, to ask for the Lord's strength to help her as well as relying on her own reserves. But Abbie had never been entirely sure how it worked. It seemed incredibly naïve to believe that an omnipotent God could be interested in the petty little concerns of Abbie Horsfall when He had a whole wide world to look after. She had to admit, though, that Peter had been restored to her, quite miraculously, and that they had had ten very happy years – so there might be something in it.

And why did she keep complaining she was on her own? she asked herself. She had lots of people who were willing to help her; Doreen and Norman Jarvis and her stepmother, Faith, and, at this end, Lily and Frank Horsfall. Abbie suddenly realised how much worse it would be for Lily and Frank to have to say goodbye to their beloved grandchildren, the only ones they had. She began to feel ashamed of her misgivings. On no account must she let her parents-in-law see she was dithering. If she became agitated and anxious, then so would they. She decided, also, that she would make sure that Sandra and Simon helped her with the practical side of the removal, the sorting out and packing up of all their belongings. Simon could make lists of what was in each packing case so it would be easier when they came to unload; he was good at lists. If they were actively involved then maybe they might forget their opposition to the move. Abbie felt that Sandie was already halfway to being won over by the thought of the Blackpool Musical Festival. Simon might prove more difficult. He was an uncomplicated lad, usually good-natured, but he could be stubborn at times.

It was the thought of her children that brought Abbie out of her doldrums. She had missed them, far more, she suspected, than they would have missed her, and as the train approached Wymondham station she was really looking forward to seeing them again. Frank Horsfall was there to meet her in his Ford car, but minus the children. Sandra was shopping in Norwich with her friends, he told her, and Simon, as Norwich City was playing away, was having a kick around on the field with his mates, but they would both be back for the tea which Lily was preparing.

'We thought you'd like a meal before you go back home,' said Frank. 'It's not easy starting from scratch when you come back from a holiday – well, I suppose it has been a sort of holiday, hasn't it? Lily's done a bit of shopping for you – some bread and a joint of meat for tomorrow. And I've been in to lay your fire; it just needs a match to it.'

How kind they both were, she thought, and how she would miss them. For the first time, however, another thought struck her. Was their kindness, perhaps, a wee bit overpowering and possessive? As though they were bent on reminding her that she was Peter's widow and, as such, she belonged to them? Now where had that thought come from? She immediately tried to dismiss it from her mind as unworthy, but a vestige of it remained and with it the realisation that maybe it was the best thing she could do, to get away and start a new life for herself.

'Hi, Mum, had a good time?' The greeting of both her offspring was casual, but only what she had anticipated. She kissed them both, but she did not expect, nor did she get, a hug in return. They were not that sort of a family, but she knew, deep down, that the three of them were very fond of one another, as much so as any family that was more demonstrative. It was just not their way to hug and kiss unduly, and Abbie knew, here again, that this was a consequence of her own rigid upbringing.

'Well, aren't you going to ask me about the house?' Abbie enquired after the two of them, with the typical self-centredness of adolescents, had told her about their own concerns. Simon had scored two goals and Sandra had bought a fluffy pale blue sweater with her saved-up pocket money.

'Oh yes, Mum,' said Sandra, as though it were the last thought on her mind. 'What about the house?' Was she really so uninterested, wondered Abbie, or was it just a front she was putting up?

'Well, I've bought one at Layton,' said Abbie. She had

already told her parents-in-law a little about the house before the children arrived home. She tried, now, to put a spark of enthusiasm into her voice, but it was difficult with Sandie observing her coolly and Simon seemingly more interested in the steak pie and chips on his plate, but glancing up at her now and again as though he might, or might not, deign to take an interest.

'Layton? Where's that?' he asked

'It's about a mile out of Blackpool,' replied Abbie.

'I thought you wanted to live in Bispham,' said Sandie with a touch of belligerence.

'The houses up there were a bit too expensive, but Layton's not far from there – it's the next suburb, actually. And it's near both your schools. Well, you know, the schools I hope you'll be going to.'

'The cemetery's at Layton,' broke in Sandie. 'I remember passing it once on the bus. Who the heck wants to live near a flipping cemetery? Ugh! How frightfully morbid.'

'The house is nowhere near the cemetery.' Abbie found she was almost shouting. 'It's right at the other end of Layton, at the top of the hill.'

'What hill?'

'Hoo Hill, I believe it's called.'

'Hoo Hill!' Both children burst out laughing. 'Fancy telling people you live on Hoo Hill.' Sandie's voice was shrill with ridicule. 'Honestly, Mum, what a stupid place to live.'

'It's not stupid at all – and please stop using that word, Sandra.' Abbie felt nearly at the point of tears. Why were they doing this to her, the little monsters? And after she had been looking forward so much to seeing them again. She had presents in her case for both of them. A green jumper for Sandra – and now Abbie had been told she had already bought herself a blue one – and a football book for Simon that he had kept going on about. They didn't deserve nice treats. Were they trying to punish her for going away and leaving them, even though they hadn't wanted to go with

47

her? Or was it the thought of moving . . . or what? She was sure they had never been as bad as this before, but then she had never left them before.

'Stop it, both of you! You're behaving very badly.' Lily Horsfall's voice was quiet but authoritative, and Abbie cast her a grateful glance. 'I'm sure your mum has found a lovely house for you all. From what she was telling your grandad and me, it sounds very nice. Now just listen properly to your mother while she tells you about it.'

'There are three bedrooms and they're all quite big . . .' Abbie's voice was strained; she could no longer force any eagerness into it. She felt deflated and so disappointed in them both, and knew that if she had had them on their own at this moment, she would really have let rip at her two children in a way she had never done before. 'In fact, the small bedroom is much bigger than the one you're in at the moment, Simon. There'll be lots of room on the walls for football posters and all that.'

'OK, Mum.' She was relieved to see he cast a mollified glance in her direction. It was not like Simon to be badly behaved. 'That sounds good.'

'There's a nice garden, not too big, all well laid out, so it shouldn't be too much trouble. Bathroom and separate toilet – that's handy. Two reception rooms.' She tried to laugh. 'I sound like an estate agent, don't I? You know what I mean – a lounge and a dining room. And a smallish kitchen – I'd have liked a bigger kitchen, but all the semis in Blackpool seem to be the same, the ones built at that time.'

'Isn't it a new house then?' asked Sandie, a little more politely.

'No, of course not. Early 1900s, but it's very well built. They were in those days.'

'Ancient,' muttered Sandie.

'And that's about all I can tell you,' Abbie concluded, 'but I've signed the contract, so that's that.' A new determination had entered her being. She was not going to allow herself to be intimidated by her son and daughter, although she suspected that this present bout of defiance was largely at Sandra's instigation and that Simon, for whatever reason, was just going along with it. Perhaps he was upset at the thought of leaving his friends and she couldn't blame him for that. However, from now on they would both have to learn that she, Abbie, was the boss.

'The house is empty,' she went on. 'What they call vacant possession, so we can move just as soon as we are ready.' The people who had bought their house in Wymondham did not intend to move in until early next year. 'I thought January would be a good time. We'll get Christmas over, and then we can make the move early in the New Year – ready for you to start at your new schools at the beginning of term.'

'Supposing they won't have us? There might not be any room.' Sandra's smirk made her mother even more determined to stamp out any nonsense.

'There'll be room somewhere,' she replied decidedly. 'There's more than one grammar school to choose from. That's the next thing I've to see to, but I'm sure your present schools will arrange the transfers. You can help me with the packing up, both of you, during the school holiday. You can sort out all your own belongings; decide what you are taking and what you're throwing away. You have both accumulated a lot of rubbish. What's more, I shall need you to help me pack up all the household goods. All right?' The new note of forcefulness in her voice must have conveyed to both of them that she would brook no disobedience.

'All right, Mum,' said Simon with a wary look first at his sister, then at his mother.

'OK, if you say so.' Sandie shrugged nonchalantly.

Abbie bit her lip. Maybe her tone had been a little too sharp. 'I realise it won't be easy, not for any of us. It's just as hard for me, you know, leaving the place where I've lived for so long – and leaving your grandma and grandad as well.'

She smiled in their direction. 'But it's something I know I've got to do, and we'll soon settle down and make new friends.'

She was aware that Lily and Frank were exchanging covert glances and they had both gone very quiet, making no attempt to join in the conversation. She looked pointedly in their direction. 'We'll be sorry to leave you, Grandma and Grandad. But you'll be able to come and visit us, whenever you like. I'm going to get a bed settee and there's really plenty of room in the new house.' She had not known what to call Peter's mother and father when she was first married. They were of the generation that did not use Christian names freely and they had never invited her to call them Lily and Frank. Nor had she felt easy calling them Mum and Dad, as Peter had done, but the advent of the grandchildren had solved the problem. Now they were Grandma and Grandad to Abbie as well as to the children.

Frank Horsfall grinned suddenly. 'We'd best tell them, hadn't we, Lily? Do you want to, or shall I?'

'Tell us what?' asked Abbie.

'Yes, come on – what's the big secret, Gran?' asked Sandie. 'What's up?'

'I'll tell them,' said her grandmother in a hushed, excited sort of voice. 'We've been having a think, your grandad and me, and we've decided there'll be nothing much to keep us in Wymondham when you've gone. We've no more children or grandchildren. There's only Frank's sister here and my brother in Great Yarmouth, but they might just as well be at the other side of the world for all we see them. So we've decided . . .'

'We've decided to come with you,' broke in Frank, a delighted beam spreading across his face from ear to ear.

'Oh, be quiet, Frank!' said his wife with a mock frown. 'You said *I* could tell them.'

'Doesn't make any difference who tells 'em, does it?' They sounded like a couple of kids scrapping, but their glee at the bombshell they were dropping was written large on both their faces. 'Yes, we've decided to move to Blackpool as well. Like Lily says, there'll be nothing much for us here when you've all moved away.'

Abbie found all she could do was stare at them, dumbfounded. 'But . . . what about all the things you do here?' she said when she had recovered her voice. 'There's your church, and Grandad's bowling club. And what about the Women's Institute, Gran? They'll miss you, won't they?'

'I dare say there are churches in Blackpool, aren't there, and bowling greens?' Was Abbie imagining it or was Lily's tone just a touch sarcastic? Some of the elation had disappeared from her mother-in-law's face and Abbie felt guilty that her initial response had been such a negative one. 'We won't be moving just yet, you know,' Lily added. 'There's the house to sell and all kinds of things to sort out. We'll let you settle down first.'

'D'you mean you're going to come and live with us, in our new house?' asked Simon.

'No, of course not,' answered Abbie quickly. 'Don't be silly, Simon. There wouldn't be room, would there? You know that.'

'You've just been saying there's plenty of room in the new house,' broke in Sandie. 'Make up your mind, Mum.' Her tone angered her mother even more and she answered more sharply than she intended.

'Well, there isn't! And don't be so cheeky, Sandra. You know perfectly well what I mean. We would make room – of course we would – if anyone wanted to come and visit us, but not for any length of time. No, Grandma and Grandad will be buying a house of their own – quite near to ours, I dare say. That was what you meant, wasn't it?' She turned to her parents-in-law. 'And what a good idea it is, too. I would never have thought of you wanting to move there as well.' Abbie was trying to inject some enthusiasm into her voice, hoping and praying it would sound convincing. 'It will be lovely to have you there. Really . . . lovely. I was just taken aback when you mentioned it at first. It was such a surprise.'

'A pleasant one, I hope?' Her mother-in-law's glance was questioning and a little unsure. Abbie smiled warmly at her. She did not have to force her smile because she really was very fond of Lily. She had grown to love both of them, possibly even more since Peter's death.

Lily had aged considerably after her son died. Her hair was now completely white and her once plump figure had lost much of its comfortable roundness. There had been a period after her son's death when she had lost interest in everything, including food and the appetising home cooking she had loved to do. Now, thanks to her supportive husband, she had regained her interest in life. She pursued her hobbies and looked after her home with a zeal that left little time for mourning, and the love she had once given to her only son she now lavished on her grandchildren and their mother. Abbie spoke quickly, trying to make amends for the hurt she might have caused.

'Yes, it was certainly a lovely surprise, Gran. It's just that we'd never thought of it, had we, Sandie . . . Simon? We'll be able to show Grandma and Grandad all the sights of Blackpool, won't we?'

'Oh, we'll be able to do that for ourselves,' replied Frank. Again, was Abbie only imagining the touch of asperity in his tone? 'We were visiting Blackpool even before you were born, Abbie, weren't we, Lily? The Tower and the Winter Gardens and walks on North Pier, and those noisy trams.' He turned to his wife, his blue eyes, so like his son's, glowing with affection. 'We'll be able to stroll down Memory Lane, won't we, love? We've had a few happy holidays in Blackpool.'

'That's good.' Abbie felt rather as though she had been put in her place. 'You'll probably know as much about the town as I do. I noticed quite a few things had changed. I don't think they have the Women's Institute in Blackpool, Gran, but perhaps you could join the Townswomen's Guild?

Faith's a member of that and I think it's like the WI in a lot of ways. I'll ask her about it if you like.'

'Yes, that would be nice, dear,' answered Lily, though not with any degree of enthusiasm. 'We know we'll have to make a new life for ourselves. It won't be easy at our age, but we thought it might be worth a try. That was what we had hoped, anyway,' she added, sounding a little uncertain.

'We'll be fine, Lily.' Frank spoke assertively. 'Things'll be a bit different, but we'll soon get used to it. I'll find a bowling club if there's one that'll have me, and you can go to your Townswomen's whatsit, and we'll try and find a church that's to our liking. And Simon and me'll be watching First Division football, won't we, lad? That can't be bad.'

'Yeah.' Simon nodded, and Abbie was glad to see he looked quite pleased at the idea. 'I suppose it might not be all that bad living in Blackpool, especially if Gran and Grandad are there. And there's Preston North End as well; they're a good team. We could go and watch them, Grandad. It's only a few miles away. Some of the lads were dead jealous when I told 'em we were going to live up north.'

'I thought they were all keen City fans,' said Abbie. 'Fair weather supporters, eh?'

'They appreciate good football, Mum,' said Simon in a superior tone, 'and those teams up north are some of the best in the country. There's Manchester United for a start, isn't there, Grandad?'

'There is indeed, lad.' Frank beamed at his grandson.

'Yes, of course.' Abbie nodded, trying to look knowledgeable. 'It's a pity you won't be able to watch Stanley Matthews, isn't it, Grandad? He's been transferred from Blackpool now, you know.'

'Aargh!' Simon gave an exaggerated moan. 'Tell us something we don't know, Mum! Anyway, he was past it. He'd been playing for the second team for ages, hadn't he, Grandad?'

'That's right. He was a wizard, though, in his time. There was nobody to touch him. There still isn't if you ask me.'

Abbie felt, again, that she had been well and truly put in her place, by her son this time, and now she was being ignored as the two men of the family started on a discussion of football technique. Her mother-in-law and Sandie were talking about the various ballrooms in Blackpool; at least, Lily was talking and Sandie, surprisingly, was showing quite a keen interest.

'I used to love listening to Reginald Dixon on the Wurlitzer,' Lily was saying. 'That's in the Tower ballroom, of course. "Mr Blackpool", they used to call him, he was that famous in the town. Yes, your grandad and me have danced to him many a time. "Oh, I do like to be beside the seaside" . . .' She suddenly burst into song then she gave a reminiscent chuckle. 'That was his signature tune. I dare say he's still there; at least I haven't heard any different.'

'Yes, he's still there, Gran,' Abbie broke in, but Lily didn't seem to have heard her.

'And then we used to go down to the aquarium and have a look at all the fish,' she continued, still talking animatedly to her granddaughter. 'That's on the ground floor of the Tower; lovely and peaceful it is down there.'

'And have you ever been to the top of the Tower, Grandma?' asked Sandie.

'Just once.' Lily nodded.

'We've never been,' said Sandie. 'That's something I'll have to do, and I shall have a ride on the Big Dipper as well. I was only a little kid the last time we went to the Pleasure Beach and I was too scared. But I'm not now. I think it'd be dead exciting.'

Abbie started to clear the pots from the table. She felt, suddenly, left out of things, a little piqued, if she were honest, that her children's upsurge of interest in Blackpool had been brought about by her parents-in-law's decision to move there as well. She knew she was being peevish, but at the moment she felt she did not want them in Blackpool, however well-meaning or helpful they might be. Was she never to be allowed to do anything on her own, for heaven's sake? She clattered the pots together at the side of the sink with unnecessary force.

'Leave those, Abbie love,' Lily called from the living room. 'I'll do them later. I didn't want you to start bothering with the washing up. You'll be wanting to get off home, won't you, to get yourselves sorted out?'

'Yes, I suppose we should, really,' replied Abbie with a great sense of relief. 'There's a lot to do at home. But I don't like leaving you with all the pots.' When she re-entered the living room the strained atmosphere she had been aware of five minutes earlier seemed to have vanished and her mother-in-law was giving her her full attention once again.

'Nonsense, what's a bit of washing up?' said Lily, fussing around, handing Sandra and Simon their coats. 'Washing up's never bothered me; that's the least of my worries. Besides, it's been lovely having you all here, and Grandad and I have really enjoyed having these two all week. They've not been a bit of trouble.'

'Thank you for having us, Grandma,' said Sandie dutifully.

'Yes. Thanks, Gran,' added Simon.

'Don't mention it – it's been a pleasure.' Lily kissed them both, then briefly put her arms round Abbie who stooped to kiss her mother-in-law's cheek. 'And thank you again for the lovely present,' whispered Lily. 'You shouldn't have, really you shouldn't, but it was so clever of you to remember my favourite perfume.' Abbie had bought her a huge gift box – already the shops were stocking up with Christmas goods – containing soap, talcum powder, toilet water and bath salts in Morny's Lily of the Valley fragrance, and a box of Terry's Spartan chocolates, the hard centres that Frank particularly enjoyed. 'You're so thoughtful, dear.'

'Not at all.' Abbie felt a little ill at ease, recalling her resentment of a few moments ago, and she was still anxious to be off. 'Come along, you two. Don't keep Grandad waiting. Have you got everything? Your duffel bags and anoraks? Those mucky football boots'll have to stand on some paper in the boot, Simon. We'll see you soon, Gran. Take care now, and thanks again. 'Bye for now.' She did not add that she was glad they had decided to move to Blackpool. To keep on saying how pleased she was might sound insincere.

'She doesn't want us there, does she?' said Lily when Frank arrived back after dropping off Abbie and the children at their home. 'I could tell. She didn't like the idea.'

'Whatever makes you say that?' said Frank in an astonished voice that would fool no one. 'She said she was pleased, didn't she? You heard her. She said what a good idea it was. She said it would be lovely.'

'Yes – after her face had dropped a mile.' Lily shook her head. 'I can't forget that look on her face, Frank, when we said we were moving to Blackpool. She looked . . . dumbstruck.'

'It was the shock, I reckon. She said it was a surprise.'

'Oh, come on, Frank, you know as well as I do that she's dead against the idea. And you noticed it – don't pretend you didn't. That's why you were so short with her.'

'Aye, happen I was, a bit. But I wouldn't go so far as to say she was dead against it.' Frank scratched his temple thoughtfully. 'She might've been looking forward to making a fresh start, having a bit more independence, like. And there's us sticking our noses in, not letting her do anything on her own.'

'Interfering, you mean?' Lily bristled a little. 'I'm sure I've never interfered in Abbie's business, not with the way she's brought up the children or anything.'

'We've never needed to, have we?' Frank said gently. 'Because she's never done anything we haven't approved of. She's a grand girl, our Abbie.'

'Oh, I agree, Frank, you know I do. Abbie's a lovely young

woman, and our Peter couldn't have had a better wife. It's just, I can't bear the thought of losing her, not after losing Peter.' Her voice faltered a little. 'I've come to love her nearly as much as I loved our son, and those two kiddies. I know Sandra can be a bit of a handful, but they're grand kids, both of 'em. And I've never had a wrong word with Abbie. You don't think she's turning against us, do you, Frank?'

'What – Abbie? No, of course not. We've given her rather a shock, that's all. Something to think about. She'll come round to the idea.'

'You don't think we've made the wrong decision then? I was looking forward to Blackpool.' Lily sounded pensive. 'But perhaps it might be better if we stayed here. We don't want any trouble.'

'There won't be any trouble. We're going and that's that. We'll just have to be careful to keep our distance and not go pushing in when we're not wanted. We'll have to buy a house far enough away from Abbie's place to give her privacy but near enough to be of help if she needs us.'

'All I ever wanted to do was to help,' said Lily. 'I remember what a comfort she was to me at first, when I was so upset about Peter. Oh dear, I wish I knew we were doing the right thing.'

'We are,' said Frank. 'Believe me, we are.' But Lily was not sure at all.

Chapter 5

'So how did it go with the dreaded in-laws?' asked Doreen. 'Did they manage to find a suitable house or will they be paying another visit to Blackpool?' She smoothed a minute crease in the piece of wallpaper she had just pressed to the wall, then stood back to admire her handiwork. 'Hmm, not at all bad, though I say it meself. It's coming on a treat, kid.'

Abbie paused for a moment, sticking her wide brush into the bucket of paste and wiping her gooey fingers down the front of her already tacky apron. She had been delegated the task of pasting whilst her friend, much more efficient at this decorating business, was involved in the more intricate job of hanging the paper and trimming the edges. She frowned at Doreen reprovingly. 'I wish you wouldn't call them that. They're OK really, and I don't mind them coming here, not now I've got used to the idea.'

'That's not what you said at first, is it? You carried on something awful when you found out what they were going to do. I remember you ringing up that first night, after they'd told you. Calling them fit to burn, you were.'

'Well, it was a shock, wasn't it? I felt as though I was being smothered, killed with kindness – you know what I mean. But I've calmed down now. I've had to put a brave face on it because Lily looked so wounded. I knew I'd hurt her so I've gone out of my way since then to show her that I don't mind them coming at all – that I'm really looking forward to it, in fact.'

'Even though you're not?'

'I didn't say that.'

'Well, did they find anywhere, then? You didn't answer my question.'

'Yes. They've settled on a little bungalow at the other end of Layton, just off Layton Road.'

'Thank God it's the other end, eh, kid? At least you haven't got them right on your doorstep.'

Abbie declined to comment on her friend's remark. 'They were undecided between two properties, like I was, if you remember,' she went on, 'and Frank kept pushing Lily to make up her mind. She seems very undecided, though, does Lily. Sometimes I think she's not at all sure, now, that she really wants to come at all.'

'But he's persuaded her, eh? So when are they moving in?'

'Sometime next month, round about Eastertime. They did the same as I did; they got a sale on their own house first before they started looking. The bungalow needs very little doing to it, so it should be quite straightforward. They were here all last week, and they've signed the contract, so that's that – there's no turning back. I wish Lily looked a little more sure about it all. I can't help thinking it's me that's put her off the idea.'

'I shouldn't think so for one moment,' said Doreen. 'It's a big step, leaving a place where you've lived for ages – you said so yourself. I notice you've decided to call them Lily and Frank now. About time, too.'

'Not to their faces, I don't. I couldn't do that.'

'Why ever not?'

'It wouldn't seem right.'

'I would. In fact, I do. Norman's mam and dad have always been Betty and Joe to me – since we got married, I mean. When I was their Land Girl they were Mr and Mrs Jarvis, naturally.'

'You're a cheeky monkey, you are, Doreen Miller. You could get away with murder.'

'I think I'd murder my in-laws if they ever decided to come and live here. No, thank you very much! Betty's far too nosy. I do sympathise with you, kid. I know exactly how you feel.'

'I've told you, I don't mind.'

'OK, if you say so.' Doreen shrugged. 'Right, we'd best get on, hadn't we? Standing around gassing won't buy the baby a new bonnet. Mix some more paste, lass, and I'll cut the next length.'

They worked steadily for the next hour and more in a companionable silence, or near silence, as it was impossible for Doreen to keep her mouth shut all the time. But she certainly did not talk as much as usual, concentrating on making a first-class job of Abbie's dining room.

'Let's just finish this wall, then we'll call it a day,' said Abbie at about four o'clock. She put her hand on her hips, easing her aching back. 'I don't know about you, but I'm feeling the strain. I'm not used to this sort of hard labour. Anyway, the kids'll be home from school before long, and you'll be wanting to get back to your brood, won't you?'

'Needs must, I suppose,' replied Doreen. 'A woman's work is never done. I'm having a break from them all soon, though. Didn't I tell you?'

'No, I don't think so.' Abbie glanced curiously at her friend, who was not looking at her as she spoke, but applying herself studiously to the task of measuring the next length of wallpaper. 'Do you mean that you and Norman are going away, like I suggested?'

'No, that's not what I said. I said *I* was having a break – *me*, not the two of us. There's nobody to look after the kids and I wouldn't ask you, not at the moment. You're far too busy.' Doreen was rattling on before Abbie had a chance to speak. 'Norman doesn't mind seeing to them for a weekend, and that's all I'll be away, just the weekend. You remember my sister Janey?'

'Of course I remember Janey. How could I forget her?'

Abbie was aware that Doreen was still not looking at her. Her eyes were fixed on the scissors as she carefully cut off the surplus edge of paper. It was a tricky job, admittedly; one slip and the whole length of paper could be ruined, but Doreen's voice sounded a tiny bit shrill and her cheeks were rather pink.

'Well, she's just moved into a new house,' Doreen continued. 'They moved before Christmas, actually, but she's only just got round to inviting me to go and stay. Since Norman's never got on all that well with our Janey, I said I'd go on my own.'

'Janey lived in Preston, didn't she? Is the new house in Preston as well?'

'Yes, just on the outskirts. It's in Ingol – a lovely little village area from what our Janey says. When I say a new house, it isn't actually new – it's quite old really, turn of the century. Dick's just had a promotion at his engineering firm. Our Janey landed on her feet all right when she married him. You remember what a flibberty-gibbet she was? But she's settled down amazingly well. She's had to, of course. They've got five kids now.'

'The same as you, then.'

'Yes.' Doreen gave an odd little laugh. 'The same as me. They're even more spread out than ours, though. Sam's seventeen now, and the youngest one's three.' Abbie recalled how Janey Miller, at the age of sixteen, had discovered she was pregnant by an American GI who had, very conveniently for him, been posted to a distant camp. Perhaps it was not to be wondered at that Norman had never got on with the young woman. At one time there had been some talk of Doreen leaving the Land Army to look after the baby, and that could well have put paid to Doreen and Norman's wedding plans as well. But all that had ended happily and Janey, as Doreen had said, had landed on her feet. 'It'll be nice to see her again,' said Doreen. 'Like I say, we don't often meet, with her and Norman not hitting it off.'

61

'And will you be seeing your other sister as well?' asked Abbie. 'Your Peggy lives in that area, doesn't she?'

'Yes. She's in Rishton, just outside Blackburn. I don't know whether Peggy'll be coming or not. She might be.' Doreen cast an uneasy look in her friend's direction, then, just as quickly, looked away. If the expression on her face was not one of guilt then Abbie would eat her hat. She continued to look fixedly at her friend.

'What are you staring at me for?' Doreen gave an embarrassed little laugh, then put down her scissors and started to take off her apron. 'I think you're right, kid. We'll call it a day now. If we start rushing we'll only go and make a mess of it. We'll finish it off tomorrow, eh?' She was pretending not to notice Abbie's intent gaze. With an air of nonchalance she shoved her rolled-up apron into her bag and changed her shabby slip-on shoes for her outdoor pair.

'Doreen, what d'you think you're playing at?' Abbie's voice was quiet, but ominous.

'What d'you mean?'

'You know very well what I mean. You're not going to see Janey at all, are you?'

'Of course I'm going to see Janey.' Doreen's voice petered out in the face of Abbie's scrutiny. 'What else would I be doing?' She paused, then: 'How do you know?' she said in a whisper.

'It's written all over your face,' said Abbie. In spite of herself she smiled a little. This was her best friend with whom she had never exchanged a cross word, not since those very early days. How could she take a high moral stand with her now and risk damaging their friendship? And yet she had to get across to her that what she was doing – or what Abbie had assumed she was doing – was wrong. And not only wrong, but foolish. 'You're too honest a person, Doreen, to tell lies successfully.'

'I thought you said, not long ago, that I could get away with murder?'

'I was joking, wasn't I? Of course you couldn't. I've told you – you're too honest, too . . . moral. At least, I always thought you were. It's that fellow at night school, isn't it? You're still seeing him then?'

Doreen nodded. ''Fraid so.'

'Oh, love, don't be silly. Just think about what you're doing. What is it you intend doing, anyway? Are you thinking of going away for the weekend together?'

Doreen nodded again. 'We planned to, yes. Please don't look at me like that, Abbie. I'm not doing any harm, honestly I'm not. It's just a bit of fun, that's all. I don't seem to have had any fun for ages, not till I met Ken. I wouldn't dream of hurting Norman if that's what you're worried about. I'd never leave him, you know. Not for good. I couldn't anyway, could I?'

'Because you're a Catholic, you mean?'

'Yes. Sometimes I wish I wasn't. It's all so rigid – mortal sins and venial sins and all that. And the priest always telling you what to do.'

'At least you can go to Confession, can't you? Get absolution.' Abbie's tone was mild; all the same Doreen retaliated.

'Are you being sarcastic? You know I don't go any more – I told you.'

'No.' Abbie shook her head, slowly and thoughtfully. 'No, I don't think I'm being sarcastic. I don't mean to be, but there's a lot I don't understand.'

'About my religion, you mean? Then that makes two of us.'

'What I'm thinking is something like this. Those of us who are not Catholics may not have it laid down in black and white, what is right and what is wrong, but most of us do try to live by some kind of moral code, just as you do. We don't have to confess to a priest, but we know when we've done something unworthy or . . . sinful. You say you don't want to hurt Norman, but he'd be dreadfully hurt if

63

he knew about this, wouldn't he?'

'He's not going to know, is he? You wouldn't tell him, would you?'

'Of course not. You know I wouldn't. I just want you to think, Doreen. There's so much at stake; your husband, your children, your business.'

'And I've told you, it's just a bit of fun. It won't lead to anything else. It can't – we both know that. We just enjoy being together and we don't see why we should deny ourselves the chance of some happiness if we can do it without anyone getting hurt.'

'You mean he's married as well?'

Doreen pulled her mouth into a moue. 'He might be.'

'He's married, isn't he?' Abbie persisted.

'OK, OK, so he's married, and so am I.' Doreen was almost shouting. 'That's why we know it can't go anywhere.'

'And I suppose he's a Catholic, too?'

'No, as a matter of fact, he isn't. Not that it matters, and not that it's anything to do with you.' Doreen's blue eyes were flashing angrily and her cheeks were flushed. 'He's not anything, as far as I know. I don't think he goes to church and that's probably very sensible of him. At least he's not all screwed up about offending the priest, or God, or . . . or . . .'

'Or his wife?' said Abbie quietly.

'There you go again! Mind your own damned business, can't you?' Doreen was really shouting now. 'We're not harming his wife, or my precious husband either. You seem to think the sun shines out of Norman's behind, but it doesn't, believe me. You want to try living with him. He's boring, dead boring, and I want a bit of excitement, that's all. Ken's wife leads her own life. She's got a shop – a fancy goods shop, if you really want to know – and she spends more time there than she does with him. Anyroad, what gives you the right to be so flaming smug and pious? You're getting to be a real prig, Abbie Horsfall. It's time you got yerself a fellow of yer own.' Doreen stopped suddenly,

64

putting her hand to her mouth. 'Oh . . . I'm sorry, kid. I didn't mean it. I didn't mean to say that.'

'It's all right,' mumbled Abbie. 'I asked for it. I shouldn't've said that about his wife. That was below the belt. Besides, as you say, it's none of my business. Look, it's not just Norman I'm concerned about. It's you as well. I don't want you to get hurt. I care about you, Doreen, and we can't fall out. Not you and me. Not after all this time.'

'If I get hurt then it will be my own fault, won't it?' said Doreen in a much more subdued tone. 'My eyes are wide open, Abbie. I just want a bit of fun, that's all. I keep telling you. There's precious little to be had at home.'

'There are your children. Sorry, sorry, I don't mean to sound pious.' Abbie raised a placatory hand. 'But it's true, isn't it? Kids can be good fun, sometimes. And I'm living here now, aren't I? We could start going out together now and again.'

'The Palace has gone.' Doreen gave a sad smile. 'And I can't see you shaking a loose leg, somehow. Anyway, you've got your new job, haven't you? That's going to take quite a lot of your time. When do you start?'

'In a week or so. I'm just waiting for the rest of my "starter pack".' Abbie was about to become a Tupperware rep. 'You could come with me, if you like. They're quite good fun, these Tupperware parties.'

'A crowd of cackling women?' Doreen raised her eyebrows. 'No thanks, luv. Anyway, I've got my night school, haven't I?'

'And Ken,' added Abbie slyly but, she hoped, not reproachfully.

'And Ken,' agreed Doreen. 'Which brings us right back to where we started. Don't worry about me, Abbie. Nobody's going to get hurt. We've only seen one another at night school so far. Well, occasionally we've been out for a drink afterwards and then he's run me back in his car. Just to the corner of the road.'

'In case Norman happens to be looking out of the window?'

'Quite so.' Doreen looked down at the floor, shuffling her feet slightly. 'I tell him there's a crowd of us going for a coffee after night school. He thinks I come home on the bus; I'm never all that late. But Ken and I . . . well . . . we decided we'd like to spend more time together. His wife's got a trade fair that weekend.'

'Which weekend is it?'

'The one after next. The middle of March. After that we'll start getting busy at the hotel as it gets towards Easter.'

'So, where are you planning on going, you and Ken?'

'Ask no questions and you'll be told no lies,' Doreen answered pertly. 'I thought you said it was none of your business.'

'It isn't, but I can't pretend I approve of what you're doing, Doreen, because I don't. You and Ken, you haven't . . . you know?'

'Oh, come on, Abbie, spit it out.' Doreen gave an ironic little laugh. 'Have we "gone all the way", you mean? That's what we used to call it, didn't we, when we were kids? P'raps they still do, I don't know.' Abbie remembered that when she was a girl, even quite a grown-up one, she had known very little about such matters. It had been Doreen who had told her what was what. Even now she found it difficult to refer to the act of love or to know what to call it. 'No, we haven't indulged in a "mortal sin". Oh, hell's bells! I can't get away from it, can I? It's there at the back of my mind all the time, though I try not to think about it. I tell myself it doesn't matter, and it doesn't,' she added defiantly. 'It's only . . .'

'A bit of fun,' Abbie finished for her. She couldn't help thinking that in the end Doreen's Catholic conscience would prevent her from committing what would, in the eyes of her Church, be an unpardonable sin.

'Look,' Doreen said wearily, 'we're both adults and we know what we're doing. Ken is a very nice chap. Not pushy or domineering or anything. He wouldn't force me to do something I wasn't happy about. It will just be nice to be together, to be able to relax away from prying eyes.'

'Are the other people at night school suspicious?'

'I don't think so. We've been very careful when there's anybody else around. We're going to Morecambe,' she added, obviously on an impulse. 'Friday night till Sunday. I'll only be away two nights.'

'Oh, I see. How are you getting there? On the train?'

'No, in Ken's car.'

'But supposing Norman wants to run you to the station? He would offer, surely? You'd be going to Preston on the train, wouldn't you? That is if you were really going to Preston.'

'We've thought of that. I'm going to travel from Central station to South station on the train – it's only one stop – then Ken's going to pick me up near there. That's where he lives, in South Shore.' Such scheming, thought Abbie, such deception. Could it really be worth it?

'And where are you staying?' she asked. 'In a hotel something like yours?'

'Ken's arranging it,' Doreen replied airily. 'A quiet B and B, I expect. Some places stay open all the year round.'

'Won't it be rather chilly in Morecambe at this time of year?'

'No worse than Blackpool, I don't suppose. It doesn't really matter what the weather's like, does it?' But Doreen, at that moment, sounded not at all elated. 'Look, I'd best be off. I'll see you tomorrow. Shall I come about the same time – one o'clockish? We should be able to finish this off in one more go.'

'Yes, that's great, Doreen. And thanks ever so much for all you've done so far. I couldn't have done it without you.'

'What are friends for? We *are* still friends, aren't we, in spite of what I've told you?'

'Of course. Always will be.' All the same, Abbie could not

put the utmost conviction into her reply and she felt, too, that Doreen's answering grin lacked a little of its usual confidence.

What a foolish girl she is, thought Abbie when her friend had departed. No longer a girl, in truth, although she guessed she and Doreen would always be girls in one another's eyes. She was old enough to know better, certainly. And what was it all about, anyway? She hadn't even said that she loved the fellow, just that she craved excitement. It was physical attraction, Abbie supposed. Sexual attraction, to put it more bluntly. This man certainly must have some sex appeal to make Doreen risk so much for the sake of a clandestine weekend. But this was something that Abbie knew little about. Doreen's taunt that she should get a fellow of her own had struck a chord in Abbie, waking her to the realisation that she had not felt the stirrings of an attraction to the opposite sex since Peter's death.

There had only ever been Peter in her life, then, for a short while when she had believed that Peter was dead, there had been Jim. They had become friendly whilst Abbie was a Land Girl, working at his parents' market garden, and, for a short time, they had been engaged. She hadn't thought of Jim for ages, but then he had never had the power to arouse her emotions and her sexual longings – to excite her, to use Doreen's word, as Peter had done. Maybe she was wrong to condemn her friend when she had had no experience herself of such a strong physical desire, at least not for years and years. Perhaps she, Abbie, was growing old and staid and frigid – was that what Doreen had been hinting at? Certainly she had never given a thought to marrying again or even having a close friendship with a man, not that the opportunity had ever arisen.

What Doreen was doing, though, was wrong. Abbie was firmly convinced of that. She was not going to let her disapproval ruin their friendship, and she would definitely not breathe a word of what she knew to Norman or to anyone, but that did not mean that she could condone it. She just hoped that in the next week and a half Doreen might have second thoughts and come to her senses.

She stood in the middle of the room gazing round at their efforts so far. She had to agree with Doreen that they were making a pretty good job of decorating the dining room. The walls had been covered in a dingy nondescript fawnish paper with an old-fashioned border of orange and brown when she took over the house. Even though it might have sufficed for the time being, Abbie had been determined to have a complete change. She had chosen, with Doreen's help, a bold design of red and black poppies on a white background for the fireplace wall, these colours being repeated in a much smaller motif on the complementary paper for the remaining three walls. With the dazzling white paintwork, most of which Abbie had managed to complete on her own, the new colour scheme would provide a most striking setting for her G-plan sideboard, table and four chairs with cherry red seats. These had been bought about seven years ago – not long before Peter's death, in fact – when such furniture was becoming popular and it was still in very good condition. The brown carpet already in the house was unobtrusive and would have to do until such time as Abbie felt she could afford to replace it.

She would get round to decorating the rest of the rooms eventually, although the time was coming when Doreen would be fully occupied with her hotel. The hall and stairs had been decorated professionally before Abbie moved in as neither she nor Doreen had wanted to risk life and limb climbing a ladder to the high ceiling. It was a pleasing aspect when the front door opened to reveal the Regency striped green and gold walls and the toning sage-green carpet. This carpeting was new; Cyril Lord's finest nylon and wool needleloom with a non-slip runner base. Cyril Lord was all the rage now; reasonably priced and hardwearing and Abbie hoped, in time, to have similar carpets laid in several more of the rooms.

Sandra already had her eye on one in a deep pink shade to match the startling wallpaper she had chosen – shocking pink, lime green and bright orange squiggles in an abstract design – for her bedroom. The rolls of paper were at the moment on the top of her wardrobe awaiting the attention of her mother. Abbie had decided, if Doreen was unavailable, that she and Sandie, with possibly a little help from Simon, would tackle the decorating of the bedrooms themselves.

She was gratified, in spite of her misgivings, that the children had settled down well, both into their new schools and into other activities as well. Simon, who had never had difficulty in making friends, already had a small group of pals with whom he kicked a ball around on a nearby field when the weather was fine – and sometimes when it was not – or, upstairs in his small room, discussed the chances of the various First Division teams at the next Saturday's fixtures. Especially Blackpool; he had switched allegiance pretty quickly and most Saturdays he headed for Bloomfield Road, his orange and white scarf slung round his neck, accompanied by the same group of lads. To their slight disgust they were made to play rugby football at their school, but Abbie guessed it did not worry them unduly. They seemed a well-adjusted set of boys and she was only too pleased that Simon was so contented.

Sandie, too, appeared reasonably settled, although Abbie had not yet met any of her new friends from school. There were one or two girls with whom her daughter seemed to get on quite well, from the little she said, but they lived in a different part of the town. Sandie met them occasionally on a Saturday afternoon for a mooch around the town shops, but she told her mother next to nothing about her doings. She was, Abbie feared, becoming somewhat secretive, but maybe this was only to be expected in her mid-teenage years.

Acquaintances of Abbie, who had girls slightly older than Sandie, had told her how difficult they could be. It seemed to be commonplace these days, teenage awkwardness and rebellion. Abbie well remembered how she, at a similar age, would never have been allowed to be difficult.

Any hint of defiance had been stamped on immediately. It was only when she was older, in her very late teens and early twenties, that she had dared to stand up for herself. But in the 1930s and 1940s, of course, 'teenagers' had not yet been invented.

Abbie was relieved that Sandra was still pursuing her musical career with some diligence. Faith had recommended a good music teacher she had heard about, and Abbie, on visiting the woman's home, had been satisfied that Mrs Blake was just the person to keep her daughter's nose to the musical grindstone. The certificates on the wall of her music room were proof of her ability and her approach seemed to be one of friendliness, but with an underlying 'stand no nonsense' manner. At all events, Sandie went for her weekly lesson after school every Thursday without any show of reluctance, calling to have her tea afterwards with her Grandad Winters and his wife Faith, as they lived not far away.

Abbie went to see her father at least a couple of times a week, either walking the good mile and a half to the Stanley Park area or getting a bus to take her halfway. She had realised how much less complicated life would be if she could drive a car and had booked a series of lessons with the British School of Motoring. Her first lesson was next week.

It was next week, too, that she was to hold her first Tupperware party, working entirely on her own without supervision. This was another reason why it was necessary for her to learn to drive. For the time being she would have to rely on taxis – or a lift from an obliging customer – to transport her various items of Tupperware to and fro. The stuff was not heavy, but it was cumbersome and there was so much of it. She already had a large box of it in the corner of her bedroom and she was awaiting some more items before she launched herself into her new – albeit part-time – career.

Chapter 6

'Does that mean you've given up on the idea of being a teacher?' Doreen had asked whilst they were decorating Abbie's dining room. 'Seeing as how you're going to be a Tupperware hostess.'

'No, not at all,' replied Abbie. 'I'm just doing the Tupperware thing for the time being, until I start college in September. That is, if I'm accepted on the course, I mustn't count my chickens. As a matter of fact I've got an interview the week after next.'

'For college, you mean?'

'Yes, it's at the Training College in Chelford. I was surprised they even granted me an interview – after all, I'm turned forty – but apparently the college is specifically for mature students so I won't be on my own. If I'm accepted, that is.'

'Of course you'll be accepted, you silly chump! Stop running yourself down. You're always doing it. If you ask me they'll be dead lucky to get somebody like you. Rather you than me though, luv.' Doreen gave a grimace. 'It takes me all my time to manage my own kids, never mind taking on a whole cartload of somebody else's. They still have such big classes, don't they? That doesn't seem to have changed much since we were kids. There's forty in our Bernie's class. It's a bit better when they get to the secondary school, of course. What age are you going to teach, then? Have you decided?'

'Juniors, I think. You know, seven to eleven year olds. I like them when they're growing up a bit, but I don't think I could cope with them at secondary school age. I definitely wouldn't fancy a classful like our Sandie, although I don't think she's any bother at school. They often behave better for somebody else, don't they?'

'Why, are you having problems with her?'

'No, not really, no more than usual. She's become rather secretive, not always telling me where she's going or who she's with. She's never late home, though, so I suppose I can't complain. I like her to be in by half-past nine during the week, when she's at school, and so far she's done as she's told.'

'What does Sandie think about your plan to become a teacher?'

There was a few seconds' silence before Abbie answered. 'I haven't told her,' she said, a little guiltily. 'I haven't told either of them, not yet.'

'What! And you're accusing *her* of being secretive?' Doreen laughed, but not unkindly. 'Honestly! You're a fine one to talk, aren't you?'

'There didn't seem to be any point in saying anything yet,' Abbie tried to explain. 'I though I'd wait and see if I'm accepted, then I'll have something more definite to tell them. They know all about the Tupperware job though. It means I'll have to leave them on their own occasionally, so I've told them I trust them to behave themselves. Sandie was quite pleased at the idea of being left in charge; she was adamant that they didn't need a "babysitter". She's fifteen now, so it's time she started taking on a bit of responsibility. You don't think it's wrong of me to leave them on their own, do you?'

'Of course not. You worry too much, Abbie. You've had to be mother and father to your two these last seven years and I know it can't have been easy. You deserve some time to yourself. Don't spend all your time working though, will you? These Tupperware parties, are they all in the evening?'

'No, only the ones where the women are working during the day. I'm hoping to have quite a few in the afternoons as well, for Women's Fellowships and Mothers' Unions and Townswomen's Guilds. Faith has quite a lot of contacts.'

'Well, I wish you luck, kid. Are you looking forward to it?'

'With mixed feelings.' Abbie gave a nervous laugh. 'I'm rather apprehensive, to tell you the truth, about being in sole charge of the party. You know, standing up in front of all those women and holding forth about the merits of Tupperware, and organising those silly games they play. I've never done that sort of thing before. I've never even chaired a church meeting or anything like that.'

'Then it'll be good practice for you, won't it, for when you start teaching?'

'Yes, that's what I've been thinking.'

'I should imagine a crowd of women are a darned sight easier to manage than a classroom full of kids.'

Doreen's words came back forcibly to Abbie the next week when she stood up in front of her first audience of women. They were gathered in the home of an obliging neighbour who, on hearing about Abbie's new venture, had willingly offered to hold a party. So, for her first foray into the world of selling, Abbie was glad she did not have to transport her goods very far, only a few doors away.

It had been Faith's idea – it was surprising how many good ideas came from her practical stepmother – that Abbie should become a Tupperware hostess. Faith was one of the few people to whom Abbie had disclosed her aspirations about going to college, at the same time saying she would need a job of some sort in the meantime, one that would fit in with the children's school hours. She didn't want Sandra and Simon to be 'latch-key kids'. It was Faith who had persuaded her, as Doreen had tried to do, that her children were growing up and that by the time she started her college course they should be old enough to fend for themselves a little more. For the time being, however, Abbie wanted a job to augment her widow's pension and help pay for the little extras in the family budget.

'I've never been anything but a doctor's or a dentist's receptionist,' she told Faith, 'apart from being in the Land Army, of course. And I don't think it would be fair to take on a post as a receptionist and then pack it in after eight or nine months.'

It was then that Faith had suggested the Tupperware job. She knew the woman who was the area manager for the firm; Faith knew a lot of people in many different spheres of life. It was this woman, Celia Jackson, who had instructed Abbie in the direct selling approach, at the same time telling her about the history of the firm.

Earl Silas Tupper was an American from New Hampshire working for the large Dupont chemical company which was experimenting with plastics before World War Two. He persuaded his bosses to sell him some of their left-over material, and so it was that eventually, after a great deal of trial and error, he developed a new plastic that was touch, lightweight, flexible and unbreakable, the hallmarks of what later became his Tupperware products. He manufactured storage containers, plates, cups and bowls, many of them with the unique air-tight and liquid-tight seal on the lids. In 1945 these Tupper plastics were introduced to the American market in hardware and department stores, but they failed to sell, because no one could work out how to operate the seal. And so, in 1951, Earl Silas Tupper took all his products off the shop shelves. He hired a woman who created the direct selling system for his newly named Tupperware; selling to customers directly in their homes. Her name was Brownie Wise and it was she who invented the sales promotions and home parties with games and competitions, and encouraged the support and training which was necessary to motivate their workers.

It was only two years since the product had been introduced to Great Britain, but already sales were booming, with thousands of demonstrators, nationwide, giving home parties each week. 'You'll love it,' Celia told Abbie with all the verve and enthusiasm of her founder. 'And the beauty of it is you can work just as much or as little as you choose. It's all up to you. Of course, the harder you work and the more parties you have, the more you sell and the more your commission will grow.'

This was the first party that Abbie had been in charge of, although she had been a spectator at two others, and Celia had convinced her – or tried to – that it would be simple, as easy as falling off a wall. She had set out her wares on the table that her neighbour, Kathleen, had provided and when it seemed as though all the women, about fifteen or so, had arrived, she stood up at the end of the room and cleared her throat. The women were chattering twenty to the dozen and, although one or two seemed to have noticed her, most of them kept on talking. Oh crumbs! thought Abbie. What on earth do I do to make them shut up? I can't clap my hands like a schoolteacher. The thought was racing through her mind that if she couldn't get the attention of a smallish group of women, however would she manage with a large class of children? It was Kathleen in the end who brought them to order.

'Ladies.' Her voice was quite loud and authoritative. 'Abbie is waiting to start now. Could you give her your attention, please? In other words, kindly shut up!'

There was a ripple of laughter and all the women looked expectantly in Abbie's direction. 'Good evening, everyone,' she began. Her voice, to her own ears, sounded high-pitched and false, so she tried to lower it a tone as Celia had suggested. It was difficult, though, because her mouth was dry and she could feel her knees trembling a little. 'My name is Abbie . . . and this is Tupperware.' She indicated the array of products at her side. 'Now, we are going to start with a little game to put us all in a party mood and to help us all to get to know one another. Kathleen,' she appealed to her saviour of before, 'I think you know what to do. Could you start us off, please? Oh, I nearly forgot to tell you. I have a box of samples here, so when it's your turn you can choose one – whichever you like – and hold it up.'

Kathleen obligingly started the ball rolling. She chose a serrated tomato cutter from the box Abbie had placed in the centre of the floor. 'My name is Kathleen,' she began. 'Her name is Abbie,' she pointed to Abbie, 'and this is Tupperware.' She held the tomato cutter aloft.

And so on. 'I am Joan, she is Kathleen, she is Abbie, and this is Tupperware.'

'My name is Betty, that's Joan, that's Kathleen, that's Abbie . . . and this is Tupperware.'

It became more difficult, of course, as the women worked their way through the box of salt pots, measuring spoons, bowl scrapers, vegetable brushes and other small items of useful kitchenware, and there were more and more names to remember. 'My name is Sheila, that's Christine, that's Julia, that's . . . Barbara . . . I think. No – you're Barbara, aren't you? That's Moira, that's . . . oh heck! I've forgotten again.' There were peals of sympathetic laughter all round.

At all events it *was* an ice-breaker, which was the intention, and as the evening progressed small prizes were handed out of the box of 'goodies' for various games. For the person who could write the longest list of boys' names beginning with T (for Tupperware), or who could remember all the small items of Tupperware displayed on a tray. Then, after Kathleen had served an appetising supper of coffee and tiny sandwiches and home-made cakes, it was time to get down to business.

Abbie, by this time much more confident, showed her captive, but very receptive, audience the various items that were for sale. The pastel-coloured bowls with the unique seal – 'Just watch while I show you, ladies. You press gently at the side, so that it "burps", to let the air out, then it is completely air-tight and liquid-tight' – which would double

78

as cereal bowls as well as food containers; the 'square rounds', ideal boxes for sandwiches; the 'Party Susan', which would hold many different kinds of salads, or hors d'oeuvres, or sweets, or whatever you wished; the colanders, salad shakers, biscuit jars, cereal containers and mixing bowls. Each guest was given a printed list on which to tick off the items she wished to order and, at the bottom, there was the question of utmost importance. *Would you be willing to hold a Tupper party?*

Anyone would have thought that these women's kitchens were completely void of any gadgets or equipment, judging by the number of goods that were ordered that night. Abbie was astounded as she collected in the forms. They must have quite a lot of 'pin money' to play around with, she decided, as Tupperware was by no means cheap, although she would not admit that to her clients. She was delighted at the orders she received and by the fact that she now had three more parties lined up. Two were afternoon parties for church groups, although these were both some months hence, and the third, in a few weeks' time, was at an address just off Whitegate Drive, quite near to Abbie's father's home.

'Phew! I'm exhausted,' she said, flopping down on to Kathleen's sofa after all the guests had departed. 'It went well though, I think – thanks to you, Kathleen. Did you think so?'

'Of course it did. You should be jolly proud of yourself,' said Kathleen. 'I know you were nervous. You didn't say so, but I could tell.'

'Oh dear! D'you think the others noticed?'

'I don't suppose so. Anyway, what does it matter? You did very well, and you've got a lot of orders, haven't you?'

'Loads. I'm really surprised.'

'Well, that's all that matters, isn't it?'

Abbie admitted to herself that it had not been half as bad as she expected, once she had got going. Things seldom were as bad as you anticipated. She recalled how she had worked herself into quite a frenzy at the thought of moving house, but in the end it had all gone smoothly. Now they were happily settled, and in a few weeks' time she would be coping, or at least helping, with another removal, that of her parents-in-law. She just wished Lily seemed a little more cheerful about it. Abbie was not sure whether she was having second thoughts or, like she herself had been, was just dreading the actual removing day. Perhaps she was sad at the thought of leaving her friends. Abbie hadn't told Doreen just how unhappy Lily had looked at times. She only hoped her mother-in-law's air of dejection was nothing to do with her. She couldn't shake off her feeling of guilt about this.

Abbie's main worry at the moment, however, concerned her friend. Oh, how she wished Doreen would see sense and cancel this clandestine weekend. But she knew it was none of her business and, whatever her feelings might be, she had to keep her nose out.

Doreen was congratulating herself on how well she had managed her getaway. It had all gone according to plan. Norman had insisted on driving her to Central station, as she had guessed he would, but fortunately he had not stayed with her as she booked her ticket to South station and not to Preston. Ken had met her outside the station as arranged and now, having traversed the minor roads of the Fylde, they were zooming along the A6 bound for Lancaster where they would branch off on the road to Morecambe. Doreen was wishing, however, that Ken would not drive quite so fast. She often told Norman he was an old slowcoach, meandering along in the inside lane as everything whipped past them, but Ken, she was now discovering, was the other extreme. He was a commercial traveller, and so he was used to driving fast, but there were times when she found herself giving a gasp of apprehension, almost of fear – she hoped Ken was not aware of this – as villages and farmsteads flashed by, with Ken barely slowing down. The approaching traffic seemed, sometimes, to miss them by mere inches, but she was not a driver herself and she supposed Ken knew what he was doing. Oh God, she tried to pray as another heavy lorry whizzed by, please don't let us have an accident. How awful it would be if Norman were to find out that way. It was something she hadn't even considered.

However, they arrived safely at the resort and Ken pulled up with a squeal of brakes outside the boarding house where he had booked a room for two nights. Lakeland View, although this was a misnomer, was in a side street just off the promenade and it appeared, on first impressions, to be clean and comfortable. Mrs Reynolds, the proprietress, showed them to their room, which had twin beds, a wash basin and ample wardrobe and drawer space.

'What a pity,' said Ken, eyeing the two single beds. He grimaced then grinned at Doreen. 'Never mind, eh, luv? We'll manage very well, won't we?' He winked at her.

'Er, yes,' said Doreen, trying to return his smile. 'Yes, it'll be fine.'

'What's up, luv? You look rather the worse for wear.'

'Nothing. Nothing at all.'

'Drive too fast for you, did I? I noticed you'd gone a bit quiet.'

'Well, a shade fast maybe. I'm not used to it, that's all. I was rather worried about getting away, you know, without anything going wrong. P'raps that's why I was quiet.'

'Well, it didn't, did it? Nothing went wrong. And we're here now and we're going to enjoy ourselves, aren't we?' Ken grinned cheerfully. 'Don't worry about my driving. I'm as safe as houses, honestly. Never had a bump yet, not in twenty years.'

Doreen was to learn that you could, in point of fact, view the Lakeland hills from the top landing window of the boarding house, if you stood on tip-toe and craned your neck. But the hills of the Lake District could be seen in all their splendour from the Morecambe promenade, and it was there that they went when they had unpacked their few belongings.

'Splendid, aren't they?' said Ken, pointing to the mountain peaks making a black silhouette against the darkening sky, which was tinged red and gold by the setting sun. 'Ever been walking up there?'

Doreen hadn't. She had never been a walker, not in the sense that Ken meant, with proper walking boots and a rucksack and all-weather clothing. She learned now that he was keen on fell walking, even climbing, an interest of his that she had known nothing about. He seemed different, somehow, this weekend; not any less likeable, she tried to tell herself, but different. She had not noticed, before, the loudness of his voice, or the sprouting of a few hairs from his nostrils, or the network of broken capillary veins that reddened his cheeks and nose, almost as though he drank too much, but she knew he didn't. Not that any of these things made any difference to the way she felt about Ken. She liked him tremendously and it was so kind of him to have brought her here this weekend; to have found such a pleasant place for them to stay and to have taken time off from his busy schedule in the north-west of England. He had assured her it was purely pleasure this weekend. There were to be no business deals conducted at the local shops on behalf of the stationery firm he worked for. Ken was such a kind man; she had always known that.

They had arrived in the late afternoon and by the time they had eaten their evening meal at the boarding house – a most satisfying meal of freshly caught fish coated in golden-brown batter, served with succulent chips, and followed by Mrs Reynolds's delicious apple pie and cream – dusk was falling.

They wandered on to the promenade again. The evening was chilly, but not unpleasantly so, and as they leaned against the railings looking out at the vast expanse of sand –

the sea went out a very long way at Morecambe – Ken put an arm around her shoulders. 'Happy, luv?' he asked.

'Yes,' Doreen replied briefly. It was funny; they didn't seem to be talking as much this weekend, as though they had run out of things to say to one another.

'Good. So am I. Let's go and have a drink, shall we? I noticed a nice little pub near the boarding house, then we can have an early night, eh? What d'you say to that?' He squeezed her shoulder, pulling her towards him and kissing her cheek.

'Yes, that's a good idea.'

He chuckled. 'You don't sound too sure.'

'Yes, I am. Really, I am.' She smiled at him. 'Come on – let's go and have that drink. I'm feeling a bit chilly.'

They had several drinks, Doreen having far more than her usual single gin and orange whilst Ken stuck to his customary beer. She knew she needed to give herself some Dutch courage. She had never done this sort of thing before, never even imagined herself in such a situation, and now that the time was drawing near . . . She looked across at Ken, tipping his head back to drain the last drop from his tankard, and in that moment she knew she couldn't go through with it.

He plonked his glass down and grinned at her. 'Come on, luv, time to go home. Well, our home for tonight, at any rate.'

They walked the hundred yards or so to the boarding house, arm in arm, letting themselves in through the front door, then mounting the stairs to their first-floor room. Once inside the room Ken did not wait for her to take off her coat. Immediately his arms went round her and he was kissing her passionately, breathtakingly, in a way he had never done before. They had kissed, but only briefly, in the car when they were saying goodnight. Doreen was taken aback, although she knew it was only what she might have expected.

'Ken,' she began when he let go of her, 'I must tell you . . .'

'What is it, luv?' He smiled at her in a curious, but kindly way. 'Feeling nervous, are you? Well there's no need to be. I know what I'm doing and nothing'll go wrong.' He patted his breast pocket, and by that she supposed he meant that he was prepared; that he had a packet of contraceptives with him. That was something that Doreen knew little about. She knew what they were, of course, but she was a Catholic, and in their view contraception was wrong. In fact, the whole thing was wrong. 'Tell you what,' Ken went on, 'I'll nip along to the bathroom and get undressed there. Leave you on your own for a bit, eh? Come on, cheer up, luv. You know how much I think about you, don't you?'

He hadn't said he loved her. He had never said that; neither had she. They were not free to do so. 'Ken,' she said again. She took a deep breath, then let it out in a long sigh. 'I can't. I'm sorry, but I can't. It's the time of the month, you see. I never know just when it's going to happen, and now it's happened.' It was a lie, all of it. She was as regular as clockwork and her period had ended last week, but he was not to know that. It was better than telling him she didn't want to, that she had changed her mind, had come to her senses.

There was a moment's silence, Ken staring at her as though he were dumbstruck, as well he might be. 'Oh I see,' he finally managed to say. 'But why didn't you tell me earlier? When we were on the promenade, or in the pub? I knew there was something the matter; you should have said.'

'I . . . I wasn't sure then,' Doreen faltered. 'I thought something might have happened, but I didn't know for sure. But I know now. I'm sorry, Ken.'

He shrugged a little offhandedly. 'It's not your fault, and it can't be helped, I suppose. It's just one of those things.' He obviously believed her, but then there was no reason for him to do otherwise. He smiled at her, but rather ruefully. 'I'm sorry too, luv. I know you must be feeling rotten. I know all about women and their period pains. Feeling a bit under the weather, are you?'

'Yes, just a bit.'

'I thought so. I realised earlier that you weren't your usual bright and breezy self. Ne'er mind, eh? We can have a kiss and a cuddle, can't we? Now, you'd best nip along to the bathroom, hadn't you, and sort yourself out. I'll get my 'jamas on and have a read of my book. Off you go, luv, and don't worry about it.'

'Thanks, Ken.' She smiled weakly at him. 'Thank you for not minding, and for everything.'

Such subterfuge, she thought, as she grabbed her night-dress and toilet bag and made a pretence of putting something inside it from out of her suitcase. She was lucky that Ken had taken it so well and not seen through her tissue of lies. She had always known he was a happy-go-lucky sort of fellow, ready and able to take things in his stride. But she would have to be careful not to get too close to him, not to sleep in the same bed, for instance, or he might discover her ruse.

Suddenly, Abbie flashed into her mind, her face a picture of shocked disapproval, her deep brown eyes clouded with concern, as they had been when Doreen had told her of her plan to go away with Ken. She loved Abbie dearly – far more, if she were honest, than she loved any of her sisters. But Abbie's naivety irritated her at times and a wicked little streak of perversity in Doreen would goad her on to shock her child-like, trusting friend who, she realised, had never really come to terms with the ways of the world. Abbie was still one of nature's innocents. In spite of having been married and brought up two children, she had never been able to entirely shake off the shackles of her restrictive childhood.

As Doreen undressed in the bathroom, donning her pink nylon nightdress, bought specially from Marks & Spencer for this – now abortive – occasion, she knew, to her chagrin, that Abbie had been right. And that she, Doreen, for whatever reason – her Catholic conscience or the recollection of her friend's disapproval – had not been able to go along with what would have been the ultimate act of wrongdoing, when it came to the crunch. But that streak of obstinacy reared its head again and she was determined she would not give Abbie the satisfaction of knowing this. She would pretend, for the time being at any rate, that they had had a wonderful weekend and that Ken had been all she ever dreamed of in a lover.

Abbie opened her door at half-past six on Saturday evening to find Norman on her doorstep in a state of extreme agitation.

'Where's Doreen?' he demanded. 'Come on, Abbie, I know you know, so don't pretend. Where is she?'

Oh, crikey! Whatever had happened? She had feared all along that Doreen's scheme was doomed for disaster. Nevertheless Abbie knew, for the moment at least, she had to plead innocence. 'Doreen?' she repeated. 'She's with her sister Janey in Preston, isn't she? Oh Norman, whatever's the matter? Come in.'

He brushed past her, making for the sitting room at the front of the house, which was where she had entertained him and Doreen when they had visited her. 'It's all a pack of lies, isn't it? You know – and now I know – that she's not in Preston at all.' He flopped down in an armchair and Abbie just stared at him, knowing she could not carry on lying any longer.

'Something's happened, hasn't it?' she said.

'It's our Paul. He's been injured in a rugby scrum, taken to hospital with concussion, and can I get hold of Doreen? Can I heck as like! I rang Janey's number, like the complete bloody fool that I am, and she doesn't know what I'm talking about. Doreen's not there, never has been; Janey has no idea where she is. But you know, don't you, Abbie?' He paused, looking at her searchingly. 'She's with him, isn't she? That chap from night school.'

Oh crumbs, he knows, thought Abbie. It sounds as though he's known for some time. But before she could answer his question, before she had thought of how best to deal with this awful situation, her mind latched on to what he had said about his son. 'Your Paul,' she said, 'you say he's been injured? How bad is he? Shouldn't you be with him, at the hospital?'

'He's come round,' said Norman, almost dismissively. 'He's OK now, at least he will be. He's in good hands, though he had me worried for a while. But he wants his mum – only natural, isn't it? But she's playing fast and loose with us all. You didn't answer my question, Abbie. She's with *him*, isn't she, that night school bloke?'

'How do you know about him?' asked Abbie, still not saying yes or no, but realising, as soon as she had said the words, that they were a dead giveaway.

'Because I've seen them together, that's why. I went to meet her from her evening class, poor bloody deluded fool that I am . . .' That was the second time he had said that, and never before had Abbie heard him swear. '. . . And there they were, coming along the street, the two of them, laughing and joking together. I dodged back out of the way. Happen I should have confronted them there and then, asked her to introduce me, but I didn't, 'cause I was suspicious, you see. So I watched them and they got into his car and drove away. She came in about an hour later; said a crowd of them had been for a drink.'

'I think there is a crowd of them, Norman,' said Abbie. 'And this sort of thing often happens after night school. They all go out for a drink.'

Norman shook his head sadly. 'Don't make excuses for her, Abbie. I know she's your friend and all that, but I've known about this for some time, had my suspicions at any rate.'

'And you never tackled her about it?'

'No. There was always the possibility I might be wrong, but I'm not, am I? She's with him this weekend, isn't she?'

Abbie nodded, though unwillingly. 'You didn't suspect, when she said she was going to Janey's? If you were having doubts . . .'

'No, the thought never entered my head that she could be guilty of such deceit. I believed she was going to her sister's. She was so convincing. Where is she then?'

'They've gone to Morecambe, I believe.'

'You believe? You know, don't you?' Abbie did not reply. 'Where in Morecambe? Where can I get hold of her?'

'I have no idea, Norman, and that's the honest truth. I don't think Doreen knew herself. She said that Ken was arranging it.'

'Oh, so he's called Ken, is he? Ken what?'

Abbie sighed. 'She just referred to him as Ken. Look, I know she's gone away with him, but I don't think there's anything in it. She said she wouldn't ever want to hurt you, Norman.'

'She didn't want to hurt me?' He gasped. 'Then what the hell is she doing now. Oh yes, I get it – I wasn't supposed to know. I shouldn't have found out – and you never thought of telling me, I suppose, what a lying, deceitful trollop of a wife I've got?' She had never seen Norman so angry. She had never seen him angry at all, Abbie realised, not even mildly so. She continued to stare at him, her lips moving sound-lessly, unable to form the words or even to think what to say to him.

'No, I'm sorry,' he said after a moment. 'It isn't your fault. She's your friend, and I dare say she swore you to secrecy, didn't she? I wouldn't have expected you to betray her, Abbie. You're too loyal a friend for that. Didn't you try to tell her, though, that what she is doing is wrong? I'm sure you must have done.'

'I did, but she wouldn't listen. I'm sorry, Norman.'

He nodded glumly. 'Stubborn as a mule at times, my Doreen.' Abbie couldn't help but notice the possessive pronoun, and she guessed that although her friend would find herself in very hot water indeed when she returned, her husband would forgive her and try to carry on as before. On the other hand, he might throw her out. Oh, what a mess and muddle it all was! If only Doreen had not had that silly craving for excitement.

Norman stood up. 'Well, that's that. I can't get in touch with her. Morecambe's a big place and I can't go knocking at all the doors in the town. I could put out an SOS on the radio, but it's not worth it, not now Paul's recovering. She'll be home tomorrow, anyway, and I'll be ready for her,' he added ominously. 'I'd best get back to the kids now.'

'What have you told them?'

'Very little. Just that I haven't been able to contact their mum. I let them think she was out somewhere with Janey. I couldn't tell them the truth.'

'No, of course not. She still loves the children. And – I believe – she still loves you, Norman.'

'Then she has a funny way of showing it.' He sighed. 'Sorry to have bothered you, Abbie.' He sounded considerably calmer now. 'At least I know now, don't I? And to be forewarned is to be forearmed, so they say.'

Poor Doreen, thought Abbie, in spite of the knowledge that her friend had brought all this upon herself. She watched as Norman walked dejectedly down the path and opened his car door, not even turning to smile or wave at her. Yes, poor Doreen; there was no way *she* could be forewarned. She would come back, all unsuspecting, on Sunday afternoon to God only knows what sort of a welcome. Abbie could have maintained that it served her right, but she could not help but feel sorry for her.

Chapter 7

Doreen was glad the weekend was almost at an end. It was Sunday morning now. There would be time for yet another walk along the prom, then after a snack lunch they would be able to set off for home.

It had not been the exciting, glamorous time she had anticipated when Ken had first mooted the idea. In fact, if she were totally honest, she had known, even as Norman was driving her to the station on Friday afternoon, that she was going through with it only out of a sense of bravado and out of defiance at the reaction of her friend. At that moment she would have given anything to have turned back, but she was unable to do so. She had told Norman she was going to see Janey, and so she had to go through with the pretence.

And from then on, or so it seemed, things had gone from bad to worse. Ken's speedy driving had been the first thing that had worried her, and throughout the weekend the fear of the journey home had niggled away at the back of her mind. A car crash with both of them ending up in hospital – or worse – and Norman's discovery of her perfidy; the anxious thoughts would not leave her alone. She knew that to have such thoughts was most unlike her usual optimistic self, but it was all part of the awful feeling of guilt which had taken hold of her. It was after his erratic antics at the wheel that she had started to 'go off' Ken. Quite rapidly she had fallen out of love – no, not love; enchantment or infatuation or whatever it had been, but certainly not love, she realised now – and she knew she could not possibly allow him to make love to her or even occupy the same bed.

They had kissed and cuddled for a while as Ken had suggested they might; after all, it was the least she could do after the trick she had played on him. Then he had given her a curious look – or was she just imagining that? – and moved back to his own bed. 'I'll read for a while. You don't mind, do you?' he said. 'The light won't disturb you?'

'No, not at all. I'll do the same,' she murmured. Ken was reading a Dennis Wheatley novel and he very quickly seemed to be engrossed in it. She had brought a *Woman's Own*, but the stories and the fashions and the problem page – what distressing and harrowing problems some folk had, to be sure – failed to capture her interest. And after they had agreed it was time to switch off the lamp between their two beds, and Ken had muttered, 'G'night, luv, sleep tight,' she found she could not get off to sleep. Ken soon dropped off, as his rhythmic snoring, much louder than Norman's, indicated, but it must have been the early hours before sleep overtook Doreen. Even then her slumber was restive and she awoke several times during the night wondering, for a moment, where she was.

The best part of the weekend was, undoubtedly, the comfort of the boarding house. Doreen found it was a home from home and she would have appreciated her stay there much more had she not been so consumed with remorse. After they had risen and dressed, Ken departing to the bathroom to leave her on her own for a while, they tucked into an appetising breakfast of bacon, egg, mushrooms, tomatoes and fried bread. Doreen tried to tell herself to enjoy it. She loved her food and there was no point in wearing sackcloth and ashes all weekend. She was stuck here for two days so it was up to her to make the best of it and pretend to Ken that she was having a good time, in spite of feeling under the weather.

She was, in truth, not feeling too well at all, but not for the reason Ken supposed. As the day progressed her sense of strangeness increased. She was in a strange place with a man who had become almost a stranger to her. Her slight headache and her feeling of disorientation were due entirely to her self-knowledge. She had done wrong; in the eyes of her Church, in the eyes of her friend, and, worst of all, she had betrayed her husband and the trust he had always had in her. Please God, she found herself praying from time to time during that long day, though she knew it was an utterly selfish prayer, don't let Norman find out. If only they could get back home without any mishaps then she would be safe and Norman would be none the wiser. She even wondered if she should confess everything to him, but just as quickly as the thought entered her head she dismissed it. No, there was no need to go to such extremes. There was no point in upsetting Norman unnecessarily, even if she could find the courage to do so. But she would start going to Confession again, she decided. She would get herself back on a proper footing in the Church.

First of all, though, there was this seemingly endless day, Saturday, to get through. They walked for miles along the promenade. It was possible to walk across Morecambe Bay at low tide, from Hest Bank to Grange-over-Sands, provided one was accompanied by an experienced guide. Ken told her this in what she thought was a wistful tone of voice, and she was sorely tempted to tell him to go and do it – it was low tide today – if that was what he really wanted, but she bit her tongue. He kept trying to jolly her along. Most likely he couldn't understand this quiet, almost unsociable companion compared with the friendly and talkative women he had met at night school. She chided herself again – Snap out of it, Doreen, for goodness' sake! – and managed to work up a little enthusiasm for their snack lunch of Morecambe Bay shrimps and crusty bread.

In the afternoon they took a bus to the nearby village of

Heysham, and after they had enjoyed another of Mrs Reynolds's well-cooked meals – Lancashire hot-pot that night, followed by gooseberry fool – they decided to go to the pictures. It was obvious by now, to both of them, that the weekend was not a riproaring success, although neither had admitted as much to the other. As Doreen sat in the stuffy darkness of the small cinema watching a *Carry On* film which did not amuse her at all, but had Ken laughing uproariously, she thought she had seldom felt so alone or so miserable. There was only tonight to get through, then tomorrow she would be able to see her family again.

'I'm sorry, Ken,' she said, as he took her arm on leaving the cinema.

'You're sorry? What for?'

'For everything. For not feeling well and because it's not been quite what we expected, has it?'

'Maybe not.' He sounded quite phlegmatic about it all. 'It's just one of those things, isn't it? Put it down to experience, luv. No harm done, eh? It's been a bit of a change at any rate. I was ready for a break.' Seemingly he was taking it all in his stride, as she guessed he was able to do with everything. He did not appear overly concerned that his plans for a weekend of passion had failed, or that the two of them had not 'hit it off' as they had done in the past. He would go back to his wife, she had no doubt, behaving in his usual carefree and jocular manner, untroubled by any pangs of conscience, unlike Doreen.

She slept reasonably well that night and they awoke in the morning to a drizzly miserable sort of day. Doreen wished they could set off for home as soon as they had eaten their breakfast, but as she had told Norman she would be arriving home later in the day, towards tea-time, she realised this would not be possible. She had no idea what Ken had told his wife to explain his absence over the weekend. Probably that he was on one of his longer sales trips; as she was away herself at a trade fair it was unlikely that she would be too concerned. They seemed to go their separate ways, from what Ken had said. It sounded like one of those modern marriages where freedom was the name of the game. Doreen found herself wondering if she was the first, or had Ken dallied with other women he had met on his selling jaunts? She came to the conclusion that he must have done, otherwise he might have been more annoyed about her supposed indisposition.

She was realising how lucky she had been with regard to this. Ken could well have turned nasty; she did not know him well enough to have discovered whether or not he had a bad temper. Fortunately, he didn't; her estimation of his personality had been right in that respect. He was, essentially, a decent sort of man, good-natured and kindly and humorous . . . but he was cheating on his wife.

As you, Doreen, are cheating on your husband, she told herself, watching Ken spreading marmalade on his second piece of toast. She had realised, belatedly, that she was not cut out for this sort of thing at all. Norman might be predictable and unexciting; she remembered telling Abbie he was boring. Not the kindest of things to say about her husband, but she had been feeling annoyed with her friend for her holier-than-thou attitude. Now Doreen was remembering that he was also loyal and trustworthy and, in his own way, a loving husband who she knew would always be there for her . . . in whatever circumstances. Even in circumstances such as these? she asked herself. Oh God, please don't let him find out, and I'll never, ever do anything like this again. It was, in fact, their complete trust in one another that had been one of the bedrocks of their marriage and she had very nearly thrown it away for . . . what? For nothing at all.

'Penny for them.' Ken's jocular voice broke into her reverie. 'You're miles away, luv. What are you thinking about?'

'Oh, nothing much. I was just thinking what a rotten sort of morning it is. Not the weather for walking on the prom. I don't suppose we'll be lingering here too long, will we?'

'A drop of rain won't hurt us,' replied Ken cheerily. 'We need some exercise to walk off this gigantic meal.' He patted his rather rotund stomach. 'We'll walk up towards Hest Bank, not much more than a mile or so – you've got your umbrella, haven't you? Then we'll have a spot of lunch, and – yes – I think we could set off back a little earlier. Mid-afternoon did you say you'd be back?'

'Yes, thereabouts.'

'Same here. I'll tell you what we'll do. We'll start off about eleven o'clock, then we can take our time. I know you don't like me driving too fast.' He grinned at her. 'So I'll try and slow down a bit, just for you. We could stop at a pub and have a bite of lunch on our way back. How about that, eh?'

'That sounds fine.' Doreen smiled back at him. She was feeling more contented now, not so disorientated and lost as she had felt all weekend. She knew it was the thought of going home to her family that had lifted her spirits. And Ken had promised to drive more slowly so that was a weight off her mind.

'You're feeling better this morning, aren't you?' said Ken. 'I can tell.'

'Yes, much better,' she agreed, but it was not for the reason he thought.

'Good . . . good.' He dabbed his sticky mouth with his serviette before rubbing his hands together in a hearty manner. 'Come on then, let's be having you. A nice brisk walk to blow the cobwebs away. Then it's "Home James, and don't spare the horses".'

'I thought you said you wouldn't drive so fast, Ken.'

'I won't. Just a figure of speech, luv. You should be used to me by now.'

But she was not used to him. She felt she had come to know him better this weekend, inevitably, as they had been together for the whole of the last two days, but that was not to say she was used to him, nor could she ever be. She had believed that she and Ken had a lot in common. Now she knew this was not so. Why, then, had they seemed to get on so well together in the night school setting? she asked herself. She did not know the answer and it was useless to worry her head about it. All she knew was that she had made a mistake, the biggest mistake of her life.

Ken was as good as his word. His driving was an example of competence and courtesy to other road-users, and Doreen found herself able to relax much more than she had done on the outward journey. They stopped at a small pub near Scorton for a sandwich lunch and arrived back in Blackpool before three o'clock. Ken dropped her outside Central station, which was where she would have arrived had she really been to Preston. She had told Norman that he must not think of meeting her; she was not sure of the times of the trains, but they would be fairly frequent from Preston, and it would be easy enough to get a taxi outside the station to take her home.

'See you at night school then?' said Ken, leaning across to kiss her cheek. 'Thanks for coming with me, luv. I've enjoyed it in spite of . . . Well, it was a change, wasn't it?'

'Yes, a very nice change. Thank you, Ken,' she replied. He really was a very generous man and had not let her pay for anything this weekend. She guessed he had an expense account and that he was not entirely honest about some of the items included on it, but that was none of her business; she doubted that she would see him again. She had evaded his question about night school. There were only a couple of classes remaining on this term's schedule, and Doreen had already made up her mind she would not be attending them.

She waited while Ken took her case out of the boot, anxious now she was back in her home town lest anyone she knew should see her, but the forecourt of the station was quiet. The holiday season had not yet started. 'There's a taxi over there, Ken. I'll go and grab it.' She seized hold of her case, eager to make a quick getaway. 'Thanks again, a lovely weekend.'

'See you on Tuesday then?'

'Mmm. See you, Ken.' She hurried away before someone else could take the taxi. 'Hornby Road, please. "Dorabella", that's the name of the hotel. It's about halfway up. I'll tell you when we get there.'

'OK, madam.' The taxi driver almost threw her case into the black cab and she scrambled in after it. 'Here on holiday, are you?'

'No, I live here. I'm going home,' she said, settling back in the seat with a feeling of intense relief. She knew she would have to start lying to Norman as soon as she arrived home, but she didn't foresee too many problems. He didn't care for Janey and wasn't likely to ask her overmuch about her sister and her family. And as for Doreen's children, well, they had never seen very much of their aunt and cousins, hardly knew them, in fact, so they would not be curious about their doings. Janey had tended to cut herself off from the rest of her family since her marriage. It might be as well, though, to put her in the picture about this weekend, in case the subject ever arose. It could prove awkward. Doreen didn't know why she hadn't thought of this before.

She paid the taxi driver, then opened the door to a silent house. 'Hello there, I'm back!' Where was everyone? Paul's music could usually be heard, echoing through the house. Doreen didn't allow it when they had visitors, but at other times she didn't mind. Perhaps he had gone out. And the younger children, of course, would be at Sunday School. 'Oh, there you are, Norman. I was just wondering—'

Her husband had appeared from the small living room at the back, but there was no welcoming smile on his face. His mouth, moreover, was set in a grim line and his eyes were cold. She had never seen him look so distant, so unfriendly. 'Why, Norman, whatever's the matter?' she asked, her heart sinking. He must have found out – but how? There was only one other person who knew about it. *Abbie*.

'Where the hell have you been?' His voice was harsh and so very unfamiliar.

Even now it was instinctive to lie. 'I've been to Janey's, in Preston. You know I have.'

'Stop lying, Doreen. It won't do any good. You haven't been anywhere near Preston. I rang Janey and she knew nothing about your visit. It was all a pack of lies. Come on, where have you really been?'

'I've been . . .' She was searching around desperately in her mind for an answer to give to him. 'I've been . . .' There was nothing for it but to tell the truth, or part of the truth, but she could not find the words.

'I'll help you, shall I?' His half-smile was contemptuous. She had never seen him like this before; she felt she did not know this assertive man at all. 'You've been to Morecambe, haven't you? To Morecambe, with your fancy man.'

'If you know where I've been then why did you ask?' Immediately she was on the defensive, though she knew she was in the wrong, so very much in the wrong. 'And he's not my fancy man. I've been away with a friend from night school. And if you want to know why I didn't tell you the truth it's because you're stuffy and old-fashioned.'

'Oh, I see. Stuffy and old-fashioned, am I? It's old-fashioned, is it, not to condone my wife carrying on with another man?'

'We're not carrying on! Nothing of the sort. We're just friends. Why were you checking up on me, anyway? Why did you ring Janey? And how did you find out where I was? No, don't answer that – I know. It was Abbie, wasn't it? She told you. A fine sort of friend she is, I must say.'

'Yes, she's a very good friend, Doreen,' said Norman, sadly as much as angrily. 'A friend who cares about you very much. And don't start blaming Abbie. She had to tell me; she had no choice.' He paused, looking at her intently, his grey eyes behind his spectacles so searching and forbidding that she felt she wanted to shrink away. She could see the hurt there, too, as he went on to say, 'You want to know why I rang Janey? I was not checking up on you, Doreen. I didn't think I would need to. I rang because Paul has had an accident. He was hurt playing rugby, and we wanted you here. Paul wanted you. He needed you, and you were—'

'Oh no! No!' Doreen gave a horrified gasp. Her hand went to her mouth. What on earth had she done? 'Paul, *Paul*! Where is he?' she cried. 'Is he in bed? I must go to him.' Frantically she dashed for the stairs, mounting them rapidly. Her voice caught in her throat as the sobs of anguish overtook her. 'Paul, I'm coming. Mum's here. I'm so sorry, love.'

'Come down, Doreen.' Norman's voice was peremptory, more than a little impatient. 'He's not up there. He's in hospital.'

'In hospital?' She turned round, clinging to the banister rail for support. 'Then he's badly injured, is he? How bad, Norman? Tell me, tell me! How bad is he?' She was almost screaming at him.

Norman gave a deep sigh. 'He's all right now. At least he will be, with a few days' rest and care. His head was kicked in the scrum and he had concussion, but he came round after an hour or two. He's twisted his leg as well, and they decided to keep him in overnight. As a matter of fact, I'm going to bring him home this afternoon. Veronica's with him now, so I'll pick them up in a little while. I was just waiting for you.'

'Norman, I'm so sorry. So very sorry.' She came dejectedly down the stairs, then stood at the bottom, her head hanging down, too ashamed to even look him in the eyes. 'What have you told the children about me? About where I've been?'

He did not answer at first. She looked up, staring at him in anguish. 'Norman, for God's sake, what have you told them?'

'Very little.' His voice was still cold, devoid of feeling. She felt she could not bear it. 'I could hardly tell them the truth, could I? That their mother is a liar and a cheat.'

'Norman, don't. Please don't say that. I'm so sorry.' She reached out a hand towards him, but he did not respond. 'It's not like you think, not at all.'

'As far as the children are concerned,' he went on, 'you were at Janey's, like you said. I let them think there was no one in when I rang. Then when Paul came round it didn't matter so much about getting in touch with you. We were all only too relieved he was getting better. I lied for you this morning, though. You don't deserve it, but I did. I told them I'd managed to contact you, and you'd be home as soon as possible. I was praying that you would be. That you hadn't decided to . . . to run off with him for good.'

'As if I would! I've told you; it isn't like that. It doesn't mean anything.' She had realised during the disastrous weekend that Ken meant little or nothing to her. It hit her even more forcibly now, but would she ever be able to make Norman believe it?

'So you keep saying. Well, you'd better get your tale ready now. The children will be home from Sunday School soon, then I'll be off to collect Paul and Veronica.'

'Shall I come with you?'

'No.' His reply was unequivocal. 'You'll stay here and prepare a nice tea for us all. We'll have to put on an act – but you're good at that, aren't you?' He sounded cynical, most unlike his usual placid self. 'It's the least we can do for our Paul, and don't you dare let them see there's anything wrong, do you hear me? The children are to know nothing about this. It's up to you and me to sort it out, later, what we are going to do about this situation. At the moment it's Paul I'm concerned about, not you. So you'd better pull yourself together and act normally.' His authoritative tone shocked her into silence. She looked at him unsurely, almost pleadingly, but he turned his back on her and walked off into the living room.

For the second time she mounted the stairs, this time carrying her suitcase. She flung it on to the bed then tipped out the contents, ramming them away into the drawers and wardrobe, shoving the dirty clothes into the linen basket, scarcely aware of what she was doing. All the while the tears of misery and self-loathing were streaming down her cheeks. Whatever had she done? And would she ever be able to put it right?

The banging of doors and the sound of shrill voices told her the three younger children were home. 'Is Mum back?' 'Where is she?' 'Are you going to fetch our Paul, Dad?'

Doreen dabbed at her face with her hanky, peering anxiously into the mirror. Her eyes still looked moist and her cheeks were a little blotchy, but it would be understandable, surely, to the children, that she should shed a few tears about Paul? 'I'm here,' she called out. 'Home safe and sound.' She took a deep breath before she walked, as composedly as she could, down the stairs.

They were all in the living room, pestering their father about Paul. 'Can we come with you to get him, Dad? Will he be off school? Lucky beggar, I wish *I* could have a week off school.'

She gave them each a quick hug. 'It's lovely to see you all again. I've missed you ever so much.' She evaded Norman's eye. 'See, I've brought you some sweets from Preston Market.' Actually they were from a sweet stall on Morecambe promenade, but Norman had ordered her to behave as though there was nothing wrong, and so she would. 'They're for you all to share, Veronica and Paul as well. Goodness me, what a time you've been having with Paul, haven't you? And to think that I was away . . .'

'You couldn't help it, Mum. You didn't know he was going to get injured.'

'You've been crying, Mum.' This was Bernie, the tender-hearted and very observant ten-year-old.

'Well, of course I've been crying, love. It was such a shock about Paul, and I was so relieved to be home again, that's all. Now, perhaps Michael could go with Daddy to the hospital. And Bernie and Teresa, you can help me to get the tea ready.'

'No, they must all stay here, Doreen.' Norman sounded as though he would allow no arguing and the children, unusually, fell silent. 'Paul will need all the back seat to himself. I'd better be off then. See you later. Cheerio.' His somewhat worried smile encompassed all the children, but not his wife, but it was only Doreen who noticed this.

'Come on, I'll make some chips,' she said with a forced brightness. 'Lots of chips – Paul's favourite. There's a tin of Spam in the cupboard and another of corned beef, and there's tomatoes and pickled onions and beetroot. And I baked before I went away so there's loads of cakes. Yes, we'll soon have a slap-up meal ready.'

Doreen's quietness, an unusual state for her to be in, went unnoticed in the excitement over Paul's homecoming. There was still a good deal of bruising around his left eye, but his eyesight, fortunately, was unimpaired, and the injury to his leg was not serious. He was cheerful and obviously pleased to be at the centre of so much attention. Doreen did not apologise to him too profusely for her absence. To do so might have drawn attention to it. She was feeling a little calmer now, though still guilt-ridden. All she wanted to do was to put the events of the weekend behind her and get back to normal living. But would it ever be possible?

'It wasn't your fault that you weren't here, Mum,' said Paul, just as one of the other children had said. But she knew she still had to face Norman's wrath, which he was keeping well hidden at the moment. 'We'll sort it out later what we are going to do about this situation,' he had said. What was in his mind? He couldn't possibly mean that he wanted their marriage to end . . . could he?

'Why, Doreen? That's what I can't understand – why?' He

must have asked her this same question a dozen times, but she could not fully explain her actions. They seemed ridiculous to her now, almost madness, to go off for the weekend with a man she hardly knew when she had a husband and five children at home. Almost as though she had wanted to live dangerously for a while, to get away from her usual humdrum existence. But she did not say this. Indeed, she did not fully understand it herself.

The children had gone to bed earlier than usual, all tired out, it seemed, by the traumatic events of the weekend, and Doreen and Norman were on their own at last. 'Why?' he asked again. 'Why did you feel the need to go off with some other fellow? To lie to me and to our children? For God's sake, Doreen, we've got five children!'

'I know, Norman, I know. And I'm sorry. I was sorry before we even got to Morecambe. I think I would have told you. I might have done, I felt so bad about it. But there was nothing in it. You've got to believe me. We didn't . . . you know. We didn't do anything. We never have. He was just . . . a friend.'

'But it's been going on a long time, hasn't it?' said Norman. 'I know. I saw you with him. I came to meet you out of night school.'

'You saw me with him?' She was astounded to hear that. 'Then why didn't you say something?'

'I kept thinking I might be mistaken. I didn't want to believe it, you see. And I really thought you had gone to Preston. I had the shock of my life when I found out you weren't there. Why, Doreen? Why did you do it?'

'I was restless, I suppose,' she told him, though she knew it was a lame sort of excuse. 'I wanted a bit of excitement.' She couldn't tell him that she found him boring and devoid of sparkle, that he made her feel she was growing old before her time, all of which she had said to Abbie. She hoped to goodness Abbie had not repeated what she had said. Besides, she was now realising that it was not true. Norman's reaction to her perfidy had shown him to have a streak of dominance and self-assertiveness of which she had not formerly been aware. Her respect for him had increased and she knew, deep down, that she still loved him: she had never stopped loving him. Their marriage had settled down into the ordinariness common to thousands of marriages, that was all that was wrong. She knew now she would be thankful for an ordinary, uneventful marriage such as theirs, if only he would forgive her.

In the end he did forgive her, as they had both known, all along, he would. There could be no other outcome for a couple such as them. Even if they were to separate – which was out of the question, anyway, with five children to consider – they both knew, according to the dictates of their Church, that they could never be divorced. They did not even discuss such extreme measures, though the unspoken threat had hung heavy in the air as they talked about what had happened to their marriage.

'Familiarity breeds contempt,' said Norman. 'It's trite, but true. I know I'm not a very exciting sort of person, but I thought you loved me. I took it for granted, I suppose.'

'I do love you, Norman,' she insisted.

'Don't our children provide enough excitement, even if I can't?' he asked. Strangely enough, Abbie had said something like that; that children could be fun if you tried to enjoy them. She, Doreen, would have to try harder to find the stimulation she craved, right here, 'in her own backyard'.

She told Norman, time and time again, that she and Ken had not committed the ultimate act of treachery, and it was this that eventually won him round. To have done *that* would have been unforgivable, not only in Norman's eyes, but in the eyes of God and of the Church. They agreed to try again. To go out together a little more – to the pictures, maybe, or for a drink at a country pub. Veronica was quite old enough to babysit the others now, and maybe they had both allowed their marriage to become humdrum. They even started to discuss plans for a family holiday – at some other place than the home of Norman's parents – between Easter and Whit. The holiday season did not get into full swing until after the Whit Weekend, and Doreen was pretty sure she had no one booked in for the first week in May. A quick look at the register told her this was so, and Norman said he would start sending for holiday brochures immediately.

'We'll take the children with us then?' she asked. She remembered Abbie suggesting that it might do her and Norman good to have a holiday on their own, but relations might be somewhat strained for a while, and the presence of the children might help to relieve any tension between the two of them. Besides, who could possibly look after five children while their parents went away? In normal circumstances she might have considered asking Abbie, but now that was completely out of the question. She was far too angry with Abbie to ask a favour of her, or to grant her any, either.

'Of course we'll take the children,' said Norman. 'We're a family, aren't we? We've got to stick together.'

Doreen could not believe she had got off so lightly. Norman had forgiven her. They still had a long way to go, but he was prepared to try and make a success of their marriage, and so was she. Now she would have to forgive herself and endeavour to put it all behind her. Abbie would say, 'I told you so. I knew it would end in disaster,' or words to that effect. Or if she didn't say it, then she would think it. Doreen was very annoyed with Abbie. She knew it was unreasonable of her to feel that way, but she couldn't help it. She had trusted Abbie with her secret. Abbie had betrayed her trust, and that, from someone who called herself a best friend, was like a mortal wound.

Chapter 8

Abbie couldn't get Doreen out of her mind. Norman had been so angry when he came round on Saturday, so hurt and angry, that she found herself quaking in sympathy with her friend when she thought about the homecoming Doreen would have had to face after her illicit weekend. Should she ring her, she wondered, and find out what had happened, or should she go round? Doreen might be in need of a shoulder to cry on. On the other hand, Abbie was still conscience-stricken about her own part in this affair. She had 'spilt the beans', although to be fair she had had no choice. Norman had already guessed, hadn't he? Surely Doreen would understand it was inevitable he would do so and that she, Abbie, could not be blamed. She had felt from the start that the whole escapade was doomed. Poor Doreen. She would give it another day, she decided on Monday. At any rate, she had her second driving lesson that afternoon. She would go and see Doreen tomorrow.

But it was Doreen who came to see her. On Tuesday morning at ten o'clock she opened the door to a pink-faced, very indignant little figure. Oh dear! Abbie found herself quailing at the mere sight of her, her blue eyes blazing with anger, her red lipsticked mouth set in a firm line.

'A fine sort of friend you've turned out to be, I must say!' Doreen launched her attack straight away. 'You *promised* you wouldn't tell Norman, and you did. I just can't believe it of you, Abbie. I trusted you.'

'Doreen, I'm sorry, really I am, but I didn't have any choice. He already knew you were seeing someone else. He'd seen you together.'

'So he told me,' Doreen snapped. 'But it's no excuse, is it? You didn't need to have landed me in it like this. You could have said – oh, I don't know – that I'd gone away on a course, or something. Huh! I might have known you'd crumble away at the slightest touch. It's just like you. You can't stick up for yourself, can you, let alone anyone else.'

'Hey, hang on a minute, that's not fair. I would have stuck up for you if I could, but it was no use. Norman had guessed where you were.'

'He didn't know I was in Morecambe, did he? *You* told him.'

'It doesn't much matter where you were, does it?' Abbie was beginning to get cross now. 'He guessed who you were with – that's more to the point. I was completely dropped on. I didn't know what to say. I had no time to think. I would have told a few lies for you if I could ... and you know I don't like telling lies.'

' "You know I don't like telling lies," ' mimicked Doreen in a silly childish sort of voice, and this, to Abbie, was the worst jibe of all. She felt her eyes becoming moist, but she angrily blinked the tears away. Doreen was being downright spiteful and ridiculous. She had never seen her like this before. Yes, she had – once, when they had first met and Doreen had thought of Abbie as the stuck-up and over-privileged doctor's daughter; the memory returned with startling clarity. But after that they had become bosom friends, inseparable and loyal to each other. She couldn't allow this to happen to them.

'Stop it, Doreen,' she said. 'There's no need for that. There's no need for any of this ... and we can't stand arguing on the doorstep. You'd better come in.'

The look Doreen gave her was malevolent. Her eyes were still smouldering with rage, as she followed Abbie through the front door and into the sitting room. She flopped down on the settee, not waiting for an invitation. 'You don't know what he was like,' she mumbled, as much to herself as to Abbie. 'He was so angry. I've never seen him like that before.'

'I do know, Doreen – I saw him, remember? But didn't he have the right to be angry?' she asked bravely.

'Oh, I suppose so.' Doreen's reply was grudging. The slump of her shoulders conveyed that she was as much dejected now as angry. 'It was the thought that you – you, of all people – had let me down that upset me as much as anything.'

'I've told you I'm sorry,' said Abbie, quite composedly, 'and I can't say any more than that. But surely you were more upset about Paul, weren't you, and about hurting Norman than you were about me. I don't matter really. It's your family that's important.'

'Of course you matter. You've always mattered – you and me.' The look Doreen gave her was still defiant, but her eyes were less angry now. There could almost be a touch of understanding there.

'How is Paul?' asked Abbie quietly. 'You must have been worried sick about him.'

'I would have been if I'd known.' Doreen gave a small sigh. 'He's all right now. He's making a rapid recovery, revelling in a week off school.' She even smiled a little. 'His music was going full blast when I came out, so that's a good sign. He's been hurt before, you know, playing rugby. It's not the first time. He goes at everything like a bull at a gate.'

'Thank goodness it was no worse then,' replied Abbie. 'And Norman?'

'What about him?' Doreen looked at her sharply.

'Well, how is he? How are things between the two of you?' She saw Doreen's lips press together and a set look came on to her face again. 'Perhaps you think it's none of my business, but you made it my business, didn't you, by

108

involving me in all this in the first place. I want things to be all right between you and Norman. Are they?'

Doreen shrugged. 'Yes, they're all right.'

'Only all right?'

'You can't expect us to be all lovey-dovey and everything straight away, can you?' She still sounded mildly aggressive. 'He says he'll *forgive* me.' She emphasised the word and there was the slightest hint of a sneer in her tone. Abbie guessed she was unwilling to put herself entirely in the wrong, although she had probably been made to eat humble pie to her husband. Judging by Norman's wrath, Abbie assumed that this would be the case. 'He wants us to carry on and make a go of things, if we can. Seems we've very little choice anyway. I knew that all along. I told you that I didn't want to hurt Norman. I only want a bit of fun, for a change.' Again she could not keep the belligerence out of her voice.

'And did you get it?'

'Did I get what?'

'Your bit of fun. With Ken. Did you have a good weekend, before you found out about Paul?'

'Before it all collapsed around my ears, you mean,' said Doreen. 'Yes, as a matter of fact, we did. We had a lovely weekend. We stayed in a first-class hotel and had the most gorgeous meals. We walked for miles along the prom and went to the pictures and to a nice little pub. And we talked and talked. It was great to be with someone who was such good fun, so lively and jolly. I told you before – we get on so well together.'

'In every way?'

'What d'you mean?'

'You know what I mean. Did you . . . well, did you? You said Ken wouldn't want you to do anything you weren't happy about.'

'Did we make love, is that what you want to know?' Doreen's bright blue eyes were ablaze with defiance. 'Come on, Abbie, why don't you come out and say it? Don't be so mealy-mouthed. Yes, as a matter of fact we did. And Ken didn't have to persuade me, because I wanted to just as much as he did. And it was great, really great.' She did not add, 'So there!' but Abbie could almost hear the words spoken silently in her friend's mind.

'Oh, I see. Well, that's that then,' she replied. She could not, in any honesty, say, 'How nice,' or 'How wonderful,' or words to that effect. Nor could she start to berate her friend. She, Abbie, had caused enough trouble already, according to Doreen, so there was no point in adding more fuel to the fire now, disapproving as she might be. And she did disapprove, most strongly. 'Does Norman know about it?' she asked.

'That, Abbie Horsfall, is none of your business,' retorted her friend. 'I told you, Norman has forgiven me and that's all there is to it. I've got to make the best of it now. I've had my fling.'

'Fair enough,' said Abbie resignedly. 'But what about Ken? Will you be seeing him again?'

'Yes, just at night school. I'll have to, won't I? And I'll have to tell him it's all over. He'll be upset, I know, but I've no choice.'

'No, I don't suppose you have,' said Abbie. 'Try and put it behind you, Doreen. You've got a good husband and lovely kids. You couldn't think of throwing all that away. It's not worth it.'

'I'm not going to, am I? I'm going to be a model little wife and mother.' Her eyes bored into Abbie's. 'Don't start preaching at me, for goodness' sake, Abbie. You're out of touch, that's the trouble with you.'

'Out of touch with what?'

'With life, with marriage. You haven't been married for ages, have you?'

'That's hardly my fault, is it?' Abbie felt hurt. She wouldn't have believed Doreen could be so heartless. 'My husband died, remember? If he'd lived we would have gone on being happy, I know we would. And I would never, ever have behaved like you did, Doreen Jarvis. You should start counting your blessings. You've still got your husband. You don't know what it's been like, being a widow for seven years, bringing up two children on my own.' She stopped short, aware that she was beginning to feel sorry for herself, and that was something she always tried hard not to do.

'All right, all right, I'm sorry.' Doreen had the grace to look a little shamefaced. 'I know you and Peter were happy, but you didn't really have time for it all to turn sour, did you?'

'And that's what you think has happened to your marriage? That it's turned sour?'

Doreen pulled her mouth into a moue. 'Gone stale, more than sour. There was never anything all that wrong, actually, between Norman and me, but like I told you once before, the gilt wears off the gingerbread. I was bored, and I fell for somebody else. It's as simple as that. It does happen, you know. It's not all that unusual. And I *do* think you're out of touch. You've been living in a backwater, haven't you, ever since you married Peter and went to live in Norfolk. You've shut yourself off from reality, down there in the country.'

'So that's what you think, is it, that I'm some sort of country bumpkin who doesn't know what's going on in the world? Wymondham isn't the country, not exactly. It's a market town, and I dare say there's as much of that sort of thing goes on down there as it does up here, if you look for it. Not that I've ever become involved in anything like that, I must admit,' she added, aware that she sounded a little smug.

'No, you wouldn't, would you, Abbie? You were always naïve. When you were a girl you were always green, compared with the rest of us, and you're not so much different now. If you were to fall in love you might understand a bit better.'

'Is that what it was? You really fell in love with that Ken?'

Doreen's lip curled a little. 'I fell *for* him. It might not have been love, but it was something. Physical attraction, sex appeal, call it what you like – but you wouldn't understand that, would you? I couldn't help myself being attracted to him. You'll know if it ever happens to you. But I don't suppose it ever will. You're so bloody prim and proper.'

Abbie felt a stab of hurt, almost like a physical pain.

'It did happen to me,' she replied slowly. 'I loved Peter, and it wasn't just sex appeal. I would have gone on loving him for ever.' She stared coldly at Doreen. 'And no, I can't imagine it ever happening again. Nor do I want it to,' she added quietly.

Doreen didn't answer. She just looked steadily and unsmilingly at her friend and Abbie could not tell what she was thinking. It was Abbie who spoke first.

'We're not going to fall out about this, are we?' she said, in spite of her hurt. 'I've said I'm sorry. I didn't mean to drop you in it. It seemed to me you were already knee-deep in the mire, weren't you?'

Doreen pulled her mouth down. 'Happen I was,' she said grudgingly. 'P'raps you thought you were doing the right thing, but you were bitter and frustrated as well, weren't you?' she added, almost under her breath.

Abbie decided to ignore Doreen's last remark. She was obviously still feeling very vindictive. 'We're still friends then?' she asked warily.

''Course we are.' But there was no warmth or enthusiasm in Doreen's answer and she did not even look at Abbie. 'Let's forget it, shall we?'

'I'll make some coffee,' said Abbie. 'You'll stay and have some?'

'Just for a little while, then I must get back to Paul; he's on his own.' They were fencing round one another, and when Abbie came back with the laden tray they were still searching for things to say.

'Thank you, no sugar. No, I won't have a biscuit, thank

you.' Doreen was answering her as though she were a new neighbour come to call or a candidate at an interview. Abbie, suddenly remembering what was to take place later that week, seized on this as a topic of conversation.

'I've got my interview on Friday. You know, at Chelford Training College.'

'Oh, good. How are you getting there?'

'On the train from Layton station. It's only a few minutes' walk from here.'

'Will you start there in September?'

'All being well, if I'm accepted.'

Doreen did not reply, as she would normally have done, 'Of course you'll be accepted; they'll be lucky to get someone like you.' Instead she said, 'You'll be able to drive there if you've passed your test by then.' But she sounded completely uninterested.

'If.' Abbie gave a little laugh which sounded forced and unreal. 'I've only had two lessons so far.'

'How's it going?'

'Oh, so-so, you know.'

Doreen nodded, then there was silence again while they both politely sipped their coffee. She did not stay long after that and no further mention was made of the reason why she had called. She did not even say, 'Good luck with the interview,' but just mumbled a sort of goodbye and left without a backward glance. She was obviously glad to get away.

Abbie, too, breathed a sigh of relief when she had gone. At least the dreaded confrontation was over and done with, and it might have been worse. The two of them were still speaking, just about, and she tried to tell herself it would get easier as time went on. Doreen was not one to bear a grudge indefinitely. It couldn't have been easy for her to accept that her romantic weekend had ended in disaster; that she had been found out and her liaison brought to an abrupt end. She had seemed to enjoy it while it lasted, though. But

Abbie had found herself shocked at Doreen's revelations, that she and Ken had actually slept together. She knew she would never feel the same way about her friend, now. How could she? Their precious friendship had been irreparably damaged.

Doreen had not asked her if she had told Sandra and Simon about the interview. It was just as well she hadn't, because so far, Abbie had not plucked up the courage to do so. She wasn't sure why she was being so hesitant. Did she fear they might think they were being neglected, while their mother went off pursuing some crazy whim of her own? Or was she afraid they might ridicule her ambition? At least, Sandie might. She was constantly jeering at things these days, very quick to condemn everything or everybody as 'stupid' if they did not fit in with her own ideas. But did she, Abbie, in point of fact have any *real* ambition to be a teacher? She acknowledged to herself that it was not an out-and-out burning ambition; it was more that it seemed like quite a good idea.

Both children gaped at her when she told them that day, over a favourite tea of spaghetti bolognese followed by lemon meringue pie.

'You want to be a teacher? In a school?' asked Simon, sounding incredulous.

'Yes, that's where teachers are usually to be found, isn't it?' Abbie allowed herself a little smile.

'I mean in a school like ours, mine and Sandie's?'

'No, not in a school like yours – not a grammar school. I'd have to have a degree for that, wouldn't I? This is just a teacher-training course. I'm thinking of training to teach Juniors, or Infants.'

'Oh no, not Infants, Mum. They're dreadful!' Sandie's voice rose in a shrill crescendo. 'They do nothing but spill their milk and wet their knickers. You can't want to do that . . . honestly!'

Abbie raised her eyebrows. 'I should hope there's a little

114

more to it than that. How come you're such an expert on Infants, anyway?'

'My friend at school, Lindsay, her sister's an Infant teacher. Well, she's training to be one at any rate. She's at college, and she had to do a School Practice, or something. She said it was awful, she had the Reception Class.'

'No doubt she'll get used to it,' said Abbie evenly. 'If she doesn't, then she's in the wrong job, isn't she? And I won't be put off. Anyway, I should imagine I know rather more about young children than Lindsay's sister. That's the good thing about going into teaching later. You've got more experience of life.' She recalled, suddenly, Doreen telling her that that was just what she hadn't got. *You're out of touch with life, Abbie.*

'Why d'you want to do it at all, Mum? You never said anything about it before. You were OK working at that dentist's place, and you've got this Tupperware thing.' Was Sandra looking resentful, or was she just curious? Abbie wasn't sure.

'I hadn't thought of it before. It was Norman who put the idea into my head, and I thought, yes, why not train for something worthwhile? I'm only in my early forties. I'll still only be forty-four, when I've finished my training.'

'How long will you be there?' asked Simon.

'Three years.'

'Three years? Gosh! You're going to be at that college place all that time?'

'Apart from the holidays, yes. They're long holidays, mind you. It used to be a two-year course not so long ago, but now it's three. That's the good thing about teaching; it fits in well with your own children's education. When you two are on holiday, I will be as well.'

'By the time you finish training we'll have left school, Mum,' Simon pointed out.

'No, you won't. You'll be sixteen, Simon. You'll be just about to go into the sixth form. Sandie'll be ready for leaving, though; probably thinking about going to college herself.'

'No fear! Not to be a teacher, anyway. As a matter of fact,' Sandie smiled a trifle smugly, 'I'm thinking of leaving when I've done my O-levels and getting a job. So it won't make any difference to me, will it?'

'We'll see about that,' said Abbie carefully. She wasn't prepared to rise to Sandie's challenge at the moment. Her news, on the whole, had been received much more easily than she had anticipated. And she needed their co-operation now. 'Anyway, the point is this; for the next three years, starting in September – that is, if I'm accepted – I'll be around for the holidays, I can promise you that. But during termtime you might have to be on your own a little more than you are at the moment. You'll be home from school earlier than me. I'll get back as soon as I can – about five o'clock, I hope, depending on the times of the trains. Will you be all right on your own for a little while? You could get your own teas, if you felt like it, instead of waiting for me.'

'Stop treating us like children, Mum,' said Sandie loftily. 'I'm fifteen now, not five, and our Simon's thirteen. We're not little kids in the babies' class. 'Course we'll be all right on our own, won't we, Si?'

'We sure will,' drawled Simon with an air of nonchalance, although, of the two, he was the one who was eyeing his mother a little unsurely.

'Yes, of course you will.' Abbie nodded confidently at them, far more so than she was feeling. 'I've always been able to trust you, haven't I? But I wouldn't want either of you to feel I was letting you down. I'm sure they'll ask me at my interview if I've children and whether I've made arrangements for them to be looked after.'

'Stop fussing, Mum.' Sandie glanced at her crossly. 'Honestly, you don't half go on! We're managing OK now, aren't we, while you're doing this Tupperware thing, so what's the difference?'

'I've only had one party so far, haven't I? And that was just down the road, near enough for you to get me if there was a crisis.'

'There isn't going to be any crisis, Mum. Anyway, we're on the phone, aren't we, so you can stop getting your knickers in a twist.'

'Sandra, honestly! I don't know where you pick up these expressions.'

'Sandra, honestly!' Sandie mimicked her mother's tone of voice and her indignant countenance. ' "I would never have got away with it when *I* was a girl. I would never have dared to speak to *my* mother like that." '

'No, I most certainly wouldn't.' Abbie found herself smiling. 'That'll do, Sandie. Anyway, you never knew your Grandma Winters.'

'Good job, too, from what I've heard,' mumbled Sandie.

'She wouldn't have put up with any cheek, I can tell you.'

'Times have changed, Mum.'

'You're telling me!' said Abbie, with feeling.

' "You young girls don't know you're born." ' Sandie was still carrying on with her mockery, but her mother knew there was no malice in it. She was showing a boldness, though, that Abbie would never have dared to display to her own parents. Nor would she even now; her father still expected, and was given, the utmost respect.

'That's enough now, Sandra,' she said calmly. 'I've always tried to be lenient with you. Don't take advantage of it, will you, there's a good girl. I'm trusting you to look after Simon. You're the eldest.'

'OK, Mum, will do.' Her daughter nodded now with no hint of derision and Abbie began to feel better about things. She couldn't help thinking, though, of the crisis that had arisen in Doreen's household when she was away from home. That had been totally unforeseen, as such calamities often are. There was no point, however, in predicting disaster, Abbie told herself. Three years was a long time to spend in a

117

state of apprehension; she would never get through the course if she was continually worrying about what might, or might not, happen.

'I still can't imagine why you want to be a teacher, Mum,' Sandie added. 'A glutton for punishment, that's what you are.'

The Training College was only five minutes' walk away from the railway station. It was easy to find, being almost in the centre of the town and just across the road from the market. Friday was a market day and Abbie glanced, in passing, at the various stalls with their gaily striped awnings. She loved markets and decided she would have a wander round later when the interview was over. She had not been feeling particularly nervous; more excited and ready to face the challenge of the day, and of the next three years, if she was lucky. Nevertheless, she felt a twinge of panic and a slight fluttering of her stomach muscles as she mounted the long flight of steps leading up to the front door of the redbrick building. It reminded her of the Blackpool Grammar School for Boys in Church Street – the school which had recently removed to Highfurlong and which Simon now attended – and she guessed that the interior would be pretty much the same as well. The style was that of the early years of the century; long corridors, half-tiled walls, lofty ceilings and windows set high up so that pupils could not be distracted by the view outside.

She took her place with a few other candidates who were seated outside what she guessed had been, at one time, the Headmaster's room. There were two other women and a man, and Abbie was encouraged to note that they were all roughly the same age as herself, give or take a few years. It was hard to guess people's ages, but she had feared, in spite of Norman's reassurance that this college was mainly for mature students, that she might appear as old as Methuselah compared with the others. The woman next to her smiled and nodded a greeting and asked if she had travelled far.

'From Blackpool,' said Abbie. 'What about you?'

'I'm what you might call a local lass,' said the woman. 'I'm from Leybridge. It's only one stop away, so it'll be handy if they decide to take me. We must have been on the same train; I didn't notice you, though. We could travel back together, perhaps? I could wait for you if I go in first. What's your name?'

'Abbie – well, Abigail really – Horsfall.'

'Oh. I'm Jean Birtles, so I'll be in before you if they take us in alphabetical order. Before anybody, I should imagine.' She looked around interestedly, but the other two people did not respond. She pulled her mouth down then grinned meaningfully at Abbie. 'Shall I wait for you, then we can tell one another how we've got on?'

Abbie hesitated. She didn't want to appear rude. At first glance she did quite like what she could see of the woman; she was chatty and friendly and probably easy to get on with. But Abbie felt she might need a little time on her own afterwards for quiet reflection, and time, also, to savour the excitement of a day in a different town with new shops and streets and markets stalls to explore. 'We don't know how long they're going to keep us, do we?' she replied. 'Perhaps we'd better just go our separate ways, but I can meet you later at the station, if you like.'

'OK, suits me.' Jean Birtles grinned again. 'Which train are you getting back?'

Abbie didn't have time to answer because a woman in a tailored costume opened the door at that moment. 'Mrs Birtles, please?' she said questioningly, and Jean stood up.

'That's me.'

'Would you come in, please?'

The other two candidates shuffled their feet, moved about in their chairs, and after a brief glance around looked down again, obviously disinclined to chatter. The woman was reading a neatly folded newspaper and the man was consulting a railway timetable. Abbie did not mind their silence if that was the way they wanted it. She was not much of an idle chatterer herself and did not often instigate a conversation with strangers, preferring someone else to take the initiative. She was content to sit and wait although she hoped it would not be too long before she was called. In the days when she had been Abigail Winters she had always been at the tail end of any list, although there had not been too many of those. Only the school registers, and the list of applicants when she had applied for the Land Army. Apart from that she could not remember ever having had an interview. Her appointment at the dentist's surgery in Wymondham had been very informal, just a brief talk with the dentist who ran the practice. She was glad her surname now came earlier in the alphabet. There were only five letters between B for Birtles and H for Horsfall, she found herself pondering, but there was no way of telling. These two, with their eyes glued to the page in front of them, might be called Davis, or Eaves, or Fisher, or Giles. In which case she would have a long wait. Doreen, she knew, would have asked them. 'Excuse me, what's your name?' she would have called out boldly.

In point of fact she waited for what must have been ten or fifteen minutes before the door opened again and a very elated-looking Jean Birtles walked out. Could she have been offered a place already? Abbie thought not; maybe it was just a sign that the interview had not been too horrendous. She did not find out the names of the silent candidates, as she, Abbie, was the next to be ushered in by the costumed lady. Nor did she have a chance to discuss times of trains with Jean.

'Good luck,' mouthed Jean Birtles, sticking her thumb in the air, and Abbie felt cheered. She began to hope that the two of them might end up on the same course or group or set, whatever it might be called.

'Come in, Mrs Horsfall. Sit down, please.' There was another woman seated behind the desk in the centre of the room, and she smiled pleasantly at Abbie. She had gold-rimmed spectacles, black hair which was swept back from her face in a French pleat and she wore a bright red dress. She might have looked formidable had it not been for her welcoming smile. The woman in the navy tailored costume, who had short iron-grey hair, sat down at the side of her and Abbie seated herself opposite them. She had no idea who these two women were; the Principal, maybe, and her deputy? At all events they looked an interesting couple and were a sharp contrast to one another.

'I am Miss Fairbrother,' said the one with the gold spectacles, 'and this is Miss Williams. We would like you to tell us a little about yourself, Mrs Horsfall.' She did not indicate what their positions were in the College. Abbie wondered if she was expected to know without being told; maybe she should have done her homework before she came. Feeling at a slight disadvantage she began to speak.

'Well, I'm a widow.' Now that sounded negative for a start, didn't it? She paused.

'Yes, we noticed that on your application form,' said Miss Fairbrother. She smiled encouragingly at Abbie. 'You have children?'

'Yes, I have two, a girl and a boy.' Abbie explained that they were now in their teens, of an age when they did not need too much supervision. She would not have dreamed of undertaking a teaching course when they were younger, she said, but she felt that now was the time for her to train for a career that would bring her satisfaction and a sense of achievement.

'And why have you chosen teaching, Mrs Horsfall?' asked Miss Williams. 'There are other careers which would, presumably, give an equal sense of fulfilment?'

But not the same long holidays, nor the hours that would fit in with my own children's needs, said a little voice in Abbie's head, which she had the sense to ignore. 'I wanted to train for teaching when I was much younger,' was what she

121

replied. It was not strictly true, but who could tell what she might have done if her mother had been less overbearing? 'But my parents . . . well, they did not altogether agree with my plans. My father was a doctor and he more or less insisted that I should work for him, which was what I did, of course. He would have liked me to be a nurse.' The two women nodded understandingly. They were both somewhat older than Abbie. No doubt they, too, remembered a time when daughters were far more subject to their parents' dictates than they were today.

'Then the war started and I joined the Land Army,' Abbie went on. 'I got married and had the children, and there just hasn't been the opportunity until now.'

'And now is a very good time,' said Miss Fairbrother. 'You are still a young woman, but not too young.' Not likely to mess up your training by getting pregnant – was that what she meant? Abbie wondered. 'Students here do two main courses and two subsidiaries,' she continued, 'as well as the Education course which is concerned with the principles of teaching. What are your interests, Mrs Horsfall?'

Music, she told them, saying she had been quite a good pianist in her youth, but was a little out of practice now. Excellent, they replied. That was a skill which would be very much in demand, especially as it was the Infant and Junior course for which she was applying. She loved literature, too, and what, at school, they had used to call Nature Study. She told them how she had missed the countryside since she returned to Blackpool. Her previous home had been in a much more rural setting.

There would be plenty of time for her to decide later on the exact courses she wished to take, they told her. Her qualifications – School Certificate passes amounting to the equivalent of eight O-levels – were more than ample for their requirements. They would let her know shortly, they said, being careful not to give anything away, but she felt she was in with a good chance.

'Thank you, Mrs Horsfall, that will be all,' said Miss Williams, rising to her feet, and Abbie felt as though the interview had flown by in just a few seconds. Commonsense told her, though, that it must have been more than a quarter of an hour. The two uncommunicative candidates had been joined by another two people now, a man and a woman. Abbie smiled vaguely in their direction, then made her way out of the building and into the street facing the market.

She realised she was hungry, although a glance at her watch told her it was only eleven-thirty, too early to have lunch. She decided to have a look round the market, then, in a little while, she would find a café. Abbie loved markets and regretted that Blackpool no longer had one. There were the two market halls, of course – St John's Market and the one in Abingdon Street – but they were there all the time and the stalls seldom changed. It was not the same as a weekly travelling market where stallholders came from the outlying district to sell their goods. She had always enjoyed Wymondham Market, and the one in nearby Norwich with its rows and rows of striped awnings had been particularly fine.

She wandered now along the aisles, between the stalls selling crockery, second-hand books, toys, cut-price electrical goods, and materials of a myriad textures and colours. There was nothing she particularly wanted to buy in this section, but still she found it fascinating. It was a unique experience, she recalled, being a market trader. When she had been in the Land Army, working on Marton Moss towards the end of the war, she had sometimes accompanied Mrs Webster on her weekly visit to Preston Market to sell their produce; the famous Blackpool tomatoes, vegetables, flowers and home-made marmalade and pickles. She felt an empathy now with the men and women manning the stalls, some stamping their feet or blowing on their hands between bouts of serving, because the March air was chilly. She remembered how her feet would be like blocks of ice on cold winter mornings, although there could be no pleasanter occupation when the weather was clement.

The pungent odour of vegetables and fruit conveyed to Abbie that she was near the food section of the market. She purchased some shiny green and red veined apples, thinking they would be crisper than the deep red ones, a fluffy white cauliflower and several large breakfast mushrooms, one as big as a small saucer; they were much tastier than the button type. Then she was tempted by the luscious pale pink ham, cut from the bone, on a farm produce stall. She bought half a pound of this – to have for tea with baked potatoes and pickles – a large chunk of creamy Lancashire cheese and a jar of home-made lemon curd. By this time her string bag, which she had tucked away inside her handbag, was cutting into her fingers with the weight and she decided she had better bring her spending spree to an end.

Another appetising smell – mingled aromas of fried onions, smoked bacon and freshly brewed coffee and tea – was wafting across from a nearby covered stall. Abbie had been hungry half an hour ago and she was more so now. She placed her order, for a bacon barmcake and a pot of tea, at the counter, then sat down on a stool at a Formica-topped table. She waited for her snack lunch, savouring the varied sights and smells and the hustle and bustle going on around her. She was experiencing a moment of deep contentment where she felt at peace with herself and with the world. Such moments were rare indeed. There was usually something to worry about; the children, Doreen, her mother-in-law, her father's health – not major worries, to be sure, and not to be compared with some of the troubles she had gone through in past years, but real enough to disturb her peace of mind. For the moment, they had vanished. Moreover, Abbie felt she was at the brink of a new and exciting episode in her life.

'Yoo-hoo, yoo-hoo.' A woman's voice, not loud or shrill, but insistent, broke into her reverie. She looked up to see her acquaintance from the College coming towards her – Jean Birtles, wasn't that what she said she was called? 'Hello again, Abbie, isn't it? Do you mind if I join you? I'm famished and this place looks as good as anywhere.'

Abbie did not mind at all. Her short period of serenity was about to be brought to an end, but what did it matter? Here was a new friend, she could feel it in her bones; one who would be part of the exciting time that lay ahead. She gestured to the stool next to her. 'Yes, come and join me. I'm so pleased to see you again. It's Jean, isn't it?'

Chapter 9

During their lunch together, Abbie learned that Jean Birtles had been married, but was now divorced. She tried not to look at her as though she had two heads. Divorce was becoming far more commonplace these days, but Abbie had never before spoken with anyone who had been through this trauma. She began to realise, listening to Jean's story, that she, Abbie, had led what might be called a sheltered life. It was true that she had encountered illness and the death of the person who had meant most to her in the world, but her life, otherwise, had gone along quite smoothly and uneventfully. You could not count the occasional outbursts of rebelliousness from Sandie; she assumed these were common to many teenagers. Doreen had told her, more than once, that she was out of touch, that she had no idea of what was going on in the world around her. Once, indeed, her friend had called her a prig and said it was time she got herself a fellow. Abbie had resented that. She had never considered her outlook to be priggish, just moral – she supposed that was the word for it – or high-principled. *Just wait till it happens to you*. She could almost hear Doreen's voice in her mind as she listened to the other woman's story.

Jean was two years older than Abbie, but Abbie thought she looked the younger of the two. She had joined the WAAF soon after the start of the war, and that was how she had met her husband, Eddie, who had been a flier, just like Abbie's husband Peter. This gave the two women an immediate empathy. Jean and Eddie had met, originally, in a Blackpool ballroom, and so had Peter and Abbie – except in their case it had been the Winter Gardens, rather than the Palace.

'Our marriage didn't last though,' Jean told her. 'We stuck it out for eight years – for the sake of the kids, I suppose – but it was a miracle it lasted so long. It was glamorous enough to start with. I had the most gorgeous wedding dress of parachute silk, and two bridesmaids, even though it was wartime. Married in 1944, we were. You could say it was one long honeymoon at first, with all the meetings and partings. You will know what I mean, of course. Not like real life at all.'

Eddie had never settled down to civilian life after a dazzling career as a fighter pilot. Reality consisted of two children, a mortgage, and a mundane job in an insurance office in Eastbourne; the prospects were good, but his heart was not in it. And his wife was no longer a saucy little Corporal in the WAAF, but a common or garden housewife.

'There's no doubt about it; there's a lot of glamour attached to a uniform,' Jean sighed. 'I think we were both disillusioned. Mind you, he'd always had a roving eye.'

Eddie had 'upped and left', as Jean put it, in 1952 when the children, a boy and a girl, were aged seven and five. He had gone off with a typist from his office and, soon afterwards, had packed in his steady job in insurance to open a travel agency on the outskirts of Eastbourne, which he was still running with his new wife.

'So I came back up north,' said Jean. 'I'd never settled down there anyroad. There's summat different about southerners, you can say what you like. They try to be friendly, but they're not like the folks up here, are they, luv?' Abbie found herself warming to Jean's homely northern accent, though she guessed it was exaggerated at times – to show she was not ashamed of her roots, maybe? Abbie doubted she would have spoken quite so broadly at the interview.

'I would have thought you'd have made friends quite easily,' said Abbie. 'You're a friendly sort of person, aren't you? Perhaps it was because you were never really happy with Eddie – was that it? And you were homesick for the north, maybe – the "hills of home", as they say. I settled down well enough in Norfolk, I must admit, and I didn't notice the people were so different. But that's because Peter and I were happy, very compatible.'

'You were one of the lucky ones,' said Jean, but not at all grudgingly; she was smiling warmly. 'I know it's very sad that your husband died, but you've only happy memories to look back on, haven't you? You know, "For ever wilt thou love and she be fair" – that sort of thing.'

Abbie nodded, recognising the quotation from *Ode on a Grecian Urn* by Keats. ' "For ever panting and for ever young",' she added. 'Not that we were all that young, Peter and I, when he died, but that's the way I like to remember him.' She was feeling that she had quite a lot in common with her new friend; already she was beginning to look upon Jean as a friend.

Jean nodded. 'I'm so glad you were happy. Me, I just spent me time being homesick. You're quite right – I *was* homesick. I couldn't wait to get back up here, so Eddie did me a favour when he buzzed off. It took a while to get it all sorted out, the divorce and everything, but it's all behind me now. I've a nice little home for me and the kids, I'm not too far from me mam and dad, and now I've got this teaching course to look forward to.'

'If we're accepted,' said Abbie.

'Of course we'll be accepted.' Jean thumped lightly on the table. 'Think positive, Abbie.'

'I'm trying to.' Abbie smiled. 'I must admit they were very encouraging at the interview. I'd be surprised if I was turned down after the leading questions they asked. What are you doing at the moment, Jean? What's your job?'

'Shorthand typist – same as I've always been.'

'But you fancy a change?'

'I fancy the good pay, short hours and long holidays!' Jean grinned. 'Only joking,' she added, noting Abbie's look of surprise. 'I know teachers work damned hard, but that's the general view, isn't it? It's something I've had in mind for quite a while, but like you, I've been waiting till the kids were old enough to fend for themselves a bit. And then . . . well, a couple of years ago I should've been getting married again, but it all came to nothing.'

'Oh. I'm sorry.'

'Don't be. I've come to the conclusion I'm better on me own. Love 'em and leave 'em, that's what I say. There's been a few since Eddie went, I must admit. I thought the last one was serious, but he went the way of all the rest. What about you, Abbie? Are you foot-loose and fancy free?'

'What, me? Oh no. There's no one else for me. There never has been, since Peter. I don't think I would want to—' She stopped lest she should sound too pious. That was what Doreen had accused her of.

'No, you've nothing to prove, have you?' said Jean. 'You've had a happy marriage. As for me . . . well, I think I was trying to prove I could make a relationship work, but it seems as though I can't. So I've given up on men. I'll concentrate on my career.'

She was a vivacious woman, several inches shorter than Abbie, with dark hair upswept in a modern, bouffant style, which made Abbie feel that her own hair, curling around her forehead and neck, was distinctly out of date. Jean's eyes were hazel – more green than brown – and held a lively, questioning look. Her slightly crooked nose and her wide mouth, revealing teeth that were a little out of line, prevented her from being beautiful or even pretty, but she was certainly one of the most attractive women Abbie had ever met, both in looks and personality. I shall be overshadowed by her, thought Abbie, the insecurity which had been the bane of her life raising its head again. She is smaller than me, but she will make more of an impression, just as Doreen always did. All the same, that did not prevent her from hoping that Jean Birtles would be her friend.

'We're going to be good friends, you and me,' said Jean, as though she were reading Abbie's mind. 'I can feel it in me bones, can't you? And we're both going to be accepted, there's no doubt about that. Now, d'you fancy a wander about Chelford before we get our train? There's nowt much to it; it's not as big as Blackpool and the shops can't compare with your RHO Hills, but it's worth a look.'

By the time she said goodbye to Jean Birtles in the mid-afternoon as she got off the train at Leybridge, Abbie felt as though she had known her for years.

She's nice, thought Jean. I like her; I hope we'll be friends. She knew, though, that she must try not to overshadow the woman with her own ebullient personality. There had been an example of that this afternoon, not that it had been Jean's fault; it was just the way it happened. They had gone into a nice little café on the main street to have a cup of tea and a cake before they went for the train. They had talked themselves dry and as they had not had an 'afters' to follow their delicious bacon barmcakes they were ready for some sustenance. The waitress had handed the bill to Jean. She hadn't asked for it and both she and Abbie had spoken when placing the order, but somehow the waitress had assumed that she was the one in charge. Why? Jean wondered. Was it because she had the most to say? The girl must have noticed her chattering twenty to the dozen whilst Abbie was mainly listening. Abbie was the sort of person who blended into the background, whereas Jean was usually the one people noticed.

Abbie hadn't appeared to mind. She had taken out her purse, even though Jean had said it was her treat, and insisted on splitting the bill fairly in two. Jean hadn't argued; she did not want her new friend to feel she was being patronised. As soon as she met her, she had known that Abbie Horsfall was a very nice person. On further acquaintance she had found her to be kindly and gentle and an excellent listener. Jean's friends needed to be good listeners; those who knew her the best had often told her so. Abbie seemed trustworthy, the sort of person to whom you could confide your secrets and feel they would not, immediately, become common gossip. Her lovely deep brown eyes reminded Jean of her cocker spaniel, Amber, who had the same trusting look and eyes of the same hue, not that she would have dreamed of saying that to Abbie. She was, Jean thought, just the teeniest bit old-fashioned. Not, however, in her dress; her sage-green semi-fitting coat with the stand-away collar had been very fashionable. It had just skimmed her knees, showing to advantage her long and shapely legs. Jean had felt slightly envious of Abbie's legs; her own were too thin and sinewy. No, it was more in her general demeanour that Abbie seemed old-fashioned, as though the worldliness around her had not affected her innate naivety. She could do more with her hair, or was that a case of sour grapes since she, Jean, was always having to mess around with hers, backcombing it to give it height and paying regular visits to the hairdresser for sets and perms. Whereas she guessed Abbie's hair curled naturally and would need little tending. Jean had to admit that the style did suit the other woman's plump and fresh-complexioned face.

Jean was aware of true beauty there, not the mere attractiveness that was more due to artifice than nature, as her own was. Jean did not spare the lipstick and powder and eye-shadow, knowing that you had to make the best of yourself, especially when you had not been given very much to start with. At all events she was hoping she had made a new friend today, although she must be careful not to lose her through too much exuberance. She felt she would like to draw Abbie out, help her to emerge from her shell. It was

Jean's opinion that there was far more to Abigail Horsfall than met the eye.

Abbie knew the next couple of weeks would be hectic ones. Her parents-in-law were moving from Wymondham into the house they had bought at the other end of Layton, she had her next Tupper party to arrange and, as it was the Easter holiday, Sandie and Simon would be at home. She thought she might take advantage of this and persuade them to help her with some decorating – of their own bedrooms, perhaps. Sandie's rolls of jazzy wallpaper were still on top of her wardrobe, all these months later. Abbie did not feel she could ask Doreen for any further help, considering their somewhat strained relations. Besides, Doreen would be fully occupied at the moment preparing for the Easter visitors, that being their first busy weekend of the season.

Mr and Mrs Horsfall made the move without a great deal of difficulty, although Lily complained, albeit mildly, that she hadn't realised the rooms were quite so small and that their cumbersome – rather old-fashioned – furniture would look top-heavy in its new surroundings. Abbie tried to convince her that this was not the case, that the less spacious accommodation would just take a bit of getting used to. Their semi in Norfolk had been a good family-sized home; too big, now, for the two of them. Abbie pointed out that the garden here was of a much more manageable size for Frank to cope with, while for Lily, the smaller rooms would not need so much cleaning, and the shops were just around the corner. In Wymondham they had been quite a distance away, which had sometimes meant that Frank had to take her in the car.

Abbie, in point of fact, had had the same opinion about the furniture as she watched the removal men stagger with it through the door of the bungalow. She had supervised the arrival of the household effects whilst Lily and Frank travelled by car, arriving only when most of it was in place; they had left a list with her saying what was to go where. Now there were the packing cases containing all their crockery, cooking utensils and ornaments to be unpacked. Lily was a great one for knick-knacks and Abbie doubted that Frank would have been able to persuade her to part with many of her treasures, despite the lack of space.

'Let's just unload the important items,' Abbie suggested. 'The pans and cups and saucers and that sort of thing. You've got the boxes labelled, I see – that was a good idea. I'll get Sandie to come down and give you a hand with the rest of the stuff tomorrow. Simon, too, unless you think he'd be in the way.'

'The lad'd never be in the way,' said Frank, 'but he'd sooner be off playing football, wouldn't he? He won't want to be bothered with a couple of old fogeys like us.'

'Nonsense, Grandad. He'd love to come and help. I don't want him to be more of a hindrance than a help, that's all. I discouraged either of them from coming today; the fewer people around the better when the removal men are at work. They'll be round to see you soon, though. They've both been excited about you moving here.' She was trying, as indeed she had been doing ever since they told her of their intended move to Blackpool, to convince them that they really were welcome here.

'That's good,' said Frank quietly. 'We neither of us want to push in where we're not wanted, do we, Lily?' Oh dear, thought Abbie. He still sounded a little disgruntled. He must be remembering her initial reception of their news. She pretended not to notice.

'No,' said Lily, even more quietly. 'No, we don't.' She appeared preoccupied, almost sad for a moment, then she looked at Abbie and smiled pensively. 'We're glad to be here, dear, and we hope you are glad, too.' She looked tired, Abbie thought. Very tired and bewildered, as well she might at the end of a long journey, surrounded by packing cases and piles of bedding and curtains and goodness knows what else.

Abbie moved across and put her arm round her, kissing her on her soft, still smooth cheek. The gesture was instinctive. So were the next words she spoke. 'It's lovely to have you with us, Mum,' she said. It was the first time, ever, she had called Peter's mother 'Mum', and she had scarcely realised she was doing so. If Lily noticed she made no comment. She just squeezed Abbie's hand briefly and Abbie noticed there were tears in her eyes.

'I'm sorry,' she said, putting a hand to her brow. 'Silly of me. I'm just a bit tired, that's all.'

'I'm not surprised,' said Abbie. 'I tell you what – shall I go and fetch us some fish and chips? There's a shop at the end of the road and I believe they're very good. I'll just put the kettle on for another cup of tea, and perhaps you could warm some plates while I'm gone. At least the cooker's working.'

'If I can find the plates,' laughed Lily, seeming a little more in control of herself now. 'Yes, fish and chips are a good idea, Abbie. It's a long time since we had our breakfast.'

Later, Abbie put up the curtains – the ones from their previous house had sufficed, although a few hems had had to be turned up – and made up their bed, putting hot water bottles at the head and foot, whilst Lily and Frank washed the few dinner pots. It was nearly tea-time before she left them, with a promise to see them soon; if not the next day then the day after that. At all events, the grandchildren would be there on the morrow.

Abbie made up her mind that she must see Lily on her own, as soon as she could, for a confidential chat. She sensed there was something troubling Lily. It could well be the strangeness of her new surroundings, or maybe she was still not entirely convinced her daughter-in-law wanted her to be there. If that was the case, then Abbie must set her fears at rest. But she felt sure it was something other than that. There was a look of fear and anxiety in Lily's eyes that she did not like at all.

She had forgotten, momentarily, that it was her next Tupper
party two days hence, so she was obliged to send a message
with Sandie that she would call and see her parents-in-law
later in the week. The party was to be held at an address just
off Whitegate Drive, quite near to the home of her father
and Faith, which was very convenient for Abbie. Especially
as Faith had already transported her boxes of merchandise
in the car to her own home, and had offered to take them to
the house where the party was being held on the said
evening.

Abbie would be relieved when she had her own vehicle.
Her driving lessons were progressing satisfactorily. She had
surprised herself at how well she was taking to driving,
mastering the gears and clutch and brake and accelerator
pedals with comparative ease, not to mention all the knobs
on the dashboard. She had thought it all looked terribly
complicated when she watched Faith or her father-in-law or
Norman driving, but it was amazing how quickly it all fell
into place. She was taking lessons in a Ford Anglia and
intended buying a car of the same model when she had
passed her test. For the moment she was forced to rely on
buses for her trips into town, and it would have to be a taxi
in future to transport her Tupperware items. She could not
expect Faith always to act as chauffeur.

'I'm awfully grateful to you, Faith,' she said as they
unloaded the boxes from the boot and back seat and started
to carry them up the path to the front door. 'The trouble
with this stuff is that it takes up so much room. It's light
enough, but it's bulky. I couldn't have managed without
you.'

'Don't mention it,' said Faith. 'I've an ulterior motive . . .
I'm coming to the party. I want to see you at work.'

'Oh, crumbs! You're not, are you? You'll make me nervous.'

'Rubbish! You'll forget I'm there. Anyway, you've done
one before, haven't you? And you did very well, too. It'll be

easier this time. It's all good practice for when you stand in front of a class.'

'So I keep being reminded.'

'You haven't heard anything yet from the College?'

'No. I'm keeping my fingers crossed. It shouldn't be long.'

It was Moira who was holding the party this time. She was a friend of Kathleen, Abbie's neighbour, who had held the first party. Abbie found herself relaxing and getting into the swing of it all far more easily this time. 'I'm Abbie,' she began, 'and this is Tupperware.'

The game proceeded. 'I am Stephanie, this is Tupperware'; 'I am Gillian . . .'; 'I am Irene . . .'; 'I am Heather . . .' and so on. 'I am Sylvia . . .' Abbie gave a slight start as she looked properly for the first time at the woman who had spoken; until that moment she had noticed her only as one of a crowd. She was slim and dark-haired, or had used to be – her hair was turning grey at the temples now. A few years older than Abbie, she had a lively, interested sort of face and intelligent dark grey eyes. Abbie knew at once who she was. Sylvia Fairfax she used to be called. Now, of course, she was Sylvia Webster. She had married Jim towards the end of the war soon after Abbie had married Peter. Jim Webster . . . to whom Abbie had briefly been engaged, during that period in her life when she had believed Peter was dead and gone from her for ever.

There had never been any animosity between the two young women, and as Abbie smiled at her now, Sylvia nodded and smiled back. They did not have a chance to speak to one another until the games were over, Abbie had done her talk about the benefits of Tupperware, and the order forms had been distributed.

Sylvia came over to her where she stood at the side of her pastel-coloured bowls and boxes and myriad containers. 'Hello, Abbie. I thought it might be you because of the unusual name, but I wasn't sure until I heard you speak.'

'Hello, Sylvia.' Abbie smiled warmly at her. 'How lovely

to see you again. I'm sorry, I didn't notice you at first amongst such a sea of faces. And I'm rather new to all this. It's only my second party and I was trying to concentrate on what I was doing. How is Jim? Are you still at the market garden on the Moss?'

'Jim's fine, thanks. Yes, we're still at the same place. Jim's parents retired and we took it over. They live in a bungalow now, not very far away from us. They're both hale and hearty, I'm pleased to say – they're well into their seventies now. Arthur still comes to help with the tomatoes now and again; he's never really wanted to let go of the reins, you know.'

It was good to hear news of Mr and Mrs Webster again. Abbie had been very fond of them both when she had worked at their market garden on Marton Moss at the latter end of the war. They had consoled her at the time of her mother's death and when it was believed that Peter had been killed. She and Jim, inevitably, had grown fond of one another, working closely together as they did, although Abbie had always felt that Jim was the more devoted of the two. She had never been entirely sure that she loved Jim as much as, maybe, she ought to do, but she had agreed to marry him believing that love would grow. Jim had been extremely tolerant and understanding when the news of Peter's miraculous escape from death had come to light, knowing that Abbie must return to the young man to whom she had previously been engaged. Mr and Mrs Webster, however, had not understood so readily.

Abbie had not seen either of them since she married Peter – nor had she seen Jim, for that matter – but she had heard news of the family, occasionally, on the grapevine. She had known that Jim had married Sylvia, who at that time had been serving in the WAAF, and that they had a son. Maybe they had more children by now? Of late she had heard little news of the Websters.

Jim and Sylvia had been friends since they were children,

too close, probably, for Jim to have realised how very fond of him Sylvia was. Abbie recalled how Sylvia, very hastily, had joined the WAAF when she, Abbie, and Jim had started to get friendly. She had felt a little guilty, but Jim had insisted that he and Sylvia were just friends and nothing more. Anyway, they had now been married for eighteen years or so and it seemed they were still happy together. Abbie hoped so.

'My husband died seven years ago,' Abbie told her, 'but we were very happy and I have a lot to be thankful for.'

'Yes, we did hear about it,' said Sylvia, 'but I didn't realise you'd come back to live in Blackpool.'

They exchanged items of news over supper, and Abbie learned that Jim and Sylvia, like herself, had two children; a boy, Ian, who was sixteen, a year older than her Sandra, and Janet, who was roughly the same age as Simon.

'You must come round and see us. Jim would be so pleased to see you again,' said Sylvia ingenuously.

Abbie nodded and smiled. 'Yes, that would be nice.' She supposed, however, that Sylvia was just being polite, that it was one of those things that people say as a matter of course, but with no real intention behind it. She excused herself and went to chat with some of the other women. She knew she must spread herself around, as the Tupperware agent, and not talk solely to one person. Sylvia would understand.

When she collected the forms a little while later she realised she had been wrong to doubt Sylvia Webster's sincerity. In the space where it said *Would you be willing to hold a Tupper party?* she had written *Yes*. Abbie remembered, then, that Sylvia had always been totally honest.

'Our phone number's on the form,' Sylvia told her. 'Do you want to ring me and arrange a date for the party, or shall we do it now?'

'I'll have a look at my diary,' said Abbie, feeling rather bemused. 'What about in a fortnight's time? Two weeks today? There is a slight snag, though.' She did not want it to look as though she were spurning Sylvia's offer, but something was becoming increasingly clear to Abbie.

'What's that?' asked Sylvia.

'Well, I live at Layton, and you're at Marton, opposite ends of the town, and I've no car.'

'Oh, I was assuming you'd driven here.'

'No, I'm learning to drive, but for the moment I have to rely on taxis or on good-natured people like my stepmother, Faith.'

'That's no problem at all,' said Sylvia. 'Jim will come and fetch you, and all your stuff as well. How about that?'

'Oh no, I couldn't possibly let you do that – let Jim do that, I mean.' Abbie was covered with confusion. 'I wasn't dropping a hint, you know. I didn't mean—'

'I know you didn't.' Sylvia laughed. 'I've known you a long time, remember.' She was looking candidly at Abbie. 'You were always a guileless sort of girl and I don't suppose you've changed all that much. I won't take no for an answer. Give us a ring nearer the time and we'll arrange for Jim to come and pick you up. And in the meantime I'll find you lots of new customers.'

'I don't know what to think,' Abbie confessed later that night to Faith. She was spending a little time with her father and his wife before going home. 'I feel completely bewildered. Jim Webster . . . after all these years. I'm not sure I like the idea of being alone with him in the car. And fancy Sylvia suggesting it!'

Faith smiled. 'It's not as though you are kids, any of you. Jim must be – what? – getting on for fifty now? Not that age makes any difference when it comes to affairs of the heart. Your father and I know that.' She looked fondly at her husband, Cedric, who was sitting and listening quietly to the conversation. 'But I should imagine Sylvia is very sure of Jim. From what I recall of him he was a very steadfast

139

young man and he won't have changed. And you were devoted to your Peter. So what does it matter? You're just a couple of old friends, aren't you, meeting again after several years.'

'I suppose so. It'll feel strange, though.'

'It might, it might not. I'm sure Jim will put you at your ease.'

'I don't like depending on people for lifts. It's not fair on them. I must admit I didn't really think about it when I took on this Tupperware thing. I was assuming, wrongly, that my parties would all be in my own area.'

'Now that's a different problem altogether, isn't it?' said Faith. 'My advice to you is to pass that test as soon as possible and get your own car. For the moment your orders can be sent to our address – your dad or I are usually in – and you can do your deliveries from here. But put in for that test; it'll solve a lot of problems when you have your own transport.'

Abbie was disturbed to see the confused look still there in her mother-in-law's eyes when she called to see her the day after the Tupper party. It disappeared, but only momentarily, as she greeted Abbie and ushered her into the small sitting room.

'How lovely to see you, dear. I've been looking forward to you coming. We're on our own, you and me, so we'll be able to have a nice chat.'

'Is Grandad out, then?'

'Yes, he's on the bowling green. It didn't take him long to get himself over there, I can tell you. He went yesterday and introduced himself and he's having a game this afternoon. I'm pleased for him; he loves his bowls. It was one of the main reasons we settled for this bungalow, with it being so near the Green.' Layton Bowling Green was, in fact, only a stone's throw away.

'Sit down, Abbie love.' Lily fussed around, plumping up a

140

cushion and straightening a cover. 'We're getting a bit more organised, as you can see. Your Sandie's been a great help, unpacking me bits and bobs, and Simon, too, bless him, although I don't think it's much of a job for a lad. He didn't seem to mind, though. They've sorted out my display cabinet, see, and they've made a good job of it an' all.'

The cabinet was crammed, as it had been at the previous house, with a floral china tea service – only brought out on special occasions; various items of EPNS silverware, many of them wedding presents, Abbie guessed – cruets and jam dishes and a large ornate teapot, never used; oddments of sherry and wine glasses; china ornaments emblazoned with the crests of seaside towns up and down the country; boxes and animal figures crafted from shells; and silver and wax flowers, some from their own wedding cake and some from that of Abbie and Peter. Several more of the treasures were displayed on the mantelpiece and windowsill; lustre vases, glass paperweights, china baskets of flowers and blue and white imitation Delftware. The three-piece suite – on which Lily's embroidered cushions and lace-edged chair back covers had been once more put in place – a large pouffe and the display cabinet were the only items of furniture in the room; even so, it appeared overcrowded.

'Nice and cosy, don't you think so, dear? I'm getting used to being a bit cramped now. Frank says I'll not notice it at all after a while. Yes, we're settling down all right.' Her voice faltered a little, however, as she sat down on the chair opposite Abbie and her anxiety was showing again. Abbie was watching her concernedly and as Lily's eyes met hers it seemed as though they were pleading with her. 'Abbie . . .' she faltered.

'Yes, what is it?' said Abbie gently. 'There's something wrong, isn't there? Is it something I've done?'

Lily shook her head. 'No, not you. It couldn't be you, Abbie dear.' She hesitated. 'Do you know, the other day you called me Mum, didn't you? And it sounded so nice, so right.

I'd always wished you would, but I knew I couldn't expect it. You had a mum of your own, didn't you, love? And I know you can only have one mother. There's nobody like your own mum.'

There certainly couldn't have been another like mine, thought Abbie, a trifle bitterly. She wondered if Lily had forgotten about Eva Winters. She surely must have known about her at the time, although she had never met her, of course. 'It's a long time since my mother died,' said Abbie. Even now she could not speak ill of her or tell Lily that she, Peter's mother, had shown her more affection than her own mother had ever done. 'And I would like to call you Mum, if you don't mind. I didn't before because of . . . well, because of Peter. You were his mum and no one else's and I thought it might upset you.'

'You could never upset me, love. Please believe that.' There were tears in the older woman's eyes now and they seemed to be tears not just of sentiment, although she appeared very touched by Abbie's suggestion. Abbie was more convinced than ever that there was something amiss.

'But I did upset you, didn't I, Mum?' she began. 'That time when you told us you were thinking of moving to Blackpool – you know, when I'd just come back from my house-hunting trip, you told us your news and I'm afraid I was rather short with you. I was sorry afterwards. I've felt awful about it ever since, but somehow I could never tell you. Is that what's been worrying you? You still think that perhaps we don't really want you here?'

'Oh no, dear. I don't think that, not now. Happen I was a bit hurt at first though.'

Abbie smiled sadly. 'You thought I'd jump at the idea, and I didn't. I'm sorry, I really am.'

'Yes, something like that. But I talked it over with Frank – I always tell him when there's something bothering me – and he made me see things a bit differently. I realised we'd been a bit pushy, like. Happen you wanted to make a fresh start, entirely on your own, and we weren't letting you do it. So we decided we'd come, but we would try to stand back a bit and not monopolise you. And now we're doing just that. At least I am. I don't know how I'd have managed without you this week, love, you and the kiddies.' Lily was visibly distressed again. Her eyes were filling up with tears and she was clenching and unclenching her hands until the knuckles were white.

'I'm glad to be able to help. And we're really glad you're here, all of us. But there's something else, isn't there? There's something wrong. Can't you tell me?'

'Yes. Yes, I must.' Lily took a great gasp of breath, then she seemed to be holding her breath before letting it go in a long, long sigh. 'Abbie,' she whispered, 'I've found a lump.'

Abbie did not need to ask what sort of lump. She already knew by the tentative way Lily's hand wandered towards her breast and then fell away again. 'Are you very sure?' she asked gently.

'Yes, I'm quite sure. I kept thinking it might go away, but they don't, do they, love?' It seemed as though Lily could speak quite rationally now she had overcome the first hurdle of actually voicing what was wrong with her.

'Have you seen a doctor, Mum?'

'No, not yet. We haven't got ourselves a doctor here yet.'

'But surely you've seen your doctor in Wymondham, haven't you? And I thought that Grandad might have—'

'Frank doesn't know about it, love.'

'He doesn't know?' Abbie was feeling more and more anxious but she knew she must be careful not to let her agitation show. 'But you just told me, not five minutes ago, that you always tell him if there's something worrying you.'

'I couldn't tell him about this.' Lily shook her head. 'He was looking forward so much to coming to Blackpool and I didn't want to do anything to spoil it. Like I said, I kept hoping it would go away, or that I was imagining things, but it's not gone away.'

Abbie felt herself go cold. 'When did you first find this lump? I'm sorry, Mum, but I've got to ask.'

'It was just after Christmas. The first week in January, round about the time you were moving here. Frank was getting really excited about the prospect of us coming as well. I didn't want to upset him.'

January . . . and it was now April. Abbie was frightened. Supposing Lily had left it too late? She had no medical knowledge to speak of, but her father had been a doctor and she knew that tumours could grow at an alarming rate. There was the chance, of course, that it might not be a malignant growth. This was what she must try to tell Lily now.

'It might just be a cyst,' she said, speaking calmly. 'I've heard about such things. It might be something quite simple, but whatever it is, you've got to go and see about it. You do realise that, don't you?'

'Yes, I know, dear.'

'There's a surgery in Lynwood Avenue; the children and I have signed on there. It's very convenient, midway between here and our house. Would you like me to go with you? We could go tomorrow morning, and I'll explain that it's neces- sary for you to see a doctor as soon as possible. Unless you'd rather Grandad went with you – Dad, I mean. I wouldn't want him to feel I was being pushy.'

'Abbie, you've no idea how much I need you now.' Lily was becoming agitated again. 'Yes, please *please* come with me. Men aren't much good anyway, are they, at this sort of thing?'

'You should have told him, though. He'll be very upset when he knows that you didn't.'

'Perhaps I should, but I did it for the best. At least, that's what I tried to tell myself. I dare say I was scared an' all. Scared of what they might have to do to me.' She shuddered. 'I'm not very brave, Abbie. Not when it comes to operations an' all that.'

144

'I don't think many of us are,' said Abbie. 'But we don't know yet, do we, what will be necessary. I'll be there with you, Mum. You don't need to feel you're on your own.'

'We'll have to stop thinking we're being pushy, won't we, love?' Lily sighed. 'We're going to need one another.'

The tears welled up in her eyes again, and Abbie rushed over to her. She knelt on the floor and took the cold hands in her own. 'Don't worry. I'll be here. I'll always be here.'

Chapter 10

'Hello, Abbie. Long time no see, eh?'

'Hello, Jim. Yes, it's been ages, hasn't it?'

The years fell away as Abbie greeted her old friend. Her one-time fiancé, she reminded herself, although that had been of short duration and, looking back now, she recalled how they had been good friends first and foremost. Jim had not changed overmuch in looks. He had always been of a slim build with somewhat angular features and he had not put on any weight with the passing years. His outdoor work kept him fit and this accounted for his ruddy complexion. His wiry hair was grey now, though, instead of dark brown; apart from that he had kept his youthful appearance.

They loaded the boxes into the boot of his Hillman car, assisted by Sandie and Simon. Abbie was pleased at her children's easy greeting of Jim. They were never tongue-tied with strangers as she remembered being at their age.

'Two nice kids you've got there,' he remarked as they set off on their journey to Marton. 'Roughly the same age as our two, Sylvia tells me. Except that we did it the other way round; a boy first then a girl a few years later. What you might call a well-planned little family – for both of us, eh, Abbie?'

'That's right.' They chatted easily – about the present time, however, and did not hark back to the old days, apart from a brief reference to their respective parents. Ian, Jim and Sylvia's son, was at Arnold School, at the south end of

Blackpool, and after taking his O-levels this summer would be going into the sixth form. Janet, their daughter, was not so academically minded, although she was doing very well at Highfield Secondary Modern School, and Jim guessed it would be Janet, rather than Ian, who would come into the family business.

'You'll be able to meet them both,' he said. 'They're in this evening – no youth clubs or badminton or whatever – but as Sylvia's got this Tupperware thing we're going to make ourselves scarce.' He laughed. 'There's a good thriller on the telly so we'll be OK.'

They were pleasant children, Abbie thought, although Ian, already almost six feet in height and with a manly air about him, could not be termed a child. Yes, the Websters were the archetype of a happy family and Abbie, looking back afterwards on the evening, felt to her surprise, and not without a little shame, that she was envious. Of what? she asked herself. She, also, had two lovely children. Jim had remarked on the fact, so they must have seemed so to him. And she certainly did not wish she were married to Jim. She had been apprehensive about meeting him again, wondering if some of the spark that must once have been between them was still there, but she had found that it was not. She liked Jim immensely, though, as she always had, and she was pleased to see that he and Sylvia were so obviously happy together. What, then, was the matter with her?

She began to realise that it was the absence of a man in her life that was niggling at her. She would not have thought, at one time, that such a thing could ever be possible. How many times had she said that she and Peter had had such an ideal marriage that she could never think of replacing him? Doreen had accused her of being smug, but her new friend, Jean Birtles, had seemed to understand. The three of them, she and Sandie and Simon, had seemed to Abbie to be a complete little unit, functioning very well on its own with just the occasional helping hand. And she had intended making herself even more independent by learning to drive.

It's all Doreen's fault, she told herself. It was Doreen who had put the silly idea into her head that she should get a fellow of her own. Relations with Doreen were still strained; at least Abbie assumed they were because she had not seen her friend at all since that morning when she had come round in high dudgeon. Sylvia and Jim, although they had welcomed her unreservedly into their home, had not suggested another meeting, and this, for some reason that she couldn't quite fathom, niggled at Abbie. The Tupper party had been successful, with a very satisfactory list of orders and the promise of two more parties, nearer to the centre of Blackpool, she was pleased to note, instead of way out in the wilds of Marton Moss.

And that, I suppose, must be the extent of my social life, Abbie bemoaned to herself; the company of a crowd of chattering women – cackling women, Doreen had called them – once a week or so. She had hardly ever been invited to supper parties or to dine with friends since Peter died because she was a woman on her own, very difficult to accommodate unless a spare man was invited along as well. This had happened, very occasionally, in Wymondham, and Abbie had hated the half-hearted attempts at matchmaking by her well-meaning neighbours and acquaintances. They had not come to anything, the men seeming as uninterested as Abbie. She knew this was largely her own fault. She was still inclined to find herself at a loss for words when confronted with a man she did not know, especially in the company of others, although women did not have the same effect on her. And here in Blackpool she had, so far, even fewer friends than she had had in Norfolk. The Tupperware women were really only clients; Kath was friendly, but that was because she was a neighbour; and Doreen ... well, Doreen didn't want to know. There was Jean, of course, but she would only become a friend if they were both accepted at the College. In her present despondent mood Abbie doubted it was likely that she would be given a place. No, there was little likelihood of any exciting invitations coming her way at the moment.

Oh, for goodness' sake, snap out of it! Abbie chastised herself the morning after her visit to the Moss. Just because you're feeling a bit lonely and your best friend's playing hard to get, that's no reason to start feeling all sorry for yourself and hard done by. What about poor Lily? If you had to face up to that, you would have something to worry about.

The doctor had seen Lily almost at once and had confirmed that there was, indeed, cause for some concern. She had had a further examination at Victoria Hospital the following week and was now on the waiting list for an operation. Abbie guessed it was an emergency operation as they had assured her she would not have to wait long. Lily was reasonably calm now she knew for certain what she had to face. Not so Frank. He had been annoyed, quite justifiably, with his wife for keeping such an important matter from him, and now he was finding it hard to hide his anxiety. Abbie called to see them almost every day. The fact that they had decided, in the beginning, to keep their distance was now forgotten by all three of them. Lily and Frank knew they needed Abbie and she was touched by their reliance upon her.

The rattle of the letter box broke into Abbie's thoughts. There was only one envelope on the carpet, an official-looking brown elongated one. She snatched it up and after making sure it was addressed to her she looked at the postmark. Chelford. It must be the one she had been waiting for. She ripped it open, then her eyes quickly scanned the page. Yes! She waved the letter aloft in her excitement and couldn't help expressing a cry of joy and relief. 'Oh, thank goodness for that!' although there was no one to hear her. She had been offered a place at Chelford Training College, starting at the end of September, 1962; that was less than five months away. Sandie and Simon had both left for school, not that they would have shared all that enthusiastically in her triumph, she knew, but she had to tell someone. At one time Doreen would have been the first person she told, but that no longer seemed such a good idea. As she stood there pondering, the phone rang. She picked it up from the meter box near the front door. 'Hello, Abbie Horsfall here.'

'Abbie, Abbie . . . I've got in! Have you?' She recognised Jean's excited voice. She had exchanged addresses and phone numbers with Jean Birtles, but they hadn't contacted one another since that first meeting in Chelford.

'Yes! I'm in as well. Oh Jean, isn't it wonderful? And how lovely to hear from you. How are you going on?'

They exchanged items of news about their families and discussed Abbie's progress with her driving lessons. Jean, surprisingly, had never learned to drive and was full of admiration for Abbie. They agreed to meet for a day in Preston, which was midway between their two towns, sometime during the summer so that they could have a natter about the college, the set books and all that sort of thing. By the time Abbie put the phone down she felt tremendously excited, far more so than she had done for years. She couldn't remember when she had felt so elated, as though she were a real part of the current scene; 'with it' was the 'in' phrase. Her former mood of irritability had completely vanished now. She found herself humming as she washed the breakfast pots and tidied the chaos left behind in the children's rooms, particularly Sandie's. They were supposed to keep their own bedrooms tidy, but more often than not they forgot, or it could be that their idea of tidiness conflicted with Abbie's. She could not be cross with them this morning, however.

She decided she would go and see her parents-in-law and tell them her good news. Lily in particular had shown a keen interest in Abbie's application for a college place. Abbie had been a little surprised at this. Lily was of the generation that believed a woman's place was in the home, but maybe she thought that being a widow put Abbie in a different category; that was what she had seemed to imply. The news of Abbie's acceptance might help to take Lily's mind off her forthcoming operation. Maybe she, too, might have had some news?

The letter confirming Lily's operation had, in fact, arrived that very day. There was a bed available for her at Victoria Hospital the third week in May. Abbie guessed it would involve a complete mastectomy, and that turned out to be the case. She had feared that Lily had left it too late; if she had sought help sooner the surgeon might not have had to take such a drastic step. She just hoped and prayed now that that was the end of it and that there would be no repercussions.

'How are you feeling, Mum?' she asked, the day after the operation. Only Frank had been allowed to see her the previous night, and now Abbie, with Sandie and Simon, had come to visit her, but only for a short while. 'That's a silly question, isn't it?' Abbie kissed her cheek and squeezed her hand. 'But it's what everyone says. I know you must be feeling pretty groggy. Thank God it's all over though.'

'Yes, thank God,' breathed Lily. 'Actually, I don't feel too bad, love. There's not nearly so much pain as I expected, but I daresay they're keeping me well doped. I feel light-headed, and a bit lop-sided,' she added with an attempt at a chuckle, which turned into a sort of sob.

'Don't worry about that, Mum,' Abbie told her, with a wary glance at Sandie and Simon who had gone rather quiet. 'They'll get you sorted out. They can do all sorts of things these days.'

'And they say I've got to have radium treatment,' said Lily, sounding a little confused. 'I thought this operation would be the end of it all.'

'I think that's pretty general,' said Abbie. 'They're just

151

making sure that all the bad cells have gone. Something like that,' she added quickly. 'You can be sure they're doing the very best they can for you.'

'I know that, love,' said Lily wearily. She looked tired and they did not stay very long after that.

'Will Gran be all right?' asked Sandie in a small voice, as they made their way back through the endless corridors. 'She's going to get better, isn't she?' Abbie knew how fond she was of Lily. Sometimes, indeed, she had felt almost jealous of Sandie's affection for her grandmother. She seemed to take her, Abbie, so much for granted.

'Of course she'll get better,' she replied quite forcefully. 'It's a big operation, but it's over and done with now. Don't you worry, love, she's going to be fine.'

And so it seemed. Lily came home after ten days and the radium treatment started soon afterwards. She was listless and inclined to be tearful at first, but as the summer progressed she gradually improved. She joined the local branch of the Townswomen's Guild and, although she was not such a leading light as she had been in the Women's Institute in Norfolk, she enjoyed the meetings and the company of the other women. Frank took her dancing in the Tower ballroom, as he had promised to do, towards the end of the summer. They went in the early evening before the floor became too crowded, and this brought a sparkle back to her eyes that had been missing for far too long.

Abbie continued to visit them nearly every day and as the summer drew to a close she began to feel less anxious about Lily. Come September she would not have nearly as much time to devote to her parents-in-law, but they both seemed to be coping well in their new surroundings. Lily appeared to be responding satisfactorily to her treatment and was almost back to her old cheerful self. All will be well, Abbie told herself. She could look forward to her new life without any qualms of conscience.

★ ★ ★

The first day at College passed in a hectic blur. Abbie wondered how she would ever remember which room she was supposed to be in and at what time. The corridors were endless and all the rooms looked alike. They were numbered, of course, but that did not help very much with the doors standing open and the numbers obscured, and with hundreds of students dashing hither and thither. They each had a timetable to follow and that should have helped, too, but to Abbie, that first day, the words and numbers seemed an incomprehensible jumble that she doubted she would ever be able to decipher.

Fortunately Jean was in the same division as herself. They had both opted for the combined Infant and Junior course and by a stroke of luck they both found themselves in Div. B. For one of the main subjects, also, they would be together as they had both chosen to do the English Literature course. For her second main subject Abbie had chosen Modern History, and Jean Arts and Crafts, but Abbie was hoping that in a day or two she would be slightly more confident at finding her way around. She couldn't expect Jean always to be there to hold her hand, but she was glad, in the beginning, of her bolstering support.

'Phew! I'm exhausted, and it's only half-past twelve,' Jean remarked as they queued at the canteen counter for their midday meal. It looked appetising enough and there seemed to be a reasonable choice of dishes. Abbie chose sausage and mash with baked beans – one of Simon's favourite meals, she thought to herself – with stewed apple and custard to follow. The treacle pudding looked good, but it would go cold while she was eating her first course – or were you supposed to go and queue up again for your pudding? These were all little details they would have to learn as they went along. Drinks – tea, coffee and hot chocolate – could be obtained from a machine in the corridor. There had been a huge crowd around it at break-time, but eventually she had managed to procure a cup of tea and Jean one of coffee. The liquids had looked indistinguishable, both in colour and in aroma – the smell was like that of pencils being sharpened in one of those whirring things that fitted on to a teacher's desk – and Abbie suspected they tasted similar as well.

'Not much like school, is it?' she remarked as they unloaded their plates and cutlery from the heavy tin trays and squeezed themselves into the last two seats around a Formica-topped table which seated six. 'I don't mean the dinners – they didn't have school dinners when I was a girl. I mean the lectures and everything. I thought we'd be sitting at desks and we'd all have to be quiet and listen, like schoolkids. They expect us to join in, don't they? To say what we think. The trouble is, I don't know what I think at the moment.'

'Same here, luv. Never mind, we're all in the same boat.' The speaker was a stocky man with grey hair who appeared to be somewhat older than Abbie and Jean. 'I've chosen Psychology for one of my options, but I'm beginning to wish I hadn't. I thought it would stretch me, get my mind ticking over, but I didn't understand a word, not one word. I just sat there trying to look intelligent.'

'I take it you've been with old man Rivers, then?' asked a black-haired woman who was sitting opposite him. She looked rather younger – mid-thirties, Abbie guessed – with a lively intelligent face and eyes almost as dark as her hair.

'Yes, that's right – Mr Rivers.'

'Then don't worry about it. Don't worry at all.' The black-haired woman reached across and patted his hand. 'Julian Rivers is noted for being incomprehensible. I'm in his second-year group now. We haven't been able to make head nor tail of him for a whole year, have we, Kay?'

The fair-haired woman next to her shook her head. 'No, we haven't, that's true enough. Our advice to you would be to swot it up on your own. You've got the set books and that's all you need. That's what we've done, haven't we, Myrtle?'

Myrtle nodded. 'There's a lot of difference in lecturers. Some are as dull as ditchwater, like old man Rivers. I'm not saying he's not brainy – in fact, he's brilliant – but he just can't put it over. Art Gillespie now, he's just the opposite.'

'You can say that again!' The fair-haired woman, Kay, raised her eyebrows meaningfully as she grinned back at Myrtle. 'Art Gillespie – he's quite something. Have any of you come across him yet?' The first-year students shook their heads.

'It rings a bell,' said Jean thoughtfully. 'Gillespie . . . Isn't that the name of our English lecturer, Abbie? But we haven't met him yet.'

'That's the one,' said Myrtle. 'We were in his group all last year, weren't we, Kay? You girls are in for a treat, I can tell you.'

'Why?' asked Abbie. 'Is he a good lecturer, or good-looking, or what?'

Myrtle pursed her lips. 'I don't know whether you'd call him good-looking, but he's very attractive, very personable.'

'And doesn't he know it!' added Kay. 'Thinks he's God's gift to women, that one.'

'Oh, come on, that's not really fair,' said Myrtle. 'His lectures are fun, you must admit, and he knows his subject through and through.'

'Certain aspects of it, yes,' said Kay.

'Sounds intriguing,' said Jean. 'We'll look forward to meeting him, won't we, Abbie? I'm Jean, by the way, and this is Abbie.'

Belatedly, they all introduced themselves. The dark woman was Myrtle and the fair one Kay; they were both second-year students. The grey-haired man was called Eric and the remaining occupant of the table was a bespectacled, much younger man called Tim whom Abbie had already noticed in her own division. Abbie was considerably heartened by the fact that many of the students were older than herself, at least they seemed so, but it was impossible to guess at people's ages. The age range of the students – a couple of hundred of them in all – was from the mid-twenties to early fifties.

Abbie was to learn, as the term progressed and she became acquainted with many of them, that the majority of the students had done other jobs before deciding to take up teaching. The exception were the younger men – Tim was one of them – who had just completed their National Service; the last call-up had been at the end of 1960. The rest came from a wide variety of occupations: office workers, librarians, clerks, shop assistants, bus drivers, factory workers. Many of them, like Abbie and Jean, had served in the war, the women as well as the men, and quite a number – again like Abbie and Jean – were housewives whose children were now old enough to be left on their own.

Lectures, Abbie had to keep reminding herself to call them lectures and not lessons, finished at half-past three, and if she didn't waste any time afterwards she was able to catch a train and arrive home well before five o'clock. If the last lecture of the day went on too long, however, she was liable to miss the train. One couldn't just get up and walk out, even though the atmosphere was quite free and easy. On the occasions that this happened she had to try to control her impatience but, as the term progressed, she learned to view her late arrival home as unavoidable. Especially as Sandie and Simon didn't seem to notice whether she was there or not.

The first time it had happened she had arrived home in a great panic, almost running all the way from the station, then apologising profusely as soon as she opened the door. 'Sandie, Simon – I'm ever so sorry. The lecture went on and on and I couldn't get away . . . Where are you?'

They were both in the sitting room watching television and, at the same time, eating their tea. Abbie, as a rule, did not approve of the television being on during mealtimes – they ate in the dining room anyway, so that precluded this

156

hasty, snack sort of meal – but under the circumstances there was little she could say. She was glad they had had the sense to make themselves something to eat; 'doorsteps' filled with luncheon meat and tomatoes, from what she could see, with brown sauce oozing from the edges. Sandie was sprawled full length on the settee whilst Simon was leaning forward, elbows on his knees, staring fixedly at the antics of some cartoon character on the screen whilst his plate balanced precariously on the arm of the chair. He didn't appear to have noticed her arrival. It was Sandie who glanced up, mumbling through a mouthful of sandwich.

'Hi, Mum. We got ourselves something to eat. D'you want a cup of tea? I was just going to make some more.' She swung her long legs off the settee and jumped to her feet. Abbie winced as Simon's plate wobbled. The last thing she wanted was HP sauce on her gold plush suite, but she was gratified at Sandie's offer.

'Yes, please, love. That would be nice.'

'Don't know why you're watching that rubbish, Si. It's time you grew up.' Sandie flicked the knob as she was passing and the screen went blank.

'Hey, I was watching that, you rotten cow.'

'Simon!' yelled his mother, dismayed both at his language and at the sight of his plate toppling to the floor as he leapt out of the chair, leaving a brown stain on her floral carpet. Fortunately the carpet was not a new one, merely the one left by the previous owners which she intended to replace. 'Now look what you've done! Sandie, bring a cloth, will you? Really, Simon, you mustn't speak to your sister like that. I've never heard such language.'

'Sorry, Mum. But she *is* a rotten so and so. She's no business to tell me what to do.'

'All right, all right. She's a bit high-handed, maybe, but I did leave her in charge. Anyway, there's no harm done. Thank goodness this stuff didn't go all over the chair.'

She stopped worrying about them after that episode. She

knew she had to let them grow up, and what did a few slapdash meals matter, or a few stains on the carpet? She didn't want to be the sort of mother who was forever nagging at her offspring, especially when she was leaving them to fend for themselves to a certain extent. When it was possible, though, they dined together in a more civilised manner; certainly at weekends and at most times during the school holidays. It was then she tried to compensate for her neglect of them during termtime by cooking the dishes she knew they liked, or by suggesting they should go on little outings together, as a family. They had quickly grown accustomed to her busy schedule, however, and did not seem to see it as neglect, which was all to the good. It just proved how adaptable kids could be, when it suited them.

Her proposal for family outings fell on deaf ears. They both had their own interests which they were pursuing single-mindedly; Simon, his football – playing or watching or studying form; Sandie, her music and the new friends she had made at school. They no longer wanted to be seen out with Mum, although Mum was useful, Abbie thought to herself philosophically, when she was needed as a chauffeur! She had now passed her driving test – at the first attempt, which was a feather in her cap – and had bought a two-year-old blue Ford Anglia. It was easy to drive and she liked the up-to-the-minute look of the forward-sloping rear window and the extra-large boot. This was especially useful for transporting her Tupperware equipment.

She had wondered whether or not to give up her party hostess work now she was at College, but after a chat with Celia, the area rep, she had decided to keep on with it, while limiting the number of engagements she undertook. She was now able to do only the evening parties – one every ten days or so, at an average – during termtime, but she would be available for afternoon work as well during the long College holidays. The extra money came in handy. Abbie had been awarded a grant for her teaching course, but there were all sorts of little extras to pay for. There were books to be purchased for her various courses. The College library was useful, but with so many students all wanting to take out the same books it paid to have one's own. Then there was the cost of running her car, although she still travelled to Chelford each day on the train, not feeling quite brave enough to tackle the road journey.

Clothes for the children were an on-going expense. Simon was growing out of everything so rapidly, although she hoped that Sandie, at five feet six inches already – only a couple of inches short of Abbie's own height – had almost stopped growing. Abbie was not much of a dressmaker. When the children were little she had, now and again, run up simple garments for them on her second-hand Singer machine, which she had acquired when Lily bought herself a new one, but Sandie now declared she 'wouldn't be seen dead!' in anything homemade. Not that Abbie would have offered; her daughter was becoming increasingly difficult to please. Most of the time, fortunately, Sandie had to wear school uniform, but she always seemed to be hankering after a new dress or skirt or pair of jeans. The newly opened Paige's fashion store was a happy hunting ground for Sandie and her friend, Lindsay. She no longer wanted to go along with her mum when choosing new clothes, so Abbie had come up with the idea of a clothing allowance which Sandie must budget herself. So far it seemed to be working quite well and was giving the girl a feeling of independence.

As for herself, Abbie looked despondently at her own collection of skirts and jumpers and dresses after her first couple of weeks at College. She decided that what she really needed was a complete new wardrobe. Her pleated Gor-ray skirts and neat little twinsets, the mid-calf-length dresses with nipped-in waists and square shoulders looked hopelessly out of date. But alas, her budget was limited. She had already splashed out on the green coat for her interview, which had also meant buying a shorter length skirt as well,

159

but she had nothing else that could be termed fashionable, or 'with it', as Sandie might say.

'What shall I do?' she said to Jean. 'I feel like Granny Groves next to some of these youngsters. Well, they're not all that young, really, but they look it with their short skirts and piled-up hair. They make me feel about ninety.'

'Actually, you don't look all that bad.' Jean pursed her lips appraisingly. 'There's nothing wrong with that skirt and blouse, but you've got a bit of a complex about it, haven't you, luv? Nobody's really bothered what we wear. Some of the blokes look like scarecrows, but I can see what you mean. The solution's simple: get yourself some new clothes.'

'I can't afford it, can I? That's what I'm trying to tell you.'

'I mean make them, not buy. You'd have to buy the material, of course, but these shift dresses are dead simple to run up on a machine. Straight up and down, and a hole cut out for the neckline – dead easy.'

'It might be dead easy for you, but it's certainly not for me. It's ages since I used my machine. It might have rusted away for all I know.'

'You've still got it, though?'

'Oh yes. I took it to Blackpool.'

'That's OK then. I'll come and help you. I'm inviting myself, if you'll have me. I'll come over to your place one weekend and we'll get cracking. We'll make you a complete new wardrobe before you can say "Jack Robinson".'

'What about your Julie and Bobby?'

'Oh, they can stay with my mam, can't they? They won't mind. Anyway, they're a bit older than your two, quite old enough to cope for the odd weekend. I say, you don't mind, do you, luv? You've got room for me? You know what I'm like. I jump right in without thinking sometimes.'

'Of course I don't mind.' Abbie laughed. 'I'm thrilled to bits. What about this coming weekend, eh? No time like the present.'

'That's OK with me. We can go across to the market on

160

Friday and get everything we need. There are some gorgeous material stalls. And we've both got a free period Friday afternoon, haven't we? Right, that's settled then.'

Chelford Market had numerous stalls piled high with bolts of dress materials: wool, cotton, linen, satin, silk, and a variety of manmade fabrics in a myriad textures and colours. There was also a stall with paper patterns and all the accessories one might require – reels of cotton, zips, buttons, press-studs, bias binding and trimmings of lace, ribbon and sequinned braid. Abbie was mesmerised by such a vast display and very glad of Jean's assistance, otherwise she might have hummed and hawed for ever. Jean decided that one simple pattern would suffice. It could be adapted, she said, for a shift-style dress with elbow-length sleeves, and also for a couple of loose pinafore dresses – very fashionable at the moment – with square or boat-shaped necklines. Abbie knew she could not have adapted it in a month of Sundays, but she bowed to Jean's superior knowledge. Jean was doing Main Course Arts and Crafts, incorporating Needlework, and Abbie could see that this must be as easy to her as falling off a wall. They chose a fine wool in cherry red for the dress, and a light tweed in a heather mixture, predominantly mauve, for one pinafore dress, and emerald-green rayon for the other.

When they boarded their usual tea-time train, they were laden down with bags. Abbie had also done her weekend shopping, as she often did, at the market. The vegetables always looked so fresh and wholesome, and there was a very good meat stall where she bought pork chops and a large chicken. She knew there would be little opportunity for shopping in Layton that weekend. They had agreed not to take any college work home. The books were too heavy with everything else there was to carry; besides, there would be no time for studying. Fortunately neither of them had any essay deadlines hanging over them and there were, as yet, no exams ahead.

Sandie and Simon were on their best behaviour and Abbie felt proud of them. 'What nice kids,' said Jean. Sandie could, indeed, pull out all the stops when she was so inclined.

By burning the midnight oil on Friday, Saturday and Sunday they managed to finish all three garments in what they considered to be record time. 'Come on then – try it on and let's have a look at you,' said Jean as midnight approached on the Sunday night. The cherry-red dress was the last one to be completed. The two pinafore dresses had been tried on the day before and declared to be a perfect fit and the height of stylishness. Even Sandie had been impressed. She would never have believed something home-made could look as good as that, she had said, with a wistful look at her mother's new gear.

'I'll make one for you if you like,' Jean promised. 'Nearer Christmas, perhaps. Just choose the material and we'll see what we can do.'

'Ooh, would you really?' Sandie sounded delighted. 'Gosh! Thanks, Jean.' She had insisted they should call her Jean. 'That'd be great. Mum's never made me anything, not since I was about six.'

'Only because I knew you'd turn your nose up at my efforts, young lady,' retorted Abbie, a little piqued at her daughter's offhandedness towards her. 'But I must agree. Jean's an expert; they're really professional.'

'You can wear all sorts of blouses and jumpers under-neath,' said Jean. 'But what would look really classy is a black turtle-neck sweater with that emerald green.'

'Oh no, not black,' said Abbie. 'Black's not my colour. Not with my dark hair and brown eyes.'

But a quick visit to Marks & Spencer late on Saturday afternoon proved that Jean was right. The black and green looked very striking together and did not make Abbie's complexion look dingy, as she had feared.

She now slipped the red dress with the elbow-length sleeves over her head. It was the new shorter length, just skimming her knees, and the loose style showed to advantage her well-rounded bust and hips.

'Oh yes,' said Jean. 'It looks great.' She grimaced slightly. 'It's not right with those slippers, though.' They both giggled as they looked at Abbie's feet in her fur-edged shabby mules. 'Put your court shoes on.'

Abbie kicked off the offending slippers and stepped into her black patent leather medium-heeled shoes. 'Oh yes!' cried Jean again, with a great deal more enthusiasm. 'Now that really *does* look terrific.'

Pleased with herself, Abbie did a little pirouette in front of the full-length wardrobe mirror. 'Mmm ... not bad. Though I say it myself, I look quite nice.'

'Quite nice? You look stunning!' said Jean. 'What I wouldn't give for a pair of legs like yours. I tell you what – when Art Gillespie sees you in that, his eyes'll pop out of his head. That'll really get him going, luv.'

'Now you're just being silly,' said Abbie. 'He would never look at me; not in a hundred years.' All the same, she could feel herself blushing. She knew that what she had just said was not strictly true. She had noticed Arthur – commonly known as Art – Gillespie's eyes upon her, more than once, during the English lectures. And, if she were honest with herself, she knew this was one of the main reasons for her wanting to change her dowdy appearance. At least, she considered herself to be dowdy. Doreen's words – 'You're prim and proper ... mealy-mouthed ... out of touch ...' – as well as being hurtful had really hit home. Abbie was dissatisfied with the way she was and knew it was time to make some changes. To re-fashion her outward appearance would be a good start.

Chapter 11

By the time she had been at College a little over a month Abbie was starting to feel as though she were part of the scene; a real student, albeit a mature one. She found that her stylish clothes were giving her a new confidence although, even before that, she had been trying to take a more active part in the lectures; to express an opinion or ask a question if something was puzzling her.

When she had been at school, she recalled, it had been the teachers who had asked the questions and the pupils who had shot up their hands to answer them, some more eagerly than others. Abbie had never been one of the first to raise her hand, even when she knew the answer, as she usually did. She had always shied away from speaking out in front of others. She had learned that a teacher usually chose the girl who had put up her hand first – an eager beaver – or, perversely, one who was looking bewildered with her hand down. And so Abbie had very rarely been called upon to speak.

Here at Chelford it was very different. There was as much time spent in discussion as there was in listening to the actual lectures. She had learned to find her way around the building much more quickly than she anticipated but to add to the confusion, several other venues were used as lecture rooms as well as the college itself. There were several terrapin classrooms, use was made of nearby church halls, and they took over the Odeon cinema when the Principal wished to give a lecture to the whole body of students.

The Principal, Dr Fortescue, was a shadowy figure, very seldom seen. Abbie had soon learned that Miss Williams, the woman with the iron-grey hair who had conducted her interview, was, in fact, the Vice Principal. It was she who had much to do with the running of the college, assisted by her clerical staff, as well as being the Education lecturer. This was one lecture, the students soon learned, for which they must turn up promptly. Miss Williams was a stickler for punctuality. Apart from that the regime was very free and easy, very different from Abbie's regimented schooldays at the select private school she had attended. Lectures were supposed to start at nine o'clock, but it was more often nine-fifteen before they got under way, except for Miss Williams's groups, of course. Abbie found it frustrating. She had to leave her house before eight o'clock each morning, and if she could make an effort to arrive on time she didn't see why the lecturers could not do the same, especially as it was invariably the same ones who exceeded their time at the end of the day. However, she was learning to look upon each day as a new experience and to not get too irritated by minor frustrations. This was a whole new way of life, totally challenging and stimulating.

Miss Williams, in particular, was an excellent lecturer, getting her points over effectively and without a great deal of waffle; this was something of which several of the male lecturers were found to be guilty. Abbie had not realised so much was involved in the education of young children. Piaget and Montessori, names she had not heard before, became familiar to her. She learned that a child's development was manifold; physical, intellectual, emotional and social were the four key words they must remember. (PIES was an easy way of committing them to memory.) Good teachers must constantly be aware of these various aspects of development in the children in their charge, so they were told. And yet, strangely enough, they were not given any instruction on how to teach; they were just lectured about the principles behind it all.

They would learn soon enough, the second-year students informed them, when it was time for their first Teaching Practice. Then they would be flung in at the deep end and expected to put into practice all the theories they had been hearing about. But that would be during the Spring term; there was no point in worrying about it yet. Before that they would be taken into various schools in the area for 'observation', so they could see how real teachers tackled the job.

It was Miss Williams who had given Abbie the encouragement she had needed to speak out in front of the others. 'What do you think, Mrs Horsfall?' she had asked persuasively, when she had seen that Abbie was dithering, wanting to express an opinion, but not sure whether or not she was brave enough to do so. The question was about 'reading readiness'. Should a teacher wait until a child showed he was ready to learn to read, or should he be taught to do so even though he might be showing no interest or aptitude? Abbie found herself saying, quite forcefully, that some children would never be 'ready' unless they were persuaded. They might be like some adults, she suggested – a little lazy and not inclined to stir themselves unless they were given a push. She was gratified when most of the others agreed with her. Yes, some children would play around all day unless they were encouraged to do otherwise. Wasn't that what school was for, anyway, so that children could learn to read and write? The three Rs – reading, writing, and arithmetic – it had been called when Abbie was a girl, but that concept now seemed to be considered old-fashioned.

Abbie was learning, to her surprise, that there was a policy of 'laissez-faire' in many primary schools in these years of the early 1960s. This free and easy approach to learning was not just confined to colleges of higher education. In infant schools, in particular, the education of the children depended largely upon the headmistress in charge or even upon the class teacher. The staff were allowed a good deal of freedom to teach in whichever way they wished. There was much talk of free activity, learning through play, and pursuing projects which, it seemed, could involve any subject under the sun, usually one in which the teacher had a particular interest. Heaven help those children who had the misfortune to have a less than competent teacher, thought Abbie. She might not have had a burning ambition to be a teacher at the beginning, but now she found herself longing to get on with the job instead of just talking about it.

It had been hard at first to get into the routine of studying again. She had not written anything other than a shopping list or a letter since she was sixteen. Now she was expected to write essays and even longer ones, known as theses. She had always been able to compose interesting letters, however – to her father and to Doreen while she lived away – and this stood her in good stead. Nor had she read anything but novels and detective stories and the odd biography since she left school. Some of the educational tomes and the set books for the English and Modern History courses she found, therefore, rather heavy going at first, but she was gradually getting established in a pattern of studying and, what was more, she was enjoying it all immensely.

Miss Fairbrother, the elegant woman with the gold spectacles who had also been at the interview, was the Drama lecturer, and so Abbie did not encounter her again. She discovered, however, that Miss Fairbrother and Miss Williams were known to be close friends. They shared a flat near the College and were rarely seen apart, except when they were lecturing. Abbie knew herself to be naïve and not very worldly wise. She had not encountered such a relationship before although she had known, in a vague sort of way, that they existed. Now she was learning to be more blasé about such matters, and about the various pairings-off that she witnessed going on around her and which often involved the married, as well as the single, students. That was not to say she approved of such goings-on, but she knew she must not adopt a high moral stance. It was none of her business how her colleagues conducted themselves. No doubt, with most of them, it was just a casual fling. She had learned her lesson with Doreen. Since she had started at College she had not seen her former friend at all.

Abbie's favourite lectures were the English ones, given by the very personable Arthur Gillespie, who preferred to be known as Art. What was more, he insisted his students should call him by his name. It was a fairly common practice at the college for Christian names to be used, by lecturers and students alike, although some of the more conventional members of staff preferred the more formal Mr, Mrs or Miss. As Myrtle and Kay had told her and Jean on that first day, Art Gillespie was 'quite something'. Abbie was not sure how to take him.

Abbie had loved reading since she was a child, and felt that the set books would widen her field of knowledge in what had always been her favourite subject at school. As well as the more traditional authors and poets – Shakespeare, Hardy, Jane Austen, Keats and Browning – they were also due to study the works of more modern writers. D.H. Lawrence, Virginia Woolf, E.M. Forster and George Orwell were some of the authors on the list, together with T.S. Eliot, Dylan Thomas, and the poets of the First World War.

The more you read the more you wanted to go on reading, Abbie discovered. On many nights, she sat up in bed till well past midnight, until the words began to blur and her eyes were heavy and could no longer focus. *Lady Chatterley's Lover* was not on the reading list, but Lawrence's novel *Women in Love* (almost as controversial) was there, along with *The Rainbow*. Abbie read these for the first time, captivated by the beauty of the language and the vividness of the descriptive passages, but also somewhat surprised by the explicit detail of some of the scenes of intimacy.

These books were ahead of their time as far as sexual content was concerned. There had been no end of a commotion over the publication of *Lady Chatterley's Lover*, but the appearance of this title on the shelves of bookshops and libraries had, as it were, opened the floodgates. Literature was becoming more permissive, Art Gillespie told them. No longer was it necessary to 'close the bedroom door', he said, and leave it to the reader's imagination as to what was going on. Some authors were becoming much more sexually explicit and he could foresee a time, in the not too distant future, when all restrictions and taboos would be laid aside.

In Art Gillespie's lectures, even more so than in those of the other tutors, the hour consisted more of discussion than of listening and taking notes. Often they would find themselves deviating from the main topic and these digressions always seemed to lead one way, to the subject of love and romance in literature and the manner in which various authors and poets dealt with this. It was in one of these discourses that Abbie had first felt Art Gillespie's eyes upon her and, to her chagrin, she felt herself blushing. Feeling she had nothing to add to the remarks of her fellow students, she had kept quiet, looking down at her notes in some discomfort lest he should ask her to voice an opinion. He did not do so, not that time, but when she ventured to look up again his eyes were still focused in her direction, an amused, though quite kindly glint in them lighting up his boyish face. She had guessed he was pretty much the same age as herself, but he had one of those puckish faces that would never look old.

A couple of weeks went by and she still had not dared to enter into any discussion on this emotive subject, although she occasionally spoke up concerning less provocative issues. As she tried to do as a schoolgirl, so she was doing now; endeavouring not to meet the eye of the teacher – in this case, the lecturer – but it was too late.

'What do you think, Abigail?' Her heart gave a jolt as Art Gillespie spoke her name. 'We haven't heard much from you about this subject, and yet I'm sure you must have some . . . er . . . experience. You are Mrs Horsfall, are you not? A married lady? Not that that is anything to go by.' His twinkling eyes now scanned the rest of the group. 'I don't suppose there are many of us, married or single, who are without some sexual knowledge.' There were a few mild titters and smiles from the students, but Abbie felt they were laughing more out of politeness than anything else and that some of them, like herself, found their English lecturer rather aggravating and far too personal at times.

'So, what do you think, Abigail?' he persisted. He was looking at her quizzically, one eyebrow raised. 'Sexual scenes in literature – that was what we were discussing, were we not? What do you think? Should they be explicit, or implicit? How much should we be told about what is going on?'

Abbie felt herself going hot, more with anger now than embarrassment. How dare he single her out like this? He was bent on making her look foolish; naïve and out of touch with what went on in the world. Doreen's words came back to her as she met his amused glance with a challenging look of her own. She found that her changed appearance – today she was wearing her new emerald-green pinafore dress and the black sweater that Jean had persuaded her would look great – was giving her the confidence she needed. That, and the fact that she was blazing mad. She took a deep breath before she spoke.

'I prefer to think of them as love scenes rather than mere sex,' she answered, her voice quiet, but assertive. 'And I happen to believe this is a private matter between the two people who are involved. I have never thought much of women – or men, for that matter – who discuss with all and sundry what goes on between them and their husband or boyfriend or whoever. As I've said, it's private, and so it should be in literature. We can use our imaginations, can't we? As you've reminded us, Mr Gillespie, we are not without experience and we can work out for ourselves what is going on "behind the bedroom door". We don't need to have every movement, every sigh and moan described to us. And that's all I have to say,' she finished abruptly.

She had surprised herself by the length of her speech and the calm way in which she had been able to present it, but now she was starting to feel flustered again. What would they all think of her, her fellow students? She was not bothered about what Art Gillespie might think, but had she made herself look silly in the eyes of her peers? Did she appear ingenuous and simple-minded to these forward-looking people?

'Good for you,' whispered Jean at her side.

'Hear hear,' said a few voices and nearly all the students were looking at her, some in surprise and some in admiration.

'Wow!' said Art Gillespie, opening his eyes wide and raising his eyebrows even higher. 'That's telling us, isn't it? Thank you very much, Mrs Horsfall, for those pithy comments.' Tit for tat, she supposed, noting his use of her formal name. She didn't know which was worse, being called Mrs Horsfall in that disdainful way, or Abigail. If the self-satisfied, conceited man had bothered to find out or listen to what went on around him, he would have known she was Abbie to her friends. Abigail belonged to the dim and distant past. Her indignation, still bubbling away inside her, forced her to speak up again.

'Just one more thing, Mr Gillespie. Could we please get back to what we were discussing before we strayed away from the subject? We were studying *The Love Song of J. Alfred Prufrock*, weren't we? I, for one, have difficulty in understanding parts of it, and as you want us to write an essay on T.S. Eliot I think we could do with a little more clarification. Time is running short.' She looked pointedly at her watch.

'Yes, you are quite right.' The look that the tutor levelled at her now had little of roguishness in it. He looked, not exactly angry, but exceedingly irritated and his greenish eyes were devoid of sparkle. 'Where were we up to? "Arms that are braceleted and white and bare . . ." if I remember correctly.'

That was the line that had caused the diversion. Art Gillespie needed little excuse to get on to what appeared to be his favourite subject. They worked through the rest of the poem, the tutor explaining to them, very ably, about the ramblings of an ageing man. Abbie had thought it was nonsense at a first reading, but Mr Gillespie's exposition made it come alive and be more meaningful. She loved the imagery of the poem, despite being unable to fully under-stand it, just as she loved T.S. Eliot's more light-hearted poems about the cats. This was a poet she had only recently discovered. The English course had introduced her to many previously unexplored avenues in literature. She was finding it all challenging and rewarding. If only Arthur Gillespie did not have such a one-track mind; and if only she did not find him so . . . disturbing.

She supposed, if she were honest, she found him physi-cally attractive. Not since Peter died had she been attracted to any man – until now. Art fascinated her. He had been quite rude to her, but she continued to be mesmerised by him. Doreen's words were still coming back to taunt her. Was she really out of touch with the world? Naïve and self-righteous and . . . frustrated? Doreen had as good as told her she was incapable of feeling a physical attraction for any man, and Abbie had piously stated, yet again, that there would never be anyone else for her but Peter. Was she ready now, she asked herself, for another friendship, a *sexual* one? She hardly dared to say the word, even to herself.

Yes, she found Art attractive, and if his surreptitious glances in her direction were anything to go by, he must find her so as well. Unless, of course, she had completely messed things up by being too outspoken. It was not just a physical attraction she felt for him though, she argued with herself. She admired him for his passion for his subject and for the way he was able to make all aspects of English literature come alive. That was because of his vibrant and often humorous personality. She was convinced there was far more to Art than his tendency to intersperse all his lectures with sexual overtones. He was, she felt sure, a very deep-thinking and, at heart – though he might sometimes give the wrong impression – a very sensitive man. She wished she could get to know him better.

Abbie paused outside the door of the sitting room listening with admiration and a certain amount of pride to Sandra's rendition of 'Rosemary', the piano solo by Frank Bridge. She had got the contrast just right – the lyrical sadness of the beginning and ending, and the crashing chords and turbulence of the middle section. It was the test piece for one of the classes Sandie was entering in the forthcoming Blackpool Musical Festival, only a couple of weeks away now. In addition to that she was working for her Grade 7 piano exam, but in spite of all this extra studying she still seemed well able to cope with her schoolwork and home-work in readiness for next year's O-level exams.

Abbie had little to grumble about at the moment with regard to her daughter, except, perhaps, her secretiveness. She still seemed unwilling to confide overmuch in her mother about her new friends and where she went with them, but she did, at least, always arrive home at the time she had been instructed. Abbie had heard no more about her threat to leave school and get a job when she was sixteen, not that there was anything wrong with that, but she was a clever and intelligent girl and Abbie did so want her to go on to college or university, to have the chance that she, Abbie, had been denied when she was a girl. She had been quite good, also, about keeping an eye on Simon and preparing their meal when her mother was late home from college; and so, all in all, there was a lot to be thankful for.

Abbie gave a start as the music on the other side of the door suddenly changed.

'Bobby's girl, I wanna be Bobby's girl.' She could hear Sandie's voice, vibrant and melodious, although she had never professed to be a singer, above the sound of the piano accompaniment.

Abbie put her hand on the door handle, ready to go in and berate her daughter, to tell her to get on with what she was supposed to be doing – practising for her exams and the Festival – then she stopped. She remembered a similar occasion when she, Abbie, had been a girl and her mother had overheard her playing 'In the Mood' or some such piece instead of getting on with her practising. Eva Winters had stormed into the room, practically slamming the piano lid down on Abbie's hands, castigating her for playing 'such disgusting rubbish', saying she would ruin her style, how such music was lewd and common and not suitable for a girl like Abigail, and so on and so on.

Abbie smiled to herself now and turned away. She would go and get on with cooking the Sunday lunch, which was what she had been doing in the first place before she was distracted by the strains of Sandie's playing. Sandie was a sensible girl, at least as far as her musical talent was concerned. She had been in the sitting room nearly an hour already, working at her set pieces, and she was entitled to a bit of light relief. Abbie had the good sense to know that playing 'pop' music, as it was called, would not do anything to damage Sandra's technique at the piano. Jazz musicians and the like often had a classical training in the first instance before veering off in a different direction. Abbie was confident that Sandie's love of the classical composers would not wane, but nevertheless, she had noted her daughter's growing awareness of what she termed the 'pop scene' and the 'charts'.

Sometimes she heard music other than that of Mozart or

Brahms issuing from the Dansette record player in Sandie's room. Though not entirely conversant with all the hits of the Top Fifty, Abbie could recognise such voices as Elvis Presley, Cliff Richard, Frank Ifield, Helen Shapiro and Susan Maugham – the original singer of 'Bobby's Girl' – and that up and coming group, The Beatles. Abbie had heard them on the radio and seen them, occasionally, on the television. Their photos were continually in the newspapers following their tour to Hamburg and their frequent appearances in the provincial cities of England, particularly Liverpool. A real set of Liverpool 'scallies' they looked in their black suits with velvet collars, shoe-string ties and mop-head haircuts, but Sandie seemed to think they were wonderful.

'They've got a new drummer now, Ringo Starr,' Abbie had overheard her saying to Simon, 'and a new manager. There'll be no holding them now, you'll see.' Abbie didn't much mind her interest so long as The Beatles didn't lure Sandie away entirely from Bach and Beethoven.

'A few of us are going to the pub on Friday night,' Jean told Abbie as they boarded the teatime train one afternoon at the very end of October. 'It's to celebrate half-term and our few days of freedom. D'you fancy coming?'

Jean had occasionally gone with a group of newfound friends, which included Eric, the middle-aged man they had met their first day at college, who was a keen admirer of Jean, to the Olde Market Inne, the aptly named pub near to the market and almost as near to the College. It was a popular rendezvous for the students and lecturers alike. Jean lived quite close to Chelford, only a short train journey distant, but Abbie lived much further away, and although she was always invited along she never accepted. It was the same today.

'No, I don't think so, thanks all the same. I don't see how I can. I have to get back to the children, as you know. I don't mind being a bit late, but I dare say you'll be making a night of it, won't you?'

'We might be. A few of us – those who don't live in Chelford – will probably go back to Eric's to have a bite to eat, then go on to the Market pub later. Oh, come on, Abbie, don't be a spoilsport.'

'I'm not.' Abbie felt a trifle indignant at her friend's remark. 'At least, I don't mean to be, but it's not so easy for me. Your kids are older than mine, and they're more used to being left.'

'Couldn't you get your mother-in-law to have them, just for once? Yes, I know she's been ill, but it might help to take her mind off things.'

'Yes, it might, and I know she wouldn't mind, but . . . oh, I don't know. I wouldn't fancy going home on a late train, and that's what it would mean.'

'You could come and stay with me and go home on Saturday morning.'

'Could I? Really?' The idea was beginning to appeal to Abbie. She had never been much of a one for pubbing, but this would be with a crowd of people she knew and whom she was beginning to like more and more – and Jean might dismiss her as a wet blanket if she went on refusing. 'It's very kind of you, Jean,' she said.

'Not at all. You put me up, didn't you, that weekend when we made the clothes. You'll come then?'

'Yes, I think so. I'll have to ask Lily and Frank. I don't know, though. Maybe I shouldn't. It's the Festival next week, you know, and I've got to make sure Sandra does her practice.'

'For heaven's sake, Abbie, give the girl a break! You fuss about her too much. Your Sandra's OK. She's a great kid. She knows what she has to do and you can be sure she'll do it. She doesn't want treating like a kid of five.'

'D'you think that's what I do? Treat her like a kid?' Strangely enough Abbie did not feel offended by her friend's words, just curious. She had tried to strike a happy medium with her children, a fine line between nagging and being too lenient. She thought she had succeeded pretty well, but perhaps others did not agree.

'No, I think you manage them jolly well, both of them. Honest, I do.' Jean patted her arm companionably. 'You're bound to be anxious, taking the part of both parents. I know what it's like, don't I? I'm in the same boat.'

'It doesn't seem to worry you as much.'

'Maybe not. But mine are just that bit older, like you say. Just . . . loosen the apron strings a bit more, eh?'

'I'll try.' Abbie grinned at her. 'Right – I'll come. You're on.'

Eric Fielding was a widower who lived in a semi-detached house on the outskirts of Chelford. Six of them, Abbie included, piled into his shooting brake when lectures ended on the Friday and he drove them to his home. It was as neat and tidy as Eric was himself, and he proceeded to make them cups of tea and sandwiches of boiled ham and tongue – Abbie guessed he had been shopping at the market during the dinner hour – laid out in symmetrical rows on blue and white willow-pattern plates. Abbie noticed that Jean, although she had purported to disparage him at first, pretending she was not interested and deeming him to be an 'old woman', nevertheless went to help him in his immaculate kitchen, and it was the two of them, later, who did the washing up. There did not appear to be any hint of romance between them, but it was obvious they got on very well together. Grey-haired, reserved – though good-natured – and quite unexceptional-looking, Abbie would never have considered him to be an ideal companion for her exuberant and charming friend. But you could never tell. He was kind-hearted and reliable, and Abbie knew that these qualities went a long way in any relationship.

They all chatted together easily, watched the early evening

news, then drove back to the centre of Chelford where Eric parked his car in the marketplace, now empty of stalls, but rapidly filling up with cars, vans and motor bikes. He was an abstemious man, as one would have guessed, and he declared he would have only one pint, then stick to orange juice, so that he could drive his friends to the station or wherever at the end of the evening, and himself home without any fear of accidents.

The Olde Market Inne was already quite crowded when they entered. It was not as old as its olde-worlde name might suggest, although the solidly built brick building had probably been there since the early years of Victoria's reign. It was a happy stamping ground for market-traders, commercial travellers and businessmen during the day, and in the evening a favourite haunt for locals who did not want to travel far from home. They did a good pub meal – chicken in a basket, scampi and chips and other reasonably priced dishes – which probably accounted for the crowds there now, many of them waiting for a table in the adjoining eating room; it was not really posh enough to be called a restaurant. The students from the nearby college helped to swell the numbers during termtime and so, all in all, it was a thriving establishment.

To add credence to its name the landlord had installed mock Tudor beams across the ceiling, along with the inevitable horse-brasses, hunting horns, Toby jugs and Dickensian prints. A log fire blazed in the huge brick fireplace and the tables, adapted from old-fashioned Singer sewing machines and surrounded by red plush-seated stools and chairs, added a unique touch. A very pleasant place to spend a few hours.

'Goodness, what a crowd,' remarked Jean. 'It'll thin out a bit when some of them go to eat. Eric and I'll get the drinks while the rest of you go and grab some seats . . . if you can find any. Yes – look – there's room over there. Just one table, and you can pinch a couple of stools from somewhere else. Go on, Abbie, get a move on or it'll have gone. Is it a shandy you're having? What about the rest of you? Right, three shandies and a pint of bitter.'

Abbie had hesitated because she had noticed, sitting at the table next to the empty one, none other than Art Gillespie. It was about a week since they had had their little contretemps, if it could be so called. Most probably it had meant nothing to him, but it had affected Abbie because she did not like to be at cross purposes with anyone. Since that occasion she had felt somewhat discomfited in his lectures, fearing that she might have spoken out of turn. He treated them as equals, admittedly, but when all was said and done he was the lecturer and they were the students. She still remembered the teachers at her school and how no one would ever have dared to challenge their say-so. He had not singled her out again either, to her slight disappointment, nor had his eyes lingered upon her as they had formerly done. If she happened to catch his eye, he looked away.

Her heart sank now as she saw him sitting on his own. There were a couple of people at his table, but they did not seem to be with him. Unusual, that, because he was a gregarious soul, often at the centre of a crowd, whether it be fellow tutors or students. The three other people who made up Abbie's little group quickly sat themselves down at the free table. None of them knew Art Gillespie, except by sight, as they were not on his course, so it was left to Abbie to go up to him and ask if she could take the two stools that were near him.

He had already noticed her and his eyes lit up with merriment as he watched her tentatively approaching his table. 'Well, hello there, Mrs Horsfall. What a nice surprise. Are you coming to join me? There's plenty of room.'

'Yes. I mean, no, not really. I'm with these people here, but there aren't enough seats.' Oh crikey! He was getting her all hot and bothered already. Why must he keep grinning like that? 'I wondered, is there anyone sitting on these stools, Mr Gillespie?'

He made an elaborate charade of staring at the stools, then he got up and peered all round and beneath them. 'No, I don't think so,' he said seriously. 'I can't see anybody sitting on them, can you? Why, did you want to borrow them? You may, as far as I'm concerned, although they don't actually belong to me, you understand, but I should imagine it will be quite in order.'

His eyes were twinkling again, and in spite of herself, she found she was smiling. 'Thanks,' she said. She shook her head. 'Silly of me, but it's what everybody says, isn't it? "Is anybody sitting there?" I'll just put them here.' She moved the two stools a few feet away to the table where the rest of the crowd were already deep in conversation. 'I'd better go and help Jean and Eric to carry the drinks. If you could just watch them for me, till I get back.'

'Oh, I'll watch them, Mrs Horsfall.' Art chuckled. 'I'll make sure they don't get up to any mischief while you're away.' Another inane remark, Abbie, she told herself as she thankfully hurried away to the bar where Jean and Eric were struggling with six glasses of various tipples.

'The stools have behaved themselves very well,' quipped Art as they returned. 'I've had my eye on them all the time and they've never moved. Joking apart, though,' he was suddenly straight-faced, 'do you think I might join you? That is, if I'm not butting in. It looks as though Dave's not coming. Dave Saunders – you know, the Rural Studies bloke – he said he might meet me here, but he wasn't a hundred per cent certain. His wife might've had other plans.' He pulled his mouth down in a grimace. 'So, if you don't mind . . .'

'No, we don't mind at all, Art.' It was Jean who replied. 'The more the merrier. Pull your chair up. I don't think you know the others, do you? Eric, Graham, Shirley and Linda.' She waved a hand in the direction of the rest of the group. 'And this, folks, in case you didn't know, is Art Gillespie, our esteemed English tutor.'

'Evening, all,' said Art. 'Nice to meet you. I've seen you around, of course, but it's only these two ladies I know intimately – Jean and Abigail. Well, not perhaps as intimately as I'd like . . .'

I wish he would stop all that suggestive nonsense, thought Abbie, seeing Jean's knowing wink at her – she only hoped Art hadn't seen it – and the way her friend wangled it so that Abbie ended up next to Art, a little apart from the others. She found, however, as soon as they all settled down and were companionably sipping their drinks, that Art was about to surprise her.

'Abigail, I owe you an apology,' he said, quietly enough for the others not to hear; they were not taking any notice anyway. He rested his hand briefly upon hers as it lay on the table, then, to her relief, moved it away. 'I know you were annoyed, and you had every reason to be, about my less than tactful remarks. I'm sorry, please believe me. I should not have singled you out the way I did. I could see you were uncomfortable and I realised – probably too late – that I might have touched a raw nerve.'

'It's all right.' Abbie shook her head dismissively. She did not use his name. It would look churlish in the face of his seemingly genuine apology to address him as Mr Gillespie, but she could not pluck up the courage to call him Art. 'I realise I overreacted and I felt bad about it afterwards. I know I must have appeared rather rude. I didn't mean to. I'm sorry as well. I'm rather touchy, I'm afraid. And maybe I haven't – what shall I say? – been around as much as some of the others. I'm not as used to such outspoken remarks.'

'And I'm a dreadful tease, I know I am,' replied Art. 'I can't seem to help it – I just love to get people going. The trouble is, I don't always know when to stop. Sometimes that sort of thing can be unkind, very thoughtless. I'm sorry if I offended you, Abigail. You don't mind me calling you Abigail, do you?'

'I've said it's OK.' Abbie smiled at him. 'I accept your

apology. It doesn't matter. I was being silly. And I'd much rather you called me Abbie. That's what my friends call me.'

'And I certainly hope I can be counted as one of them, Abbie,' he interrupted. His intent look disturbed her and she hurried on.

'I haven't been called Abigail for years, not since my mother was alive. She always insisted on calling me Abigail – and I hated it.'

Art gave a slow smile. 'What's in a name? Some might say a lot. It's odd how names often seem to fit the personalities, although our parents could have no idea when they named us how we would turn out. Abigail . . .' He pursed his lips slightly and put his head on one side. 'I find it quite charming, actually. Quaint and a little old-fashioned.'

'You're saying it suits me?' Abbie answered quickly and a trifle edgily.

'Now don't start getting all huffy again. I didn't say that. I thought we'd agreed on Abbie anyway? On condition that you call me Art. It isn't so difficult, surely? Everyone else seems to manage it.'

'All right, Art.' She found herself smiling at him much more easily now. 'I must admit it's an improvement on Arthur, isn't it?'

He grimaced. 'You could say so! Like you, I hated my name; that's why I changed it – well, abbreviated it. But my mother still insists on calling me Arthur. Mothers always do, don't they? She was a lover of *Idylls of the King*, but I never reckoned much to his name. Now, if she'd called me Lancelot, that would have been more like it. Lance . . . that might have suited me.'

'I think Art suits you very well,' said Abbie. He was a mite full of himself, she suspected, but she was glad that the tension between them had disappeared.

There was a moment's silence before Art spoke again. Jean and the rest of her friends seemed to be leaving Abbie and Art to their own devices, as though they were not really a part of the group, or maybe it was because the two of them were finding plenty to say to one another. 'Tell me,' he asked, 'is there a Mr Horsfall? Or is he, perhaps, no longer with you? Forgive me asking, Abbie, but I can't help being curious.'

'My husband died,' she replied. 'Nearly eight years ago. We were very happy; tremendously happy. And there has never been anyone else,' she added simply.

'Oh, I see. I am so sorry.' Once again he covered her hand with his own, then quickly took it away. 'I had no idea you were a widow. I'm not surprised you were offended at my crass remarks, especially as you say you were so happy together.' He sounded very humble.

'There's no need to apologise,' she said. 'You weren't to know. Why should you?' She had stated on her application form that she was a widow and it would be in the college records, but he would not have needed to see these, only a list of the students in his various groups and whether they were Mr, Mrs or Miss.

'It's sometimes as well to know,' he replied, 'although it's not supposed to be any of our business. I might have guessed you were not divorced. You look a very settled sort of person, very serene.'

'As serene as I can be with two teenage children to contend with,' she told him, laughing a little. 'They're not bad kids, though, all in all.' He seemed interested in Sandie's prowess on the piano and Simon's passion for football.

'I'm a rugger man myself,' he told her, which did not surprise her. He had played at school, then at college, and still played occasionally for a local team although advancing years – at least for a rugger player – were taking their toll. She learned that he had joined the Army at the start of the war, taking part, eventually, in the D-Day landing and coming through it all unscathed. After the war he had decided to train as a teacher which had led, eventually, to lecturing.

'You are not from round here, though?' asked Abbie. She could detect no trace of a Lancashire accent. His voice seemed to be accentless, almost refined, although it was possible he had worked at making it so.

'No, I'm from much further north,' he answered carefully.

'Scotland?'

'No, not quite so far. North Yorkshire, actually, getting on towards County Durham. My mother still lives there. I taught for a while up there . . .' He hesitated. 'But things didn't work out, so I decided to go for a complete change. That's why I'm here, lecturing to you lot.' He seemed unwilling to elaborate about his early teaching. 'I got myself a nice little bachelor pad, a self-contained flat just outside Chelford, and so here I am.' He grinned at her.

Abbie was not an overly curious person, but she did not hesitate to say, 'You are a bachelor, then?' After all, he had not been slow to ask about her marital status.

'That's what I call myself,' he replied. 'I'm divorced actually, quite a while ago.' He shrugged. 'It was not important, not like your marriage. You still miss him, I dare say? You're sure to. Eight years is not such a long time, not in the general scheme of things.'

She admired his frankness. 'Yes, I do. I do miss Peter, but I am not grieving any more. I have so much to remember, so much that was good.' She went on to tell him about Peter's war service, about how he had been believed dead, but had then, miraculously, been found alive. And how he had died, ultimately, as a result of his war wounds.

'I was one of the lucky ones,' he remarked, 'coming through it all with not so much as a scratch.'

'Mental scars, though, perhaps?' she asked. 'You must have seen things you'd rather forget.'

'Bad memories fade,' he said. 'I'm not one to dwell on the past. I'm happy in the here and now. And I hope you are, too, Abbie.' His eyes, green and intent, looked deeply into hers for a moment. 'Now, how about another drink – the same again? A lemonade shandy, isn't it? I'd better stick to that myself, I think, seeing that I've to drive home. Tell me, how are you getting home tonight? Could I drive you somewhere?'

'Oh no, thanks all the same. I'm staying at Jean's home tonight, in Leybridge. Eric is driving us to the station, and I'm going home to Blackpool tomorrow.'

'Yes, I knew you lived in Blackpool. It's one of my favourite places, but I haven't been there for ages. I must visit it again – soon.' Again his eyes bored into hers and she found it hard to look away. 'We must meet for another drink, Abbie. After half-term. We'll arrange something. Not here, though. Somewhere different, right?'

'Yes, all right,' she answered, a little weakly. It was more than likely that he didn't mean it, that he was just being polite. Especially as he turned away now, to the rest of the group. 'Now, what are you having, folks?' he said. 'This one's on me.'

For the remainder of the evening, until they all departed at closing time, Art Gillespie joined in with the students' chatter, mainly about college and the various courses and tutors. He did not single Abbie out again and his goodbye to her was casual, including her along with the others. Yes, he was just being polite, she decided, in showing an interest in her. She didn't mean anything to him. Why should she? She wasn't his type at all. So why did she now feel so deflated?

Chapter 12

To Abbie's relief Jean did not tease her about her tête-à-tête with Art Gillespie. Abbie had feared that she might well do so; her friend had mentioned before how his eyes lingered on her when he was lecturing. But apart from saying, with a grin, 'You've made up your little difference of opinion then, you and Art?' Jean left well alone. No doubt she had noticed, as had Abbie, that his parting from her had been perfunctory, as though she were just one of his students and nothing more.

'Yes,' Abbie replied casually. 'He said he was sorry. That surprised me, I must admit. I'd have thought he was too big-headed to apologise, but he's OK when you get to know him better. Quite friendly and easy to talk to. And I said I was sorry, too, for overreacting, so that's that. All sorted out.' She had no intention of telling Jean about his suggestion that she should have a drink with him sometime, or his saying that he would like to visit Blackpool again. She was seeing them for what they were, anyway; throwaway remarks that were not meant to be taken seriously.

Jean seemed far more intent, on the short journey from Chelford to Leybridge, on talking about Eric; about what a kind and considerate man he was – Abbie had already realised that – and how droll and amusing he could be when you got to know him properly. Abbie decided that he must have hidden depths because she had always found him to be something of a sobersides, quite lacking in humour, in fact.

She realised, though, that people could be quite different when you got closer to them and a few more veils of their outward persona were stripped away. She had not suspected, for instance, that Art could be so sympathetic and concerned about hurting another's feelings. But there was not much point in thinking about him, not now. She tried to push him to the back of her mind and concentrate on what Jean was saying.

'Eric has asked me to go out with him on Monday. We thought we might have a run out into the country and then climb up to Rivington Pike. I haven't been up there for ages, not since I was a girl.'

'So you've said you'll go with him then?'

'Of course. Why not? He's good company and we get on very well. I know what you're thinking, Abbie.'

'What? I'm not thinking anything.'

'Well, I know what I said about him, that he was an old fusspot, far too pernickety for the likes of me, but I'm changing my mind. I'm allowed to change my mind, aren't I?'

'Of course.' Abbie laughed. 'I've just changed my mind . . . about Art.'

'You see, I've come to the conclusion that Eric's like that because he's been on his own for so long. It's five years since his wife died and he's had to get used to coping. Apparently he did all the cooking and housework when she was ill.'

'So he's a good catch for any woman?'

'You could say so. Not that there's anything like that. How could there be? I've only known him a few weeks.'

'It seems longer though, doesn't it, Jean? We've only been at Chelford a few weeks, just half a term, but it seems like ages and ages, doesn't it?'

'It sure does. I suppose it's seeing people every day and discussing things the way we do. We feel as though we've known them for ever. It seems like two different worlds we're living in; home and College. Hard to adapt, sometimes, isn't it, to make the switch from one to the other? Do you find that, Abbie?'

'Yes, I do. I suppose that's why I've tried extra hard, when I'm there, to make sure the children aren't suffering in any way. Not that they seem to be. They didn't mind staying at their grandparents' tonight. They were quite pleased about it, in fact. It's a change for them and Lily always makes a big fuss of them.'

'She's keeping well, is she, your mother-in-law? Quite recovered from the operation?'

'She seems to be, touch wood.' Abbie automatically tapped her fingers on the window frame. She knew, though, that it would take more than a silly superstition to ensure Lily's recovery. That depended on whether the operation had been performed in time or whether the disease had spread. Abbie experienced a moment's panic – a shudder, as though a goose were walking over her grave – which she hid from Jean. She and Lily had become very close of late, ever since Abbie had started, belatedly, to call the woman 'Mum'. Lily had been immeasurably touched and it marked the start of a much more affectionate relationship, as though she were, indeed, Abbie's real mother. 'She's a lovely person,' she said now. 'Do you know, I was quite set against it for a while when I knew they were coming to live in Blackpool, but I know now that it was the best thing that could have happened . . . for all of us. They're wonderful grandparents. And there's my own father, of course, and Faith. I'm very lucky.'

'No more lucky than they are, having you,' replied Jean. 'Oh, shucks! We're getting all maudlin, aren't we? This won't do. Come on, stir your stumps – we're here. I say, I'm ever so pleased you decided to come and stay tonight. Isn't it fun? Just as though we're a couple of teenagers staying together after a dance.' The train stopped and they alighted, the only two passengers to do so at the small station. 'Hmm . . . I doubt we'll get a taxi,' said Jean, staring around doubtfully.

'It's rather late. How are you for walking? It's not all that far, but it's a bit dark and lonely. Still, we'll look after one another, won't we? Come on, best foot forward.'

Abbie was relieved it wasn't any further. She hadn't thought to change back into her more comfortable shoes and her best black patent ones, though not all that high, were starting to pinch. Jean's home, in the centre of a crescent of terraced houses, was in a semi-rural setting, about half a mile from the station. Opposite was a stream and a field and a small coppice. Dark and lonely, as Jean had said, but quite enchanting. Abbie recalled how she and Peter had lived in just such a countrified setting in Norfolk. Since moving to Blackpool she had had to acclimatise to a much more bustling, noisy environment although the avenue where she lived was reasonably quiet. For a moment she felt quite nostalgic, even a little envious.

Jean's daughter, Julie, had gone to stay with a friend for the weekend, so Abbie was given her room. She was glad about this. If she had shared with Jean she doubted they would have got any sleep at all, but would have stayed awake talking all night, like the teenagers to whom Jean had compared them. Even so, it was after one o'clock when they went to bed and after two cups of Nescafé Abbie found it hard to settle. The bed was comfortable, though, and Julie had left her bedroom in a reasonably tidy state; tidier than Sandie's was at times.

The rest of Jean's house, however, could not be termed spick and span. It was not dirty, but extremely disorganised, everything existing in what Abbie termed comfortable clutter. Newspaper stuffed down the side of chairs, the detritus of everyday living – letters, gloves, library books, magazines, keys and loose change – accumulated on the sideboard, and, in the kitchen, pots left draining, a pile of ironing sitting on the Formica table and another pile of washing in the basket in the corner. Abbie could not help comparing it with the preciseness – Jean would, only a short while ago, have called it the pernicketiness – of Eric Fielding's home. And what would Eric think of Jean's way of living, were he ever to come here? Still, they did say that opposites were attracted; just think of herself and Art. No, best not to think of him at all, she told herself, thumping her pillow and trying to settle down for sleep, which did come, eventually.

She departed early the next morning, although Jean would have kept her there talking all day if she had had her way. Abbie insisted, however, on catching an early train and Bobby, Jean's son, ran her to the station in the firm's van. He was apprenticed to an electrician and, to his delight, had recently not only passed his driving test, but had been granted a vehicle. Abbie found him a most pleasant and amiable lad, very much like his mother, both in looks and temperament. She had not yet met Julie, who Jean had once said was rather a handful. Maybe it was true that girls were harder to bring up than boys? Abbie had certainly found it to be so.

Sandra, however, was on her best behaviour, ready and waiting with her bag packed when Abbie went to collect her and Simon. They could have walked home, but Abbie liked to keep in touch with her driving – she still thought it was a miracle she had passed her test first time – and she wanted to make sure that Lily was all right. Lily assured her that she was perfectly well, saying she had enjoyed having the children and they had not been a scrap of trouble, but Abbie thought her mother-in-law looked strained and she had not regained any of her lost weight, as the doctor had advised her to try and do. I shouldn't have left them, Abbie chided herself with a pang of self-reproach. Even the slightest exertion seemed too much for Lily these days.

'Gran's fine, honest she is,' Sandie tried to reassure her, when she said as much to her daughter. 'She gets tired, but it's not long since she had that big operation, Mum, and all that treatment. It's sure to have taken it out of her. She's a lot older than you, remember.'

'Yes, I suppose so, love,' Abbie replied. 'I just felt a little guilty at leaving you with her, that's all.'

'We were no trouble, Mum – she told you that. We helped her.'

'Yes, I know you did, dear, but it's extra beds to change and extra cooking and washing up, isn't it?'

'Oh, stop fussing, Mum,' retorted Sandie. 'Gran enjoyed having us, and we enjoyed it as well. I'd have stayed another night, but I've got to get home to do my piano practice, haven't I? It's nearly here, Mum – the Festival. I feel dead excited.' Sandie's brown eyes were alight with enthusiasm. She was more elated than Abbie had seen her in ages.

'I'm glad you're looking forward to it, love,' she replied. 'So am I. You've worked hard and you deserve to do well.'

Sandra was growing up, as was revealed by her perceptive remark about her gran's illness, but she could also be very childlike at times. Her excitement at the forthcoming Musical Festival reminded Abbie of how, as a little girl, Sandie had looked forward to a birthday party or Christmas. She might have expected her daughter to be more casual about it – she, who all too often condemned things as *bo-o-ring* – but Sandie was a volatile girl with pronounced highs and lows of mood. She was proving much easier to get on with these days, thank goodness. Even if the respite should prove to be of short duration, Abbie was thankful for small mercies.

She was glad, too, that Blackpool Musical Festival coincided with her short half-term holiday from College as it meant she could attend both the piano classes in which Sandie was taking part. Fortunately the piano classes were always at the beginning of the week; Abbie was due back at College on Thursday.

Sandie, for once, seemed grateful for the offer of a ride in her mother's car on the morning of the Festival. Abbie could tell she was a little nervous although she was trying to hide this beneath a show of indifference. The excitement that had buoyed her up for the last two days had given way to a fatalistic attitude. 'Mrs Blake says exams are more important than festivals,' she told her mother. 'She says it doesn't matter if I don't come in the first three. It's only one person's opinion, anyway.'

'You'll do fine, love. I know you will.' Abbie smiled at her, feeling so anxious for her. 'And remember what I've always told you. You can only . . .'

'. . . do your best,' Sandie finished with a grin. 'Yes, I know, Mum. So you keep saying.'

Abbie was fortunate to find a space in Cedar Square, just opposite the Winter Gardens. The parking spots were filling up rapidly and the scene outside the Gardens was one of bustle and quiet excitement as children of all ages, both boys and girls, were arriving clutching music cases. Some were on their own, others were accompanied by parents, predominantly mothers, or by their music teachers. Mrs Blake had said she would meet them in the Spanish Hall, where Sandie's class was to be held, at ten o'clock or thereabouts. It all depended on how long the previous class went on. Abbie had wondered if Sandie might object to having her mother with her as well as her music teacher, but she didn't appear to mind.

They walked through the Floral Hall with its palm trees and statues and glass-canopied roof, the main thoroughfare of the Gardens through which one must pass on the way to the Empress Ballroom, the Indian Lounge, the theatre and the Olympia – the place where exhibitions were held. Abbie had been in the Gardens before, of course, to the cinema or a season show, but it was not as familiar to her as the Palace, now, alas, demolished. The Winter Gardens was a truly magnificent building, the pride of Blackpool when it was built in 1878 and still very popular today for concerts and conferences, dog shows and cat shows, competitive ballroom dancing, the Home and Beauty Exhibition, and the annual Musical Festival.

They climbed the stairs to the Spanish Hall, waiting outside with a few other people until one of the competitors in the Twelve and Under class had finished playing, then creeping in to take their places, quite near the front. Mrs Blake was there before them and had saved seats for them.

'Not nervous, are you, Sandra?' she whispered.

'No, not really,' Sandie replied, politely and with a brief smile. Abbie doubted that she would have had the same reaction, had she asked such a question. She had not done so, considering it pointless and apt to annoy. Mothers learned which remarks not to make, although Abbie feared she didn't always get it right. She was rather surprised at Mrs Blake who was a mother herself, of grown-up children, but maybe she was only trying to put the girl at her ease.

Abbie gazed around at the wonders of the Spanish Hall. She had been there only once before. It was a popular place for dinner dances, and she and Peter had indulged themselves one Saturday evening when on holiday in the town, her father and Faith looking after the small children. Sandie had been about five, she recalled; it must be more than ten years ago. She had thought then that it was a fascinating place, though somewhat gimmicky. The glazed roof was painted in a semblance of sky, sunshine and clouds, and the walls and balconies were decorated to represent a Spanish scene with quaint little houses, courtyards, churches and pine trees. At the end where the grand piano was situated was a magnificent pillared gateway in a mock Byzantine style.

There were still four more competitors to play in the class for much younger pianists, twelve years of age and under. The set piece was part of a sonata by Clementi and the four children who performed it were of varying ability. Two of them tackled the runs with ease, whilst the other two stumbled a little, possibly through nervousness, but it was obvious they did not possess the same technique or the self-confidence required.

The adjudicator, a homely middle-aged man, made only brief general comments before giving the marks. There had been fifteen competitors so time did not allow for a lengthy appraisal of each. The winner was a serious-looking boy who did not seem at all surprised to have won, and who received his silver trophy with a quiet smile of thanks. He was the one who had played before Abbie and Sandie came in and Mrs Blake pronounced that he was 'Quite brilliant – such technique. He could go far.'

A tiny little girl, whom they had all heard play, came second and seemed delighted at her success, and it was a girl, too, who was placed third. 'Now, I don't agree with that at all,' whispered Mrs Blake. 'She wasn't a patch on that boy – look, the one with the big glasses. He looks disappointed, poor little chap. Still, you can never tell with festivals, and it's only one person's opinion when all's said and done. Good luck, Sandra,' she said, as an important-looking woman, wearing a large badge which proclaimed she was a Steward, stood up to announce the next class. 'Piano solo for local competitors, sixteen years and under.'

Sandie was the third to play out of sixteen entrants. The local competitors came from Blackpool and the Fylde area, from Fleetwood in the north to Lytham St Annes in the south, and the inland villages. Tomorrow the open class would take place, which would include competitors from all over the country, including the Isle of Man – Blackpool was a popular place with Manxites, being just a boat trip across the Irish Sea – and the competition would be much stiffer. Sandie felt reasonably confident as she walked out to take her place at the grand piano. She did not carry her music, as she had opted to play from memory. This took some courage. There was always the fear that her mind would suddenly go blank, but the general opinion was that adjudicators looked favourably on those who did not use music. Besides, she knew that if she was ever to become a really good pianist it was something she had to train herself to do. What's more, the first two competitors had used their music, which had strengthened her resolve.

If only her mother and Mrs Blake would not keep saying, 'Do your best, Sandra; it doesn't matter so long as you do your best.' What a stupid thing to say! Of course she would do her best, and of course it mattered. It would matter to her if she made a muck-up of it. It would damage her pride – and that of her mother and Mrs Blake as well; there was no point in them pretending otherwise. They would be squirming with embarrassment if she forgot her piece in the middle or played a cacophony of wrong notes, imagining the smugness of those parents and teachers whose pupils had performed perfectly. But she wasn't going to forget or fumble the runs and twiddly bits. She knew the piece inside out, for heaven's sake, and she was going to give a superb performance.

She sat on the piano stool and flexed her fingers, waiting for the adjudicator to ping on his little bell. The piano was a Bechstein grand, highly polished, and when she began to play she noticed she could see her fingers reflected in the mirror-like surface of the lid. The tone was different from that of her upright Brinsmead piano at home – a workaday instrument compared with this classy aristocrat of pianos – much more mellow and resonant. It took a few moments to get used to the feel and sound of an unfamiliar instrument – it was better to have a go on it first, but that was not always possible – but she soon became accustomed to its strangeness and she found that her nervousness, that slight fluttering in her stomach, had disappeared.

The piece was the first movement of a sonata by Haydn, an Allegro, to be played *con brio*, with fire. She gave it all the brilliance she could. It was full of runs and embellishments and trills, and she knew these had to be played smoothly and sound effortless, although it had, in truth, taken a great deal of effort and weeks of practice to produce what sounded like musical simplicity. Her memory did not fail her and she felt, when she reached the last crescendo and final chords, that she had given a creditable performance. The applause of the audience, some fifty or more, consisting mainly of other competitors, parents and teachers, told her that they thought so too.

'Well done,' whispered her mother, smiling, and, 'That was very good, Sandra. I think it was the best you've ever played it,' said Mrs Blake.

Sandie almost collapsed into her seat with a sigh of relief. She scarcely heard the next competitor, so pleased was she to have got it over and without disgracing herself. Then she pulled herself together and started to listen and compare; one with another and them all, of course, with herself, although this was difficult – you could not truly assess how well you had played. She was aware that some, quite frankly, were not up to the standard required for a competitive festival, although there were only a very few like this and she decided that they were probably suffering from nerves. Sandie found she was not gloating at the other competitors' mistakes as she might well have been, but was feeling for them, putting herself into their shoes. Maybe they had not practised as much as she had done or did not have such a good music teacher as Mrs Blake. She knew a few of the other competitors, but not well. None of Sandie's particular friends played the piano, so she never made too much of it, emphasising to them rather how she shared their interest in pop music. There were two more girls from her school there, one younger, and one slightly older who was in the sixth form.

And, of course, she knew none of the boys. Hers was a single-sex school – most schools were – and their contacts with the opposite sex were few and far between. There were fewer boys than girls in the class, which was often the case. One of the boys who had played was from Blackpool Grammar School and two were from Arnold School; she could tell by their ties. They would be going back to their schools this afternoon, most likely, as she would be, but

Sandie had decided not to wear her school uniform, at least not all of it; it was far too childish. She was wearing her green sweater and had brought her blouse and blue striped tie in a bag to change into later in the cloakroom.

It was when the last but one competitor took his place at the piano that Sandie really began to sit up and take notice. He was another Arnold School boy, as denoted by his green striped tie, but there was little of the schoolboy about this young man. He was tall and of slim build with straight, almost black hair which he wore rather long, and angular features in a face which looked very mature for his sixteen years; he could not be any more than that. Sandie thought he was incredibly handsome, so serious, though.

When he began to play she – almost – forgot what he looked like. His playing was brilliant; there was no other word for it. Sandie had mastered the tricky runs and musical ornaments well, she knew she had, but this young man made the piano sing out in a way none of the others had done, the cadences and triplets and chords falling from his fingers like a rippling waterfall of sound, rich and mellow and melodious. Needless to say he played from memory, never stumbling at all, and with the utmost confidence. When he had finished there was a few seconds' awed silence before everyone burst into loud applause. He acknowledged this with a nod and a shy smile which transformed his serious face and made him, Sandie thought, look even more handsome.

'Gosh!' she whispered to her mother and Mrs Blake. 'Wasn't he great? I think I might as well go home.' For this lad, undoubtedly, would be the winner.

'Don't be silly, Sandra,' said Mrs Blake. 'You've done very well, hasn't she, Mrs Horsfall? He's older than you, anyway, anyone can see that. He looks more than sixteen to me.'

'Yes, he's probably nearly seventeen,' Sandie whispered back. 'But it doesn't matter, does it? Even if he's seventeen tomorrow he's still got a right to be in this class.'

She felt sorry for the last competitor. Anything would be an anti-climax after that, unless the girl was equally brilliant. Which she wasn't. She played competently, using her music, and there was a burst of sympathetic applause when she finished. There could be no doubt as to the result of this class; the first place, at any rate. The adjudicator, as before, made general remarks in a kindly and helpful manner, not being over-critical of anyone. Sandie liked him; he reminded her a little of her Grandad Horsfall, though rather younger – a nice amiable man. She thought she might be in with a chance, though not for the first place, when he commented on her accuracy and her attention to detail, though he was not over-generous in his praise. That, obviously, was not his way. He could do no other, though, than commend competitor number fifteen for his outstanding performance. 'A young man who could go far,' he said.

He, of course, was the winner. His name was Gregory Matthews, which Sandie had already known from the programme. To her delight she was placed second and she walked out to the front, feeling as though she was walking in a dream, to accept her certificate and prize money. The boy from the Grammar School was given third place and the three of them stood there shyly, smiling at one another. Sandie was about to return to her place when a photographer appeared. 'Hold on a minute, young men, and you, young lady. Let's have a picture for the *Gazette*.'

They stood and smiled at the camera, Gregory Matthews in the centre, holding his silver cup, Sandie on one side and the other boy, Michael James, on the other. The *Gazette* photographer took details of their names and their schools for the caption which would appear in the Blackpool paper, beneath the photograph. Sandie thought belatedly that maybe she should have been wearing her school shirt and tie, as the boys were, but she knew that her bright green sweater enhanced the colour of her hair, which was a sort of fairish, sandy colour, like her name, and showed to its best advantage her developing figure. Not too much so, however, her mother would have been very quick to tell her if it was too revealing. She was even more pleased she was wearing it when Gregory actually spoke to her. She knew she looked older than her fifteen years. Maybe he might think she was as old as he was?

'Well done, Sandra,' he said. 'I'd got you picked out as a winner as soon as I heard you. Not easy, is it, to master all those runs? But you did it really well.'

'Oh thank you,' she breathed, feeling all fluttery inside. 'Not as well as you, though. You were . . . you were brilliant!'

'Thank you.' He smiled, causing her stomach to turn a somersault. 'Are you competing tomorrow, in the open class?'

'Yes, I am. Are you? Well, of course, you must be.'

'Yes. There'll be much stiffer competition for us tomorrow.'

'Yes there will.'

'See you then, Sandra. See you tomorrow.'

'Yes. See you, Gregory.'

She stepped aside as two people came forward to join him, one obviously his mother – she was so much like him – with her face wreathed in smiles, and a man of about the same age who she guessed might be his father. Still feeling as though she were walking on air she went back to her mother and Mrs Blake.

'That's Mr Hendy, his music teacher,' said Mrs Blake. 'Duncan Hendy. I know him by sight, but that's all. He must be feeling very proud, but no more proud than we are of you, Sandra dear. You've done very well – hasn't she, Mrs Horsfall?'

'Yes, indeed she has.' Mum was looking like the cat that had got the cream, Sandie thought. Her brown eyes were shining with a delight that she knew she did not always evoke in her mother. She was glad she had done something to please her for once. 'And we mustn't forget to thank you

199

as well, Mrs Blake. Isn't that right, Sandie? She's come on in leaps and bounds since we moved to Blackpool, and it's all thanks to you.'

'Not at all. It's been a pleasure to teach her. I wish all my pupils were so keen to learn. I wish I didn't have to . . .' Mrs Blake paused, then shook her head. 'No, never mind. I've something to tell you both, but it can wait till another time. I'm in rather a rush now; some shopping to do before I go home. Now, the class tomorrow is at two o'clock, Sandra. It's in the theatre, so you'll be playing on the stage. That'll be quite an experience for you, dear. And I'm so pleased you've got second place today. You deserve it. See you tomorrow then, and you as well, Mrs Horsfall? Cheerio, then.'

'She seems in a hurry to be off,' remarked Abbie. 'I wonder what she was going to tell us? I don't suppose it was anything very important. Now, what are you going to do, Sandie? Are you going straight back to school? You'll be there in time for your dinner if you go now.'

'Just a minute, Mum. I think Paula's waiting to speak to me.' The girl from the sixth form who had also competed in the class, and had been placed fourth, was hovering.

'Hiya, Sandra,' she said. She did not know Sandie well. 'Do you fancy coming with me for a quick lunch before we go back to school, or are you going with your mum?'

'No, it's all right.' Abbie smiled at them both. 'I think that's a good idea. You go with your friend, Sandie. Wait a minute – let me treat you both to some lunch.' She opened her purse and handed Sandie a pound note. 'Keep the change. You've done very well, both of you.'

'Gosh! Isn't she nice, your mum?' said Paula as they both hurried away.

'She's all right,' replied Sandie with a slight shrug.

'My mum couldn't come this morning, she's working,' said Paula, sounding a mite regretful. 'My music teacher came, but it's not the same.'

'You've not got your school uniform on either,' said

Sandie, looking closely at Paula. The girl was wearing a red sweater under her navy coat. 'Have you got it with you?'

'Yeah, it's here, in my bag. My blouse and tie and jumper.'

'Same here,' said Sandie. 'Shall we get changed now, before we go out?'

'No, let's spin it out a bit longer,' said Paula, grinning. 'Where d'you fancy going for your lunch? I think Marks and Spencer is as good as anywhere.'

'Me too.' Sandie nodded. 'And it's only just down the road.' They turned left out of the Gardens entrance, heading towards the popular store. 'I don't think they've got a cloakroom, though, to get changed in.'

'Ne'er mind. We can go in the lavs in Talbot Square,' said Paula. 'Come on, I'm starving, aren't you? You did ever so well, by the way, coming second. You're a brilliant pianist.'

Sandie felt ten feet tall. That was praise indeed, especially from a sixth former. It was turning out to be a fantastic day. She had come second in her class, she was on the way to making a new friend – and they were pinching a bit of time away from school – and Gregory Matthews had spoken to her. What's more, she was going to see him again tomorrow . . .

Chapter 13

Abbie felt a wee bit deflated when Sandie had gone. She had seemed in such a hurry to get away, she and her friend, Paula. But that was the way of it, Abbie supposed. Girls of Sandie's age didn't want to spend much time hanging around with their mothers. That Paula seemed a nice sort of girl, quiet and respectful. Abbie hadn't heard Sandie mention her before, but then she never talked all that much about her schoolfriends. Maybe she should encourage her to invite one, or more, of them to come to her home now and again. For tea, perhaps, when she, Abbie, was not at college. Although she could well imagine Sandie scoffing at the idea of a tea party. 'Just as though I'm a little kid, Mum.'

Mrs Blake, too, had seemed anxious to depart at the end of Sandie's class, leaving Abbie on her own with this odd feeling of anti-climax. The next class, for piano duettists of fourteen and under, was about to start and she wondered if she should stay and listen. It didn't hold the same interest, though, when you did not know any of the competitors. No, she would go and have a browse round the shops, she decided, and treat herself to some lunch. She pushed her festival programme into her bag and hurried off, just as the steward stood up to announce the next class.

Blackpool town centre was not very busy on this Monday morning. The Lights had finished recently, so there were no late-season holidaymakers sauntering around, getting in the way of residents who were in a hurry to do their shopping, as was often the case. Not that Abbie was in a hurry today, nor had she any vital shopping to do. It was nice to be able to take her time wandering around the shops and she began to enjoy her rare time of leisure.

After a cursory look around Marks & Spencer and Little-woods, Abbie realised she was feeling hungry. She had only had a slice of toast for breakfast, which was all she ever had, but today she had not even eaten all of that; she had been all keyed-up in sympathy with Sandie. She decided she would go to Lockhart's café on the corner of Bank Hey Street. She remembered going there with Doreen when they were house-hunting; it was a nice comfortable sort of place, not too posh, but not too 'snackbar-ish'. To her surprise it was already quite busy in the upstairs restaurant although it was not yet half-past twelve. There were still a few vacant tables, however, and she sat down at an empty one tucked away in a corner.

She studied the menu. There was a good selection of reasonably priced dishes – roast beef, or roast pork, plus all the trimmings, steak and kidney pie, omelettes of various kinds, pork chop and chips, gammon with pineapple, bat-tered haddock or cod. Abbie was quite spoilt for choice. What a treat it was to choose something she had not cooked herself and to eat it in such pleasant surroundings. She didn't count the canteen meals at college. They were well cooked, but much of a muchness, and after a while their stodginess and sameness began to pall and the level of noise was apt to give you indigestion.

She finally made her decision as she saw the waitress, in her black dress and starched white apron and cap, hurrying towards her, pad and pencil at the ready. 'Gammon and pineapple, with chips and peas,' she told her. 'And a pot of tea for one, please.' The tea arrived first, and quite quickly, too, as was usually the case in cafés such as this. That was not strictly correct, Abbie supposed – you should have your tea or coffee at the end of the meal, not before – but it gave you something to do while you were waiting and helped to make the waiting time seem not so long.

She poured out her tea, noting that the restaurant was filling up rapidly now. There were several people with music cases, some accompanied by children; this was obviously a popular place with the festival-goers. There were even a few people waiting at the entrance until a place was vacant. She was not terribly pleased when the waitress approached her and asked, 'Would you mind sharing your table, madam?' She had been enjoying her solitude and did not relish the thought of making polite conversation with a stranger, but she could do no other than say, 'No, of course not.'

She recognised at once the man who was approaching her table; he was quite a tall fellow with greying hair and an aristocratic face – one you would not easily forget. He looked pleasant, though, and not at all standoffish. It was the music teacher of the boy who had won the cup. What had Mrs Blake said his name was? Henderson? Something like that.

He was smiling rather ruefully. 'I'm so sorry to barge in on you like this,' he said, 'but the waitress said you wouldn't mind.'

'No, not at all,' Abbie said quickly, smiling back at him.

He took off his fawn raincoat, hanging it on a nearby coat-stand with curving branches, then sat down in the chair opposite Abbie. 'It's awfully kind of you to share your table. I daresay you were enjoying your privacy, weren't you? The problem is, I'm in rather a hurry. I want to get back for the afternoon session at the Festival.' He looked more closely at Abbie. 'I saw you there earlier on, didn't I?'

'Yes, that's right, you did. My daughter came second in the class, and your pupil came first, didn't he? I must congratulate you. He was brilliant; we all thought so.'

'Thank you – thank you very much. How nice of you to say so.' He looked genuinely pleased. 'There is often jealousy, I know, and backbiting about who should, or should not, have won. It's inclined to put me off festivals, but they're good experience, especially for youngsters such as Greg Matthews. He's a natural, that boy. I feel I haven't done all that much really, he's so very talented.'

'But his talent needs nurturing, bringing out, surely?'

'Yes, of course. But he has a talent that's quite rare and I'm very proud to be his teacher. Your girl came second, you say? Yes, I remember her. Sandra, isn't it?'

'Yes, Sandra Horsfall. She likes to be called Sandie.'

'She gave a very good performance. She's a talented girl, too. She has a good music teacher, has she? Well, I suppose she must have.'

'Yes – Mrs Blake. It was she who told me, actually, that you were the boy's music teacher, or I wouldn't have known. You know her, do you?'

'Only a little. Our paths cross now and again at festivals and exams. I must admit I didn't notice her there this morning, but I was rather preoccupied. I noticed you, though, Mrs Horsfall.' He smiled at her in a friendly way. 'Yes, I believe Mrs Blake is a very good teacher. But didn't I hear she was leaving Blackpool? Something about going to live nearer her daughter? Oh . . . excuse me a moment.' The waitress had come with Abbie's meal and also to take his order. He had scarcely looked at the menu and he did not bother to do so now. 'That looks good,' he said, eyeing Abbie's gammon and chips. 'I'll have the same, please. And a pot of tea. Thank you very much.'

'What was that you were saying about Mrs Blake?' asked Abbie. 'I'm sorry, I didn't quite catch your name. Mr Henderson, is it?'

'Hendy,' he replied. 'Duncan Hendy.' He held out his hand across the table. 'How do you do? And you are Mrs Horsfall, aren't you?'

'Yes, Abbie Horsfall,' she said, feeling his firm warm handclasp. 'You said Mrs Blake was leaving Blackpool?'

'So I've heard. Do eat your meal, Mrs Horsfall. Don't let it go cold. It may be only a rumour, of course, but the person who told me did so in good faith. But I'm surprised you didn't know, with your daughter being her pupil. I thought she might have told you.'

Abbie took a mouthful of the moist pink gammon and decided it was very good indeed, then a succulent golden-brown chip. 'I think she was about to tell us,' she said, between mouthfuls. 'She said she had some news, but it could wait. Maybe she doesn't want to tell Sandie until the Festival is over that she might have to find another teacher. It's sure to upset her a little – Sandie, I mean. They seem to get on quite well, and my daughter isn't always the easiest of girls, I have to admit. You know what teenagers are like.'

'I do indeed, Mrs Horsfall.'

She liked his quiet unassuming smile. She felt sure he was an excellent teacher, despite what he said about the boy's natural talent, but he appeared so modest. She liked, too, his casual mode of dress, nothing flamboyant – a tweedy sports jacket, cream shirt and diagonally striped tie in pleasing autumnal shades of gold, russet and dark brown. She wondered . . .

'Mr Hendy,' she said on impulse, 'do you think, if it's true about Mrs Blake, that you might consider taking my daughter on as a pupil? She's passed her Grade Six and she works very hard, most of the time. That is, if you've room for her. I realise you probably have a great many pupils.'

'Not so many that I couldn't fit in your Sandra . . . Sandie,' he replied. 'Let's see what happens, shall we? I'll give you my address, then Sandie could come along and see me. It's up to her really, isn't it? She may prefer another lady teacher.'

'I don't think she'd mind,' said Abbie. 'Oh look, here's your tea, and it looks like your meal as well. That's quick service.'

He was so easy to talk to. She had finished eating first,

and at his gentle questioning she told him about her teacher training course, about her own love of music and her somewhat limited ability as a pianist, 'although I was quite good when I was younger.' And that she was a widow.

She learned that he, too, was a widower. She guessed him to be a few years her senior – in his mid to late forties, maybe. He had lived in Blackpool all his life and his home now was in a quiet avenue near to Stanley Park, not very far from where her father and Faith lived.

'Do you teach the piano full time?' she asked. 'Or do you do something else as well?'

'Oh, I'm a sort of Jack of all trades,' he laughed. 'All connected with music, though. I have a part-time post as a music teacher in schools. A peripatetic teacher, they call me. Sounds painful, doesn't it?'

She grinned. 'Yes, I know what it means, though. You travel around, don't you, to various schools? I must confess I hadn't heard the word until I started training myself. Do you teach the piano in schools, then?'

'A little, out of school hours – mostly singing lessons, though, and some music theory. Then I have my own private pupils on Saturdays and early evenings. I keep Sundays free because I play the organ at the local church. And from time to time I play for functions in hotels – dances and civic dinners and that sort of thing – sometimes on the piano, and sometimes on the organ. A Hammond organ or something similar, very different from the church organ, of course.'

A talented man, she thought, very much so. Peter, too, had played the church organ and had been quite an accomplished pianist. When she had met him again in Norfolk, after their first abortive meetings in Blackpool, he had been playing in a small RAF band and she, a Land Girl, had been billeted at a nearby hostel. Peter had not made a career out of his musical ability, however, as this man, Duncan Hendy, had done.

She would have liked to go on talking to him, but she

knew, when she had finished her meal, that she really should leave. It wasn't as if they were friends or even acquaintances, just a couple of people who happened to have shared a table, although there was the possibility they might meet again if he became Sandie's music teacher. She motioned to the waitress and settled her bill, then rose and put on her coat.

'Don't rush away on my account,' said Mr Hendy. 'It was your table anyway, wasn't it? I'm the intruder.'

'No, you're not. Not at all. I've enjoyed talking to you, Mr Hendy. But I really must go.'

'Not as much as I have enjoyed it, I can assure you, Mrs Horsfall.' He reached into his jacket pocket, taking out his wallet and extracting a small card. 'Here is my address, just in case you decide to allow me to teach your daughter. I would consider it a privilege but, as I said, it's up to Sandra. I'll see you again tomorrow, maybe? I take it she's competing in the open class?'

'Yes, so she is.' Abbie had forgotten that momentarily, and she realised that the thought of seeing him again was very pleasant. 'Well, goodbye then, Mr Hendy.' She held out her hand. 'It's been nice meeting you.'

'It has, hasn't it? Very nice.' He smiled warmly, half-rising from his seat as he shook her hand. 'Goodbye, Mrs Horsfall. It won't be long before I go myself. I have two more pupils competing this afternoon. Till tomorrow, then.'

Next to Lockhart's café was RHO Hills, Blackpool's leading department store, one of Abbie's favourite places, with four floors and a basement full of tempting merchandise. Not that she often ventured further than the ground floor unless she wanted to purchase a dress for a special occasion, maybe, or an item of furniture; their range of goods was extensive. The ground floor was a delight to the eye with its multifarious displays of bags, scarves and gloves, costume jewellery, beauty preparations and luxury items for the home – mirrors, pictures, vases, ornaments and the like. The aroma, too, was quite heavenly; the mixed fragrance of face powder, nail varnish and expensive perfume. There was usually a woman to be seen being made up by a beautician and other elegantly dressed ladies trying out the latest shades of lipstick or eye-shadow.

Abbie fingered the silken scarves and looked longingly at the fine kid gloves. A little out of her price range though, those gloves, and she already had a black pair and a brown pair, somewhat worn, but they would suffice. On an impulse she treated herself to a scarf with a swirly design of varied greens and yellows which would go well with the sage-green coat she was wearing. And that called for a new lipstick; it was ages since she had bought one and Sandie had told her that the pinky-red one she always wore was not very 'with it'. She reached for a Max Factor sample in a coppery-orange shade and was just trying it on the back of her hand when she heard a voice behind her. 'Can I help you, Modom? That is one of our new autumn shades.' She gave a slight start. Officious sales ladies always intimidated her, but this didn't sound like one of those. The voice was familiar. She turned round to see Doreen smiling at her. A little uncertainly, to be sure, but at least she had spoken to her, she might well have pretended she hadn't noticed her.

'Hello there, Abbie. How're you doing?' Doreen sounded quite cheerful, but it could have been bravado.

Abbie put the lipstick down. 'Doreen, how nice to see you. It's been ages. How are you?'

'Oh, you know, not so dusty.' The saleswoman was eyeing them a trifle disdainfully. 'Are you going to buy that lipstick?' asked Doreen. 'Come on, make up yer mind. I'm just going for a coffee in the basement. Want to come?'

Abbie hesitated – Doreen had not sounded over-enthusiastic – then said, 'Yes, I will.' She paid for the lipstick then accompanied Doreen to the basement café. She hadn't the heart to tell her she had just had a pot of tea. It was good to see her old friend again and she hoped the former uneasiness that had marred their relationship might disappear over a cup of coffee and a chat. There was still a certain wariness in Doreen's eyes, but at least this was a start.

'So, how's tricks?' Doreen asked as they drank their coffee. 'Enjoying college, are you?'

'Yes, it's great,' replied Abbie, but she did not want to say too much about that. It was not something she and Doreen had in common and she did so hope they would be able to get back on their old footing. 'It's half-term though now, so I'm able to spend more time at home. I've just been to the Musical Festival – well, earlier on this morning. Our Sandie came second in her piano class. That's probably why I'm feeling so pleased with myself.'

'Yes, you're certainly looking all bright-eyed and bushy-tailed,' said Doreen, though a trifle waspishly.

Abbie thought her friend, on the contrary, was looking a little unkempt, as though she was not taking quite the same care with her appearance as she had used to do. Her blonde hair, curling untidily around her coat collar, was dark at the roots – she had been a natural blonde when she was younger – and she had put on a little more weight.

'That's great news about Sandie, you must be very proud of her.'

She did not sound all that interested, however. Abbie remembered how Doreen had always thought it rather odd that Sandie should pursue her musical studies with such dedication, and be encouraged to do so by her mother. The implication was that the girl had enough on her plate with her school work and should be urged to spend her leisure time enjoying herself.

'I was hoping your Sandie and our Veronica might've got friendly, with you coming to live in Blackpool,' she continued, 'but you can't choose their friends for them, can you? They're at different schools, of course.'

'Yes, that's true,' Abbie agreed. 'I don't see much of our Sandie's friends. There was a girl at the Festival this morning

– Paula, she seemed nice enough – but they're very secretive, aren't they?'

'I'll say they are! Has Sandie got a boyfriend yet?'

'Give her time, she's only fifteen – well, sixteen in January. But I must admit she looks older. No, there are no boys on the scene, not that I know of. But then I don't know very much. What about Veronica? Let's see, she must be seventeen now.'

'Yes, seventeen last month, but there's no boyfriend yet. I wish there was. I told you, didn't I, about her religious craze? Well, it's not abating at all. I say to her it's a wonder she doesn't take her bed and sleep there, at the church. She's always there, when she's not at school. If it's not Mass then it's some discussion group or other, or the Youth Club.'

'She could do a lot worse,' said Abbie gently. 'Maybe there is a boy, though, if you say she goes to the Youth Club. Perhaps that's the big attraction.'

'I doubt it. I would know, wouldn't I?' Doreen looked a little uncertain. 'But, as you say, they're so damned secretive. Anyway, never mind them. How about you? There's no dashing male swept you off your feet at that college of yours?' Did Abbie only imagine the touch of asperity in her friend's voice?

'No, nothing like that,' she answered quickly. 'There are quite a lot of men, of course, but no.' She remembered Art Gillespie and his vague invitation, but immediately closed her mind to the thought. 'What about you and Norman? You're getting on all right now, are you?' It was a bold question, she realised, considering the altercation they had had when Doreen had accused Abbie of betraying her, but she had to ask, if there was to be any hope of them getting back to normal.

'Yes, we're OK,' replied Doreen. 'We have to be, don't we?' She sounded a little edgy. 'We had a good holiday earlier this year, all of us, in North Wales. And Norman and I are having a couple of days in London after Christmas. His

211

parents are coming down to look after the children. I don't know why we didn't think of it before. So . . . yes, we're getting along quite well.'

There was a pregnant pause for several seconds, and Abbie began to feel sorry she had mentioned Norman. Maybe Doreen was still blaming her for telling tales to her husband. Maybe it was too soon for them to get back to their former footing. She was, therefore, surprised when Doreen said, quite out of the blue, 'Are you still doing your Tupperware parties?'

'Yes, now and again,' replied Abbie. 'Not as much, of course, with college and everything.'

'Would you like to do one for me, sometime before Christmas? We could make it a bit of a party. I'll provide some special eats and a bottle or two of bubbly – sparkling wine, I mean, not champers, I can't run to that. To be quite honest, we've all been asked to help with fundraising for our church, and I thought, Oh dear, what on earth can I do? Then I thought about you and your Tupper parties and I knew you wouldn't mind. I'll charge 'em for the supper and we'll have a raffle and a Tombola stall. It should make a good bit of money for the church, and you'll be able to sell some of your stuff, won't you? You could bring Sandie along and I'll make sure our Veronica's there. How about it?'

'Yes, it's not a bad idea,' said Abbie. She felt, however, that she was being manipulated and that the one to gain most from the evening would not be herself, but Doreen – or Doreen's church. It was because of this that she said yes. She was not a Catholic, but it was all in a good cause.

'We'll put the girls in charge of the buffet,' said Doreen. 'Pay 'em a few bob. They won't refuse with Christmas coming up.'

'It had better be fairly early in December.' Abbie was determined that Doreen was not going to have everything her own way. 'Then people can perhaps buy a few bits and bobs for Christmas. If it's any later I'm afraid I'll be too busy with my college work.'

They settled on a date, the first Friday in December, before they left the store and went their separate ways. Abbie drove home with mixed feelings. It had been a most eventful day, what with Sandie's success and a conciliatory meeting with her old friend . . . or had it been? She was not too sure about that. And in between there'd been a very pleasant lunch companion. She remembered she would be seeing Duncan Hendy again tomorrow.

Sandie was almost, though not quite, as successful the following day. In the open pianoforte class, again for competitors of sixteen and under, she was placed third and Gregory Matthews, to the surprise of many people, was given second place, the trophy going to a girl from Manchester. It was a different adjudicator this time. Maybe he had liked the girl's rather different interpretation of the piece entitled 'Rosemary' by Frank Bridge; maybe it was expedient to award the trophy to someone outside of Blackpool, or maybe the girl from Manchester had just been the best.

Sandie was well pleased with her result, but she did think that Gregory should have won, as he had the day before. She would have liked to tell him so when they went forward to collect their certificates, but it would have seemed rather rude to the girl who had won – whom Sandie did, in all fairness, congratulate – and there was not the same opportunity this time for them to speak together. They were not asked to pose for a photograph and, to her slight disappointment, Gregory Matthews hurried away with his music teacher.

'Well done, Sandra,' said Mrs Blake. 'I'm proud of you and I know your mother is, too.' Mum, indeed, had been in a very good mood altogether since yesterday. It was a long time since Sandie had seen her quite so happy. She couldn't seem to stop smiling and Sandie was glad she had, at last, done something to please her.

'You're not wanting to dash away, are you?' Mrs Blake went on. 'I was wondering . . . would you come and have a cup of tea with me in the Indian lounge? There's something I want to tell you both.'

And over a pot of tea and fancy cakes – Mrs Blake's treat – the music teacher told them that she was leaving Blackpool. She and her husband were moving to the Midlands to be nearer their married daughter, who apparently needed some help with her children. 'I feel I must put my family first,' she explained. 'You, as a mother, will understand that, won't you, Mrs Horsfall?'

Abbie agreed that it was true, but Sandie thought her mother's reaction was a shade cool, and was surprised to hear her say that she had already heard the news. Trust her to be so blatantly honest; never could she tell even a half lie or dissemble in any way.

'I'm sure I don't know who you've heard it from,' said Mrs Blake, rather huffily.

And, 'Why didn't you tell me, Mum?' asked Sandie, almost at the same time.

Abbie explained that she had not wanted Sandie to be worried in any way until she had finished both her Festival classes. As if I would be, thought Sandie. What does it matter who teaches me the piano? She knew she was doing well and she knew also that although Mrs Blake was a good teacher, she, Sandie, had achieved much of her success through her own efforts. She was rather sorry, though not unduly so, at the thought of Mrs Blake going. She wasn't such a bad old thing; a bit strict and inclined to fuss, but on the whole the two of them had got on quite well together. It would mean a change of music teacher. I wonder . . . thought Sandie.

Her eyes wandered to the table a few yards away where Gregory Matthews was sitting with his teacher, drinking tea and eating cakes, as the three of them were doing. He looked a nice man, that Mr Hendy or whatever his name was, quite good-looking, too, for an old fellow – and if she were to start going to him for lessons there was a chance she might come across . . .

'Sandie, are you listening?' said her mother. 'You're not, are you? You were miles away. Mrs Blake was just saying that you have two lessons left this term,' her mother paid for her lessons ten at a time, 'so that will take you to the middle of November.'

'Sidney and I hope to move down to Wolverhampton in mid-December, so we'll be well settled there in time for Christmas,' said Mrs Blake.

'You've bought a house down there, have you?' asked Sandie.

'No. My daughter has had an extension built and we'll be living there. I'll be looking after the children while she's at work. She's a teacher, you see.'

'And have you sold your house here?'

'Sandie, don't be so nosy,' said her mother. 'It's really none of our business, is it? What we are concerned about is fixing you up with another music teacher. I was wondering . . .'

Sandie saw, to her surprise, that her mother's eyes were also wandering in the direction of Gregory and his teacher. 'As a matter of fact, I met that gentleman over there, Mr Hendy, at lunchtime yesterday, quite by accident, and he said . . .'

'Oh, so that's how you found out, is it?' said Mrs Blake. 'And they say women gossip.' She was smiling, but it was a rather tight-lipped smile.

'Yes, indeed,' said Abbie. Her own smile was quite guileless. 'But it wasn't just gossip, was it? It happened to be true.' She turned to her daughter. 'He's offered to teach you, Sandie, but of course it would be up to you to decide.'

'Well, I must say he's been quick off the mark,' said Mrs

Blake. 'Talk about dead men's shoes! Actually, I am handing over my pupils – those who wish it, that is – to a young woman I used to teach. She has done very well and now she's started taking pupils of her own. I thought it would be a boost for her, but of course it's up to you to make your own arrangements. Now, if you'll excuse me, I have some shopping to do. I'll just settle the bill then I must be off.

'I'll see you as usual on Thursday, Sandra,' she said as she stood up to take her leave. 'And I really am very proud of you, my dear. You've done remarkably well.'

'Thank you . . . and thank you for the tea and cakes,' said Sandie.

'It's the least I could do. Goodbye, Mrs Horsfall, good-bye, Sandra.'

'Oh dear, do you think I've upset her?' said Abbie. 'She seems a bit miffed. Perhaps I shouldn't have said that about Mr Hendy and the lessons. But you know me, Sandie. I always believe in being straight with people. I wouldn't want her to think I was being deceitful or anything like that.'

'Mum, you couldn't be deceitful if your life depended on it,' said Sandie. 'You're an open book. And I think it's a great idea about Mr Hendy. He must be a wonderful teacher. You've heard that boy, Gregory Whatsit.' She mustn't appear to be too interested in him or her mother might become suspicious. 'Come on, let's go and ask him now, shall we? Quick, before he decides to go.'

'Well, we could go across now, I suppose, and I could introduce you,' said Abbie, a shade doubtfully. 'But we'd have to go and see him at his home and make proper arrangements. Perhaps we'd better wait.'

'Oh, come on, Mum. Stop dithering.' Sandie was already on her way across the room so Abbie had no choice but to follow her.

'Hello again, Mrs Horsfall.' Duncan Hendy looked up with a welcoming smile. 'And this, of course, is Sandra, isn't it? Congratulations, my dear. You've done very well, today and yesterday.' He held out his hand and Sandie shook it. He had a firm handclasp and nice kind blue-ish eyes.

'Thank you.' She smiled back shyly at him, although she was not, as a rule, so bashful. She knew it was because Gregory was also looking at her. She glanced quickly across at him. 'Congratulations to you, too, Gregory,' she said, 'once again.'

'Thanks.' The boy grinned. 'And to you as well. Getting to be a habit, isn't it?' Her heart turned a somersault as his blue eyes – a brighter blue than those of his teacher – met and held hers. 'I'm usually called Greg,' he said.

'Sit down,' said Mr Hendy, gesturing towards two empty chairs. 'Come and join us.' But Abbie said no, they were not stopping.

'I've just come to tell you, Mr Hendy, that Sandie and I – well, we'd like to take you up on your offer. You know, what we were talking about yesterday. Mrs Blake has just told us she's leaving, so perhaps we could come and see you sometime?'

'Yes, that's fine,' said Mr Hendy, smiling at them both. 'You've got my card, Mrs Horsfall, and it has my telephone number on it. Give me a ring and we'll make an appointment. No, that sounds too formal, doesn't it? We'll arrange a date for you both to come and see me.'

'I say, are you thinking of having lessons with Duncan?' asked Gregory. 'That would be great, Sandra. He's terrific.'

'With Mr Hendy . . . yes,' faltered Sandie. 'That is, if he has room for me. I'm called Sandie, by the way.'

'We'll make room for you, Sandie, have no fear,' said Duncan Hendy.

'See you around then, Sandie,' said Greg, as they said their goodbyes. Her mother was fidgeting like a cat on hot bricks, saying that they really must be going.

'Yes, see you,' replied Sandie.

'Goodbye, Mrs Horsfall, lovely to see you again. Goodbye, Sandie.'

Sandie could not help but notice the look of admiration in the man's eyes. Crikey! She thought. Mum's made a conquest. Not that it would make any difference. Her mother would never, ever look at any other man, not in that way. Sandie's father had been dead for nearly eight years and her mum had never shown any interest at all in men. And it was too late now; Mum was turned forty. Duncan Hendy would be wasting his time.

But as for Greg Matthews and herself . . . Well, that was a different story altogether.

Chapter 14

By the end of the week Abbie was back at College. It seemed as though she were moving back into a totally different world and, very soon, the events of the long half-term weekend which she had spent in Blackpool began to recede to the back of her mind. She was pleased she had seen Doreen again, although she felt there was still some resentment lingering between them, but back at College there was her newer friend, Jean, with whom, if she were honest with herself, she had much more in common. There was also Art Gillespie.

She attended his first lecture of the half-term determined to keep a firm check on her silly thoughts. For heaven's sake, she told herself, she was a woman in her early forties, not a teenager with a crush on a man who happened to have glanced in her direction. She had two children and a home to look after, as well as, sometime in the future, a new career to embark upon. Besides, she was a widow with very happy memories and Peter was the only man she would ever love.

So when she became aware of Art's eyes wandering towards her she told herself she was imagining things and kept her own eyes firmly glued to the notes in front of her.

He caught up with her at lunchtime in the canteen. Jean saw him approaching their table and she got up, collecting her books together. 'Jean, don't!' whispered Abbie frantically. 'Don't go. I don't want to be left alone with him.'

'And I don't want to play gooseberry,' Jean whispered

back. 'I've seen him looking at you. He wants to be alone with you.' She rolled her eyes. 'Just watch it, that's all.'

'Hi there, Abigail. No, I must remember to call you Abbie, mustn't I?' He sat down next to her and she was relieved, in a way, that they were the only two at the table. 'You seem rather aloof today. Is something the matter?'

'No, there's nothing the matter, nothing at all. I'm just getting used to being back here, I suppose.' She smiled weakly at him. 'It's like moving onto a different planet after being at home for a few days.'

'You enjoyed your break then? Your time with your family?'

'Yes, very much so. It was Blackpool Musical Festival and my daughter, Sandra, was very successful. She plays the piano – I think I mentioned it before – and she came second in one class and third in another. So I'm feeling very proud of her.' Now why am I telling him all this? she wondered, noting his slow smile and the half-amused glint in his eyes. At all events, he would not be interested.

It seemed that he was, however. His expression changed to one of genuine attentiveness. 'Great!' he said. 'Quite an achievement. I know the competition can be tough at these festivals. She must be a talented girl. And how about your son, the lad who is interested in football – you see, I've remembered. How is he?'

'Simon? Oh, he's fine, thanks. Blackpool was playing at home on Saturday, so that's all he was bothered about. I didn't want him to feel his nose was being pushed out, with all the excitement about his sister, but Simon's not like that, I'm glad to say. He's quite easygoing. Sandra's the one who can be a bit of a handful.'

'Can't they all, at that age. Did you say she was fifteen?'

'Yes, sixteen in January.'

'A difficult time for girls. A time when they are becoming more aware of everything, particularly the opposite sex. Yes, it's a difficult time for them, and for their parents – or so I've been told.'

220

'Yes, I've been warned it could get worse before it gets better with Sandie. That's the way of it with teenage girls. There are no boys around at the moment, though.'

'You mean none that you know of. There will be, believe me, if she's a normal girl.'

'Of course she's normal! It's just that she's only fifteen and . . . and she's a very clever girl. She works hard at school.'

'Hey, hey, don't get on your high horse. I wasn't suggesting that your Sandie isn't a perfectly normal girl. And if she's anything like her mother,' he cast a sidelong glance at her from beneath his slightly lowered eyelids, 'then she must be a very attractive one.'

'She looks like her father, actually.'

He laughed. 'I'm just trying to warn you, that's all. Fifteen is plenty old enough, and being clever is no drawback, believe me. The clever ones are often the worst.'

'You seem to know a lot about girls,' observed Abbie drily.

'A little, yes,' Art replied with a slight shrug. 'Don't worry, my dear.' He smiled at her disarmingly. 'Your daughter will be fine. She's a very well brought-up young lady, I'm sure. Anyway, *revenons à nos moutons* as the French say. Let's get back to the subject.'

I do know what it means, thought Abbie, with a touch of pique. Does he think I'm a complete ignoramus?

'And the subject is you and me.' He leaned more closely towards her. 'How about coming for a drink with me? I asked you before, remember?'

Abbie stared at him, completely nonplussed. 'Yes, I know you did, Art, but I didn't think you meant it.'

'You thought I was just being polite, did you? Believe me, I was not. Art Gillespie doesn't say things he doesn't mean, at least, not very often. Will you come, Abbie?'

'I'd like to, yes.' She hesitated a little. What on earth was she to do? On no account must she sound too eager, but to refuse outright would sound as if she thought he was suggesting something improper. He was probably only trying to be friendly, nothing more. 'It's rather difficult though,' she went on. 'It's quite a long journey home, nearly an hour on the train, and the nights are getting darker now. I wouldn't want to be out late, walking home on my own from the station.'

'I quite understand,' said Art, with a humorous glint in his eye. 'Maybe an afternoon would suit you better. I have a free afternoon on Tuesday, so we could go and have lunch somewhere out in the country, perhaps – have a drink and a chat, get to know each other a little better – then I can run you back to the station at the end of the afternoon to catch your usual train. How does that sound?'

'Fine,' she answered, 'except that you may be free, but I'm not. I've two lectures.'

'What are they?'

'PE and Rural Studies.'

'You can be indisposed for PE, can't you? Not much in your line, anyway, I would have thought, prancing around in gym knickers – sorry, shorts. And Dave Saunders won't notice if you're not there for his lecture. They're not absolutely compulsory, you know. We do try to treat you like the mature students you are.'

'Yes, I know, but it's noted, isn't it, if we keep missing lectures? I'm surprised at you anyway, Mr Gillespie, encouraging me to play wag.'

He grinned at her. 'You'll come then? Please say you will.'

'Yes, I'll come,' she replied. PE was her least favourite subject, as it was with many of the maturer women who were not particularly athletic, and there were often a few absentees claiming a sore foot or a sprained wrist or general indisposition. She quite enjoyed Rural Studies, but it was not a main subject lecture and she doubted that she would be missed.

Jean raised her eyebrows when Abbie told her of Art's invitation, but forbore to comment, save to say, 'Just watch it, kid.' No doubt she thinks I'm old enough to look after myself, thought Abbie, which I am. It isn't as if I'm a teenager going on my first date. All the same, that was what she felt like through a couple of restless nights.

Art drove a Triumph Herald, a snazzy little two-seater, which got her from the college to the outskirts of Chelford faster than she had ever travelled in her life.

The country pub he took her to was in a small hamlet which Abbie had never heard of before. The barman, however, greeted him by name. 'Nah then, Art, how're yer doing, lad?' Art told her it was a pub he and his rugby-playing friends often used. The dishes of the day were written up on a blackboard, reminding Abbie of school. She chose Welsh rarebit, not feeling she could tackle the steak and ale pie which Art had chosen for himself. She was still feeling very nervous about what she was doing, having lunch in a pub with a man she did not really know very well and missing her lectures, to boot.

The meal arrived fairly quickly as the place was almost deserted. They ate it at a small round table tucked away in a corner. The cheese on toast was delicious; piping hot and well cooked, although there wasn't much that could go wrong with Welsh rarebit. Abbie found herself relaxing, especially after she had drunk the sherry which Art had bought her before the meal, and had taken a few sips of her shandy.

'I remember you were drinking shandies at the Market Inne,' he said. 'You see, I remember everything about you, Abbie.'

They did not talk much over the meal. Art was tucking into his with obvious relish, and after they had finished eating he seemed anxious to be on his way. The pub would be closing soon anyway; the landlord was clearing away and sending out Time, Please signals. Abbie remembered how Art had said he would run her to the station in time to catch the train. What did he have in mind for the rest of the afternoon? she wondered. Unsophisticated woman that she was, she had forgotten about pubs closing after lunch.

'We'll have a little run through the country,' he said as they zoomed out of the car park. 'OK with you, Abbie?'

'Yes, OK,' she replied, hoping he would not drive too fast along the winding country lanes. She was not a particularly good traveller and she wanted to keep her lunch and her shandy down.

'Where are we going? Why have we come here?' she asked as they entered the main street of a much larger village. She could tell from the signposts that they were heading back towards Chelford.

'Wait and see.' Art turned to grin at her, then he drove through the village and stopped the car outside a row of semi-detached houses just past the shops and the church. 'I was wondering if you would like to come and take a look at my place? My bachelor pad.'

Abbie felt panic rising into her throat. The alarm must have shown on her face because he went on, very quickly, 'If you don't want to, then of course I understand. But I can assure you, my dear Abbie, that you don't need to worry, not at all. I just thought we could have a nice little chat – get to know one another better. That was what I said at the beginning, wasn't it, that I wanted to get to know you?'

But you didn't mention taking me to your flat, thought Abbie. Was that what he had intended all along? Was it a case of the spider and the fly? No, you're being ridiculous, she told herself, and what an idiot she would look if she refused to go with him. If she asked him to take her back to the station now, it would be the end of everything between them before it had even begun. 'All right then,' she said. 'That would be very nice. It was just a bit unexpected, that's all. But I mustn't be too long. I'll have to catch my train.'

'Don't worry, Abbie,' Art laughed. 'I won't let you miss your train.'

Her legs felt a little wobbly as she followed him up the path through the somewhat overgrown garden to the front door. Both the upstairs and the downstairs, which was the part that Art lived in, had been converted into self-contained flats.

He invited her to take off her coat, then he showed her into his living room, a light and spacious room into which the afternoon sun was flooding. He adjusted the floor-length curtains, which were in a geometric design of black, white and red, so that the sun would not be in their eyes, then invited her to sit on the settee, a large three-seater covered in a rough oatmeal-coloured fabric. It was very comfortable, but low-sprung, and she felt her long legs shoot out in front of her. Decorously she tucked them to one side as Art sat down in one of the matching armchairs. She looked around. The fitted carpet was of a darker oatmeal shade and the dining furniture was of the Ercol design; a table, four chairs and a sideboard in light oak, simple and unembellished. There was a set of bookshelves reaching from floor to ceiling crammed with books of all kinds and, on the bottom shelf, a row of LPs. It was the books and the rack of newspapers and magazines at the side of the stone fireplace which gave the room its lived-in appearance, otherwise it might have seemed stark and austere. There were no ornaments or plants or photographs, the only picture on the wall being a rather strange abstract design, a copy of a Picasso or something similar, she guessed.

'You approve of my bachelor pad, then?' asked Art. 'Yes, you have a good look round, I don't mind.'

'Sorry,' said Abbie. 'I didn't mean to appear rude, but I always take an interest in where people live. I like to picture them in their own surroundings, if you know what I mean. Yes, I do approve, very much so. Rather more than a pad, though, isn't it? It's very impressive. And so tidy.'

'For a man, you mean?' He laughed. 'I have to admit I couldn't live in a tip, and I'm quite used to looking after myself now. The garden is another story – you'll have noticed it. I'm not a gardener at all; it just doesn't interest me. It's as much as I can do to cut the lawn and trim the hedge. I have to do it once in a while or I'd have the neighbours complaining.'

'What about the people in the upstairs flat?'

'Oh, they're an elderly couple. So any gardening that is done is largely up to me. But, as I say, it's not one of my priorities.'

'What are your priorities then?'

'Oh, my work at the college.' He nodded straightfacedly and, she guessed, with a touch of irony, although she had to admit he was a good tutor and seemed conscientious enough; she had never known him to miss a lecture. 'Playing rugby,' he went on. 'Drinking with my mates – in moderation, of course.'

He gave a wry grin and she smiled back. 'Of course.'

'Listening to music, reading . . . I'm a pretty average sort of bloke really.' He waved his hand airily at the rows of books and records. 'You'll find my tastes are fairly wide-ranging – nothing too erudite, especially in music. Now, my priority at the moment is to make you welcome, Abbie. How about a drink and some background music?'

'Yes, I'd like that, thank you.' She was not sure what he meant by a drink; a cup of tea or coffee or something stronger? She would have to be careful. She had already had that sherry, followed by a shandy.

He gave a little laugh. 'There's nothing to thank me for, yet. Anyway, it should be me that's thanking you, for agreeing to come here to my humble abode.' He looked at her steadily, not at all mockingly as she felt he did at times, but with an intensity that disconcerted her a little. 'Now, Abbie, what's your tipple? I think I have most things. Whisky, gin, vodka, Martini? Or perhaps you'd like another shandy?'

'Oh no, no, thank you. That's more of a pub drink, isn't

it? I mean, that's what I've had on the rare occasions I've been with Jean and the rest of them. That's what they drink and I never know what to ask for.' She could have kicked herself as soon as she said it. She kept trying to act with a degree of sophistication and then, suddenly, her old insecurity would surface. Peter had always ordered for her when they had been out anywhere – usually a sweet sherry or a small port and lemon – but since he had died, and until she started at college, Abbie had scarcely been in a pub at all. And she had never been alone with a man in his sitting room, accepting a drink from him.

'I'll have a vodka and tonic, please,' she said with a show of worldliness. She had heard women asking for such a drink. 'Just a small one, if you don't mind.'

'Certainly, and much more ladylike than a shandy, if you don't mind me saying so. Much more "you", my dear. I'll have a whisky and dry ginger, my favourite poison. Not too much though. Don't worry, Abbie, I know I have to get you to the station all in one piece, but there's plenty of time. Time to relax and enjoy ourselves.'

The top of the sideboard pulled down to reveal a well-stocked drinks compartment. Art deftly poured the drinks into plain heavy glass tumblers and handed one to her. 'Cheers,' he said. 'Here's to us.' He smiled, raising one eyebrow.

'Cheers,' she replied, and took a sip of the liquor she had not tasted before. She found it quite pleasant, though it tasted of nothing really, she thought.

'Now, how about some nice soothing music. Frank Sinatra do for you? All women like Frank Sinatra, don't they?'

'Yes, they seem to,' replied Abbie. She did not say that she preferred Bing Crosby, knowing that would sound very 'square'.

'And is he to your liking as well?'

'Yes, very much so,' she replied, hoping she sounded enthusiastic.

The record was a long-player of the singer's best-known hits. Art placed it on the turntable of his stereogram, which was of the same light oak as the rest of the furniture, then took the opportunity to change his seat, coming to sit next to Abbie on the three-seater settee. There was a nest of tables to hand and he pulled out the smallest one, placing it in front of them.

'Sit back and relax, make yourself at home,' he told her, leaning back against the cushions and stretching his arm, behind her, along the length of the settee. She had been perched on the edge of the seat, cradling her glass, but she put her drink down now and tried to do as he had suggested, sitting well back with her shoulders against the cushions. She was aware of the nearness of his arm although he was not actually touching her.

'You make me feel so young,' sang Frank Sinatra, and Abbie found herself gradually relaxing, chatting inconsequentially to Art, against the background of the music, about such subjects as Art's favourite film, *Casablanca*, which he alleged to have seen ten times, and about some of the folk at college. He seemed curious about Jean's friendship with Eric.

'I'm surprised at you listening to gossip,' she told him lightly. 'I thought you would have been far too lofty to concern yourself with the students' affairs. Not that Jean and Eric are having an affair,' she added hastily. 'Far be it from me to start a rumour.'

'As if you would,' he smiled, his hand briefly closing round her shoulder then moving away again. 'No, you're not one for tittle-tattle, I know that. Nor am I, believe me, but I've noticed them together, Jean and that Eric bloke, and I know she's a good friend of yours. She's a livewire, isn't she, and he seems such an old stick-in-the-mud. Still, you never can tell.'

He told her also, strictly on the QT, that his mate, Dave Saunders, was henpecked.

'I thought you didn't gossip,' Abbie teased him. She was feeling quite euphoric now, although whether it was due to the drink or the music or Art's easy chatter she was not sure; possibly a combination of them all.

'I don't,' he said. 'It's a fact. Poor old Dave has to toe the line. Marion doesn't give him much leeway.'

'Family man, is he?'

'Yes, they have three children – the youngest one's not at school yet. Dave's had his wings clipped, sure enough.'

'He doesn't look as though he minds,' observed Abbie. 'He seems a very carefree sort of man to me, always happy and smiling.'

'Maybe he is, when he gets away from the battleground.' Art grinned. 'Only joking,' he added, but she wondered if that was, in truth, his view of marriage. He had been married himself. He had told her so, briefly, that night in the pub, but had made no further reference to his ex-wife. She did not know if there were any children. She doubted that there were. No, she couldn't see Art as a family man, not even as a 'weekend father'.

'You've gone all pensive on me again,' said Art. His hand that had been lying along the settee was now stroking her hair, then he ran his fingers lightly down the length of her cheek. 'You're probably right. Dave might be quite happy with his lot. It's just me; I'm an old cynic at times. Anyway, never mind him, or Jean or Eric or any of them. Let's just think about us.'

He drew his arm away from behind her then, in a sudden movement. He clasped both her hands tightly in his own. The look in his eyes, no longer joking but fervent, disturbed her, but it was not an unpleasant feeling. She felt excited, expectant and a little . . . could it be amorous? She only knew she had not felt like this for ages and she quickly pushed away any thought of when it might have been. She was aware, as Art continued to look at her, of Frank Sinatra singing about 'Nancy, with the Laughing Face'.

'If I don't see her each day I miss her,' he sang, and Art was singing along with him, very softly, almost under his breath. He took hold of her face, gently cupping it between his hands. 'I would miss you, Abbie, if you were not there,' he said. 'I look for you each time I come into the room, and when I see you sitting there I know that all's right with my world. Didn't you realise how I feel about you, Abigail?' His tone was a little teasing, but so very tender.

'No, not really,' she murmured.

'Let me show you then.' His hand cradled the back of her head and then, still very gently, he kissed her. When he kissed her the second time she felt her lips opening beneath his and her arms instinctively went round him, just as his encircled her. They embraced for several moments and Abbie felt a strange contentment. It was lovely to be needed, to be wanted, to be special to someone again. Fleetingly she felt his hand cup her breast, but it was such a transient touch that she wondered, afterwards, if she had imagined it.

They drew apart and he offered her another drink. She opted for orange juice and he did the same. They sat companionably, saying little, as Frank Sinatra went on to sing about 'Stella By Starlight'.

'We must do this again,' said Art as the record came to an end and he stood up to remove it from the turntable. 'What do you say, Abbie?'

'Yes, that would be very nice,' she said. 'Thank you. I've really enjoyed it.'

'So have I, Abigail. So have I.' His engaging smile would have melted even the iciest heart and Abbie's was far from cold. 'You mustn't mind me calling you Abigail,' he went on. 'I know you said you don't like it, but I find it quite charming. A quaint, winsome sort of name. It suits you so well.'

'If you say so, but I still prefer Abbie.'

'Then perhaps I could use it just when we're alone together? Abbie is so ordinary, and you – well, you are quite unique.'

She smiled, not knowing what to say. It was a long time since she had been made to feel so special. Just as quickly Art's sentimental mood changed to one of practicality. 'Now, we don't want you to miss your train, do we? Let me get your coat, then we'd better be off.' He kissed her briefly as he helped her on with her coat, then again as he said goodbye to her at the station. He parked on the forecourt and did not offer to come to the platform with her.

'See you tomorrow at the lecture,' he said. 'But we'll do this again – soon, I hope?'

'Yes, I hope so, Art,' she replied. 'Goodbye, then. See you tomorrow.'

Jean was not on the train, nor anyone else she knew. Maybe her friend's last lecture had overrun. At all events Abbie was glad of the solitude. She felt completely bewildered. In fact, she was beginning to wonder if she had dreamed it all.

Sandie was anxious to be off with the old and on with the new. Once she had discovered that Mrs Blake was leaving she began to look forward to her lessons with Mr Hendy. She had been with her mother to his house near Stanley Park and they had arranged that her lessons were to be each Saturday morning, from eleven till twelve o'clock. Her mother, and Sandie, too, had been impressed by his framed diplomas, for the organ as well as the piano, that hung on the walls of his music room, and by the piano itself. It was a baby grand, a Steinway, which took up most of the space in the small room. Duncan Hendy had invited Sandie to try it and she sat down and played a few bars of a Debussy arabesque. The tone was magnificent, though rather resonant in such an enclosed space.

'You'll do well there, Sandie, I'm sure,' her mother had said as they drove back home. 'And I don't think Mr Hendy will be thinking of leaving. He told me he had lived in

Blackpool all his life, so he's hardly likely to break the habits of a lifetime.'

Sandie had noticed the courteous regard with which Duncan Hendy had treated her mother. She had fancied there was a touch of admiration in his glance, as there had been that time when they had met at the Winter Gardens. She was tempted to say, 'Watch it, Mum! He's trying to get off with you.' But her mother would only have said, 'Don't be so silly, Sandra!' or something of the sort. Best not to upset her when things were going well; her mum did not always appreciate Sandie's quirky sense of humour. Still, the idea really was quite amusing. They were both *far* too old for that sort of thing, especially him, Duncan Hendy. Sandie guessed he must be getting on for fifty. Half a century!

'Yes, I'm looking forward to it, Mum,' was all she said, so docilely that her mother gave her an odd look.

She decided to go on her bike, which was the way she, and most teenagers, travelled around. The journey was not much further than the distance she rode to school each day and was in the same direction. Her music case just fitted into the large saddle bag and she wore jeans so there was no danger of her clothes getting entangled with the spokes of the wheels. It was a nuisance sometimes with her school skirt and coat, but they were not allowed, of course, to wear trousers at school, not even for travelling to and fro. Mr Hendy had told her she could leave her bike at the back of the house – it would be safer there – and then she was to enter by the back door which he always left unlocked.

There was another bike, a boy's or a man's model, with dropped handlebars like the ones on her own, already propped against the wall by the door. Sandie gave a gasp of expectation. Could it be . . .? No, probably not, she told herself; there must be lots of other lads as well as Greg Matthews who had lessons with Mr Hendy. It was most likely some spotty thirteen year old. She entered through the kitchen, a very tidy one and small, like their own, and

Duncan Hendy, having heard the door open and close, met her in the hallway.

'Hello there, Sandie.' She liked the way he had remembered to call her Sandie and not Sandra. 'You're nice and early, that's good. I do like my pupils to be punctual. Greg and I haven't quite finished yet – just another five minutes or so – so if you could just wait in here . . .'

So it was him after all. There couldn't be more than one Greg, surely, having music lessons there. Sandie felt a surge of excitement, especially when the sound of a well-known Chopin waltz reached her ears. Whoever was playing the piano in the next room was certainly no novice. It must be him. Supposing he went out the back way though, without seeing her? After all, there was no reason why Mr Hendy should let his pupils meet one another. Mrs Blake's policy had seemed to be to keep her pupils apart. Sandie glanced round the room. It was at the back of the house and was obviously Mr Hendy's dining-cum-living room. It was functional, rather than comfortable, she thought at a first glance, with none of the little homely touches to be found in her own home, like flowering plants, books, photos and personal ornaments. There wasn't even a television set, at least not in this room. She perched on the edge of the armchair, which seemed comfortable enough, but she was too keyed-up to relax.

After a few minutes the Chopin waltz, so expertly played, reached its climax. There was the sound of muffled voices, then, a few seconds later, Duncan Hendy put his head round the door. 'Sandie, come and say hello to Greg. You two have met before, haven't you, so I can't let him dash away without seeing you. I'm afraid it's a case of hello and goodbye, though. He'll always be leaving just as you're arriving.'

'Unless we make some other arrangements,' said Greg, smiling at Sandie in that nice friendly way she remembered and which made her stomach turn somersaults. 'Hi there, Sandie. Good to see you again. I'll see you around, perhaps?'

233

'Hello, Greg. Yes, see you, perhaps,' she repeated, although she didn't really know what he meant. It seemed that it might be, as Mr Hendy had said, a question of hello and goodbye, one going out and the other coming in, like the old man and woman in the weather-house her gran had.

'Cheerio, then. Good luck with the lessons,' he said breezily. 'Not that you need luck, do you, but you know what I mean. Bye for now. See you, Sandie.'

'Yes, see you, Greg.'

She felt a bit deflated, but she had the good sense to know she must not let it show. And Mr Hendy turned out to be such an excellent teacher, as she had guessed he would be, so full of zest and love for his subject that she felt herself being swept along with him on a tide of enthusiasm. Mrs Blake had been good, but Mr Hendy was better, ten times so, it seemed to Sandie. She knew he would be able to bring out the very best in her, and by the end of the lesson she had even begun to change her mind about the Bach prelude and fugue she was studying. She had to admit that previously, she had found them tedious, but Mr Hendy made them come alive and be meaningful, and she began to appreciate for the first time the genius behind Bach's contrapuntal melodies and what a pleasure they would be to play, once you understood them.

She had almost forgotten Greg Matthews, so involved had she become in the new things she was learning. It was even more of a surprise, therefore, after saying goodbye to Mr Hendy and wheeling her bike to the front of the house, to find Greg waiting for her. He was seated on his own bike, propped up against the kerb, leaning forward on the handlebars.

'Hello again, Sandie,' he grinned. 'I thought I'd come and meet you.' He lifted his leg high over the crossbar and wheeled the machine on to the pavement.

'Hello, Greg. What a surprise.' Sandie was surprised, in fact, that she could find the breath to answer him. 'I didn't ·

expect to see you again, not so soon. Do you live near here, then?'

'No, not really. I live at the other end of Whitegate Drive, near to the Oxford cinema. Do you know it?' She nodded, although the area, Marton, was not all that familiar to her. 'It's not far on a bike. No, I've come because I wanted to ask you something. Are you doing anything tonight?'

Her heart missed a beat. Could he possibly be asking her for a date? So soon? She could hardly believe it. She knew she should play it cool – that was what it said in all the magazines – and pretend that she already had an engagement, or that she would have to put off something quite important. But the truth was she was doing nothing this evening. Her friend, Lindsay, had to go to a family party, or else they might have been going to the pictures.

'Why?' she asked, and then, terrified lest he should think better of it, 'No, I'm not doing anything special.'

'Come on, let's walk up here a bit and I'll tell you all about it.' Greg started to push his bicycle along the avenue and she pushed hers alongside him. 'I'm in a group, you see,' he began, 'me and three more lads, and we're playing tonight at this church hall. It's our first booking, actually, and I wondered . . . well, would you like to come?'

'A group?' She stared at him in amazement. 'You mean like The Beatles? And you play the piano for them?'

Greg smiled and shook his head. 'No, not the piano. I play a guitar, like the others. Well, one of them plays the drums, like Ringo Starr. And we sing a bit. Yes, I suppose we are something like The Beatles. You like them, do you?'

''Course I do! They were on the telly the other night, on *Ready, Steady, Go.*' Sandie was mystified, though. She had thought Greg would have been dedicated to his piano lessons and classical music to the exclusion of everything else, and now he was telling her he was part of the pop scene, that he actually played a guitar! She could scarcely believe it. 'Does Mr Hendy know?' she asked.

'No.' Greg laughed. 'I've not seen any reason to tell him, not yet, so you mustn't let the cat out of the bag. Not that it matters, really. It's only a bit of fun – a bit of light relief, you might say. My parents don't mind, so I don't see why Duncan should object. What about your parents? Do you think they'll let you come tonight? That is, if you want to?'

'Yes, I'd like to come,' she replied, though trying to sound dead casual. 'And Mum won't mind. There's only my mother. My father died,' she added, 'quite a while ago.'

'Oh, I'm sorry. I didn't know.'

'Yes, well . . .' She smiled rather nervously at him. 'Mum's OK really. A bit of a fusspot, you know how they can be, but she'll let me go.' Sandie was already wondering how best to get round her mother. Honesty might be the best policy. (*You know I always like you to tell the truth, Sandra . . .*)

'I wondered, with you being younger than me,' Greg said.

'Not all that much,' she retorted. 'I'm nearly sixteen, and you can't have been seventeen for very long, can you, 'cause of those piano classes?'

'I was seventeen last week, actually,' he said. 'So I only just squeezed into the sixteen and under class. I'll be in the adult class next year.'

'You'll still do brilliantly, I know you will,' said Sandie, then, fearing the remark might sound too much like hero worship, she added, 'Mr Hendy makes you work hard, doesn't he? I can tell that already.'

'Yes, he's a slave-driver, all right,' laughed Greg, not sounding as though he minded very much. 'But he inspires you, makes you want to succeed, that's what's so good about him. There's no other teacher can hold a candle to Duncan, as far as I'm concerned.'

'I've noticed you call him Duncan,' said Sandie. 'You've known him a long time, have you?'

'It seems like for ever. I've been having lessons with him since I was seven years old, but even before that, he was a sort of honorary uncle. He and his wife were friends of my parents – well, Duncan still is, of course. I used to call him Uncle Duncan, but then he asked me to drop the uncle bit, it was too much of a mouthful. It is, when you think about it.'

'Uncle Duncan. Yes, it's rather a tongue-twister, isn't it?' Sandie laughed. She felt too much in awe of her new teacher at the moment to imagine herself ever calling him anything but Mr Hendy. She was not usually so awe-inspired by adults – schoolteachers and the like – but Duncan Hendy was something different. 'His wife died, did she?' she asked.

'Yes, about five years ago. She died following an operation. Duncan was dreadfully upset at the time, and for ages afterwards.'

'Did they have any family?'

'No, there are no children. But he has quite a lot of friends and he gradually pulled himself together.' Sandie noticed that Greg had quite a mature way of speaking. If she had not known his age she would have guessed him to be at least a couple of years older; he looked older and he acted older, too. She wondered if he were an only child who had spent a lot of his time with his parents, maybe, but it was too soon to ask. 'He plays the piano, and the organ as well, you know, for hotel dances and parties,' he went on, still speaking of Duncan Hendy. 'He's not such a purist that he can't let his hair down now and again. You should hear him playing jazz – it's quite something.'

'So he shouldn't really object if you do the same, should he?' observed Sandie. 'I don't mean jazz – rock and roll, or whatever it is you play.'

'It used to be called skiffle, in the beginning,' said Greg, 'and it did have its roots in Negro jazz. No, maybe Duncan wouldn't object, but I prefer to keep it under wraps just for the moment. Anyway, never mind about him. You'll come tonight then, will you?'

'Yes, but you haven't told me where it is yet,' replied Sandie. 'Not right down Marton way, is it?'

'You make it sound as though Marton's the back of beyond,' Greg teased her.

'Well, I suppose it is to me. It would mean two buses from Layton, but I could manage it,' she decided, not wanting him to think she was backing out.

'Actually, it's right here,' said Greg. 'That's why I've brought you this way, to show you.' They had been walking down a road that led away from the Stanley Park gates and there was a church hall on the right. 'There, see? That building. It's a dance the Youth Club are holding and they've asked us to do a couple of spots. You should be able to get here easily enough, shouldn't you? It's quite near your school.'

'I go to school on my bike,' said Sandie, 'but my mother's not so keen on me going out on it in the dark.' She stopped; that sounded too childish.

'I don't blame her,' said Greg, as though he were her uncle or something. 'Listen, if you get yourself here, we'll see you get back home all right. We could take you back in the van.'

'Do you drive?' asked Sandie, impressed.

'No, I don't, not yet, but I'm thinking of learning. That's why I said "we". The van belongs to Mike's dad – Mike's one of the group – and he lets us borrow it to transport our gear. Don't worry, Sandie, tell your mum I'll see you safely home. Right, I'd better say cheerio now. See you later then, OK?' He mounted his bike and, with a cheery wave, rode away.

'Yes, OK, Greg. See you.'

Sandie cycled home in a daze. What should she say to her mother? She could say she was going to the pictures with a friend from school. She did not always reveal her exact whereabouts to her mother, and Mum, to give her her due, did not fuss too much, provided she knew who she was with and she got home at a reasonable hour. But this time it was different. She had the promise of a lift home in Greg's friend's van – pity it wasn't just with Greg, but it was a start,

238

she supposed – and she could hardly refuse. She didn't want to refuse. But Mum was sure to find out how she had come home. Besides, if she were to see Greg again, and again, her mother would have to know about it. Yes, honesty would most probably be the best policy.

Chapter 15

It was all happening much sooner than Abbie had expected. Art had warned her that it might, that Sandie probably already had boyfriends that she, Abbie, knew nothing about. And now, sure enough, here she was, asking if she could go to some dance or other with a boy they didn't know, a boy who played in some sort of a group, like those strange Beatle lads. Abbie did not want to refuse to let her go, not outright. There might be all sorts of ructions if she were too heavy-handed with Sandie, but she did think that she had every right, as a mother, to lay down certain conditions.

'But he isn't just a boy that we don't know.' Sandie stood in the middle of the dining room, arguing her point, whilst her mother was trying to set the table. She had had to walk round her twice already. 'It's Greg Matthews. You do know him. You remember him, Mum? The boy who won at the Festival. You said how brilliant he was. You said—'

'Don't keep telling me what I said, Sandra. Yes, he may well be a brilliant pianist, but we don't know him, do we? We don't know what he's like as a person. Not like we know . . . well, lots of other people.' To her annoyance Abbie could not think of a good example, and she did want to be fair. She had to admit that this Greg Matthews seemed, on first acquaintance, to be a very nice sort of lad, just the sort that any mother might choose for her daughter. But Sandie was still so young.

'Yes, he seems all right,' she said, a trifle grudgingly, 'from the little I've seen of him. Although I am rather surprised he's wasting his time playing in a group instead of concentrating on his proper studies.' Abbie was aware of Sandie's indrawn breath and she decided not to pursue that line. 'However, that's none of my business; it's up to his parents. There will be some other girls there that you know, won't there, Sandie? It won't be just you and this Gregory?'

''Course there will, Mum,' replied Sandie quickly. 'There'll be lots of girls there that I know. Quite a few girls in our year go to that church. They're sure to be there. And I won't be spending all that much time with Greg, will I? He'll be playing with his group. So can I go then?' Her blue eyes were shining with anticipation. 'You'll let me go, Mum?'

'Yes, on one condition,' said Abbie carefully. 'And that is, that I take you in the car and bring you back.'

'Oh, Mum. No!' The light in Sandie's eyes changed in an instant and now they were blazing with annoyance. 'You can't do that. You'll make me look such an idiot, like a little kid being collected from a tea party. No, I won't let you do that. I'd rather not go at all if you're going to treat me like a child.'

'Sandie, you are only fifteen. I can't let you go wandering off in the dark to a strange part of Blackpool.'

'It isn't a strange part,' said Sandie petulantly. 'It's quite near where Grandad and Auntie Faith live, actually, so why do you say it's strange? There's nothing wrong with it, and I know the way there. I can get a bus.'

'Yes, I know, love. I know it's a perfectly respectable area. I didn't mean there was anything wrong with it, but there's no bus that goes all the way there. You'd have to walk part of the way, and I can't let you do that. You're only fifteen and—'

'You're only fifteen, you're only fifteen,' Sandie mimicked. 'That's all I ever hear.'

'Yes, and just let me remind you that I had to do as I was told when I was nineteen, never mind fifteen,' retorted

Abbie. 'Even when I'd joined up and left home I had to—'

'Oh, please, not that again! Tell me the old, old story.' Sandie put her hands to her ears and Abbie felt, for a moment, an urge to strike out at her daughter. But she did not do so. She just stared back at her across the dining table, almost disliking her in that instant. Sandie sometimes had that effect on her. Abbie knew, deep down, that she loved Sandra very much and always would. But liking, that was a different thing altogether. She was learning, at least as far as Sandie was concerned, that you did not always like your offspring. The moment passed, and Abbie started to see her daughter again as she really was – a child who was not getting all her own way. But although she was only fifteen she did look quite a lot older. Abbie knew she must try to reason with her, remembering how she had suffered as a girl – a much older girl – at the hands of her own mother, and how she had resolved, ages ago, that no daughter of hers would ever be subjected to such severity.

'Don't be cheeky, Sandra,' she said, quite mildly. She could not let her off without some sort of reprimand, although there was nothing to be gained by reading the riot act. 'You won't get anywhere with me if you're going to be insolent. I know you've heard it all before. My mother wouldn't admit I was grown-up even after I'd joined the Land Army. And that's why I do try to be reasonable with you, love, even though you may not think so. Any mother worth her salt would agree with me about this. You've never been to this place before. We don't really know who's going to be there, or what will be going on.'

'It's a church youth club, Mum. They're hardly likely to be rolling around drunk or having wild orgies.'

'That will do, Sandra. As I've said, I'm willing to let you go, provided you go there and back in my car.' Sandie was still regarding her sullenly, but with not quite the same degree of insolence. She narrowed her eyes as though she was weighing something up in her mind.

'I suppose you could go and see Grandad,' she said, 'and drop me off on the way there. But Greg'll bring me back, he and his friend. He's promised – he said I was to tell you he'd see me safely home.'

'Well, that certainly sounds as though he's a thoughtful sort of boy,' agreed Abbie, 'and very polite, too. But I'm going to insist, Sandie, that I bring you home as well as taking you.' She raised an admonitory hand as Sandie, again, opened her mouth to protest. 'That's my last word on it. If you keep arguing you won't go at all; it's as simple as that. I'm not going to let you ride around in a van with a crowd of lads we don't know, no matter how nice and polite they might be.' She took a deep breath. So far, so good. Sandie did seem to be coming round, the resentment gradually leaving her face. 'You can explain to Gregory that I have gone to see your grandad and that it only makes sense for me to pick you up on the way home. That was a good idea of yours, to go and see my father and Faith. I'll take Simon with me as well.'

'You won't know what time to come for me, though, will you?'

'Oh, don't you worry about that.' Abbie smiled. 'I'll be there at half-past ten. I'll wait at the other side of the road, but if you're a few minutes later it doesn't matter. I'm not going to insist on a ten o'clock deadline like my mother used to do. And say thank you to Greg for offering, won't you? Tell him your mum says thank you.'

'Yeah – but no thanks,' said Sandie sarcastically.

Abbie decided to ignore it. She looked steadily at her daughter.

'I've told you what I think. He seems a nice boy, but we'll just have to wait and see, won't we? Now, you can come and help me to carry the dishes in. I've just heard Simon come in and he'll be ravenous as usual. It's steak and mushroom pie today, homemade. That's one of your favourites, isn't it?' Abbie was gratified now to see Sandie's face relax into a sort of smile.

And with that, Sandie knew she must be content. Trust Mum to make a fuss, but she hadn't really expected her to react any other way and it wasn't as bad as it might have been. She could have said, 'No, you're not going. You're far too young to be thinking about boys.' Sandie knew that although there were quite a few girls in her form at school, like Cheryl, Vicky and that crowd, who boasted about their boyfriends – even bragged about how far they had gone with them – there were others whose mothers were far stricter than her own. There was Rebecca, whose parents made her go to church with them twice every Sunday and was never even allowed to go to the pictures or to dances. And Constance, whose mother was a Jehovah's Witness and made her go round with her from door to door. So, by comparison, her own mother did not seem so bad.

Sandie and her special friend, Lindsay, and a few more in their little group often talked about boys, but none of them really knew any all that well. In fact, up till now they had enjoyed one another's company without bothering themselves too much about lads. It was their view that Cheryl and Vicky and co. were rather fast, and they didn't believe half they said, anyway. Only when she had encountered Greg Matthews had Sandie really become aware of 'the opposite sex', which was what they called it in magazines. She couldn't imagine herself ever doing with him what Cheryl boasted she had done with that Jeff she went on about, nor did she particularly want to think of Greg like that. The thought of that made her feel a bit, well, frightened, almost. But she did want to get to know him better.

In a way she was glad her mother was taking her, although she would not have admitted it, not in a million years. It would have been a bit scary walking through streets she didn't know all that well in the dark. As it was, she had to go into the church hall on her own, but she was hoping Greg would be there to meet her, although he hadn't actually said he would, or that she would see someone else she knew.

It was a pity about the coming home part, but it wasn't as though she would have been on her own with Greg. She might have been shoved in the back of the van with a load of guitars and drums and microphones for all she knew. The important thing was that Greg had asked her to go. She would be seeing him tonight. Now she had to decide what to wear.

She settled on her red felt circular skirt with a black polo-necked jumper and black low-heeled patent leather shoes. And her one pair of tights which she had bought last weekend from Marks & Spencer and found to be very comfortable. She had been unsure at first as to whether she should wear them over or under her panties, but she and Lindsay, who had also bought a pair, decided after a discussion that they had better go over. You could always wear another pair of pants over the lot to keep them in place, although that would be rather a performance when you went to the toilet. All in all, though, these new tights seemed much easier to wear than stockings which were always laddering and suspenders which were always popping undone. To say nothing of the draught up your skirt in the winter. Sandie, so far, had only worn stockings occasionally at weekends, as at school she still wore socks, like all the girls did. But she decided that tights would most definitely be the garment for the future. Perhaps even her mother might be persuaded to wear them. She was sure that Jean, that 'with it' friend of hers from college, would do so.

Sandie made a hasty exit from her mother's Ford Anglia. She was relieved that Abbie had not attempted to give her a kiss or make too much fuss. 'Have a nice time, dear. See you at half-past ten, or a bit later, perhaps. Enjoy yourself.'

'Yes, see you, Mum. 'Bye, Simon.'

She looked around a little hesitantly as she entered the foyer of the church hall. There was a middle-aged woman sitting at a small table with a glass dish of money and a pile of tickets in front of her, and a group of girls crowded around, but there was no one that Sandie knew.

'Now dear,' said the woman, smiling at her in a friendly manner. 'Have you got a ticket?'

'Er, no, I haven't,' said Sandie. 'I didn't realise you needed one.'

'Not to worry. Most of 'em have just paid at the door. That'll be two shillings, please.'

Sandie opened her shoulder bag and took a florin from her purse. Greg didn't offer to buy me a ticket, she thought wryly, but it didn't worry her overmuch. She knew that lads often said, 'See you inside,' in a cavalier fashion – indicating that they didn't intend to pay – especially to girls they rather fancied, but did not want to get too serious about. This much she had picked up from the gossip at school, though not from any personal experience. Greg hadn't actually said, 'See you inside,' and whether he fancied her or not she didn't really know, but he was sure to be there, somewhere, because of playing with his group.

'You can leave your coat in the cloakroom,' said the woman in charge of the money. She indicated a small room to the right. 'You haven't been here before, have you?' Sandie shook her head. 'Don't look so worried, love. They're a nice friendly lot, and perhaps you'll meet somebody you know.'

Sandie hadn't been aware that she looked as worried as she felt. Not exactly worried, but a little unsure of herself and that was an unusual state of affairs for Sandra Horsfall. She could normally cope with new situations and new people and had made friends at school without any problems.

'Sandie – fancy seeing you here! I didn't know you were coming.' Sandie turned round from hanging her coat on a peg to see Paula Walters smiling at her. Paula was the sixth-form girl with whom she had had lunch on the day of the Festival. Since that day, however, she had seen her only in passing, in the school corridor or grounds, just to smile at and say hello. Sixth formers, who considered themselves very much the 'elite', did not associate too much with girls lower down the school, although Sandie knew that Paula could be friendly enough when she tried. At all events she was very pleased to see her now.

'Hi there, Paula,' she said. 'Gosh, am I glad to see you. I don't know anybody here. I've never been before, you see.'

'No, I thought I hadn't seen you around at church or anything.'

'Do you go to this church, then?'

'Yes, I do,' replied Paula. 'I'm in the youth choir, so I go most Sunday mornings, when we're asked to sing, and I'm in the Youth Club, too, How did you know about this dance then?'

'Somebody asked me to come,' said Sandie. 'It was Greg Matthews, actually. You know, the boy who plays the piano. His group's performing here tonight, so he asked me if I'd like to come and hear them.'

'You as well?' Paula laughed. 'Greg's been asking everybody. He asked me, but I told him I already knew about it, with going to this church and everything.'

'Oh, I see.' Sandie felt as though the bright bubble of expectation in which she had been existing had suddenly burst. 'You know Greg then?'

'Yes, he lives in the next avenue. I've known him since we were kids. I thought I'd mentioned it when we met at the Festival?'

'Yes, you might have done.' Sandie did remember something of the sort, although they hadn't talked about him very much. She had not wanted to share her blossoming attraction towards Greg with anyone, nor did she now want it to look as though she cared. 'He and I share the same music teacher now,' she said. 'That'll be why he asked me. I've only just got to know him, as a matter of fact.' She gave a slight shrug. 'Are they any good, this group of his?'

Paula lifted her shoulders in a more pronounced shrug. 'Search me. It's their debut, isn't it? That's why he's so excited about it. Tony – he's the one that plays the drums – he goes to this church, well, to the Youth Club anyway, and he wangled it for them to play here tonight. So your guess is as good as mine. I should think they'll be pretty good. Greg's a whizz-kid on the piano, so if he's as good on the guitar . . . Let's go and see if we can find anybody else we know. There are usually some girls from your form here.'

The church hall was similar to the ones Sandie had known before. Large and featureless, just a rectangular room with a bare wooden floor and a curtainless stage at one end and with stacking chairs to one side, which the young people were now separating and placing in little groups around the perimeter of what would be the dance floor. A few clusters of balloons had been pinned to the walls between the windows which were curtained in an uninteresting shade of green rayon.

There were four young men on the stage, busying themselves with microphones and drums and amplifiers. Sandie's heart missed a beat as she recognised Greg, although he was barely distinguishable from the other lads at a distance, dressed as they all were entirely in black; black closely fitting jeans and black polo-necked jumpers, almost identical to the one Sandie was wearing. Two of the others had dark hair, though not quite so dark as Greg's, and the third lad, a rather shorter young man, had hair which could only be termed red. *The Blue Notes*, it said on a placard to the side of the stage.

'That's what they call themselves,' said Paula, following the direction of Sandie's eyes. 'Tony told me. That's Tony, the little one with the ginger hair. Don't look so worried.' She laughed and gave Sandie's arm a nudge. 'Greg'll come and speak to you in a little while, when they've got themselves organised.'

'I'm not bothered, honestly I'm not,' Sandie protested.

'Oh, come on, I can tell you like him,' said Paula. 'Can't say I blame you. I like him, too – well, you know what I mean. I just *like* him, that's all – but then I've known him for ever. You're in with a chance, aren't you, if you've got the same music teacher?'

Sandie laughed – carelessly, she hoped. 'I've told you, I've only just got to know him. Who do you go to, anyway, for your piano lessons?' she asked, in an attempt to change the subject.

'Oh, a woman called Mrs Carson. She's not as good as Mr Hendy, but I've been going there ages and it wouldn't seem right to leave her. Besides, I'm not nearly as good as you and Greg. I expect you'll be going on to a music college when you leave school, won't you? I know Greg is hoping to.'

Sandie hadn't known that, but then she knew very little about him as yet. 'I don't know,' she said. 'I haven't decided what I'm going to do. But you're pretty good yourself. You came fourth at the Festival, didn't you?'

'Yes, by some fluke,' Paula grinned. 'I'm good enough for what I want to do, and that is to be an Infant teacher. You need to be able to play the piano for that.'

'Yes, that's what my mum says. Did I tell you she's training to be a teacher? She's at Chelford Training College.'

Sandie found Paula Walters very friendly and easy to talk to, as were her two friends, also from the sixth form, who joined their little group. Two girls from Sandie's form were there as well. They expressed surprise and pleasure, too, at seeing her there, and the six of them, fifth and sixth formers alike, got on well together for the rest of the evening, with none of the restraint and the sense of hierarchy that existed at school.

'Hello there, Sandie. Glad you could make it.' Greg came over to their group just as the young man in charge of the entertainment was about to put on the first record. 'Hi, Paula – didn't know you two knew each other. Of course, you're at the same school, aren't you? Hello, Brenda . . . Sheila . . .' He seemed to know most of them. His greeting was warm and friendly, but not directed at any one of them in particular.

'Hi, Greg.' Paula spoke to him with the ease of long familiarity. 'How are you feeling? Nervous?'

'What, me? Never!' he joked.

'You must be. Anyway, good luck. No – break a leg, that's what they say, isn't it? Come and have a dance with us later, eh?'

'Yeah, will do. I'd better get our first spot over and done with before I start leaping around and break a leg too literally. See you later, girls.'

'Nice, i'n't he?' said Marcia to Brenda. They were the other two who were in Sandie's form. 'Didn't know you knew him, Bren. And you an' all, Sandie. You're a dark horse. I'd better stick around with you two. On the other hand, I don't want any competition, do I?' She giggled. It was all very light-hearted and Sandie began to enjoy herself, far more than she had thought she was going to at first, when she had found out she was not the only pebble on Greg Matthews's beach.

They danced to records which were a mixture of new and old. The dancing, too, was something of a hotch-potch; it was very much a do-as-you-please sort of evening. You could make an attempt at a waltz or quickstep or something called a slow foxtrot – that was what Paula said it was called – or you could do your own version of the Twist or rock and roll, dancing in a group or facing one other person, trying to make your movements complement theirs. Some of the records had been in the recent Top Twenty; Elvis singing 'Return to Sender', Rolf Harris's 'Sun Arise', and, of course, The Beatles' first hit single, 'Love Me Do'. 'The Tennessee Wig Walk', a hit from the 1950s, with everyone joining in with the actions and words, proved to be very popular, as did some of the older numbers of Guy Mitchell.

'She wears red feathers and a hula hula skirt . . .' Sandie sang along to the record as she jiggled around the floor with

Paula in their own version of a quickstep. There were a lot of girls dancing together as the girls by far outnumbered the boys who were present. She was enjoying herself immensely, although the best part of the evening, the first public appearance of The Blue Notes, was yet to come. Very soon, in fact, as the four lads were now making their way on to the stage.

'And now, ladies and gentlemen, boys and girls, the moment we've all been waiting for,' said the young man who was acting as the compère. 'We are delighted to welcome The Blue Notes in their first public performance. Here they are – Dave, Mike, Greg and Tony. Please give a big hand to . . . *The Blue Notes*.'

'Good evening, everyone,' said the spokesman for the group when the applause had died down. It was not Greg, but a shorter, more heavily built lad – the one called Dave, according to Paula, who seemed to know quite a lot about them all. 'This first number might be called our signature tune, "Singing the Blues". OK, lads – take it away!'

The number was not a new one, but it had been given a modern treatment by the group; extremely soulful and with a slow beat. They were really good, thought Sandie, leaning forward eagerly in her seat, her eyes not just on Greg, but on the other members of the quartet who she could tell were just as talented – well, almost – as Greg. Dave, Mike and Greg played electric guitars, their instruments and their voices, too, harmonising well together, whilst the ginger-haired Tony provided a very expert rhythmic accompaniment on the drums.

Here was a group, Sandie thought, who had their own style and did not seek to imitate any of the others. Their rendition of 'I can't give you anything but love, baby' led to whistles of appreciation from the lads in the audience and a few screams from the girls, and by the end of the song most of the audience were on their feet swaying to the music. There followed two numbers the lads had written themselves. For the first of the two, 'Blue Note Jazz', Greg changed his guitar for the somewhat tinny upright piano at the side of the stage. Its less than perfect tone, however, only added to rather than detracted from the style of the music. It was an instrumental piece with no lyrics and Sandie guessed, although she did not know for sure, that it might have been composed by Greg. He appeared lost in the music as he played, without any copy in front of him, his head uplifted and an almost rapturous expression on his face.

The end of the piece was greeted with tumultuous applause which the other three members of the group seemed happy for Greg to receive. They gestured towards him whilst the audience clapped and clapped and Greg took a bow on his own.

'He must have written that one himself,' said Sandie to Paula, at her side. She was unable to keep the elation from her voice, although she had been trying, all evening, to play down the attraction she felt towards Greg.

'Yeah, quite some guy, isn't he?' Paula nudged her teasingly, and Sandie suddenly didn't care who knew how she felt. She thought she was falling in love with him; in fact, she had already done so.

The second of the two numbers The Blue Notes had written was quite different in style, a catchy little song called, 'She's Waiting Round the Corner'. This ended the first spot, and an interval followed in which tea or soft drinks and biscuits were served.

'You've got a nice voice,' said Paula to Sandie as they stood at the side of the room drinking their orange juice. 'I heard you singing along to those Guy Mitchell songs.'

'Yes, they're years old, but I like them,' said Sandie. 'That's one thing my mum and I seem to agree about. She's quite a Guy Mitchell fan. My voice isn't all that great, though. I've never had singing lessons.'

'It's better than mine, and I'm in the youth choir,' Paula

told her. 'I say, would you like to come and join us? We're looking for new members and I know they'd be pleased to have you. It's a nice lively church, too. The Youth Club quite often have dances, like this one, and concerts and things. Unless maybe you already belong to a church?'

'No, I don't, actually,' replied Sandie. 'When I lived in Norfolk we all used to go, but since we moved to Blackpool we haven't been anywhere. Well, we went to the local church a couple of times, but we didn't care for it much. The people weren't very welcoming, not like they seem to be here. This is a Methodist church, though, isn't it? I was Church of England, you see – confirmed and all that.'

'Not to worry,' said Paula. 'It doesn't matter. Would you like to join then, our Youth Club and choir? We meet on a Wednesday night and we have our choir practice first. There's usually something on a Saturday night, as well.'

'Yes, I might,' replied Sandie. She was, in truth, quite taken with the idea. She had missed the Youth Club she had used to belong to in Wymondham. She and Lindsay and the rest of their little group did not belong to anything in particular and spent much of their time drifting into coffee bars or wandering aimlessly through the streets. In the summertime, that was; now that winter was coming there was really very little for them to do. Perhaps Lindsay could be persuaded to join as well, the Youth Club, at any rate; she wouldn't be interested in the singing. 'It's quite a way from where I live, though,' she said. 'I'm not quite sure how I would get here.'

'How did you get here tonight?'

'My mum brought me in the car. And she's taking me home as well.' Sandie pulled a face. 'She insisted – you know what they're like. She's gone to see my grandad, actually. He lives fairly near here, so I'd no choice. That reminds me – I'll have to tell Greg. He promised to take me home in the van – Mike's dad's van, I mean – but Mum wouldn't hear of it.'

'Oh, I say, poor you! What a shame. Never mind, there'll

be plenty more chances for you. I wonder . . . D'you think there'd be room in the van for me? They've got to go my way to drop Greg off. I think I'll ask them.'

Sandie didn't like the sound of that at all, but she knew she must not let it show. 'How did you get here?' she asked.

'Tram along Whitegate Drive,' said Paula. 'They're taking them off soon, the trams, but there'll be buses running instead. It's quite easy to get here, but I never say no to a lift, especially with four gorgeous males like these. Oh look, here's Greg. Tell him you can't go with them, and ask will I do instead? No, don't say that. I'll ask him when you've finished talking to him.'

Paula, in all fairness, did move away with a sly wink at her new friend, and so Sandie was able to offer her congratulations to Greg on her own.

'You were great,' she said. 'I'd no idea you'd be so good. All of you,' she added. 'I can't wait to hear you again. You've another spot, haven't you?'

'Yes, in about half an hour. It won't be so nerve-racking next time,' he laughed. 'The first time's always the worst. But before that we'll have a dance, shall we? After all, I did ask you to come.' She noticed again what a bright blue his eyes were as he smiled at her. At that moment it seemed as though he had eyes only for her.

'I'm ever so glad I came,' she said. 'Thank you for asking me. And my mother says thank you for offering to take me home, that it was very kind of you, but she's coming to pick me up. She's gone to visit my grandad, you see,' she explained hurriedly, 'and it's on her way home. So I won't be able to come with you.'

'Oh, what a pity.' Greg's blue eyes twinkled at Sandie in a way she found utterly heart-rending, especially as she could not accept his offer. 'But there's always another time, isn't there, Sandie?'

Paula was hovering and as Sandie could think of nothing else to say to him she felt obliged to move away. She went to

254

talk to Brenda and Marcia. 'Yes, OK, I'll ask them, but I know it'll be all right,' she heard Greg say to Paula as she walked away. Not with any degree of enthusiasm, she thought, but the fact remained – and it rankled – that it was Paula who was getting the ride home and not her.

Greg danced with Sandie twice; once to a rock and roll record and once to a quickstep rhythm in which she tried bravely to follow his lead. She felt they were well-matched; she was a tall girl for her age and their eyes were almost on a level. His closeness overwhelmed her. It was the nearest she had ever been to a boy; she couldn't count the dances with the lads back in Norfolk, callow fifteen year olds who hadn't meant a thing to her.

He danced with some of the other girls as well. With Paula, who was small and dark and scarcely came up to his shoulder, and with Marcia, who had had her eye on him all evening and could hardly contain her delight at having him to herself, if only for a few minutes.

The Blue Notes performed again, just as masterfully as before, and this brought the evening to a close, except for the singing of 'Auld Lang Syne', followed by 'God Save the Queen'. Sandie glanced at the clock on the wall. It was twenty minutes to eleven and her mother would have been waiting for ten minutes. She had said it didn't matter if she was a little late, but Sandie didn't want to risk making her too cross. Mum might come in useful for running her here again, especially if she joined the choir and Youth Club that Paula had talked about. Sandie had realised that it was not a bad thing to have a grandparent living in this area. She was sure her grandad and Auntie Faith would let her stay there overnight occasionally. Her mother wouldn't fuss too much if she thought she was in safe hands.

Greg was busy with the other lads, getting all their equipment together. 'Bye, Greg,' she said. 'I'm going now. Thanks for inviting me – you were great. See you soon, perhaps.'

'Yes, sure. See you soon, Sandie. Thanks for coming.' His smile was as bright as ever. She did get the impression that she might mean something to him. But there was Paula, quietly waiting for her lift.

''Bye, Paula,' she said. 'I'm ever so glad you were here.' Because she *was* glad. 'And thanks for telling me about the choir and everything. I'll probably join. See you.'

She waved more cheerfully than she was feeling as she made her exit. It was such an anti-climax to be driven home by her mother. She hoped nobody saw her getting into Mum's car. To her surprise, however, there were other mothers, and fathers, too, parked alongside the church buildings, waiting for their daughters. It seemed as though she was not the only one to be treated like a little kid.

Chapter 16

It was a long time since Sandie had seen Veronica Jarvis, Doreen's daughter. Mum had said she hoped the two of them might become friends when they moved to Blackpool, but it hadn't worked out that way at all. Something seemed to have gone wrong between her mother and Auntie Doreen – that was what she had always called her – although Sandie had never found out what it was. Now, however, they seemed to be friends again and Mum was organising this Tupper party for her. What's more, she wanted to drag Sandie along.

'Aw, Mum, do I have to?' the girl protested. 'Honestly! A flipping Tupper party with a load of old women! Well, middle-aged, anyway,' she amended, seeing the look on her mother's face. 'Not much in my line, is it?'

'Not even middle-aged, Sandra, thank you very much,' retorted her mother. 'I don't consider myself middle-aged, and your Auntie Doreen certainly doesn't. I'm not asking you to take part, am I? Didn't you hear what I said? Doreen thought it would be a good idea for you and Veronica to be in charge of the buffet supper.'

'Yes, I heard you, Mum.'

'We'll pay you, of course. That was Doreen's idea, too, and I'm sure a little extra pocket money wouldn't go amiss.'

'But I don't know Veronica. I've hardly seen her since we were kids. Anyway, I've got my own friends.'

'Yes, I know you have, dear, but there's no limit to the

257

number of friends we can have, is there? The two of you will get along very well, I'm sure.'

Sandie had realised there was no point in arguing any further, besides, she wanted to keep on the right side of her mother. And it had turned out, after all, to be just as Mum had said. She had found that she did get on very well with Veronica Jarvis. Veronica was very much like her mother in looks, smallish and fair-haired and with big blue eyes; very pretty, too. Doreen was still pretty, Sandie thought, although she had become rather plump. When she was younger she had been quite stunning. Sandie knew this from photos she had seen, and Veronica looked just like her mother had done at a similar age. She was a few inches shorter than Sandie, although she was more than a year older, and this extra year gave her an air of sophistication that Sandie felt she, herself, lacked. Veronica seemed to envy her height, however.

'I wish I was tall like you,' she said as they stood side by side in front of the long mirror in Veronica's bedroom. 'That's why I backcomb my hair, to give me extra height.' Although it did, in fact, look rather like a bird's nest. 'Yours is dead cool, isn't it – long and straight and a gorgeous colour, too.' Sandie was pleased. She had decided to let her hair grow and now it reached to her shoulders. 'I wish I could wear mine like that, but it's so fine, you see. I have to have it permed to give it a bit of body. You don't, do you?'

'No, I don't bother with perms,' replied Sandie. 'It's quite thick; I don't think I need one. I wear it tied back for school.'

Veronica looked at her appraisingly, her head to one side. 'I think a spot of green eye-shadow would suit you,' she said. 'You do wear make-up, don't you?'

'Yes, of course,' said Sandie, who, so far, had not progressed beyond lipstick and powder.

'Here, try this,' the other girl said. 'I'll put it on for you. Close your eyes.' Sandie did so whilst Veronica smoothed on some of the sea-green powder from a minute compact. 'There . . . have a look.'

'Yes, it looks quite nice,' said Sandie, peering at herself in the mirror. Her brown eyes looked darker and seemed to shine more.

She was surprised Veronica took so much interest in make-up and hair and all that. Sandie knew she went to a Catholic school and, from what Mum had said, she was quite religiously inclined. Sure enough, a statuette of the Virgin Mary stood on a little table in the corner of the room, with a vase of small button chrysanths in front of it. It didn't seem to add up, somehow. And Sandie was sure they would not be allowed to wear make-up at Veronica's school, any more than they were at hers.

'Come on, we'd better go and get this supper organised,' said Veronica, 'or they'll start nattering. I like your green sweater, by the way, and it's just the same colour as that eye-shadow.'

The supper was more or less ready in the kitchen. It was up to them to add the finishing touches. The sandwiches, cakes and biscuits needed arranging on plates and the sausage rolls and mince pies had to be warmed through in the oven ready to be served to the guests at nine o'clock.

'These are good,' said Veronica, sampling a second chocolate finger biscuit. 'Go on, have one.'

'Well, just one then,' said Sandie. 'We'd better not have anything else though. They'll probably have counted.'

'Mum said we could help ourselves when it's suppertime,' said Veronica. 'It's no more than we deserve. I expect they'll want us to help with the washing up as well.' She took a pile of salmon sandwiches from their greaseproof paper wrapping and arranged them in a fan shape on a large plate. Sandie did the same with the meat-paste ones, then they skewered some tiny pieces of cheese and pineapple chunks on to cocktail sticks and placed them on a small dish.

'Oh yes, *very* artistic,' giggled Veronica. She paused for a moment, then said, 'Sandie, have you got a boyfriend?'

Sandie was surprised by the suddenness of the question. 'Sort of,' she replied. 'Although I've not known him long.' She didn't want to appear lacking in front of her new, more sophisticated friend. 'Why?' she enquired. 'Have you?'

That was all that was needed to start Veronica off. Sandie guessed that was why she had asked the question in the first place, because she wanted to talk about her own love interest. She finished arranging the home-made buns and fairy cakes on a plate, then she looked across at Sandie, smiling in a confidential way. 'Well,' she began, her blue eyes opening wide, 'I have and I haven't. What I mean is, it has to be a secret at the moment, but there is . . . somebody. I know he feels the same way as I do, but we can't tell anybody yet because of who he is.'

Sandie was puzzled. 'What's the big secret?' she asked. 'He's not *married*, is he?'

'No, of course he isn't,' said Veronica huffily.

'Then what's the big deal?'

'Promise you won't tell.'

'Of course I won't tell. We don't know any of the same people, do we, so there's nobody *to* tell.'

'I don't want my mother to find out, not yet.'

'Why not? You've said he's not married, so what does it matter? You're plenty old enough to have a boyfriend, aren't you?'

'Well, it's the curate, you see. At our church.' Veronica's voice had dropped almost to a whisper, although there was nobody to listen. There were sounds of merriment coming from the lounge where the Tupper party was going on. Veronica's brothers and sisters were all in their own rooms, or out somewhere, and her dad was watching television in the living room. There was no way they could be overheard.

'What? You mean he's a priest? One of those fellows you call Father?' Sandie knew that was what they called them in the Catholic Church, although the mode of address was frowned upon, rather, in some of the Protestant churches. Sandie's gran had explained to her that she, personally, didn't think it was right to address anyone as Father, except God Himself; apart from your own earthly father, that was.

'Yes, Father O'Reilly,' said Veronica. 'His name's Dominic,' she added with a quiet smile.

'How long have you known him?'

'About a year. I knew right from the start that I liked him. And then I began to help him at the Youth Club. He asked me if I would actually. We organise discussion groups and debates, Dominic and me, and all that sort of thing, you know.' Sandie didn't know. She felt completely bewildered.

'But it's no use, is it?' she said. She knew very little about the Catholic faith, but surely priests were not allowed to marry, or to have any sort of romantic relationship with a woman. 'You wouldn't be able to . . . He hasn't done anything, has he? I mean . . . you haven't . . .?'

Veronica looked coy. 'No,' she replied, blushing a little. 'He hasn't even kissed me – yet, but he holds on to my arm when we walk home. He brings me home sometimes, you see. He's a very upright sort of young man.'

'How old is he?' Sandie asked.

'He's twenty-four.' That sounded very old to Sandie. 'He wouldn't do anything wrong, but I know he feels the same way as I do. I know he likes me a lot – I can tell. And I happen to know he thinks it's all wrong that priests have to be celibate.' Sandie frowned a little, feeling perplexed. She must look that word up in the dictionary when she got home. 'That means they can't get married,' Veronica went on to explain.

'What are you going to do about it then?'

'There's nothing I can do, is there?' said Veronica. 'All I can do is wait and hope . . . and say a little prayer,' she added, a trifle piously. 'Now it's your turn. Tell me about your boyfriend.'

'Well, he goes to the same music teacher as I do,' said

Sandie. 'That's how I met him. He's a fantastic pianist.' She was determined not to be outdone by Veronica's startling revelations. 'He met me out of my lesson last Saturday and asked me to go to this dance with him. He plays in a group, you see – something like The Beatles, and they're every bit as good. Anyway, I'll be seeing him again tomorrow. We both have our lessons on Saturday morning, so I expect we'll be going out again tomorrow night,' she added casually.

She expected nothing of the sort, not really, but you never knew. 'He's ever so good-looking,' she went on. 'Tall and dark and . . . well, he's just very nice.'

'What's he called?'

'Gregory Matthews. Greg.'

'That's nice. I say, Sandie, you'll keep it to yourself, won't you, about what I told you? I haven't told anyone else. Well, only a couple of girls at school.'

'Yes, I've said I will,' replied Sandie. 'Honest.'

Abbie was astounded, but very pleased, when Sandie confided in her. It was more than a week after the Tupper party at Doreen's when her daughter said, while they were washing up after their evening meal, 'Mum, can I tell you something? But you've got to promise me you won't tell anybody else. Especially not Auntie Doreen.'

Abbie looked at her in bewilderment. 'Doreen? What has she got to do with it? No, I won't tell. What is it, love? What do you want to tell me?'

'Well, you see, it's about Veronica. She made me promise I wouldn't tell anybody, and she doesn't want her mum to know; not yet, she said. But I don't think it matters if I tell you, Mum, because it isn't as if you were a schoolkid who can't keep a secret. Promise me, though. Promise me on your honour that you won't say anything.'

'No, I won't say anything. But I don't know what I'm promising about, do I? What is it, love? What's the matter with Veronica?' Abbie thought she could guess. A secret, something she didn't want her mother to know. It could only mean the girl was pregnant. Doreen would have to know soon, surely.

It was something of a relief to hear Sandie say, 'She's got friendly with a priest at her church. He's the curate and he's called Father O'Reilly – Dominic, she calls him. Well it seems as though they're getting keen on one another. And it's wrong, isn't it, Mum? Priests aren't supposed to have wives or girlfriends.'

'Oh dearie me,' Abbie sighed. 'Yes, you're quite right, Sandie. It *is* wrong, and Doreen would be dreadfully upset if she knew about it. I can quite understand that Veronica doesn't want her mother to know, the silly girl. Do you think she's just imagined it? Perhaps she thinks this priest is keen on her when all he's doing is trying to be kind?'

'I don't know, Mum.' Sandie shook her head. 'She says he takes her home from the Youth Club and that he holds her arm. She reckons he feels just the same way as she does, and that he likes her a lot. It would cause ever such a scandal, wouldn't it, if there really was something going on?'

'Yes, it would,' replied Abbie. 'We'll just have to hope it's all in her mind.' Abbie remembered now how Doreen had told her about the girl's excessive zeal concerning her faith. That was over a year ago. Could it all be because of this Father O'Reilly? 'It sounds to me as though she's got herself into rather a pickle. Or will do if she carries on with it. Doreen really ought to know about it,' she added thoughtfully.

'Mum – no, no! You promised!' Sandie yelled at her. 'I wouldn't have told you if I'd thought—'

'It's all right, love. Calm down.' Abbie sighed. 'I won't breathe a word, honestly I won't. As a matter of fact, I've learned my lesson about telling Doreen anything, or Norman, to be more precise. She and I had a bit of a fall-out not long ago, you see.'

'Yes, I thought you did. What was it about? You never said.'

'And I still can't say, Sandie. It was just that Doreen was behaving rather foolishly – like mother, like daughter, I suppose – and I didn't really approve of what she was doing.'

'She's got another fellow, you mean?' Sandie was agog with interest.

'I didn't say that, did I? She was . . . well, she was gadding about a bit, and Norman found out and then I got involved, even though I didn't want to. It was all rather unpleasant. No, you can rest assured that I won't say a word to Doreen about all this.' Abbie was aware, in spite of the recent Tupper party and the surface friendliness, that she and Doreen had not regained their former intimacy. Close confidences of any kind were not on the cards at the moment. 'I should try and forget it, if I were you; Veronica was showing off a bit, maybe. If there is anything . . . well, it's sure to come to a head, and we're just as well keeping out of it. I don't want to do anything to upset Doreen, not again.'

'But you've got Jean at college now, haven't you, Mum? And other new friends as well. You don't see as much of Doreen.'

'When you make new friends you don't forget the old ones,' said Abbie. 'I told you the other day – there's no limit to the number of friends we can have. You're getting quite friendly with this Paula, aren't you? But that doesn't mean that you drop the others, does it?'

'No, of course it doesn't. But Lindsay was a bit miffed when I told her about Paula and she said I was getting too big for my boots. I expect it's because Paula's in the sixth form.'

'Oh dear. It sounds as though she's a bit jealous, that's all. Paula seems a nice girl. I thought so when I saw her at the Festival. I think it's a good idea for you to join that Youth Club and choir. It's nice to belong to something and it's handy that Grandad and Auntie Faith live quite near.

They've said you can stay there on Youth Club nights if you want to.

'You've changed your tune, Mum. You weren't all that keen on me going to that dance, were you, not at first?'

'No, but it was because I didn't want you wandering around in the dark on your own. I don't mind if I know where you are, and it's at a church hall – that's all to the good – and I've already said Paula's a nice sort of girl. What about Greg Matthews? Will you be seeing him again?'

Abbie hardly dared to ask the question. Sandie had been so much more open of late, and now there was this revelation about Veronica. She had also told her, rather more guardedly, about the group, The Blue Notes, and how well they had performed at that dance. Abbie felt that her daughter's affected nonchalance was just a front to disguise her interest in Greg Matthews. She didn't want her to clam up again, but she was anxious to know whether it was because of this boy that Sandie was so keen to join. 'Is Greg a member of the Youth Club?' she asked now, a little apprehensive of the reaction she might evoke.

'No, he's not,' replied Sandie edgily. 'The group just played there, that's all. I'll be seeing him every Saturday, won't I, because I have the next music lesson. But he's not asked me to go out with him, if that's what you mean. Just shut up about him, can't you? I'm not bothered about Greg Matthews.'

'Oh, all right. I only asked,' said Abbie. 'Never mind, love. You're rather young anyway to be thinking about boys. Wait till you're sixteen. You will be, very soon.'

'And what's suddenly going to happen when I'm sixteen? The entire male population of Blackpool will be falling at my feet, will they?'

'Don't be silly, Sandra.'

'And you'd let me go out with them, would you . . . *if I was sixteen*?'

'Stop shouting, Sandra. I don't know why you're so cross

all of a sudden. It's just that sixteen sounds so much more grown-up than fifteen; a sort of milestone in a girl's life. And I know you're growing up, love. I wouldn't want you to stay a little girl for ever.'

'Huh! It sounds like it! It's "Wait till you're sixteen", then it'll be "Wait till you're seventeen", and "Wait till you're eighteen". I couldn't care less about boys anyway. It's you that brought the subject up, not me, harping on about Greg Matthews, and I've told you – I DON'T CARE!'

'And I've told *you* to stop shouting at me, Sandra! If this is the way you're going to carry on every time we have a conversation then there's not much point in me trying to talk to you at all.'

'Don't try then. Just shut up!'

'Sandra! How dare you?'

The girl did have the grace to look a little shamefaced. 'Sorry, Mum,' she mumbled. 'But you keep on and on at me.'

'I'm only trying to show an interest. And you do have a good deal of freedom, a lot more than some girls of your age.' Abbie bit her tongue. She knew she must not start on the tack of 'When I was your age . . .' or it would lead to even more ructions. 'We'll say no more about it at the moment, but please try to remember that I'm only thinking of what's best for you. I do have your interests at heart, even though you may think I'm just a nagging old fusspot.'

'I haven't said that.'

'You don't need to. I know what you think. Anyway, that's that. Thank you for telling me about Veronica. That's what we were talking about in the first place, isn't it? I will respect your confidence, don't worry.'

'OK, Mum. Thanks. And . . . I'm sorry.'

'Let's leave it at that, shall we?'

Sandie nodded. 'I'll have to go now. Some homework to do,' she mumbled as she made a hasty exit through the kitchen door.

Abbie put her head in her hands and gave a long

shuddering sigh. No matter how hard she tried, any conversation she had with her daughter seemed to lead, inevitably, to a row. And it was all about nothing, really. Sandie was at a difficult age, she supposed; teenage hormones and all that. But how long was it likely to continue? Women's problems always seemed to be connected with a 'difficult age', or 'the time of the month'. Abbie had been having a few difficulties herself in that direction lately. Her monthly periods had always been as regular as clockwork, but now, these last few months, she had found she was apt to be late, or early. She had also been experiencing what was now being called 'pre-menstrual tension'; a feeling of depression and sometimes of irritability before the monthly event. It was something she had not known before. It was not serious enough to see the doctor about and so she had tried, largely, to ignore it, wondering if it might even be the sign of an early 'change of life'. Surely not? She was only forty-two, or would be in January. She and Sandie both had their birthdays in that month.

Abbie had to admit to herself, however, that her up and down moods were most probably due to the state of her emotions as much as to bodily changes. It was Art Gillespie. The fellow was getting to her. Although she tried to pretend to herself – and to Jean – that theirs was just a casual friendship, she was allowing herself to become emotionally involved.

She had been to his flat twice more since that first time. On that occasion, she felt she had been tricked into going there, but she couldn't hide behind that excuse any longer. Both times she had protested, though somewhat half-heartedly, saying she had an important lecture or a train to catch, but both times Art had talked her round as she knew, deep down, she had always intended him to.

They had sat on the settee, listening to music and chatting and drinking coffee. Abbie had refused an alcoholic drink this time, knowing she must keep a clear head, and Art, smilingly, had gone along with her decision, choosing to drink coffee as well. His amorous cravings, however, were not alcohol-induced, as he soon began to show, and neither were Abbie's, she realised, as she found herself responding to his kisses. This time his hands explored her body, her breasts beneath her close-fitting jumper, then the length of her thighs. She was surprised when he stopped, and she was aware, too, of a tinge of disappointment in herself although she would not have let him go the whole way, to use the teenage phraseology.

'You're so lovely, Abigail,' he had said, 'but we must be sensible. I know you're an honourable woman.' She was never sure whether or not he was teasing her, although there was nothing in his serious expression, at that moment, to indicate this.

The next time she had accepted a vodka and tonic. Why not? she thought. In for a penny, in for a pound. She was a mature woman, she knew what she was doing, and it was a long time since she had had any sort of romantic involvement. Whether she would have gone ahead and let him make love to her in the fullest sense, or not, she did not know because, once again, it was Art who called a halt.

'I am growing very fond of you, Abigail,' he had said, gently stroking her cheek. 'But the time is not ripe, not yet. We mustn't spoil anything. Now, what about a cup of coffee before I run you to the station? You mustn't miss your train.'

Again she was aware of a feeling of frustration and unfulfilment, a feeling which continued and one which was not helping in her dealings with her daughter. Sandra was difficult, admittedly, and needed to be put in her place for speaking to her mother in such an insolent manner, but Abbie knew she no longer had the same patience with her as she had once had. What was more, she could empathise with the girl if she was experiencing pangs of the heart about this lad, Greg Matthews, as Abbie guessed she was. Abbie, too, was experiencing similar emotions, although she could not admit it to anyone, certainly not to her daughter. There were some things a mother could not tell her daughter, just as there were things that a daughter would never, ever tell her mother. Sandie wouldn't believe it, anyway. Abbie felt briefly amused at the thought. For most of the time, however, she was not amused at all, just perplexed and frustrated. What was Art's game? she wondered. And why could she not summon up the sense and the courage to put a stop to it, whatever it was? The truth was, she was fascinated by him and, she feared, very close to falling in love with him. There were times, what was more, when she was convinced he felt the same . . .

Sandie was angry with her mother for making her lose her temper, and when she had been getting on so well with her, too. Mum had been great about that business with Veronica and Sandie knew she would keep her word and not blab about it. She knew that she had not kept her own promise to Veronica, who had begged her not to tell, and felt a bit rotten about that, but she had been so bothered she had had to confide in someone. And then Mum had to go and ruin it all by harping on about Greg and her only being fifteen and all that rubbish. She was only too well aware that Greg thought of her as a kid. She was sure that was the reason he hadn't asked her out again, and she had a sneaking feeling he had only asked her to go to that stupid dance because he wanted to show off with that stupid group of his.

She had seen him at the end of his music lesson the following week, and they had exchanged a few words. 'Hello', and, 'Glad you enjoyed the dance', and 'Cheerio, see you . . .' and that sort of thing.

'So you've been tripping the light fantastic, you and Greg, have you?' asked Mr Hendy, when Greg had gone. And when Sandie looked mystified: 'He mentioned a dance – not that it's any of my business.'

'Oh yes. I was at a dance at the Youth Club I belong to

and Greg was there, too.' She knew she must not mention the group.

'Oh, I see. I'm glad you two are getting to know one another. I like my pupils to be friendly. Now, how are you getting on with the Mendelssohn? Let's start with that, shall we?'

She had hoped Greg might be there to meet her when she finished her lesson, but was doomed to disappointment. As she was the following week. She had been tempted to tell Duncan Hendy about The Blue Notes, but knew that would be a very childish and unpleasant thing to do. This was the reason, though, that she was so bad-tempered with her mother.

She knew, if she were honest, that Mum was being quite reasonable and that life in general was not at all bad. She had been to the Youth Club and to choir practice a couple of times and thoroughly enjoyed it. Mum had insisted on taking her and bringing her back, but Sandie had not argued because it was quite decent of her really, and she had found that other parents did the same, those of girls who lived a distance away, at any rate. She was staying at Grandad's next weekend because there was a dance on the Saturday night and then, on the Sunday, the youth choir was singing at the morning service. It was what they called a Sunday Special leading up to Christmas.

Her friend, Lindsay, had soon got over her sulks regarding Paula and had agreed to join the Youth Club – but not the choir – as she lived quite close to Marton. Christmas was coming, which was always quite a jolly sort of time even though you had to spend most of it with your family. Then there would be two weeks' holiday from school. Yes, things were not too bad on the whole . . . if only, just for a little while, she could get Greg Matthews out of her mind.

Abbie spent Christmas quietly with her family and found, to her relief, that she was able to push all thoughts of Art

Gillespie to the far recesses of her mind. She had decided to stand firm and so had steadfastly refused when he had suggested another visit to his flat. She had noticed, subsequently, a slight coolness in his manner towards her, although he had, a few days later, invited her to have a lunchtime drink with him in the Market Inne to celebrate the end of term. When she had arrived, however, she discovered that it was not to be a cosy tête-à-tête with just the two of them. Dave Saunders, Art's friend from the teaching staff, was there, as well as several students, a couple of whom Abbie had never spoken to before. Art did not treat her as anything more than a friend, for which she was relieved. She did not want their relationship to become a subject for gossip, not that anyone would care overmuch; liaisons between students and, less frequently, between students and lecturers were fairly commonplace and were either disregarded or treated as a nine days' wonder.

She could not help but be a trifle piqued by Art's attitude, although she knew he might consider she had asked for it. They saw one another again, in the same public house, on the very last day of term; Art was with a small group of tutors and Abbie with a larger group of students. Lectures had finished at midday, but the revelry at the Market Inne went on into the middle of the afternoon. Abbie waved to him as she made her exit with Jean and Eric, who was running them to the station, and Art cheerily returned her wave, though turning back almost at once to his group of friends. Abbie felt as though she had been summarily dismissed, and Jean and Eric's farewell to one another at the station did not help to make her feel any better. They kissed affectionately, Jean no longer trying to disguise the fact that they were a couple; she told Abbie on the journey home that she had invited Eric to join her and her family for Christmas Day.

Abbie had invited her father and Faith and her parents-in-law to her home for Christmas Day. The two couples had always got on quite well together on the few occasions they had met and now they were all living in Blackpool they saw one another a little more frequently. Faith had encouraged Lily to join her local branch of the Townswomen's Guild which gave the two women something in common. And the two men, though they could not be called bosom pals, seemed to like one another well enough. Abbie was aware that Frank Horsfall, a joiner by trade – what her mother had once referred to disparagingly as a 'jobbing carpenter' – had at one time been a little in awe of Cedric Winters because of his impressive standing as a doctor. But all that had disappeared with the retirement of the two men, who found they had enough in common to sustain a conversation. Most of their talk seemed to be about the local football team. Frank was now a keen supporter of Blackpool, having switched allegiance very quickly from Norwich City. Cedric was unable to attend matches now, but took a vicarious interest in 'The Seasiders'.

Abbie smiled to herself as she heard snatches of the conversation drifting through to the kitchen. The three male members of the family – her father, her father-in-law and her son – were discussing tactics and transfers and chances of promotion or relegation as though their lives depended on it. They had all listened intently to the Queen's speech – Sandie and Simon rather less intently – and then the four females had adjourned to the kitchen. This would be the way of things in houses all over the land, Abbie supposed; the womenfolk donning pinnies to wash up the dinner pots and then starting to prepare another gargantuan meal – the Christmas tea – which it was doubtful anyone would be able to eat, whilst the menfolk sat back taking their ease.

'Faith and I will wash up,' Abbie told Lily and Sandie. 'There's not really room for four of us in this small kitchen; we'll be falling over one another.' She was rather surprised that Sandie had followed the rest of the women to the kitchen, but the girl did seem to be on her best behaviour today. 'You two might as well go and join the men.'

'Oh no, I'd like to help,' said Lily. 'You've made up such a lovely meal, Abbie dear.'

'It's only boring football they're talking about,' said Sandie. 'It might be more interesting to wash up.' Some of the girls in her year took an active interest in football, attending matches with as much enthusiasm as the boys, but it had little appeal for Sandie. Abbie was relieved about that as she had quite enough on her plate with her schoolwork and music lessons, and now this added interest of the Youth Club and choir.

'It's kind of you both to offer,' said Abbie, 'but we can manage, honestly. Why not go and have a game of Scrabble?' This had been one of Sandie's Christmas presents. 'I'll let you know when we want the table setting for tea. You could do that, if you really want to help.'

'OK, great.' Sandie grinned, glad to be let off the hook, in spite of her offer. 'Come on, Gran. You can play Scrabble, can't you?'

'I think so, dear, but I won't be as good as you.'

''Course you will. It's dead easy.'

'Those two get on well together, don't they?' Faith remarked as Lily and Sandie went off companionably.

'Yes, they always have,' replied Abbie. 'I sometimes think she takes more notice of her gran than she does of me. Sandie and I . . . well, sparks fly sometimes, to say the least.'

'It's her age,' said Faith, with a shrug. 'She's a good kid, though. I don't think you have any need to worry about Sandie.'

'You don't see her all the time,' said Abbie darkly. 'She can give a good impression when she wants to. No, maybe that's not fair. I dare say she could be a lot worse.'

'And Lily seems to have recovered from her operation, doesn't she?'

'Yes, thank God. The radium treatment seems to have done the trick. She was very tired for a while, but she's picking up again now. What about Dad? He's keeping well, isn't he? You would tell me, Faith, wouldn't you, if there was anything wrong?'

'Of course. You know I would. I'm pleased to say he's as fit as a fiddle, so long as he doesn't overdo things and remembers to take his medication. I have to remind him sometimes. Yes, your father's on an even keel. And what about you? Glad to be away from college for a while, are you?'

Abbie thought again how her life seemed to be compartmentalised between home and college and how, when she was in one, it was easy to forget the other. She said as much now to Faith. Her stepmother showed keen interest, as she always did, when Abbie told her about a forthcoming trip to London which had been planned for her Modern History group. They were to visit the capital for a long weekend towards the end of January, staying in an hotel off the Bayswater Road and visiting places of historical interest: the Houses of Parliament, the Imperial War Museum, Kensington Palace and the London Museum. They were also going to see *The Mousetrap* which had been running in the West End for ten years.

'Our last chance to see it, most probably,' said Abbie.

'You go ahead and have a good time,' said Faith. 'I know it's an educational visit, but I expect you'll get some time to yourselves as well. Make the most of it, Abbie; you deserve it. And you know Sandie and Simon are very welcome to stay with us if you would like them to.'

Chapter 17

The weather was bitterly cold. The snow, which had fallen soon after Christmas, was still lying around in frozen heaps in the middle of January, an unusual occurrence in Blackpool where it usually melted very quickly in the salty sea air. Conditions for drivers and pedestrians alike were dangerous and Abbie was glad of the comfort of the train back and forth to Chelford each day. She hoped the weather would improve by the end of the month for the visit to London. It was a treacherous time of the year to plan a journey anywhere, but the latter part of the term would be hectic with teaching practices for the various year groups.

It was during the second week back at college that Art joined her in the canteen towards the end of the lunch break. Jean, as usual, when she saw him approaching, got up and walked away. Although she had said very little, Abbie knew that she did not approve of her friendship with the English tutor; a friendship, however, which seemed to be on the wane. Art had scarcely acknowledged her since the start of the new term. She had been half-expecting another invitation to his flat, or a suggestion that she might join him for a drink at the Market Inne. She could not make up her mind, though, whether she would accept or reject his offer; but such ponderings were immaterial because the invitation had not been forthcoming.

'And what have I done to annoy the fair Jean?' asked Art,

sitting down at her side. 'Methinks the lady does not care for me. Or is there something my best friends won't tell me?'

'No, it's certainly not that,' said Abbie, although she did not smile at him as welcomingly as she might once have done. Art was always immaculate in appearance, scrupulously clean and well-groomed. 'I expect she's gone to find her friend – you know, Eric. She said something about meeting him in the library after lunch.'

'Ah yes, the sober-faced Eric. It isn't that she doesn't approve of me, then? Or of me . . . and you, perhaps?'

'That I can't say,' replied Abbie, 'because I don't know. Perhaps you'd better ask her.'

'Hey, hey, what's eating you?' Art put his hand over hers. She did not pull away, but she was relieved when he removed it. You never knew who might be watching. 'Annoyed with me, are you?'

'No, why should I be?'

'I'm sure I can't imagine. Unless you think I've been neglecting you?'

'Why should I think that?'

'Because it's true, Abigail. We haven't had any of our little meetings lately, have we? Is that what you're annoyed about?'

'I'm not annoyed – I've told you.'

'Oh, come on. You've as many prickles as Mrs Tiggy Winkle. But I've come to say I'm sorry, and that there was a reason for it, for me not inviting you round to my place.'

'Oh? I doubt if I'd have come anyway, not in this weather. I've been trying to catch an earlier train home whenever I can.'

'My sister's been staying with me since Christmas. She's recovering from 'flu and she wanted a change of scenery. It wouldn't be the same with someone else there . . . would it, Abigail?'

She didn't answer his question. Indeed, there was no answer, at least not one that she could think of that would be appropriate, that would let him see she was not the sort of woman to be trifled with. She knew she was unskilled, alas, in the art of repartee, unlike her friend, Jean, who always seemed able to think of a suitable rejoinder. Instead, 'I didn't know you had a sister,' she remarked.

'Oh, yes – didn't I mention her? Brenda is five years younger than me. She lives near my mother.'

'Married, is she?'

'Not any more. She has been.'

'So she's here on her own?'

'Yes, all on her own. Why – does it matter?'

'No, not really.' Abbie reflected that there was a great deal she didn't know about Art Gillespie. She had not known, for instance, that he had a sister. She was sure he had never mentioned one. Why was it that she found it hard to believe him? And yet it would be such a silly thing to lie about. She noticed a flicker of annoyance on his face for a moment, which just as quickly turned to a dazzling smile.

'She'll be going back next week. Anyway, never mind about her. What I've really come to tell you, apart from saying I'm sorry, is that I'm coming to London with you. Is that good news or isn't it? I hope you will think it is.'

'*You're* coming? But how? Why? I thought it was just for—'

'For you and your history cronies? Well, primarily, it is, but also for a few selected members of staff, one of whom has decided that she can't go. When Ralph asked me if I would like to go instead, I jumped at the chance. What's the matter, Abigail? You don't look exactly thrilled at the prospect of having my company. Aren't you pleased?'

'Yes, I'm pleased – if it's what you want to do. Why didn't you decide at the beginning that you wanted to go?'

'One has to be invited, my dear. Which I have been, now. A personal invitation from Dr Ralph Jefferson, none other.'

'But what about your own lectures while you're away?'

'Oh, for heaven's sake, Abbie, don't you think that's been taken care of? Someone'll stand in for me. Why the inquisition,

anyway? I must say I expected a more enthusiastic response.'
He was looking annoyed again – angry, almost. He stared at
Abbie, his grey eyes as cold and hard as granite, then the
warmth crept back into them and he smiled, placing his hand
once more over hers. 'Oh, come on, Abigail. I thought you'd be
pleased. I've been longing to tell you. It'll be a good chance for
us to get to know one another better, won't it? I'm sorry I've
neglected you lately; I've already said I'm sorry, haven't I? With
my sister being over and everything. But you must remember
you turned me down before Christmas, didn't you? It made me
wonder if you really did like me.'

'Of course I like you, Art. And of course I'm pleased
you're coming to London.' Her feelings towards him were
ambivalent. At times she told herself she must stand firm,
that he was only playing some sort of game with her and
that it would, in the end, lead to nothing; or worse, to her
being hurt and rejected. But when he smiled at her as he was
doing now she found herself longing to believe in his
sincerity. Why should he not be sincere, anyway? It was
reasonable enough that he would not ask her round when he
had a member of his family there; also, as he had reminded
her, she had been playing hard to get. It was generous of him
to give her another chance. A man as attractive as Art must
surely be able to have his pick of women. She did not often
let herself dwell on the question, Why me then? She convinced herself, rather, that he must have some feelings for
her, of liking, or even the beginnings of love . . . or simply
lust? Again, she did not allow herself to dwell on this last
possibility.

She smiled at him now, at the same time extricating her
hand from his grasp, as she told him she was pleased about
his news. 'You mean you'll be coming on all the visits with
us? And our trip to the theatre, and everything?'

'Yes, Abigail, absolutely everything. The same hotel even.
The same corridor as you, I hope; adjoining rooms,
maybe . . . but perhaps that's hoping for too much.' He gave

a little laugh as she lowered her eyes. 'We'll have a ball, Abbie. I dare say it's a long time since you were able to shake a loose leg, isn't it?'

'It is indeed,' she replied. 'But it is supposed to be an educational visit, isn't it? We'll have to take notes, do some work . . .'

'It's not exactly a school visit, Abigail. Walking in a crocodile, lights out by ten and all that sort of thing. You're a big girl now, don't forget. What you do in your spare time – and there'll be enough of that, don't you worry – is your own affair. Well, I must love you and leave you now, I'm afraid. Some books to collect for my next lecture.' He squeezed her shoulder as he rose to his feet. 'And if we can manage a little get-together, just you and me, before our London adventure, well, all to the good, eh? See you, Abigail. Cheerio for now.' He winked at her expressively as he took his leave.

She realised she was smiling to herself as she walked from the canteen a few moments later, and she quickly rearranged her features into a semblance of solemnity. It was true what Art said; she *was* a big girl now, a mature woman, in fact, well able to look after herself and deserving, also, of a share of fun and freedom. For years, following Peter's death, she had had no fun at all, except with her children, of course; Christmas and birthdays, holidays and outings all planned with them in mind. Scarcely any freedom either, regulating her hours, days and weeks to fit in with her children's requirements. Since starting college she had thrown off the restraints somewhat and had started to enjoy herself in a more adult way. Maybe it was time to take a step further, to throw caution to the winds. Go for it, Abbie, she told herself now. She had only one life, and it was half over. It was time to start living that life to the full.

It was the following Saturday when Sandie came home from her music lesson in a state of great excitement. Abbie could tell she was trying to impart her news in a casual manner, but the brightness of her eyes and the slight flush to her cheeks gave her away.

'Mum, Mr Hendy's had a good idea,' she began. 'At least,' she gave a slight shrug, 'he thinks it's a good idea, but he said I had to tell you about it and see what you think. He wants Greg and me to play duets together. He says it would be good practice for both of us, and we could go in for festivals and . . .' She hesitated. 'What d'you think, Mum?'

'Well, yes, I suppose it would be all right, Sandie,' Abbie replied. 'But how will you manage? Will you have a lesson together, or what?'

'Greg has the hour before me,' said Sandie, 'so if I go a bit earlier – say quarter of an hour – and he stays a bit later, we can manage it like that. That's what Mr Hendy suggested.'

'But you'll need to practise together as well?'

'Yeah, 'course we will. But he could come here sometimes, couldn't he? And I could go to his house.'

'Where does he live?'

'Somewhere near the Oxford cinema – you know, the other end of Whitegate Drive.'

'Oh dear. It's a long way, Sandie.'

'It's not all that far. I've got my bike, and it won't always be winter. Anyway, Mr Hendy says he'd like to see you, then he can tell you a bit more about it. He said he'd ring you and arrange a meeting.'

'Oh, very well then. Although I don't see why he can't talk to me about it over the phone. If he rings I hope it will be soon, that's all. I'm going on my history trip next weekend, you know.'

'Yes, and I'm going to Grandad and Aunty Faith's. I hadn't forgotten, Mum.'

Abbie had intended, originally, for both children to stay with Lily and Frank Horsfall for the weekend, but her father's home was nearer to this youth club that Sandie had become interested in, also to Duncan Hendy's house where she would be going on Saturday morning for her lesson. So only Simon would be staying with her parents-in-law. Both sets of relatives liked to feel they were helping Abbie and this arrangement seemed agreeable to everyone.

'So you'll go and see Mr Hendy, will you, Mum?'

'Yes, I'll do that, dear, provided we can arrange a suitable time. Greg seems a nice sort of boy,' she added, 'and you're both very good pianists; you should be able to help one another quite a lot.'

'Mmm, yes. Mum,' said Sandie, 'you won't say anything to Mr Hendy about Greg's group, will you? You see, he doesn't know about it yet, and Greg said I wasn't to say anything.'

'No, dear, of course not. But I don't see why it has to be kept a secret, if they're as good as you say they are. No, I won't say anything, I promise.'

She refrained from reminding Sandie about her tender years, or of the dangers of becoming involved with boys at too young an age. Besides, Sandie had turned sixteen now, the age that her mother had mentioned was a kind of watershed in a girl's life. She could hardly go back on her word now. It was only a joint music lesson that was being suggested, after all, and time spent practising together. Ah well. Que sera sera, as Doris Day was continually singing on the radio. Sandie was growing up, and no matter how much her mother fretted about her she could not prevent what Fate might have in store.

Abbie went round to see Duncan Hendy the very next day; he had rung her almost immediately. It was Sunday afternoon, a period he kept free from music lessons. This time he showed her, not into his music room, as he had done before, but into his upstairs sitting room, a cosy place with a coal fire burning brightly. The deep golden velvet curtains, already drawn to keep out the early dusk, toned with the gold brocade of the three-piece suite and the leaf-patterned carpet of russet and brown.

281

'What a charming room.' Abbie could not help the spontaneous remark as she glanced around. And what a contrast with the stark surroundings of Art Gillespie's bachelor pad, was her next thought.

'Thank you. I'm glad you like it.' Duncan smiled at her. 'Do sit down, Mrs Horsfall. Let me take your coat or else you won't feel the benefit when you go out again. I hope you'll have a cup of tea with me while you're here. And I hope you didn't mind me suggesting you should come here. It's such a cold day to be out, although the roads are clearer now for driving, aren't they?' The thaw had set in at last and Abbie hoped it would continue and clear away the last vestiges of snow before her London trip at the end of the week. 'I could have come to see you, of course,' he continued, 'but I know you have your family to look after and . . . Anyway, you're here now, aren't you, and I'm very pleased to see you again, Mrs Horsfall.'

'And I'm pleased too,' Abbie replied. She smiled at him. 'My name's Abbie. That's what most people call me.'

'Yes, I remembered your name.' Duncan's blue eyes were looking right into hers. 'I will call you Abbie, if I may. And I'm Duncan, but of course you know that. Some of my pupils call me by my first name – the older ones, that is. I encourage them to do so. I think it makes for a more friendly relationship in some ways and I haven't found that they take advantage of it. After all, they're not at school when they come here, are they?'

'It's the same at my college,' replied Abbie. 'It's all Christian names there, for tutors and students, except for the ones who are sticklers for tradition. I couldn't get used to it at first, but it's a sign of the times, isn't it? It's a much more free and easy age we're living in.'

'Your daughter still calls me Mr Hendy,' laughed Duncan. 'But then she hasn't known me long, has she? She still seems – what can I say – a little in awe of me.'

'She admires your ability as a teacher and as a pianist,'

said Abbie. 'I shouldn't worry, if I were you. It isn't often that Sandie has so much regard for authority. She can be very quick to condemn if there's anything she doesn't approve of.'

'It's Sandie I wanted to see you about, of course,' Duncan went on. 'Sandie and Greg. You will know about my suggestion that they should play duets together?' Abbie nodded. 'Well, I just wanted to set your mind at rest, to assure you that you need have no doubts or fears, none at all, about Greg Matthews. He is one of the nicest young men you could ever wish to meet. I've known his family for years. Sybil – that was my wife – and I were very friendly with Hazel and Alan, Greg's parents, and I've been very pleased to watch the way Greg has matured. Yes, he's a very nice young man, so you don't need to worry about him leading Sandie astray or anything like that. I know how mothers worry – they're bound to. I'm sure I would worry, too, if I were a father. Which, alas, I am not.' He looked pensive for a moment. 'I'm sort of honorary uncle to Greg, though. I like to think I've helped a little in his development.'

'I'm sure you have,' replied Abbie warmly. 'No, I'm not worried about Greg, well, just a little, I suppose. Sandie hasn't known many boys, but she's bound to start showing an interest in them some time. I don't really know him, of course, but I got the impression he was a nice sort of boy when I saw him at the Festival. Thank you for reassuring me. And I think the duet idea is a very good one, so long as . . .' She hesitated. 'I was going to say so long as that's all they get up to.' She smiled. 'But we can't really do anything about that, can we? It's just that . . . well, I think our Sandie's rather smitten with him. You know what I mean.'

'Who could blame her? He's a very personable lad. But he's got both feet firmly on the ground, don't you worry. Greg wouldn't do anything silly; I feel confident of that. It isn't that I want to throw them together, but they are my most talented pupils and playing duets does help one's technique. You have to listen carefully and think about the other person, not just about yourself. I'm sure it will be beneficial for both of them. Now, I'll go and make us a pot of tea then we can talk some more. Make yourself at home, Abbie. There's the Sunday paper if you wish to look at it. I won't be long.'

The paper was the *Sunday Observer*, too wordy for Abbie to peruse at that moment with so much on her mind. Instead she glanced round at Duncan's belongings; his books, ornaments and photographs which helped to make the room look so lived-in and welcoming. The large glass-fronted bookcase contained, on the bottom shelf, volumes about the lives and works of various composers as well as the musician's Bible, the *Oxford Companion to Music*. On the other shelves were a set of leather-bound classics including Dickens, Hardy and Trollope, as well as several novels by Kingsley Amis, Ernest Hemingway and E.M. Forster. There was also a good selection of detective novels by Agatha Christie, Ngaio Marsh and Dorothy Sayers, most of them in the familiar green Penguin cover; a few of the James Bond novels as well.

He had a wide-ranging taste in literature, Abbie decided, quite similar to her own except possibly for the Ian Fleming books, which she guessed she would find too far-fetched to believe.

There were some Royal Doulton character figures on the top of the bookcase and on the mantelshelf; a fisherman, a woman selling balloons, a Chelsea pensioner and a jolly man holding a tankard, whom she took to be Falstaff. There were a few photographs, some of them in silver frames, and Abbie stood up to take a closer look. A wedding photograph, though not an over-large one, showed a much younger Duncan and a very pretty young woman. Her hair seemed to be very fair, from what Abbie could tell from the black and white photo, and she had an air of fragility. The same woman – Sybil, he had called her – featured in a larger studio portrait. There was also a casual snapshot of a little boy, whom she took to be Greg Matthews, with Duncan, and a couple of sepia photographs – Duncan's parents when young, maybe, and one of a family group. She sat down again hurriedly in case Duncan should return; not that she was doing anything wrong, but she did not want him to think she was snooping. The few pictures on the walls – prints, not originals, of course – were very pleasing to the eye and were ones Abbie might have chosen for herself: a study of wild geese in flight by Peter Scott, a Parisian scene of a flower stall near the Seine, and an Impressionist painting which she thought was by Monet.

'Tea up.' Duncan was back sooner than she expected – he must have prepared everything in readiness beforehand – with a laden tray, and she quickly got up again to close the door behind him. 'Thanks, Abbie. There's a nest of tables there if you could just . . . Thanks. I'll put the tray on this larger one, then you can have the small one for your cup and plate. There we are.'

The china was Royal Albert, a pretty pattern of red and yellow roses. A woman's taste, thought Abbie, rather than that of a man living alone, but then Duncan was not a bachelor. He was a widower and the tea service, like the silver-plated teapot, had probably been a wedding present or chosen by his wife, Sybil. There were paper napkins, too – these of a more utilitarian white – and a sponge cake sprinkled with sugar, cut into small wedges.

'This is delicious,' said Abbie. It really was as good, if not better, than any she could have made herself. 'Did you . . .?' She stopped, wondering if she was being too nosy.

'Did I make it?' Duncan chuckled. 'Not on your life! I can cook, after a fashion, and I look after myself reasonably well – I've had to since Sybil died – but I'm not skilled in the culinary arts, not by any means. No, my cleaning lady made it. She comes in twice a week to "do" for me. Mrs Warburton is more of a friend and neighbour, rather than a charwoman, and she insists on making a bit extra when she's baking for her own family. She spoils me really. Have another piece, Abbie.'

'No, thank you, I mustn't. I'll be making tea when I get home for Sandie and Simon and myself. I won't eat very much, though, because we have a big meal at lunchtime on a Sunday. But the children always seem to be hungry, no matter what time of the day it is.'

'And does Sandie help in the kitchen?'

'Only when she's forced to,' Abbie admitted. 'Like all teenage girls, I dare say. I don't insist on her helping me too much; she's all her studying to do. It's her GCE year and I want her to do well, and then there's her music, of course . . .'

They talked a little about the music lessons, then the conversation drifted on to Duncan's other occupation: his freelance work as a pianist and organist for many of the town's social functions.

'I enjoy it,' he told Abbie, 'and it gets me out in the evenings. At one time, soon after my wife died, I used to sit there brooding. I didn't want to go anywhere.'

'I know the feeling. I was just the same at first, when Peter died.' Abbie's smile was one of empathy.

'Of course. You understand, don't you? Anyway, I soon realised it was no use sitting around and feeling sorry for myself. I had a talent I could use and it was up to me to use it to the full. And now . . . well, I've had to put a curb on the number of engagements I take, or I could be out nearly every night.'

Abbie nodded understandingly. There was a silence, quite a companionable one, before Duncan spoke again. 'They always invite me to take a guest along if I'm playing at a dinner, but I have never done so, not yet. I usually come home when I've done my bit.' He paused, looking at Abbie thoughtfully before he continued. 'I'm playing at the Savoy Hotel in the middle of February – St Valentine's Day, to be exact. It's for a local businessmen's club and, for once, their wives or ladyfriends are invited. I wonder . . . Abbie, would you do me the honour of accompanying me, of being my guest?'

At first she was taken aback, too surprised to say anything, but when she answered she knew she was going to accept. This wasn't Art Gillespie inviting her to a clandestine meeting in his flat, but a highly respectable man asking her to attend what she guessed would be a very pleasant social occasion, the sort of event she had not been to for years and years.

'I'd love to go with you, Duncan,' she replied, using his name for the very first time. 'Thank you for inviting me. I feel very honoured.'

'I can assure you the honour will be all mine, Abbie.' His blue eyes were glowing with kindliness and pleasure as he smiled at her, holding hers in a gaze from which she found it hard to break away. She looked down after a moment, folding her paper napkin into a small square.

'It's a while since I've been to such an occasion. I shall have to get my glad rags out.' She knew she would, in fact, have to buy a new dress, something suitable for evening wear, which at the moment she did not possess. 'Will it be a formal occasion? Long dresses, evening suits and all that?'

'It's up to the individual really,' Duncan replied. 'The ladies usually like to dress up for such events, and the men wear dinner jackets if they wish, or lounge suits. I wear my evening suit, being in the public eye, you see.' He laughed.

'And you'll be playing the piano, will you?' asked Abbie. 'For the dancing?' She had accepted his invitation; all the same she did not relish the thought of sitting on her own all evening whilst he was otherwise engaged.

'Oh no,' Duncan replied. 'Don't worry, I won't leave you on your own. I just play light incidental music during the reception, and I accompany the fellow who sings the toast to the ladies; that's at the end of the meal. Then the dancing

287

starts. They have a three-piece band for that – nothing to do with me. That's the time I usually go home from these dos unless there's someone there I know quite well. But this time, I'm pleased to say, I won't be on my own.'

He smiled at her.

'I'll look forward to it,' Abbie said courteously.

'Yes, and so will I. We can arrange details nearer the time. I will come and pick you up at home, of course.'

They talked for a little while of more mundane matters: the arrangements for Sandie's extended music lessons for which, he insisted, she was to pay no extra. He would not be teaching longer hours, just teaching two pupils together instead of one. He told her, also, of the venue for Sandie's next music exam which would take place in April.

Abbie pondered, as she drove home, about Duncan's real motive in asking her there this afternoon. She guessed it was chiefly to invite her to the St Valentine's Day dinner, the matter of Sandie's lesson and duet playing being merely incidental. She was rather surprised at his invitation, after such a short acquaintanceship, but she guessed he did not know many women socially. He had told her how he had tended to keep to himself after his wife died. However, she was pleased and flattered to be asked out. Duncan was a very pleasant man and she would enjoy his company.

It was just over a fortnight, she realised, to the dinner. She would need, not only a new dress, but new shoes and an evening bag. The thought cheered her. It wasn't often she had a good excuse to spend money on herself. But her purchases would have to wait until she returned from London. That was the event that was looming large in her mind at the moment.

Chapter 18

The weather was still cold, but not the same piercing cold-ness that the thawing wind had brought, numbing your fingers and taking your breath away, when the party of history students and tutors boarded the train on Friday morning, the last weekend in January. It was doubtful if Abbie would have felt the cold anyway; she was too over-wrought. It was not a feeling that could be termed excite-ment. It was more of apprehension at leaving the children, although she knew they would be well looked after by her relatives, combined with nervousness at having the first holiday – well, a holiday of sorts – that she had ever taken on her own. Above all there was that feeling of suspense, tinged with anxiety, as she wondered what would happen this weekend between herself and Art Gillespie.

The train, fortunately, was a through one from Chelford, taking them via Wigan and Crewe to Euston station. The journey took four hours and they had all brought sand-wiches and flasks of tea or coffee to sustain them. There were fifteen of them in all, twelve students and three lectur-ers, those being Dr Ralph Jefferson, Miss Eileen Cardwell, who was another member of the History Department, aged fiftyish and a spinster, and Art Gillespie.

Abbie sat at a table for four with three other students from her group – Vera, a woman of roughly her own age with whom she had always got on reasonably well, and two much younger men who had done their National Service in the last call-up and then gone straight to college. Art had acknowledged her with a nod and a brief 'Hello', as they all stood on Chelford station awaiting the train, and he smiled at her as they took their seats; he was seated at the table across the aisle from Abbie with his two colleagues.

She had been to London only twice before, once with Peter, soon after the war ended when the city had still been heavily scarred by bomb damage, and again a few years later when Sandra and Simon were small, but old enough to appreciate such attractions as Buckingham Palace, the Changing of the Guard and Madame Tussaud's. She had been thrilled both times at the feeling that she was in the big city, the heart of Great Britain. London had an ambience that was all its own; the hustle and bustle of the crowds, combined with the sense that momentous events had taken place here and, indeed, were still happening. The historical figures who had walked through its streets, lived in its mansions and palaces and taken their ease in its verdant parks had left their mark on the city, not only in the myriad statues that abounded, but also in the very atmosphere of the place.

Abbie felt the same sense of fascination now, as then, as they boarded the Tube train at Euston. Her earlier misgivings had gradually dispersed as the journey progressed, the easy chatter of her companions helping to calm her anxieties. The churned-up feeling in the pit of her stomach had gone now and she was determined to enjoy herself. She had loved the Underground when she had travelled on it before. It made her feel she was, if only for a short while, like a real Londoner; without the bored expression, however, which most of them wore, having to do the selfsame journey day in and day out. Nor did they have, like her, to glance continually at the map above their head lest they should miss the stop where they had to change trains. Dr Jefferson was in charge that day, however, and he escorted them competently to their exit point, Lancaster Gate.

When they emerged on to the busy Bayswater Road, across it they could see the pleasant greenness of Hyde Park at the point where it merged with Kensington Gardens. Their hotel was situated in a quiet square only a few minutes' walk away. Abbie was relieved, when she had collected her key at the reception desk and travelled up to the second floor in the somewhat antiquated lift, to kick off her shoes and dive into her case to find her slippers. She would wear her flat-heeled shoes whilst she was in London – she remembered how a visit to the city always involved walking for miles – but she had wanted to look smart for the journey. She didn't really know why as most of the students were dressed in a much more casual manner than herself. Old habits died hard, though; she had always tried to look her best when travelling.

She had paid extra for a single room, although several of the students were sharing, and she was glad of this now. She didn't feel like chattering as she had a slight headache after the journey and needed a little space, both of room and of time, in which to unwind. She dissolved a couple of soluble aspirin tablets in a tumbler of water. It was luxury, to have her own washbasin, toilet and shower, minuscule though the cubicle might be. It was a relief to know that she didn't need to trek the length of the corridor. Not many hotels had had this facility the last time she visited the city.

She sat on the single bed for a few moments waiting for her headache to clear. The room was not large and by no means elegantly furnished, but it was clean and the bed seemed comfortable. The small built-in wardrobe and the chest of drawers with a swing mirror were adequate for the clothing she had brought. She hung her few garments now on the wire coat hangers and placed her underwear and bits and pieces in the drawers. The rest of the afternoon was free for the students to do as they pleased. As Art had reminded her, it was not exactly a school visit with its accompanying restrictions. She had arranged to meet Vera and two more women from their group in the foyer at three o'clock.

'D'you fancy getting the Tube up to Oxford Street?' asked Vera when they were all assembled. 'It's only a couple of stops. We could have a look at the big shops – Selfridges and John Lewis's and Marks and Sparks.'

But the others demurred. The afternoon was well advanced and it would mean travelling back in the rush hour. There was a meal booked for all the party at the hotel this evening, for seven o'clock, which would be followed by an introductory lecture by Dr Jefferson.

'No, let's just go to the park,' said Doris, another of the group. 'It'll be dark soon anyway, and I want to have a look at Peter Pan's statue. I remember seeing it when I was a kid.'

That was their first call – Peter Pan, surrounded by a variety of small animals and fairy folk sculpted in bronze, standing on his plinth by the Long Water. They were the only ones gazing at him on this chilly winter afternoon. All the children would be at school and there were not many adults, either, walking along the paths that led through the park. The Round Pond, too, was deserted; no children or sailing boats or nannies with prams in evidence, and by the time they reached this point it was quite dark. Kathleen, the fourth member of the little group, wanted to take a look at Prince Albert on his throne overlooking the Albert Hall – like Doris with Peter Pan, she had remembered him from childhood – and when they had done that they hastily retraced their footsteps, anxious lest they should find themselves locked in the park.

Abbie felt exhilarated when she arrived back at the hotel and was more than ready for her evening meal. They had not even had a cup of tea since they arrived in London and there had been no snack bars open in the almost deserted park. She took a quick shower, then put on clean underwear and the red dress Jean had helped her to make and which she had only worn a couple of times, during the Christmas season. She was not displeased with the reflection that smiled back at her through the full-length wardrobe mirror. Her dark hair was newly washed; she had done it the night before with a special Amami shampoo that was said to bring out the highlights, and she fancied it did look glossier, with a slight chestnut tinge. She had applied rather more lipstick than normal, a bright red shade which matched her dress, and then, fearful that she might look cheap and tarty, had wiped some of it off again. She had noticed that her daughter had started to wear just a touch of eye-shadow now when she went out of an evening. Abbie had made no comment; Sandie was sixteen and quite old enough for a little more make-up, so long as she had the good sense not to wear it at school. Secretly, she had thought how attractive it looked and mused that what suited Sandie might well suit her; their eyes were the same shade of brown. So for the first time tonight she had applied the merest touch of green eye-shadow to her eyelids. The effect was pleasing. That was why she was smiling. She hoped that other people, one person in particular, of course, might think she looked more attractive than usual this evening.

She pulled a face at herself. Oh, for heaven's sake, stop behaving like a love-sick teenager, she told her reflection. The butterflies in her stomach had started dancing again as she wondered, half in hope, half in trepidation, what might happen later. She slipped her feet into her black patent court shoes, picked up her bag and her room key and made her way downstairs.

Her friends were there already in the small bar area and they had saved her a place and ordered her a medium sherry. 'Cheers.' She raised her glass, glancing round, not too obviously, she hoped, to see who else was there.

Art was standing at the bar with Ralph Jefferson, and Eileen Cardwell, the third member of the teaching staff, was seated with a group of students. Art did not even acknowledge Abbie's presence. She tried to tell herself that it was because he did not want to single her out for attention. It was her friends who commented on her appearance, telling her how very attractive she looked.

'You look years younger,' said Kathleen, who was in her mid-thirties. 'It must be that eye-shadow. You don't usually wear it, do you?'

'No, it's just an experiment,' laughed Abbie. 'It was my daughter who gave me the idea. I noticed how nice she looked.'

'And so do you,' agreed Vera. It was not quite the same, receiving compliments from one's own sex, but it gave Abbie more confidence as she took her place at the dinner table. Besides, the night was still young.

There were three tables laid for the college group, each seating five people, and it seemed to have been agreed by the tutors that they would take a table each. She found herself holding her breath, but it was Dr Jefferson who sat down with her and her three companions. Either Art had been pipped at the post, or he did not wish to sit there. She felt her spirits plummet as she saw him laughing and chatting with the two younger men and a couple of women students. Particularly with one of them, she could not help but notice – Carol Pearson, a vivacious blonde-haired woman in her early thirties. Abbie did not know her well. Carol was in the Modern History group, of course, like all the others who were there, but she had never conversed with her very much. She tried not to watch, lest the others should notice, concentrating instead on the more serious, erudite talk of their history tutor.

He was not a man given to much levity, but she found herself enjoying his tales of previous visits he had made to the city, and his particular interest in the London of Charles Dickens's time. A visit had been planned to Dickens House for Monday morning, before they caught the train back home later in the day. A bonus for those who were also English Literature students and, Abbie surmised, the reason that Art Gillespie had been invited along, although he had said it was an afterthought.

The four women did not need to say very much as Dr Jefferson, like most of his profession, was a garrulous man with an unending fund of anecdotes. Abbie concentrated as much on her meal as on the talk. She was enjoying her dinner, more because of her hunger than of the quality of the food. It was, in truth, a stereotyped sort of meal, a table d'hôte menu put on by the hotel to oblige the college party. It was quite palatable, however, if somewhat predictable – tomato soup, roast chicken with potatoes, peas and carrots, followed by peach melba. Another set meal had been ordered for Sunday, but tomorrow, Saturday, it would be up to the students to make their own arrangements as this was the evening of their theatre visit.

They all assembled in an adjoining room for the lecture by Dr Jefferson. This took about an hour, during which he told them of the things to look out for on their various visits and supplied them with questionnaires. He concentrated mainly on the Houses of Parliament which they were to visit the following morning.

'A little drink before bedtime? What do you say, girls?' asked Doris when the talk and the subsequent discussion had finished. It seemed as though the four of them, Abbie, Vera, Kathleen and Doris, were forming a little clique, although they had not been particularly friendly at college. Abbie wondered how she would manage to break free of them should the need arise.

'Yes, good idea. Why not?' they answered her.

After a couple of drinks they decided they were ready to retire for the night. It had been a busy day with an early start, and they would need to rise early again the next morning to prepare for a hectic schedule.

'Goodnight, Vera. See you in the morning.' Abbie left her friend, who also had a single room on the same floor – Doris and Kathleen were sharing on the floor below – and went to her own room at the end of the corridor. She felt more than a little deflated. Art had not even glanced in her direction whilst they were in the bar although he must have known she was there. Was it all over? she wondered. But then it hadn't really begun, had it? Not properly. Their few meetings had been clandestine ones, although Abbie guessed that was more her fault than Art's. They had not managed a meeting before this trip, as Art had proposed. Abbie had needed to get home early on the day he had suggested as it was Sandie's youth club night, and this may have displeased him.

She took off her red dress and hung it in the wardrobe, exchanged her stylish shoes for comfy slippers, then put on her woollen dressing gown. Now she had come upstairs she realised she was not yet tired enough to go to sleep. Maybe a spell with her Agatha Christie book would divert her mind from things she did not want to think about and help to make her more sleepy. There was an armchair of sorts and she settled down to have a good read.

Some ten minutes later there was a knock on the door, not a loud one. Abbie's heart skipped a beat and her hand went automatically to the belt of her red dressing gown, pulling it tighter, although she told herself it was probably only Vera wanting to borrow something.

'Who is it?' she called a little nervously, going to the door.

'It's me. Let me in, Abbie, please.' The voice was definitely Art's. He was speaking in a loud whisper and sounded quite agitated.

She opened the door hesitantly and he came in, hurrying past her with a bottle in his hand. 'Thank goodness you're still up. I thought Ralph and Eileen were never going to call it a day. He's like a long-playing record when he gets going. I didn't want them to see me getting this.' He held up the bottle of Liebfraumilch. 'To your taste, I hope? They didn't have much choice at the bar.'

Abbie was not a connoisseur by any means, but she thought it was a German white wine and that she had had it before. 'Yes, that's lovely,' she said. 'But . . .' She stopped.

How silly it would sound if she said she'd already had quite enough to drink. She had only had a small port and lemon and a pineapple juice since her dinner. 'I wasn't expecting you, as you can see.' She indicated, slightly embarrassedly, her dressing gown, although she was, below that, fully clothed apart from her dress.

'And very charming you look, too, Abigail,' said Art. 'I'm sorry I couldn't speak to you earlier – you know how it is. Anyway, I though we could have a little drink together, a toast to the success of our weekend. What do you say?'

'I say yes. That would be very nice, thank you.' He laughed in that teasing way he had, as though he found her slightly amusing.

'I've brought a glass.' He held up the standard hotel tumbler from his room. 'I expect you've got your own, haven't you?'

'Yes, of course.' She hurried to the cubicle to get it. It was holding her toothbrush and toothpaste, so she quickly took them out and rinsed it under the tap. 'There, all prepared.' She tried to match his bantering tone. 'I don't suppose you remembered to bring a corkscrew, did you?'

'Ah, that's where you're wrong, Abigail my dear.' He sat on the edge of the bed, putting his glass down on the bedside table and drawing a corkscrew from his pocket. 'Prepared for any eventuality, that's Art Gillespie. A real Boy Scout, you might say. I brought this from home; I guessed I might need it.' He expertly drew out the cork, then reached for Abbie's glass which he almost filled, then poured the same amount into his own. She refrained from saying it was too much; he might not notice if she did not drink it all.

'Cheers, Abigail. Here's to us.' He raised his glass and she did the same, sitting down in the armchair while he perched on the bed.

'Yes, cheers.' She sipped at the wine which was very pleasant; not too dry for her taste.

'So you're enjoying yourself, are you? So far, so good, hmmm?'

'Yes, very good, Art.' She found herself relaxing, although she had experienced a moment of panic when he walked in. 'Yes, I'm enjoying myself,' she told him.

'That's good. And I want you to enjoy yourself even more. What I've really come to ask you is will you have dinner with me tomorrow night, after the theatre? We've got seats for the first house, I believe?'

'Yes, thank you. That would be lovely.' She answered without hesitation, then, remembering another occasion when she had thought he was inviting just her for a drink and had found this was not the case, she asked, 'Just you and me, you mean?'

'Of course there'll be just you and me. Who else?' he replied. 'We'll be able to find a nice cosy little restaurant on the Haymarket or somewhere near. Then we can take a taxi back here; no messing about on the Tube.'

'That'll be lovely,' she said again. 'Thank you, Art. I'll look forward to it.'

'How about coming here then and saying thank you properly?' He patted the folk-weave counterpane. 'Come on. Come and sit beside me, Abigail. It's been a long time, hasn't it?'

She sat down next to him and he put his glass down in a decisive way before taking her in his arms. His lips came down on hers and she knew that this was what she had been anticipating; she realised, moreover, that it was what she had been longing for. She did not protest when he fondled her breasts, nor when he untied her dressing gown and pulled it off her shoulders.

'You're so beautiful, Abigail,' he said, gazing at her for a moment as she sat there in her lace-edged slip. He pushed her back against the pillow and she felt his hands travelling the length of her body, pulling up her slip and, fleetingly, caressing the most intimate part of her. Then, to her astonishment, he called a halt, as he had done before on the occasions she had visited his flat.

'I think we'll wait until tomorrow,' he said, pulling her upright again. 'It's late and I'm not . . . What I mean is, I didn't intend to do this, not tonight, but I find I can't help myself. You're so lovely, so . . . irresistible. I want you to be sure, Abigail. As sure as I am. I don't want you to have any regrets.'

'I'm sure, Art,' she replied, half-smiling, half-frowning. She was blessed if she could understand him at times.

'Till tomorrow, then.' He stood up, then putting his hands on her shoulders, he stooped and kissed her again briefly. 'It will be all the better for waiting,' he whispered, stroking her cheek. 'Goodnight, Abigail. Sleep well. See you in the morning. Don't get up. I'll see myself out.'

'You've forgotten the wine.'

'Oh yes, so I have. Never mind. Put the cork back in and we'll finish it tomorrow night.' He winked. 'Goodnight then.'

He opened then closed the door quietly behind him. So that was that. Abbie felt stunned, scarcely able to believe what had happened. Art was an enigma if ever there was one. She knew she had been ready to give herself to him tonight, that she would undoubtedly have done so if he had not put a stop to their lovemaking. Why had he done that? she wondered. Was it true what he said, that he wanted her to be very sure before committing herself? Possibly, but it occurred to her, with a sudden flash of intuition, that what he was doing was working her up to such a state of anticipation that, the next time, she would be powerless to resist him.

I shall never sleep tonight, she thought as she undressed and washed, her mind a maelstrom of confusing impressions. She got into bed, then noticed the half tumbler of wine on her bedside table. On an impulse she gulped it down in just a few swallows. She put out the light and settled herself on the pillows, quite prepared for a sleepless night. The next thing she was aware of was the piercing ring of her travel alarm clock telling her it was seven o'clock.

The group had an early breakfast, then a journey by Tube to Westminster. What a thrill it was to emerge from the station and see Big Ben towering above them. Abbie knew, of course, that the name of the building was really St Stephen's Tower, but everyone called it Big Ben. Their first visit of the day was to the Houses of Parliament, open to the public on Saturdays and on other days when the houses were not in session.

Abbie had never been a very political sort of person, tending to trust whichever government was in power to do the best they could for the country. At this present time, 1963, the Conservatives had held office for years and years, ever since the early 1950s, and were now under the leadership of Harold Macmillan. 'You've never had it so good' was a slogan continually being quoted, but Macmillan's government was, in truth, experiencing certain difficulties in Europe. Abbie had found herself taking more interest since embarking on this Modern History course, and she knew that the Foreign Secretary, Edward Heath's, attempts to negotiate Britain's entry into the European Economic Community – usually known as the Common Market – were being repeatedly vetoed by France.

The group entered the Palace of Westminster through the door in the Victoria Tower, and from there ascended the Royal Staircase to the Norman Porch. Abbie was overawed by the thought that it was this very staircase that the Queen walked up on the occasion of the State Opening of Parliament. As they entered the Queen's Robing Room, then the Royal Gallery with its huge frescoes of the battle-scenes of Waterloo and Trafalgar, and the full-length portraits of former kings and queens, her feeling of reverence increased. The members of the group spoke to one another in whispers, following the guide books in their hands for such information as they would require; the voice of a resident guide quoting facts and figures would have seemed too intrusive.

There were a few audible gasps at the sight of the House of Lords with its rich dark red benches, elaborate mahogany carvings, stained-glass windows and, surpassing all, the magnificent gilded throne and canopy. What a contrast was the House of Commons; a visual anti-climax with benches of dark green leather, windows of clear glass and a simple wooden ceiling. Westminster Hall, the oldest part of the Palace, where the tour ended, evoked in all the members of the group a sense of homage and the utmost respect, and it was here that the feeling of history was most perceptible. Here, from the thirteenth until the nineteenth century, were the chief law courts of England; and it was here that the misguided, but always well-meaning, Charles Stuart had been declared 'a tyrant, traitor, murderer and public enemy to the good people of this nation', and had been sentenced to death.

Later that morning they visited the Banqueting House, from a window of which the unfortunate King had stepped out on to the scaffold and thus to his death. It was hard to return to reality, to the here and now, to the London traffic rushing along Whitehall and the usual crowds of tourists – despite the coldness of the day – crowding round the guardsman on his horse outside the Admiralty building.

Abbie and her friends walked through Admiralty Arch and crossed Horse Guards Parade. They were to meet the other members of the group at two o'clock outside Kensington Palace, their venue for the afternoon, and until then their time was their own. Abbie had not had a chance to speak to Art. She had noticed, to her slight annoyance, that Carol Pearson, the young woman with whom he had been sitting at dinner last night, had tagged herself on to him; at least, she assumed it was Carol's doing and not Art's. But it was her, Abbie, whom he had asked to have dinner with him, wasn't it? She hugged the thought to herself, although it occurred to her that she would have to break the news to her three colleagues . . . and come in for a certain amount of ribbing, no doubt.

She did so as they sat in a crowded snack bar on Piccadilly partaking of their midday lunch of ham and salad rolls and frothy coffee. Their comments were predictable, but by no means malicious or envious; just the good-humoured banter she had expected.

'Still waters run deep, eh, Abbie? Didn't realise you knew him all that well.'

'My goodness, you're a dark horse, aren't you?'

'How long've you been keeping him to yourself?'

'I haven't,' she began. 'We get on quite well, that's all. I'm one of his English students, but I don't know why he's asked me and not anyone else. Probably because I'm the only one here who's in his group, apart from a couple of the men, of course.'

'And it wouldn't be the same, would it, inviting two fellows to have dinner with him?' Vera winked. 'Go for it, Abbie. I hope you have a great time.' Doris and Kathleen agreed; they all wished her well. As far as she knew her three companions were all married – reasonably happily, she assumed. At least, none of them seemed to go in for the flirtatious behaviour that was rife amongst some of the students.

'I bet Carol Pearson would like to be in your shoes,' Kathleen commented. 'She was all over him when we were in the Parliament building. Did you notice?'

'Women do seem to like him,' Abbie answered non-committally. 'He has that way with him, you know; he's something of a ladies' man. But he's really very nice when you get to know him. I think it's all a front,' she added, a little unsurely.

Kathleen rolled her eyes at the other two, but they made no comment. Abbie knew that her friend, Jean, would be warning her to watch her step. But Jean wasn't here.

Kensington Palace, the venue for the afternoon visit, was not all that far from their hotel. After they had visited the modest royal palace of William and Mary and seen the room where Victoria was first informed – whilst in her night attire – that she was now Queen of England, they took a quick tour round the London Museum which was housed on the ground floor of the Palace.

'I don't know about you, but I feel supersaturated with all this bumf,' said Doris as they made their way back through the park. 'I can't tell whether I'm on my head or my heels.'

'I don't know about my heels, but my feet are killing me,' replied Vera. 'Talk about foot-slogging. I say, d'you think we could get a cup of tea in the bar? My tongue's hanging out for one.'

The hotel staff were very obliging. The women had not realised, the day before, that tea and coffee could be purchased during the day, but all they had time for was a quick cuppa before changing into their glad rags for the evening's theatre visit.

Abbie showered and put on her red dress, as she had done the previous night, then brushed her hair and carefully applied her make-up, paying particular attention to the green eye-shadow which her friends had commented on. She was trying to ignore the dull ache in the pit of her stomach. It must be nerves, she told herself. It couldn't be anything else. There was over a week to go before her period was due.

They had been instructed to meet in the foyer of the theatre at least fifteen minutes before the play was due to start. To Abbie's relief, Art was already there, and he seemed to be on his own.

'Go on,' said Vera, giving her a slight shove. 'You'll be sitting with him, won't you?'

'Ah, Abigail, there you are. I've been waiting for you.' He stepped forward and took her arm, seemingly not worried about what the rest of the party might think. 'Ralph has the tickets, so we'll make sure we have seats together. Thank you, Ralph. I'll take mine and Abbie's.' No one appeared to be surprised they were going in together, or even to take any notice, except for Carol Pearson. The look she levelled at Abbie as they entered the auditorium was quite vitriolic. Abbie was shaken, but she tried to push the thought of the jealous woman to the back of her mind. She had other things to worry about, chiefly the ache in her stomach which was not abating.

'Norman, look! Look who's over there! It's Abbie Horsfall. Well, fancy that. What on earth is she doing here, and who's that man with her?'

From their corner table in the restaurant on the Haymarket Doreen had been watching all the comings and goings. She had not seen Abbie and her companion come in because she had been preoccupied with staring at an overdressed young woman and her male escort at a nearby table. She was sure she had seen her on the telly, but she couldn't quite place her. Was she one of those quiz-show hostesses? But when she looked round again, there was Abbie . . . and with a very dishy-looking man.

'Why don't you go over and say hello to her,' suggested Norman. 'Then you could find out who is with her. It'll be something to do with that college of hers, I dare say. Happen he's one of her fellow students.'

'Oh no, I can't do that,' said Doreen hurriedly. 'In fact, I don't want her to see us. Don't keep staring, Norman. Abbie and me, we're still . . . well, we're still far from right with one another. Not the good friends we used to be.' She gave a shrug. 'A pity, but there it is.'

'And whose fault is that?' asked Norman.

'Well, I hope you're not suggesting it's mine,' retorted Doreen. 'Except I suppose it might be, just a bit,' she added as her husband gave her a questioning look. 'Anyway, never mind about all that now. You and me are OK, aren't we?

That's the main thing. No, I wouldn't dream of going and barging in.' But in spite of telling her husband not to stare, Doreen was doing just that.

'I say, Norman,' Doreen then said slowly, 'that fellow she's with – he looks familiar. I'm sure I've seen him somewhere before.'

'You can't have done. How can you? He'll be one of Abbie's cronies from that college of hers.'

'But I have. I know I have.' Doreen's brow was creased in thought as she stared at the man in question. 'I've seen him somewhere . . . now, where can it be?' She gasped as the memory suddenly came back to her. 'Oh, Norman. Oh no! It's that teacher from our Veronica's school – you know, when we lived in Northallerton. The one that was in all that trouble about those girls. Mr . . . what was he called? Gillespie, that's it – don't you remember? Archibald Gillespie, that was his name. And that's him . . . over there with Abbie.'

Chapter 19

The restaurant on the Haymarket was a cosy sort of place, just right for an intimate evening or late-night supper. The cosiness was effected not by the smallness of the room – it was, in fact, quite a large place – but by the subdued lighting, the candles in balloon-shaped glasses, the wooden panelling on the walls and the high-backed partitions which partially hid the small tables set for two at the sides of the room. There were larger tables, to seat four, six, or more, in the centre of the room and these were occupied by family groups or by those who enjoyed being seen by others. It was a popular place for theatre-goers, for a meal before or after the performance, and was frequented, too, by the actors who were appearing at the myriad theatres in the vicinity.

Art had already booked their table, which was just as well because the place was filling up rapidly. It was by far the most sophisticated restaurant that Abbie had ever been in, and she knew that normally she would have been thrilled by the tasteful surroundings and by the thought that Art had chosen her, of all people, to be with him this evening.

But she was not enjoying it at all, because the worst thing that could have possibly happened had done so. The nagging ache in her abdomen had increased during the play and so, during the interval, she had excused herself and hurried to the Ladies' Room. It was as she had feared; her period had started over a week early. She made herself comfortable – she was always prepared for an emergency even though it was unexpected – then went back to her seat in the theatre, wondering how on earth she was going to tell Art.

Should she tell him straight away? No, that wouldn't be feasible, surrounded as they were by their colleagues. Or when they got to the restaurant? Or should she wait until they arrived back at the hotel . . . and were in her bedroom? She was under no illusions as to what Art intended to be the climax of the evening. She was going to find it very awkward to tell him anyway. Abbie still looked upon it as a very personal and private matter. When she had been a girl, in her severely restricted background, her mother had regarded a monthly period almost as a shameful happening, not to be mentioned even to other girls, let alone to a member of the opposite sex. When she had met Doreen she had learned to be rather more open about such things. There had been very little, in fact, that she had not discussed, at one time or another, with her friend during those happy days of real friendship.

'What's the matter, Abigail?' Art leaned across the restaurant table and took hold of her hand. 'You've gone all quiet on me. You've a habit of doing this, haven't you? You're not scared of me, are you? Surely not – you've known me long enough now.' He smiled at her, so very winningly. 'Long enough to know how much I care about you, and that I would never do anything to hurt you. If there's anything wrong, you must tell me.'

'No, there's nothing wrong, Art,' she replied, trying to smile back at him. 'I have a slight headache, that's all. I'll take a couple of tablets and perhaps they'll clear it.' She couldn't tell him yet; he was being so kind and thoughtful and she found herself wondering why she had ever doubted his sincerity. It was true that she had a headache as well as the other niggling pain. A couple of aspirin should do the trick and, she hoped, make her feel more relaxed as well. It would be a pity to spoil the enjoyment of the meal. She was sure the food, like the surroundings, would be luxurious. She

307

decided to put off the evil moment for as long as she could.

'Yes, take your pills, there's a good girl.' He patted her hand. 'We don't want anything to spoil our evening, do we?' He turned to the wine waiter who was hovering with a list as long as his arm. 'Red wine, of course, as we are both having steak.' He chose a French one with a long name.

'I don't think I had better have any wine,' said Abbie as the waiter hurried away. She was not keen on red wine anyway, but Art had not consulted her. 'Not with having the tablets.'

'Nonsense,' he replied, but quite good-humouredly. 'It won't do you any harm. The aspirin will have been absorbed by the time you've eaten that.' He pointed to her starter of seafood cocktail which the waiter had just brought. 'Go on – live dangerously, Abigail.'

The mixture of seafoods – prawns and tiny morsels of crab and lobster in a tangy pink sauce – was delicious. So was the Steak Diane served with potato croquettes, asparagus tips and broccoli. By the time Abbie had finished her main course and, at Art's insistence, drunk a glass of wine, she was beginning to feel much better. Her headache and the other pain had receded. She felt much more relaxed, too, although she knew she still had to tell Art the dreaded truth. The wine, though, was dulling her consciousness, making everything seem a little unreal. She knew she could not possibly manage a sweet course – a pudding, as Art had called it; she guessed this must be the correct word – so she did not order one. But he insisted she should share with him the pancakes steeped in brandy and served with huge dollops of fluffy cream, which he had ordered for himself.

He pierced little pieces of the confection on his fork and fed them to Abbie across the table, as though she were a small child. Normally she would have abhorred such behaviour, feeling that everyone must be looking at them, but she realised she was going along with him almost without caring, even giggling a little as he said, 'Open wide, there's a good girl.'

'They're scrumptious,' she said, her voice sounding louder than she intended.

'Sure you wouldn't like a plateful to yourself? I can order some more.'

'Oh no, I really couldn't eat another mouthful. I'm so full I could burst.' She patted her stomach in a very unladylike way. The remark, in fact, was a trifle uncouth, not one she would normally have used, but then things were not normal at all. She was feeling very topsy-turvy and inside-out and as though everything was a muddle. She had enough of a grasp on reality, however, to know that Art was grinning at her in a very suggestive way. Oh, bloody hell! she thought recklessly. She could guess what was on his mind. She knew she must drink the black coffee which had now arrived, without any cream if she could stomach it, and try to get a grip on herself.

'Are you sure it's him?' asked Norman.

'Of course I'm sure,' Doreen replied. 'I'd know him anywhere. That cheeky little-boy look he has, and those devil's eyebrows. It's him all right.'

'But you didn't recognise him at first.'

'That's because I haven't given him a thought for years. Why should I? And I certainly didn't expect to see him here with Abbie. What the devil *is* he doing here? He must be at that college of hers, I suppose.'

'Not as a student, surely?'

'No, of course not. He must be a teacher there – a lecturer, or whatever they call 'em. Would you credit it? After all that happened.'

'He wouldn't have been able to get another job, surely?'

'Well, he must've done, mustn't he? He could talk his way out of anything, from what I can remember of him. He must've pulled the wool over their eyes, at this college he's at.

Most probably they know nothing about all that other business.'

Doreen was continuing to watch her friend, with that philanderer, at the other side of the restaurant. They were on to their main course now. Abbie was sipping at a glass of red wine and smiling across at him. She certainly wouldn't be smiling if she knew what sort of a creep was sitting opposite her. Doreen felt she ought to warn her, but how? She could go across and make herself known to the pair of them; tell that Gillespie she remembered him from his time at Northallerton because he had taught English to her daughter, Veronica. That would put the wind up him all right! But no; she decided she couldn't do it. It wouldn't do any good, would it, except to warn Gillespie that she was on to him.

Nor could she tell Abbie, here and now, that the man she was with was a rotter, a seducer of young girls. A wife-beater, too, if rumours – and there had been plenty of them at the time – were to be believed. She would just have to hope that Abbie had enough commonsense to see through him before she did anything silly. She would definitely put her in the picture as soon as they all got back to Blackpool. She did still care about her friend and Abbie had always been so naïve and trusting.

'Perhaps he's a reformed character, eh?' said Norman. 'It's quite a while ago now, love.'

'Reformed character, my Aunt Fanny!' Doreen spluttered. 'A leopard can't change its spots. No, he was a real bad 'un. And it's *not* all that long ago either. Let's see, our Veronica was in her first year at the Grammar School. It wasn't all that long before we moved to Blackpool. About six years ago, it'll be.'

'But he was never convicted, was he?'

'That was a fluke, if you ask me. He was damned lucky to get away with it. It was only because the girl involved was turned sixteen and she was known to have a bad reputation.

There had been others, though, but they didn't want to give evidence, or so I heard.'

'Aye, I know there were a lot of tales going around at the time.'

'Not just tales, Norman. It wasn't a tale that he beat his wife up when she found out about him, although she must have known what he was like, surely. Mrs Morrison, your mother's friend, lived in the same street as them. Don't you remember?'

'Yes, happen I do. But what are we going to do about Abbie? That's more to the point.'

'I can't tell her now, can I?' fretted Doreen. 'I can't just prance over there and say hello to her, can I? Thank goodness she hasn't spotted us.'

'She's too preoccupied,' Norman said wryly.

'Yes, that's what's worrying me,' said Doreen. 'But I'll tell her about him when we get home, just as soon as I can. It'll be hard, but I'll have to do it.'

'Tit for tat,' said Norman, laughing.

'What do you mean?' Doreen looked at him sharply.

'Well, I'm sure Abbie had something to say to you, didn't she, about a certain fellow at night school?' There was a twinkle in his eye – all that was behind them now – but Doreen did not respond to it.

'It's not the same thing at all,' she snapped. 'Abbie's heading for disaster, and I've got to warn her. I only hope I'm not too late.' She glanced across the restaurant to where Abbie and that fellow were giggling away at something. Doreen could hardly bear to look at them. 'I've finished my coffee now, Norman,' she said. 'Let's settle the bill as soon as we can and get away. Abbie's got her back to us and she won't notice us if we get out quickly. Come on – hurry up. I don't want her to see us.'

The black coffee had cleared most of the wooziness in her head, but had also brought her back to a reality she would

311

rather not face. Art would be annoyed with her; there was no doubt in her mind about that. But just how vexed he would be or what form his annoyance might take she had no means of telling. She did not know him well enough.

His arm slid round her as they sat in the back of the taxi, but she did not turn towards him lest he should try to kiss her. She just stared out of the window at the lights of Regent Street.

'What's the matter?' he said, squeezing her shoulder. 'Don't tell me you're tired. Or are you worried that the taxi driver might be watching us?'

'A bit of both, I suppose,' she answered, quite flatly. It didn't matter now if Art thought her standoffish. There was no point in going along with his amorous overtures only to let him down later.

'Hey, come on. We can't have this.' He turned his head and lightly kissed her cheek. 'You were OK while we were in the restaurant. In fact, I've never known you to be so uninhibited.' He lowered his voice. 'You're not having second thoughts, are you? I've told you, Abbie – there's no need to be afraid of me.' His fingers stroked her cheek and neck. 'You're not afraid, are you?'

'No, of course I'm not,' she replied, but her voice, even to herself, sounded unconvincing. 'It's just that . . .'

'It's just that what? That you're changing your mind? Going all prissy and prudish on me?' He withdrew his arm. 'I might have known. Yes. I might have bloody well known.'

'Art, hush! Keep your voice down.' She was aware of the taxi driver craning his ears. 'It's not like that. It's not what you think at all.'

'Oh, isn't it? I know what I think,' he muttered. He stared moodily out of the window and they did not speak again until they reached the hotel. Art paid the taxi driver then strode off through the swing door leaving Abbie to follow along behind him. They collected their room keys from the receptionist, still without speaking to one another.

Abbie was the first to break the silence as they walked towards the lift. 'Art, listen to me. I've told you – it's not what you think at all. I'm not changing my mind. I'm not having second thoughts.' The lift creaked to a halt and Art pressed the button to open the doors, still not looking at her or answering her.

'Look – come to my room and I'll explain.'

'Oh yes?' he said. He raised one eyebrow, half smiling in that teasing way she had seen many times before, but this time there was no humorous glint in his eyes. They were cold, unfeeling. But she knew she had to explain. At least she owed him that. She opened her door and he followed her inside.

'Art, I'm terribly sorry.' She reached out and took hold of his arm, but he made no move towards her. 'It's hard for me to tell you this, but something has happened.'

'Oh, and what might that be?' He was not even smiling now, just looking at her quizzically with his eyes half-closed.

'It's . . . well, it's the time of the month. You know what I mean.' Never in her life had Abbie felt more embarrassed. 'It happened suddenly. I wasn't expecting it, and so—'

'And so you can't go to bed with me. How very convenient for you.' Abbie had seen his eyes flare with annoyance before, but never so much as now. She was half afraid of him, but she was angry too, angry that he did not believe her – it was obvious that he didn't – and this gave her the courage to go on.

'Are you telling me you don't believe me? I'm not in the habit of telling lies.'

'No, you wouldn't, would you? Not you, Miss Holier-than-thou, Miss Goody-Two-Shoes. All I know is that you've led me up the garden path, good and proper. But it's just what I might have expected from you.'

'Art, stop it!' she cried. 'It's the truth. I'm telling you the truth. I started . . . I started with a period.' She shocked even herself by daring to say the word. 'Why do you think

313

I went out when we were in the theatre? And that's why I wasn't feeling too well when we got to the restaurant. I'm sorry, Art. I'm really sorry, but there's nothing I can do about it.'

He took a step towards her. She saw him raise a clenched fist as if to strike her and she tottered back towards the bed. She felt herself collapsing on to it, more afraid than she had ever been in her life. What an idiot I have been to land myself in such a situation, the thought flashed through her mind. But who would have thought that Art could turn so nasty. Just as suddenly, however, as the rage had come upon him, did it seem to leave him. His hand dropped to his side and he looked at her impassively. He shrugged his shoulders. 'Very well, if you say so, Abigail. For what it's worth, I believe you.' Again he could not resist that mocking grin. 'You would *never* tell a lie, would you? But it's worked out very conveniently for you, hasn't it? I'll say goodnight then. I'll be seeing you around.'

As the door closed behind him she felt herself trembling, her hands and her legs, all her body felt weak and wobbly, then the tears began to flow. She buried her head in the pillow and cried and cried. Gradually her tremors began to lessen and her fears evaporated. What had she been frightened of anyway? she asked herself. Art would not have dared to hit her, would he? But in that moment, no more than a few seconds it had been, she had felt terrified of him. She tried to tell herself now that it was quite understandable he would be annoyed and frustrated. She couldn't blame him for doubting her word. There was no way of proving it was the truth, and, as he had said, it seemed that it had happened very conveniently. And what else could he have done, under the circumstances, except say goodnight and leave her? She did not want to admit to herself that a kinder, more sympathetic man might have tried to comfort her a little, to stay with her for a while, to say that it didn't matter. But perhaps he had been just as embarrassed by the situation as she had. Maybe that was why he had acted so brusquely and disappeared so suddenly.

She pulled herself off the bed, undressed and hung up her clothes, cleaned off her make-up and had a wash. As normality returned – it had, all told, been an incredible, unreal sort of evening – her overriding feeling was one of relief. Art had been right in saying things had worked out conveniently for her. As she got into bed and prepared herself for sleep she wondered, when it came to the crunch – and if she had not started with her period – if she would have gone through with it. Something, deep down, told her the answer was no. How much greater Art's anger might have been then. It came to her with sudden clarity that she was not in love with Art Gillespie as she had once thought she was. She doubted she had ever been. She doubted, now, that she even liked him.

'So how did your evening go? Did you have a good time?'

Her friends, at the breakfast table, were very curious, as she had feared they might be. Breakfast in the hotel was an informal meal at which all the guests sat where they pleased and ate at whatever time they wished, between the hours of seven and nine o'clock. Abbie was relieved that Dr Jefferson, their companion at the evening meal, was not there. Probably he had eaten early and already departed. Neither, to her even greater relief, was Art anywhere to be seen.

Abbie decided she would be as truthful as it was possible to be, without giving too much away. She did not know Vera, Kathleen and Doris well enough to admit to the extent of her humiliation, and she certainly did not want to start any rumours about Art Gillespie, although she was beginning to see him as the 'not very nice' person that Jean had always considered him to be.

'You could say it was good in parts, like the curate's egg,' she laughed. 'I enjoyed the play, didn't you?'

Here they were on safe ground and they all agreed that

315

The Mousetrap had been a first-rate play.

'But it's not the play we're interested in,' said Vera, winking slyly at the other two. 'What about you and lover-boy? Did you enjoy your cosy little meal and, er, what came afterwards?'

'We had a very nice meal, yes, thank you,' said Abbie, looking down at her plate of bacon, sausage, egg and tomato and thinking it was very palatable, just as much as the meal the night before. She was feeling better this morning, in body if not in spirit. Her headache and the usual 'time of the month' pain had gone. She just hoped she would not come into contact with Art Gillespie, although she knew she could not avoid him for ever.

'But nothing happened afterwards,' she said calmly. She noticed the grins they were exchanging and she even smiled herself. 'I know what you're thinking, but honestly, it didn't. Nor did I expect it to. I told you, Art just asked me to go for a meal with him because he knows me better than some of the others, with me being in his English group. That's all. I don't think you could even call us good friends. We're just . . . tutor and student.' And that was all they would be from now on, she thought to herself. They could certainly never be friends.

'Oh, go on! We'll believe you, thousands wouldn't,' laughed Doris. Then she added seriously, 'As a matter of fact, I do believe you, Abbie. I could never see him as your type. A bit too flashy and full of himself. At least, that's how he comes across, although we don't really know him, do we, girls?' She glanced at the other two. 'Not like Abbie does.'

'I don't know him all that well either,' said Abbie carelessly. She was anxious to bring this conversation to a close. 'We had a nice meal, then we came back to the hotel and went to our rooms. It was quite late actually. To tell the truth, I was jolly glad to get away from him.' She leaned across the table, speaking in a confidential tone. 'I'd started with a period, you see, while we were in the theatre, so I was glad to see the back of him and get to bed.'

'Oh dear, poor you. Feeling better now, are you?' Her friends were immediately sympathetic, and they moved away from the subject of the disastrous evening to the programme for the day.

The morning was free, to allow those who wished to do so to attend church. Abbie and her friends opted instead for a little sightseeing. They went to Buckingham Palace, St James's Park, Trafalgar Square, then took a walk along the Embankment before having a snack lunch at a pub just off the Strand. Their venue for the afternoon was the Imperial War Museum, quite a way out on Lambeth Road. They were to meet there at two-thirty, it being thought that, by now, they should all be quite capable of sorting out the intricacies of Tube travel for themselves.

Art did not glance in Abbie's direction once that afternoon, nor for the rest of their stay in London. Carol Pearson was his constant companion, not only at the evening meal at the hotel, but on the remainder of the visits. She sat with him, too, on the train journey back to Chelford. They were not within view of Abbie, but she could hear their laughter ringing out from further down the carriage. She was relieved when most of the students and tutors left the train at Wigan, Chelford or Preston and she was on her own to complete her journey to Blackpool. She couldn't wait to see Sandie and Simon again, although she was sure they would have had a most enjoyable time in her absence. As for her return to college, the very next day, with an English lecture almost the first of the morning – well, she would put that right out of her mind for the moment.

It was Wednesday evening when she opened her front door to see Doreen standing there.

'Doreen, how lovely to see you,' she greeted her. 'What a nice surprise. On your own, are you?'

'Yes, Norman's just dropped me off. He said he'd call back

317

for me in an hour or so, if that's OK. He's gone to call on a friend who lives not far away.'

'He could have come with you, couldn't he? I'm always pleased to see Norman.' Abbie looked curiously at her friend. She seemed a little jumpy and not too sure of herself but, of course, things were still not quite right between them. 'Was there something special you wanted to see me about? It isn't that I'm not pleased to see you, Doreen, but . . .'

Doreen nodded. 'Yes, there is really,' she said as she followed Abbie through the door and into the sitting room. 'Are you on your own?'

'Yes. Sandie's at her Youth Club. She stays at my father's on a Wednesday because it's quite near. And Simon's gone to see a friend.'

'And you're not busy, are you, with your college work?' Doreen sat down on the settee. 'Homework, or whatever you call it. I don't want to disturb you.'

'No, not at the moment. Doreen, what is it?' Abbie's thoughts immediately flew to Veronica. Had Doreen found out about the girl's friendship with the Catholic priest? Yes, most probably that was it. Her friend's words, therefore, came as a complete shock.

'We saw you in London,' said Doreen, quite bluntly. 'Norman and me. We saw you in that restaurant on the Haymarket. On Saturday night, it was.'

'Good heavens! What a coincidence. You mentioned you were going to London, but I didn't realise we'd be there at the same time. I'd forgotten for the moment.' Abbie stared at her in some amazement. 'I didn't see you there. Why didn't you come over and say hello? I was with a friend. Well, he's not exactly a friend. As a matter of fact, he's my English tutor, that's all.'

'Yes, Archie Gillespie,' said Doreen grimly. 'I know him. At least, I used to know him. Know *of* him, to be more correct. And I certainly hope that's all it is, Abbie, that he's

318

just your tutor because – well – there's a lot about him that you obviously don't know.'

Abbie's immediate reaction was one of resentment. 'And you obviously don't know him all that well,' she retorted, 'because his name's not Archie – it's Art, short for Arthur. He *is* called Gillespie, though, but I'd like to hear how you come to know so much about him, or think you do.'

'Well, he was Archie Gillespie sure enough when he taught at our Veronica's school,' Doreen said steadily, 'when we were living in Northallerton. It was Archie, short for Archibald. And that's the name that was in the papers when he was had up in court.'

'In court?' repeated Abbie, her blood turning cold. 'What for? When was it? How long ago?'

'Oh, it'll be six year ago, or summat like that. Our Veronica was about eleven, in her first year at the Grammar School; that's where he was teaching, that Gillespie chap.' Doreen leaned forward in her chair. 'And d'you want to know why he was had up in court? I don't like having to tell you this, Abbie, but I know I've got to. It was for molesting young girls, that's why.'

Abbie could not have said, in all fairness, that Doreen was gloating. She looked quite upset and she was not smiling, but there was a certain something in her tone, a sort of . . . self-satisfaction which made Abbie respond vehemently.

'But how could he have got another job – as a lecturer of all things – if he was guilty of what you're saying?'

'Abbie, listen to me,' said Doreen. 'I could tell that you and this fellow were a little more than just friends. I'm right, aren't I?'

Not any more we're not, thought Abbie. We're not even friends. But she did not answer. She just stared fixedly at her friend.

'Anyway,' Doreen continued, 'there was a great to-do about it. It was all in the papers, about him appearing in court and that. But he got away with it.'

'So, he wasn't convicted then? Abbie sounded deliberately sarcastic, although her heart had sunk.

'He should've been,' said Doreen grimly. 'Everybody thought so. He only got off because the girl had a bad reputation and she was turned sixteen. He had a good record at the school – some folk stuck up for him, I've got to say that. But there had been others that didn't want all the publicity. Other young girls, apparently.'

Abbie continued to stare, silently, at Doreen. She did not doubt that every word she was speaking was the truth and what was more, after the events of the previous weekend, it did not surprise her.

'You know he's divorced, do you? You must know that,' Doreen continued.

'Yes, I believe so,' Abbie muttered.

'Well, that was because he knocked her about. She got a divorce on the grounds of cruelty. That was when he upped and left – got himself a job at that there college, I dare say. We never knew what had become of him. Good riddance to bad rubbish, that was what most people said.' Her voice altered, became more gentle. 'I just thought you ought to know, Abbie. I wouldn't like to see you get hurt, that's all.'

It was at that moment that Abbie burst into tears. She could not contain herself any longer. Doreen was at her side in an instant, her arm around her, finding a handkerchief to dry her tears. 'Come on, love, don't get upset,' she said. 'He's not worth it. I was real worried about telling you. I thought you might think it was "tit for tat" or something like that – you know, after that thing with Ken in Morecambe. But I knew I had to tell you about him. You weren't more than friends, were you? You said he was your English tutor. He wasn't . . . anything else?'

Abbie smiled weakly through her tears. 'Who's not able to get the words out now? You mean were we lovers? No, as a matter of fact, we weren't, but it wasn't for the want of trying, on his part at any rate. I've been such a fool, Doreen.'

She shook her head and she could feel her eyes filling with tears again.

'Hey, come on, come on,' said Doreen. 'Some good's going to come out of all this. We're going to be friends again, you and me, real close friends, like we always used to be. I've been a fool as well. I certainly was with Ken, but I've been even more foolish falling out with you. Oh Abbie, I'm sorry, love. I blamed you for ages afterwards for saying something to Norman, but I knew all the time you'd had no choice.'

'And I'm glad you've told me now, about Art,' said Abbie, sniffing back her tears. 'Or Archie, or whatever he's called. That's another of his lies, I suppose. Oh Doreen, I had an awful time last weekend.'

'Want to tell me about it?'

Abbie nodded. She told her friend everything that had happened; how she and Art had got friendly and that she had truly believed – or had convinced herself – he was sincere. Then about how she had suddenly started with a period in London and how angry Art had been. 'I know now he didn't care about me at all,' she said, 'but I was lucky, really, because it meant I couldn't go through with it. I don't suppose I would have done anyway, then he'd have been even more angry.'

'That's really ironic,' said Doreen, with a faint smile. 'Quite a coincidence, actually.'

'What is?' asked Abbie.

'Well, you know what I told you about Ken and me in Morecambe?'

Abbie frowned. 'What did you tell me?'

'That we'd made love and everything and that I'd had a wonderful time. Well, we didn't. I lied about it 'cause I was mad with you. Actually it was a pretty rotten weekend. I realised when I got to Morecambe that I couldn't do it, so I pretended I'd suddenly started my period, like you did. Except that you really had, but I was lying about that as well. The only difference was that Ken was OK about it. He was quite a decent bloke really, not like that Gillespie fellow. Oh, I do hope he gets his come-uppance for treating you like that.'

Abbie gave a weak smile. 'He's already got another woman in tow – Carol Pearson, she's called – but I think he might've met his match there. Anyway, never mind about him. I can't tell you how pleased I am that we're friends again. And we mustn't fall out again, ever. You'll stay a little while, won't you? I'll go and make us some coffee.'

'Forget him, that's my advice,' Doreen said later, as they drank their coffee. 'I know you've got to go on seeing him, but you'll come through it, of course you will. And as for that Carol woman – well, it sounds as though they're two of a kind. I hope they tear one another to shreds.'

Abbie was beginning to feel much, much better. 'I think I knew all along he was completely wrong for me, though I wouldn't admit it. I was flattered, I suppose. It was nice to be noticed, to be made a fuss of. But all the time he was just using me.'

'Forget him,' said Doreen again. 'There'll be others, an attractive woman like you. You always used to say there would only ever be Peter. But he wouldn't have wanted you to be on your own, you know.'

'I know,' said Abbie. 'And it's been long enough now. As a matter of fact . . .' She smiled suddenly, remembering Duncan Hendy's invitation. In the trauma of the past week she had almost forgotten about it. 'A very nice man has asked me to go out with him. A dinner and dance, it is, on St Valentine's Day.'

'Oh, I say, that's great. Who is he? Another bloke from college?'

'No, it's Sandie's music teacher, actually,' said Abbie. 'Duncan Hendy. He's very nice. Definitely. Very nice indeed. We're just friends,' she added, as Doreen rolled her eyes, 'that's all. He's a widower and he wanted a partner for this do.'

322

'It's a good start,' said her friend. 'What are you going to wear? Is it a posh sort of do?'

'Yes, and I was wondering if you'd come with me to buy a dress?'

'Don't tell me you haven't got your frock yet? The fourteenth is only the week after next. Yes, I'd love to come with you. What about Saturday afternoon? It'll be busy then, I know, but you haven't much time, have you? I say, kid, isn't it exciting?'

'Yes, I suppose it is.'

'Come on, you'll enjoy it,' urged Doreen. 'A chance to dress up, a nice meal, good company.'

'Mmm. I'll enjoy it when I get there, I dare say. It's certainly been a long time since I went to a function like that – ages and ages.'

'Then it's high time you started,' said Doreen briskly. 'What does your Sandie have to say about you going out with her music teacher?'

'Don't say it like that, Doreen, as if there's something going on. I've told you, he's a friend, that's all. Well, hardly that even. I've only met him a few times. As a matter of fact, I haven't told Sandie yet.'

'Why ever not?'

'Because there's not really anything to tell her. And other things have been preying on my mind. But not any more.' Abbie gave a decisive nod. 'I'm going to think positive.'

'That's the spirit.'

'I'll tell her tomorrow. Actually, we're getting on quite well at the moment, Sandie and I. She's full of beans, not that I'm under any illusions. It's nothing I've done. It's because of this new boyfriend of hers, Greg Matthews. Well, I don't know whether you could call him a boyfriend, or whether he's just a friend who just happens to be a boy, if you see what I mean. They play duets together.'

'At least you know what she's doing and who she's with. You like him, do you?'

'Yes, he seems a very nice lad; very polite and thoughtful.'

'I only wish I knew what our Veronica was up to. I'm sure there must be a lad, the amount of time she spends at that church – she's there at the moment – but she's so damned secretive.'

'Have you asked her if she's got a boyfriend?'

'Yes, I've tried, but I don't want to appear too nosy. After all, she is seventeen, plenty old enough to have a boyfriend, but if she has, then why haven't we met him? She just fobs me off, says she's at some meeting or other, or at Youth Club.'

'You've not noticed her with anyone, when you've been at church with her?'

'No, not really. We don't always attend the same services, though. There seems to be a crowd of youngsters; they hang around with that young curate we've got, Father O'Reilly. He's done a lot for the youth of the church, I must say.'

Abbie caught her breath. She was almost tempted to say something to Doreen, to drop a hint at least. But she knew she must respect Sandie's confidence; besides, too much trouble had been caused already between her and Doreen. She was delighted they were friends again and it must stay that way. So she held her tongue.

'She can't come to any harm, can she, not so long as she's at church,' said Doreen. 'That's what I keep trying to tell myself. So long as that's really where she is.'

'I'm sure it is,' said Abbie.

Chapter 20

'Tell me the latest then. How are you getting on with old Arty-Crafty? Any more developments?'

'You could say so. Yes, you could definitely say things are developing very nicely. He's invited me to go for a drink tonight – not to the Market Inne, "somewhere more secluded", those were his words – and then back to his flat.'

Abbie, closeted in one of the cubicles in the ladies' toilet, recognised the husky, slightly sensual voice of Carol Pearson. She did not recognise the other voice, but Carol had many friends, or hangers-on, and always seemed to be at the centre of a crowd of laughing, loudly talking women . . . or men. Normally Abbie would have flushed the toilet and gone out to wash her hands – which, she presumed, was what the two women were doing; washing their hands and titivating their hair and make-up – but under the circumstances she decided to stay where she was. They would only stop talking when she emerged, and that could prove very embarrassing. Carol must have known about Abbie's erstwhile friendship with Art – she remembered the look the girl had given her in the theatre – but not too much about it, she hoped. She was not at all surprised to hear that Carol and Art were now keeping company.

'We spent some time together in London, of course. The Sunday night, the last night we were there, we went for a drink, then he came back to my room – I told you about that, didn't I? Well, it was inevitable what was going to happen, and it did, but I thought that might be it. You know, just a holiday fling. Mutual satisfaction, you might say, and I tell you what, Linda, it was certainly satisfying.'

'I can imagine.' There was a suggestive laugh. 'I wouldn't mind a session with him myself if I got half a chance.'

'Hey, lay off! He's mine, or it's heading that way at any rate. Like I say, I thought that would be it when we got back to college, but it seems as though he's pretty keen.'

'And you like him, do you?'

'I'm not in love with him, if that's what you mean. Yes, I like him. He's friendly and sexy and good fun to be with, and I like what he can do for me – not half! But I think we both know the score. Don't suppose anything will come of it, not permanently, but you never can tell.'

'He's been married, hasn't he?'

'So I believe. He's had a lot of women, I'm pretty sure of that. I'm under no illusions. Stands to reason, doesn't it, dishy fellow like that?'

'Mmm, yes. Didn't you say he was friendly with that woman in his English class, Abbie something or other. I can't see that myself. Not that I know her, but she seems such a shy sort of person. Rather prim and proper, really.'

Abbie stiffened, hardly daring to breathe. It was always said that eavesdroppers heard no good about themselves. She hadn't intended to eavesdrop. She didn't want to be there at all and she didn't want to hear what they were saying, but she had no choice.

'She's a wimp, if you ask me. Abbie Horsfall, that's what she's called. A real wet blanket.'

'I think she looks rather nice. Quiet, you know, but nice. That's why I'm surprised about her and Art Gillespie. If it was true.'

'It was true all right.' Abbie could hear Carol's derisive tone, then her sniggering laugh. 'She hung on to him like a leech, poor demented woman. He told me, you see, that he regarded her as a challenge. There she was in his English group, he said, positively dying for it, her tongue hanging out for him, but so stiff and starchy underneath it all, so he thought he'd string her along a bit.'

'That's not very nice.'

'Well, I don't suppose he *is* very nice, is he? Don't worry, Linda. I'm not very nice either, not when it comes to getting what I want, and at the moment I want him. Anyway, he thought he'd see if he could seduce her. He likes a challenge, does Art. Give her a good seeing-to, was what he said, or words to that effect, you know. He thought that was what she was short of.'

'Poor Abbie.'

'Poor Abbie, my arse! She deserved all she got, the silly cow.'

'Why, what did she get? Did he manage to . . .? Not that it's any of my business, and I really do feel sorry for her.'

'No, he didn't make it with her and he gave it up as a bad job. She pretended it was the time of the month – went all prudish and holier-than-thou on him. He'd taken her for a meal, set it all up very nicely, and then . . . nothing. Sweet Fanny Adams. She's lucky she didn't get raped, that's all I can say.'

'Carol, that's dreadful! I don't like the sound of that at all.'

'Well, he didn't, did he? He just gave her up as a bad job. He turned to me instead, and I didn't say no, I can tell you.'

'And you don't mind, knowing you're – well, one of a long line?'

'Why should I? I haven't exactly lived in a nunnery, you know. And that silly cow can't complain. He wined and dined her, made a fuss of her. Apparently she's been to his flat a few times.'

'So he must have liked her, in spite of what he said to you.'

'I doubt it. Anyway, never mind about her.'

'I can't help feeling sorry for her.'

'Oh, forget her. She's not worth it. Just think about me, tonight. Hey, come on, Linda. Look at the time. Our first lecture'll be starting.'

The voices died away and still Abbie stayed there in the tiny cubicle, devastated by what she had heard. She had already come round to the conclusion that Art was no good and she was well rid of him, but this was too much to bear. That she had been used in that way by an unscrupulous, pleasure-seeking man, seen as a challenge. The ultimate challenge, no doubt, if he had thought her so prim and proper, stiff and starchy; those were the words that those women had used about her, that Carol and Linda, whoever she was. Abbie thought she could put a face to her. One of Carol's hangers-on, but a good deal nicer than Carol. Linda had said she felt sorry for her, but that was the last thing Abbie wanted, people to feel sorry for her because she was naïve and unworldly and trusting. She had certainly been far too trusting, that was for sure.

She felt too stunned even to cry. Her head was thumping and her legs felt like jelly. Eventually she pulled herself together and came out of the cubicle, automatically washing her hands and drying them and glancing in the mirror, as she always did, to see if her hair was tidy. Startled brown eyes in a chalk-white face stared back at her, her normal rosiness having drained away.

She picked up her bag of books and hurried along to the library. She had a free period at the start of the afternoon, her next lecture, Education, beginning at half-past two. Half-past two came and went and still Abbie did not move. She sat in a leather armchair – there were two of them at the far end of the room, in a little alcove away from the tables and the shelves of books – not heeding the handful of students working or browsing through the books. It was there that Jean found her when the lecture came to an end.

'Abbie, what on earth are you doing here, all on your own? I've been looking everywhere for you. You've missed the

Education lecture . . . Why, whatever's the matter? Oh, Abbie love, what is it?' Jean knelt down by the armchair and took hold of Abbie's hands. There was no one to see them. The library was usually deserted on a Friday afternoon, the students, by and large, more concerned with the coming weekend than with studying.

It was then that Abbie burst into tears. 'Oh Jean, I've been such a fool. You were right all along. He's no good, he's just a philanderer. I've been such an idiot to be taken in with him, to even think . . .'

'Why, what's happened? It's Art you're talking about, isn't it? What has he done?' Abbie did not answer. She just stared at her friend, the tears rolling down her cheeks, her hands clasping Jean's tightly. 'I always suspected he was two-faced, to say the least,' Jean went on, 'but I didn't like to blacken his name too much to you. I thought you knew what you were doing and that you were sensible enough to sort things out for yourself.' Her voice petered away as she looked at Abbie's woe-begone face. 'What is it? What has he done? Whatever it is, I can tell you he's not worth getting so upset about.'

'Oh Jean, I'll never be able to look anybody in the face again. I heard that Carol Pearson talking about me, when I was in the loo. She was talking to that Linda she goes around with . . .'

Gradually it all poured out of her, all the misery and hurt and humiliation, and the truth, too, that she had deep down suspected all along – that Art Gillespie was an out and out cad. Jean had not asked her a great deal about the weekend in London and Abbie, trying to forget the embarrassment of it, had been relieved. She told her everything now and gradually, as she talked and talked, her tears stopped. She did not feel like weeping any more. She felt angry – with Art, with herself, with Carol – but she felt stupid, too, a complete and utter fool not to have realised all along what Art's game really was.

'He was just laughing at me, Jean,' she kept saying. 'Just trying to – what is it they say now? – to score with me. Whatever am I going to do? They'll all be laughing at me, that Carol and all her cronies, and Art. Is that how everybody sees me – as old-fashioned and prudish? I know that's what our Sandie says. "You're not with it, Mum." '

Jean smiled. 'That's what teenagers all say. My two say it to me. No, Abbie, it is not what everyone thinks about you. You've made lots of new friends here, haven't you? Come on now, haven't you?' she repeated when Abbie did not answer. Abbie nodded. 'Well, there you are then. And those friends who know you best, like I do, they love you because you're just the way you are. You're honest, Abbie, as honest as the day is long, and kind and sympathetic and friendly. And you're not old-fashioned. Never let it be said! Just look at you, for goodness' sake. You're a real fashion plate these days.'

Jean was trying to jolly her along and Abbie did smile a little. 'My clothes are a bit more fashionable now, I know. But it's inside me, isn't it, Jean? It's what I'm like inside. I know I've never been able to throw off the restraints of my upbringing – I doubt if I ever will – the way I look at things. Yes, maybe I am prim and prudish. I'm not surprised that's how people see me.'

'They don't, I tell you. Anyway, you had a damn good try at letting your hair down with Art Gillespie, didn't you, even though it didn't quite work out?' Jean grinned. 'He must've thought you were pretty hot stuff, babe, or he'd've dropped you a good deal sooner, wouldn't he?'

Abbie half-smiled. 'He might have done, I don't know. I would never have gone along with it, Jean, not the whole way, I'm sure I wouldn't. That period was a blessing in disguise.'

'Forget it,' Jean advised. 'Put it all behind you, and forget him. He's not worth it. And as for Carol Pearson, she's not worth that much.' Jean snapped her fingers together. 'A proper little trollop, she is. Just hold your head up high, Abbie love, and show them they don't worry you in the slightest. Don't let them get to you. Those two deserve one another, if you ask me. As a matter of fact, I'll tell you something else now. I wasn't going to, but the way things have worked out it's better you should know. Eric saw him just after Christmas. He was in Chelford with a young woman who was certainly not his sister. You know what he told you, that his sister was staying with him? Well, whoever she was, she was *not* his sister.'

Abbie sighed. 'Nothing surprises me, not any more. Thanks for listening anyway. I feel much better than I did. I still feel I can't face anybody, but it's the weekend. Perhaps by Monday . . .' She glanced at her watch. 'Goodness me! It's turned three o'clock. The next lecture'll have started.'

'Not to worry,' said Jean. 'We won't be missed; it's only Social Studies. And do you know what we're going to do now, you and me?' She rose to her feet. 'We're going home. Come on, get your things together and if we're quick we might be able to catch an earlier train. You're in no fit state to go to a lecture. We'll say you weren't feeling well and I was looking after you, if anybody asks. Which they won't.'

'Hadn't you better wait and tell Eric? He'll wonder where you are.' All the same, going home was a jolly good idea. Abbie stood up, gathering together her books and shoulder bag.

'I'll ring him tonight and explain. Don't worry, I won't tell him everything.'

'It doesn't matter if you do. I don't mind Eric knowing. He's nice, Jean. You're very lucky.'

'Yes, I suppose I am.' Jean grinned. 'Now, take Eric, for instance. He's old-fashioned, a bit set in his ways, you might say. But he's not bothered what people think about him. And I'm not bothered because . . . well, I love him, I suppose.' She stopped as though she had said too much. She laughed a little self-consciously. 'Come on, let's get our coats and we'll see if we can catch that train . . .'

'Are you all right, Mum?' asked Sandie as they were finishing their evening meal. It was unusual for the girl to be so solicitous about her mother's well-being, and Abbie was touched. This was the second time she had asked the question since Abbie came home.

'Yes, I'm all right, thanks, love,' she replied. 'Just a slight headache, that's all.'

'Are you sure?'

'Yes, of course I'm sure. Why?' Abbie smiled at her. 'Do I look peculiar or something?'

'No, just a bit pale. But you're very quiet. I just wondered . . . that's all.'

'That's kind of you, dear, but I'm OK, really I am. I had a headache, as I said, so that's why I decided to come home early.' She grinned roguishly at her daughter. 'Skipped a lecture actually. Isn't that dreadful?'

'Wicked, Mum.' Sandie grinned back at her. 'You're lucky you can get away with it. We can't, that's for sure. It's more like a bloomin' prison than a school.' Abbie knew this was not true. Sandie's school was quite flexible in outlook while still maintaining discipline and a high standard of work and achievement. She knew Sandie was happy there, though she had to have her little grumble now and again like all teenagers were apt to do. She was only too pleased that her daughter was talking to her in such a friendly manner.

'I suppose it's different at college, isn't it?' Sandie asked now. 'They let you do as you like, do they?'

'Not exactly, I wouldn't say that, but it's certainly a good deal more free and easy than school. Of course, we're all mature students at Chelford so that makes a difference. They can't very well treat us like kids, can they? You're very interested in college all of a sudden, Sandie. Why is that? Are you thinking you might go yourself?'

'I might.' Sandie shrugged. 'Don't know yet. Haven't decided.'

'Well, that's a change, anyway.' Abbie smiled at her. 'The last I heard, you were talking about leaving after your O-levels and getting a job.'

'Oh, I was only a kid when I said that, wasn't I?' Abbie knew Sandie would never admit she had only said it to rile her mother, but it was gratifying enough that she seemed to be changing her mind. 'I'm thinking about music college, actually. Mr Hendy says I've got the ability.'

'I'm sure you have, love,' replied Abbie. She also knew that Greg Matthews was thinking along the same lines, but she decided to make no comment about that. He was Sandie's first boyfriend – if that, indeed, was what he was; Abbie was not sure.

At all events, he would probably be the first of many. He seemed to be having a good influence on her, so Abbie had nothing to complain about. Sandie was more diligent with her piano practice now, in addition to the time the pair of them spent playing duets.

'You've improved tremendously since you started with Mr Hendy,' Abbie told her. 'I just hope it's not too much for you, with your O-levels and everything.'

''Course not. It's a doddle, Mum,' said Sandie airily. Abbie doubted it was as simple as all that, but Sandie certainly seemed to take exams and homework and piano practice in her stride, to say nothing of her leisure activities.

Simon, who had been sitting there not speaking, mainly because he was scoffing a second helping of apple pie, gave a loud sigh. 'D'you mind if I go out, Mum? I'm fed up with all this college talk. I said I'd go round to Jimmy's. He's got some new football cards and we're going to do a swap.'

'Yes, that's all right, dear. Sandie and I'll do the washing up, seeing as how you set the table for me. And I can see you've filled the coal scuttle – good lad. Take care crossing the road, won't you? I might be out when you get back, so

333

make sure you've got your key. I won't be very long though.'

'I'll be here, Si,' said Sandie. 'I'm not going out, but take your key. I don't want disturbing if I'm practising. Where are you going, Mum?' she asked as Simon went out.

'I thought I'd go round to Doreen's,' said Abbie. 'We don't often see one another since I started college. She was in London the same time as I was, and I know she'll be dying to tell me all about it.' What Abbie really wanted to do was to tell her friend of this latest revelation concerning Art Gillespie and his duplicity. She felt she owed her that. They would be going shopping tomorrow for Abbie's dress for the St Valentine's Day dinner, but there would be no time to talk then.

'You didn't see her down there, though, did you?' asked Sandie.

'No, of course not,' said Abbie. 'London's a big place, and we'd be doing different things, wouldn't we? Ours was an educational trip.'

'You didn't tell me and Simon very much about it,' said Sandie. 'Didn't you enjoy it?'

'Yes. I did enjoy myself,' said Abbie, 'but I didn't really think it would interest you all that much, mainly visiting historical buildings. You'd have been more interested in Carnaby Street or Biba, wouldn't you, love?'

'Surprised you've heard of them, Mum.'

'Oh, you'd be amazed at the things I know about.'

'You didn't see Carnaby Street? No, you'd have said, wouldn't you?'

'No, love. There was very little time for doing anything that wasn't on the schedule. We went to the theatre – I told you that – but that was all.' Abbie wondered now if she would ever have told Sandie about her friendship with Art Gillespie, if it had progressed. She knew, with a feeling of guilt and self-disgust, that she would have found it very difficult to do so. She knew, therefore, that it had been wrong, right from the start, if she felt so ashamed that she could not tell her daughter. 'Come on, Sandie,' she said quickly, jumping to her feet and starting to clear the table. 'We'll get this lot sorted, and then I'll get off to see Doreen. The roads are clear, but there might be a frost later and I don't want the car to freeze over.'

'Mum, you won't say anything to Doreen, will you?' asked Sandie as they washed up. 'You know, about Veronica, what I was telling you about her and that priest fellow.'

'No, love, of course I won't,' said Abbie. 'You told me in confidence. Still, Veronica won't be able to keep it a secret for ever, will she?'

'Your headache's gone now, has it?'

'Yes, it has, actually.' Abbie realised she was feeling much better, much brighter altogether. It was always a relief when she and Sandie were on good terms and they seemed to be at the moment, amazingly so. And it was great to be proper friends with Doreen again.

Chapter 21

'That's cool, Mum, real cool,' said Sandie. 'You look smashing, honestly you do.'

Abbie was pleased – delighted, in fact – at her daughter's reaction to her new clothes. Doreen had helped her to choose the dress that afternoon from Diana Warren's exclusive shop in the arcade near the promenade, and then, to complete the ensemble, they'd found toning shoes and an evening bag in Vernon Humpage's shoe shop. Abbie felt rather guilty, although there was really no need, as Doreen kept telling her, because she had never in her life spent so much money on clothes.

The dress was of a double-crepe fabric with a silky feel, in turquoise green; Abbie favoured greens, of any shade, knowing they suited her colouring. It had a cowl bodice which draped becomingly over her rather ample bust, a deep waistband decorated with a flower and bow of the same material, and an ankle-length wrap-over skirt. She was now regarding herself, almost with amazement, in her full-length wardrobe mirror, with Sandie agog at the change in her mother's appearance.

'You'll knock him for six, Mum,' she said now. 'He won't be able to keep his eyes off you.'

'Don't be silly, Sandie,' said her mother, a little embarrassed.

There had been a slight edge to Sandie's voice that Abbie could not help but notice. She had told her, when she returned home from town with all her shopping, where she had been and the reason for all the new 'gear'.

'I've got a date,' she had said with a laugh – best to make a joke of it, 'with your Mr Hendy. So I thought I'd better treat myself to a new frock.'

Sandie's expression had changed in an instant from one of curiosity – she had obviously been dying to see what was in all the bags – to one of wariness, almost of resentment, Abbie felt, though she told herself she was probably imagining that.

'You're going out with Mr Hendy? Why? Where are you going?'

Abbie gave a little laugh, a carefree one, she hoped, though to her ears it sounded a mite forced. 'Why? Because he's asked me, that's why. We're going to a dinner and dance at the Savoy Hotel – next Thursday, actually. He's playing the piano there, part of the time, and he asked me if I would go along as his partner. Nice of him, wasn't it?'

'Mmm. Yes, I suppose it was.' Sandie had given her an odd sort of look that she could not define.

'You don't object, do you?' Abbie wished, afterwards, she had not asked the question. After all, it was nothing whatsoever to do with Sandra who she chose to go out with.

'No, why should I mind?' Sandie gave a shrug. 'Come on, let's have a look at your dress then.' She peeped in the large carrier bag. 'Nice colour anyway. You like green, don't you, Mum?'

'Yes, I do. I'll try it on for you after tea, then you can tell me what you think.'

Simon had accepted the news of his mother's outing with his usual good-humoured indifference, and Sandie's moment of pique, or whatever it had been, seemed to have vanished by the time Abbie held her impromptu mannequin parade. When she told her mother she looked 'smashing – real cool', she certainly sounded sincere and Abbie believed her. She made a hasty exit, however, off to her youth club, refusing her mother's offer of a lift there in the car. Abbie had stopped worrying, as she had done at first, that this Methodist church and its activities that Sandie had taken such a shine to was not in their own area. It was near her father's house, where Sandie sometimes stayed the night instead of coming home, so that was a point in its favour. Besides, the girl was sixteen and maturing very quickly. Abbie knew she had to let her off her apron strings. To fuss and worry only made Sandie more resentful.

Sandie was not very pleased about her mother going out with Mr Hendy, although she was not sure why. It was making her feel all cross inside and that upset her because everything had been going so well for her. She and Greg were becoming much more friendly and she would be seeing him tonight at the Youth Club. He had started coming to the meetings on Wednesday and Saturday nights when he did not have a booking with his group, and that had been at Sandie's suggestion.

It had been after the first of their duet lessons that he had started to show more interest in her again. They had had a quarter-hour session together and found they had an excellent rapport – on the keyboard, that was – but Sandie was sure they would get on in other ways as well, if only Greg could see it. He must have hung around while she had the rest of her lesson, because when she came out he was there waiting for her, leaning on the handlebars of his bike, as he had been that first time.

'We didn't arrange a practice time, did we?' he began, and Sandie had found it hard not to keep the excitement out of her voice as she replied.

'No, we didn't.' She hoped she sounded casual enough. Since that dance – the occasion of the group's debut – it had seemed as though he wasn't bothered about her. She mustn't let him imagine she was easy to get. 'Why, what do you suggest?'

'Do you think I could come round to your house

sometime? Or would your mother object?'

'No, why should she? She knows we've got to practise together, doesn't she?'

'Yes, of course, but to be quite honest, that's why I haven't seen you very much lately, Sandie. I wanted to see you, but I thought your mother might not like it. She came to pick you up after that dance, didn't she, and – well, you are younger than me.'

'Not all that much! I'm sixteen now, and you're only seventeen. Anyway,' Sandie shrugged, 'I thought you didn't want anything to do with me. You invited me to that dance, then I found you'd invited loads of other girls as well.'

'Not loads. Only Paula, and I've known her for ages, and one or two others. It was only because I wanted a good crowd there for our first performance.'

'And it was great, Greg, really it was.' Sandie found herself thawing, in fact she was feeling all warm inside as they began to wheel their bicycles along the pavement.

'Good, I'm glad you thought so. We've had a few more bookings since then. I do want to go on seeing you, Sandie. When Duncan mentioned the duet lessons it seemed like fate somehow. So, can I come round to your place then? What about Sunday afternoon?'

And that was how their friendship had started. That was all it was at the moment, a friendship, but she knew he liked her a lot and she knew that some of the other girls were quite jealous of her. She found she could chat to him easily about all sorts of things, and decided to tell him about her mother and Mr Hendy.

'Guess what?' she said to him later that evening. They were sitting drinking lemonade after a gruelling game of table tennis. 'My mum's got a date with Duncan.' She called him Duncan when speaking of him to Greg, but never to his face. 'What d'you think about that? I was flabbergasted when she told me. Honestly, can you believe it?'

'Yes, I can, actually,' said Greg. 'Your mum's a very

attractive lady so I'm not surprised at all. And I'm very pleased. It's high time Duncan started looking around. He's been on his own for ages. I know my parents have told him so more than once.'

'What d'you mean, looking around?' Sandie's voice was sharp and Greg frowned a little.

'You know – started thinking about getting married again. My mother says a lot of women would jump at the chance.'

'Well, my mum wouldn't, I can tell you that. She'd never get married again, she said so. She loved my father too much.' She had never actually said so to Sandie, but Sandie had heard her saying something of the sort to Doreen, how there would never be anybody else for her but Peter. It was ages ago, admittedly, when Sandie was only a little girl. All the same, the whole idea of her mother ever marrying again was preposterous.

'Hey, steady on.' Greg put a hand on her arm. 'What's eating you? I never said they were going to get married. I only said . . .'

'Yes, you did. You said it was time Duncan got married again. You said . . .'

'You're twisting things, Sandie. I only said he'd been on his own a long time, which he has. What's the matter anyway? It sounds as though you don't like the idea of your mum going out with him. I would have thought you'd have been pleased for her.'

'Well, yes, I am, really. It was just a surprise, that's all.'

Sandie knew she must try to sound agreeable, as though she didn't mind about it, in front of Greg. She wanted him to think well of her because she did like him very much indeed. He always walked her back to her grandad's house when she stayed the night there, and the last time, when he had said goodnight to her at the gate, he had kissed her. Just a quick kiss it had been, on the side of her mouth, but it was a start. It had left her wanting much more, but she knew she must show the best side of herself and not appear peevish or grudging, or Greg might well decide he didn't like her very much after all. There were plenty of other girls – she suspected Paula was one of them and Marcia another – who would be only too happy to encourage Greg Matthews to look their way.

'Where are they going anyway, your mum and Duncan?' Greg asked now.

'Oh, to some dinner and dance or other,' replied Sandie, sounding as though it couldn't matter less, and then, with a shade more enthusiasm, 'I think it's at the Savoy Hotel – next Thursday,' she said. 'Duncan's playing the piano there.'

'St Valentine's Day?'

'Yes, it is actually. Why?'

'My parents'll be there as well,' said Greg. 'It's the local businessmen's club that my dad belongs to. They always have a do on St Valentine's Day. Fancy that. Your mum will be able to meet my mum and dad.'

'Yeah, great.' Sandie was a little in awe of Greg's father although his mother was nice enough. She had made her very welcome last Sunday afternoon, when she had been there to play duets; but his father, a chartered accountant – far more interested in facts and figures than in music and the arts, Greg had told her – had seemed rather aloof and unfriendly. 'It'll be nice for her to meet some different people,' she said now, trying to sound more gracious. 'She doesn't go out much, except to college or to see her friend, Doreen. Look, the table's free again. D'you fancy another game?'

'No, not really. Paula's over there. Perhaps she'll play with you. I'll go and have a chat to some of the lads. See you later.'

Oh dear! She gazed after him thoughtfully. Greg must have thought she was being nasty and peevish, saying that about her mother and Duncan, although she was sure she hadn't said anything too terrible and anyway, she couldn't help how she felt. Greg was such a nice lad though. He always saw the best in people and never said anything wrong about anyone. She did so want him to go on liking her. She would have to try extra hard; later on tonight, perhaps, when the dancing started.

Looking back on it afterwards, Abbie realised she had not enjoyed herself so much for ages. She had, if she were honest, been a little nervous at the thought of going to a smart social occasion with a man she did not know very well, and mixing with people who might well be much more sophisticated and grand than she was. Fortunately, the experience had turned out to be a happy one. The folk there, the ones she met at any rate, were very charming and friendly, and welcomed her into their midst without any restraints.

Her dress, too, was a success, she felt. It was a semi-formal affair, but most of the men had opted for evening suits and the ladies for long dresses. Abbie felt quietly confident, knowing she looked good.

'You look very nice,' Duncan had said when he came to call for her, smiling at her warmly and, she could tell, with a touch of admiration in his eyes. 'That is one of my favourite colours. It suits you, Abbie.' He had not told her she looked lovely or beautiful – he was a quiet, somewhat reserved man and she knew already that that would not have been his way with someone he did not yet know very well – but it was sufficient to give her the boost of self-confidence she needed. She had vowed to herself that she would put all thoughts of Art Gillespie right out of her mind, but she could not help comparing Duncan's modest compliment on her appearance with what she guessed would have been Art's reaction. 'Wow! You look ravishing,' or words to that effect, he would have said, undressing her metaphorically as he looked her up and down. But she had learned, to her cost, that Art's words were shallow and meaningless – downright lies, many of them – and she wondered now how she could ever have been taken in by them.

As for Duncan, he looked handsome in his evening suit, very dignified and suave, but of course she knew she could not tell him so. When they arrived at the Savoy Hotel on the North Promenade, early because of Duncan's musical commitment, he introduced her at once to Hazel and Alan Matthews, Greg's parents. Sandie had already told her that they would be there. So Sandie and Greg must have been discussing her 'date' with Duncan, she realised. She wondered what they had said about it. Sandie had not mentioned it again until this evening when she had said, rather tersely, 'Have a nice time, Mum,' before disappearing upstairs to do her homework. But she had, at least, agreed to look after Simon in her mother's absence and the pair of them had washed up their own tea things with a fairly good grace whilst Abbie got ready.

She had seen Hazel Matthews before, at the Musical Festival, although the two women, on that occasion, had done nothing more than nod and smile at each other. Hazel, now, took her under her wing immediately and Abbie thought what a pleasant and likeable woman she was, very much like her son in appearance with the same dark hair, though in her case very slightly greying, and friendly blue eyes. She was much shorter than Greg and inclined towards plumpness. He obviously took after his father with regard to his height and build, both of them being tall and slender. Abbie found, however, that she did not warm to Mr Matthews – or Alan, as Duncan had introduced him – the way she did to his wife. He seemed to be weighing her up, but she guessed that was what he did with everyone he met, not just herself. She knew he was an accountant, used to assessing clients and their propensities. At all events, he was hospitable enough, settling the two women at a small table and hurrying off to get them each a drink whilst Duncan seated himself at the grand piano.

The sweet sherry and the soothing music which Duncan was playing helped Abbie to relax into her surroundings.

Crowds of folk mingled around, some of them stopping at the Matthews' table where they were introduced to Abbie, whilst Duncan played a selection of light music by Ivor Novello, Cole Porter, Jerome Kern. Easy to listen to, gentle and melodious tunes rippling from his fingertips like a smoothly flowing stream.

'Versatile, isn't he?' said Hazel, smiling approvingly. 'It never ceases to amaze me how Duncan can turn his hand to anything – this sort of music or the classical composers, or jazz. Whatever it is, he plays so professionally. Have you ever heard him play Chopin, Abbie? Now, that is quite something.'

'No, I haven't,' replied Abbie. 'As a matter of fact, this is the first time I've heard him play anything at all. I don't know him very well. We only met because he's my daughter's music teacher . . . but you know that, of course, don't you?'

'Indeed we do,' replied Hazel. 'Sandie is a lovely girl, Abbie. You must be very proud of her. So polite and respectful, isn't she?'

'Some of the time.' Abbie grinned. Sandie was obviously trying to create a good impression and who could blame her, but those were not adjectives she would have chosen to describe her daughter. It was gratifying to know that that was how she appeared to others. 'She's like a lot of teenagers, I dare say. She can be difficult, but yes, I do feel proud of her sometimes.'

'She's a credit to you.'

'Thank you. And your son, Gregory, is a credit to you. I was very impressed when I met him. Duncan,' she still felt a little awkward at using his name, 'assured me I had no need to worry about the two of them being together – you know, playing duets. He said Greg was very trustworthy, that I need have no fear about him leading her astray.'

'I should hope not, indeed,' said Alan Matthews sharply. 'My son knows how to behave himself.'

'I'm sure he does, Mr Matthews, er, Alan,' said Abbie

hastily. Oh dear! Whatever had she said? She hoped she hadn't gone and put her foot in it. 'I didn't mean to suggest otherwise.'

'Of course you didn't,' said Hazel in a placatory tone. She smiled sympathetically at Abbie. 'I know exactly what you meant. It's a great responsibility bringing up a daughter, more so sometimes than a son. You're bound to be concerned about them, when they start getting interested in boys . . . and everything. I must admit I was relieved when Alison – that's our daughter – was happily married and settled down. Not that I wanted to lose her, but she'd had quite a few boyfriends, and . . . well, you worry sometimes, don't you?'

'Oh, I didn't realise you had a daughter as well?'

'Yes, there are just the two of them, Alison and Gregory. Alison's six years older than Greg. She has a little girl now – Susan. She's nearly twelve months old.'

'So you're grandparents,' said Abbie. 'That's nice.'

'Yes, it is nice, isn't it, Alan?' Hazel looked meaningfully at her husband who had gone rather quiet. 'Susan's a lovely child, isn't she?'

He nodded unsmilingly. 'Yes, she is. Alison married too early for my liking, though. She was only twenty-one; far too young, in my opinion. I only hope Gregory has the good sense not to do the same thing. We have high hopes for that boy, Abbie. I expect Duncan has told you, hasn't he, that Gregory has ambitions to go to music college. There's a very good one in Manchester, I believe. Duncan has every confidence he will get a place there.'

'Yes, I did know about that,' replied Abbie. 'Your son is a very accomplished pianist. I'm sure he will be successful in whatever he decides to do.' She was determined, however, not to be intimidated by the man. And she, too, had aspirations for her daughter. 'I'm hoping Sandra may go to college as well,' she went on. 'Music college, maybe. It's early days yet for her to make a decision. She's certainly

345

improved, though, since she's been with Duncan. He's quite an inspiration to them, isn't he?'

Alan nodded again, a little more agreeably this time. 'He's a good chap all round, is Duncan. We've known him for years, haven't we, Hazel?'

'Yes, indeed, both he and Sybil, of course. That was a tragedy, but we're pleased to see he's picking up the pieces at last and moving on. It's taken a while, but he's getting there. He talks a lot about you, Abbie. More than he has about anyone. He's a reticent sort of man, quite cautious, really, but you seem to have touched a spark in him.'

'I've only met him on a few occasions,' replied Abbie, a little discomfited. 'I like him, of course. He's such a pleasant man, you can't help but like him. But I don't really know him all that well.'

'It's a start,' said Hazel, 'and a propitious one, I'm sure. We certainly hope we'll be seeing you again, Abbie. You and Duncan must both come and have a meal with us before long, mustn't they, Alan?'

'A splendid idea,' said Alan. He sounded, to Abbie's surprise, as though he meant it. 'We would love to have you. We'll sort something out later with Duncan. Listen to him now,' he chuckled. 'He's well into the pop scene, or whatever they call it, is old Duncan.'

Duncan was now playing one of Frank Ifield's hit songs, 'I Remember You – oo' which he followed with a jazzed-up rendition of 'Return To Sender'. Abbie thought that was one of Elvis Presley's songs although she wasn't well up in what they called the Top Twenty or the Hit Parade. Neither, it appeared, was Alan, although his wife seemed a little more knowledgeable. Abbie guessed it was something of an act with him; that he was professing to have no interest whatsoever in such an inconsequential subject as music, be it pop or classical, except, of course, with regard to his son's talent. This he recognised, at the same time making it clear that his own mind was a much more factual one – and, therefore, superior? – dealing with the statistics and actualities of life rather than the creative arts which were, he deemed, purely recreational. Some of this Abbie gathered that first evening, more of it later as she got to know him better.

'Not that it means much to me,' he said now, in a dismissive tone, with regard to Duncan's recital. 'They all sound alike, these pop tunes, or whatever they call them. I can tell the difference between those and the classical stuff though, and I'll tell you something.' He actually smiled and Abbie thought how much more pleasant he looked when he did so. He leaned across the table, addressing Abbie in a confidential tone. 'What they were playing the other day, our Greg and your girl Sandie, well if that was Bach or Beethoven I'll eat my hat.' He gave a chuckle. 'Talk about being led astray – and I know you didn't mean anything by your remark earlier, Abbie, please don't think I don't under- stand, because I do. As Hazel told you, we've got a daughter of our own. Anyway, I don't know who was leading whom astray with this duet playing, but they were fairly making the place shake. If that was what Duncan had told them to practise, then I'm a Dutchman!'

Hazel smiled. 'Yes, I heard them too. It was the Telstar theme they were playing. You know, The Tornados have had a hit with it.'

'There you are, you see – my wife knows far more about it than I do. Quite an expert on the pop scene, is Hazel.' Alan's tone was jocular, though just the slightest bit contemptuous.

Hazel ignored him. 'They were playing it very well, I thought. Then they started on that "Venus in Blue Jeans" tune. I thought I'd let them have their fun. They'd already done their serious practice; I recognised one of Greig's dances, and something by Schubert, I think.'

'You play yourself, do you?' asked Abbie.

'I used to, ages ago, but I'm afraid I've lost much of my technique over the years.'

'It's the same with me,' said Abbie. 'You do lose it if you

347

don't keep up with the practice, don't you? And as you get older there just isn't the time, unless you're doing it for a living, of course. Yes, I agree with you about the pop music. I don't suppose it can do any harm, can it? I've been in two minds whether to say something to Sandie when I've heard her playing other things, but it would only make matters worse, knowing Sandie. Anyway, your Gregory has his group, hasn't he? You approve of that, do you?'

'Yes, I don't mind,' replied Hazel. 'It's just a few lads having a bit of harmless fun, from what I can tell.'

'Sandie says they're very good.'

'Yes, maybe they are. I've heard them practising, and I must admit I was quite impressed. So long as it doesn't interfere with Greg's serious studies. The other lads are not music students in the way Gregory is, you see. I gather it's just a hobby with them. But they're getting a few bookings here and there, so they can't be so bad.'

'It just sounds like a hideous din to me,' said Alan. 'It doesn't seem to be affecting Gregory's studies, though – his schoolwork and his piano playing. If it did I'd soon have something to say.'

'Is Duncan still in the dark about it?' asked Abbie. 'I mean, Sandie insisted that I mustn't say anything, that Mr Hendy had no idea about the group and Greg didn't want him to know.'

Hazel grinned. 'There's not much that Duncan doesn't know. He's pretty shrewd. Yes, he knows about it, not from our telling, I can assure you, but he's found out somehow. Greg thinks he still doesn't know, but I expect the truth will come to light soon. Duncan won't mind – well, listen to him; he's no room to talk, has he? – so long as this group doesn't start getting too important. Lots of jazz musicians have had a classical training anyway, or so Greg tells me. Oh, I think things are moving. They're starting to go into dinner. You'll be sitting with us, of course, you and Duncan. Here he comes, see?'

Duncan took Abbie's arm as they entered the elegant dining room. The tables seated eight, so there were two other couples with them as well as the Matthewses. Another accountant, Abbie gathered from the conversation, and an estate agent, both with their wives, or Abbie presumed they were their wives; but it was Duncan, on one side of her, and Alan on the other with whom she conversed most of the time.

The meal was superb. It consisted of six courses – hors d'oeuvres, soup, poached salmon, sorbet, roast turkey, and a delicious raspberry meringue – more courses than Abbie had ever experienced at a dinner, but the helpings were of a moderate size and she enjoyed it all without feeling too greedy. At the end of the meal the waiters came round with coffee and dishes of chocolate mints.

'Excuse me, won't you?' said Duncan. 'I'll see you later. Duty calls.'

He took his place at the piano – an upright piano this time, at the end of the room – and accompanied the portly baritone who sang a sentimental song for the benefit of the ladies who were present. It was one which Abbie had not heard before, but which, Hazel whispered, was always sung on this occasion, consisting of flowery phrases extolling the beauty and goodness of the ladies. 'And here's to their health in a song,' the baritone warbled at the end of each verse whilst the gentlemen stood and raised their glasses of champagne, doing homage to their wives or lady friends. She was thoroughly enjoying the whole evening and the ambience of the surroundings, but Abbie could not help feeling that this was a trifle mawkish. 'Yuck!' was what Sandie would have said, and Abbie wondered, fleetingly, how many of these men were, indeed, with their wives. Most of them, she decided charitably, but how well were they getting on with them after what must be many years of marriage? She guessed she was one of the youngest women present. Many of the guests were quite middle-aged or elderly. Hazel and

Alan were fiftyish, about the same age as Duncan. With those two it seemed to be a case of opposites being attracted; they obviously got on well together in spite of their differences.

She did not doubt the sincerity of Duncan when he returned to the table, raising his glass to her in his own private toast. 'To us,' he said quietly. 'To you and me, Abbie. Thank you for coming. I've enjoyed it far more than I can say. It has made such a difference to the evening, having you with me.'

'Yes, to us, Duncan,' she replied, though a little diffidently. She did not want to appear too eager – look what a mess she had made of things with Art Gillespie. The thought, unbidden, entered her mind that she must not give him the impression she was too keen. But she felt, to her surprise, that this could well be the start of something; something very good. 'Thank you for inviting me,' she said, smiling at him. 'I've enjoyed it too, very much.'

'And the night is still young,' he whispered, resting his hand lightly upon hers. He soon withdrew it, but not before Hazel had noticed and grinned knowingly at Abbie. She smiled back with an attempt at nonchalance. She was well aware that Hazel and Alan, particularly Hazel, might well be indulging in a little match-making, hoping that she and Duncan might become more than just friends.

At the start of the evening, Abbie could not have said they were close friends, just acquaintances who had met a few times and found their meetings agreeable. By the time Duncan drove her home, however, at just turned midnight, she felt they were very good friends indeed. It was as though she had known him for ages; they were able to talk together freely and were finding more and more things they had in common. There was an easiness between them, a compatibility that was something Abbie had not experienced with anyone since Peter died.

It had been like that when she first met Peter, she

350

reminisced later that night as she lay, wide-awake, in her bed. She had been a shy and awkward girl, Peter not much more experienced either in the ways of the world, when they had first met in the Palace ballroom in the early years of the war; but they had recognised in each other that affinity, that twinning of kindred spirits. Circumstances had separated them for a couple of years, but it had been even more apparent, when they had met again at the RAF camp in Norfolk, that they belonged together.

There could never be anyone else for her but Peter. So she had told Doreen, and others, and so she had convinced herself . . . until now. It was not exactly the same, of course. She knew she would never again experience that blissful feeling of being head over heels in love or the rapture she had known in Peter's embrace. She was not imagining for one moment that she had fallen in love with Duncan, or he with her. They were both older and supposedly wiser, although a passing thought of her involvement with Art Gillespie reminded her that she had been far from wise just lately. These things took time when you were older. You could not go rushing headlong into a romantic relationship as you might have done when you were younger. But all the signs were there that this friendship might develop.

Duncan's commitment had ended with his playing of the song to the ladies, and he was free to devote the rest of the evening to her, which he did with great pleasure. He danced with her several times. The dances were mainly traditional ones, such as the waltz and the slow foxtrot, but there was a fifteen-minute session of rock and roll as well, in which Abbie danced with a verve and enjoyment that surprised even her. Duncan, too, was not so serious-minded as he appeared to be on a first acquaintance, but was ready to let his hair down with the best of them.

He had kissed her lightly on the cheek, just a friendly kiss, when he stopped the car outside her house. She did not invite him in for a nightcap as she would like to have done. It was late and she had to go to college in the morning and, she guessed, he would have a teaching appointment. Besides, it might have seemed too presumptuous; she did not want him to think she was rushing things.

'Goodnight, Abbie. Thank you for a lovely evening,' he said. 'I'll see you next week then? I'll come and pick you up to go to Alan and Hazel's. I think she said seven o'clock, but I'll give you a ring before then. Goodnight, my dear.'

'Goodnight, Duncan,' she replied. 'And thank you, too. It's been lovely.'

It had, indeed, been a lovely, lovely evening.

She had but a few hours' sleep before the alarm clock rudely awakened her. Then it was downstairs for a hurried breakfast, a quick goodbye to the children, then the usual rush for the train. There had been little time to converse with Sandie and Simon at the breakfast table, but that was nothing unusual. Sandie, in particular, wandered around in a zombie-like state in the morning. But at least she had managed to say, 'Did you have a good time, Mum?' and Abbie had told her that she had. 'Good, that's great.' The girl's rejoinder had been laconic, but that was only to be expected so early in the morning.

Abbie could not quite make up her mind, however, on the morning following the St Valentine's dance, and on subsequent occasions, whether she was imagining the indifference, verging on hostility, which appeared on her daughter's face and was to be heard in her tone of voice whenever Duncan Hendy was mentioned. After all, why should it matter to Sandie? But Abbie had a feeling that it did matter; that it mattered quite a lot.

Chapter 22

Abbie and Duncan's next outing was to the Matthewses' home, the week following the dance, where Hazel entertained them to a delightful meal; she was well known, apparently, for her expertise in the kitchen. Abbie commented on the fact that Greg was not dining with them, and Hazel said he was out somewhere practising with his group. Duncan seemed to be well aware of his star pupil's alternative interest now, and not to mind.

Sandie and Simon were at home on their own. Abbie had cooked them one of their favourite dishes of spaghetti bolognese and they had dined alone because, she told them, she would eating later, with Duncan, at the home of Greg's parents. Simon had not seemed to mind, but there had been a slight narrowing of her eyes and fleeting look of animosity on Sandie's face.

As she ate the succulent duck in orange sauce and the tempting selection of vegetables and sauté potatoes Abbie pondered on the possibility of a return visit to her home for the Matthewses, and Duncan, of course. She knew that nothing she cooked could come up to the standard of this delicious dish, but that was not her chief concern. Should she invite Greg as well, she wondered, and, with her children present, make it a more family occasion? Or should it be a more intimate meal, just for the four of them, as this one was? If they were all invited it might be a way of bringing Sandie round from whatever it was that was troubling her.

Abbie could not understand the girl's resentment, for that was what it seemed to be, that she resented her mother's friendship with Duncan. Why on earth should she feel like that? It wasn't as if Sandie herself was being neglected in any way, and her father had been dead for ages. Abbie guessed that this must be at the root of the problem. Sandie had always been her Daddy's girl. Sometimes, Abbie had felt excluded from the close bond between the two of them, and it had taken the little girl, who had been just eight years old, a very long time to get over her father's death. And here was Abbie, showing an interest in another man.

Abbie's thoughts turned again to Art Gillespie. How would Sandra have reacted, she wondered, if *that* relationship had continued? Very unfavourably, no doubt, and who could have blamed her? Art Gillespie was a man who would never have been accepted, in any way, into her family life, whereas Sandie knew Duncan and she liked him. He was her music teacher, for goodness' sake! Why, then, should there be any problem?

'You're very quiet, Abbie,' said Duncan, at her side. 'I'm sorry, my dear. You don't know the people we are talking about, do you? It was rather rude of us, I dare say.' Engrossed in her own thoughts, Abbie had only been half-listening to the conversation going on around her, about some mutual friends of Duncan and of the Matthewses who were, at the present moment, enjoying a cruise of the Greek islands.

'Not at all,' she said now, smiling at him, then at Hazel and Alan. 'I'm quiet only because I am enjoying this delicious duckling so much – I'm savouring every mouthful, Hazel – and I was thinking to myself how nice it all sounded – the Greek islands, and then mainland Greece and Athens. I've only been abroad once,' she continued, trying to make up for her silence, 'when the children were small and when Peter was alive. We went to Brittany. The children loved it at Dinard, mainly because of the sand and the sea, of course.

After Peter died I could never pluck up the courage, some-how, to take them abroad on my own. And the sand and the sea at Blackpool were just as appealing to them.' She laughed. 'It was quite useful, when we were in Norfolk, having a father who lived at the seaside.'

'It's the same with us, isn't it, Hazel?' said Alan. 'We're never short of visitors in the summer – my brother and his family, and Hazel's sister. It's a nice cheap holiday for them. Don't get me wrong, though, we love having them.'

'And where do *you* go for your holidays?' Abbie asked them.

She gathered that Duncan had not been away very much since his wife died, but Hazel and Alan told her they usually went touring in the car, to the Scottish Highlands, the Lake District or the Welsh border country. Greg had always accompanied them, his mother said, until last year when he had gone camping with a group of friends. 'So there's just Alan and me now,' she commented. 'That's the end of our family holidays, I suppose. There comes a time when you have to let your children go their own way, don't you, Abbie? Especially when it comes to holidays.'

'Er . . . yes, that's true,' replied Abbie. Since they had been living in Blackpool she had not even thought about holidays. It had not seemed necessary with the town and all its attractions still proving something of a novelty, to the children at least. But the time would come when the subject of holidays would inevitably crop up, and she could not see Sandie – or Simon, for that matter – wanting to fit in with her plans. Her children would want to pursue their own interests without their mother's involvement – or what they might term interference.

These thoughts returned to Abbie later that evening after she had said goodnight to Duncan. Again he had kissed her on the cheek and again she had made the decision not to invite him into her home. The thought had occurred to her and it was very appealing, then she had decided . . . not yet;

next time, maybe. Her courage had failed her. Sandie and Simon might still be up, or if not up, then still awake. What might they think? But did it really matter what they thought, she asked herself as she sat by the dwindling embers of the fire, contemplating the delightful evening she had just spent in Duncan's company. She had her own life to lead. Surely it was time for her to be thinking about herself, to be looking forward to the time – a long time ahead though it might be – when her children had left home. It was unlikely that when Sandra or Simon wanted to leave home and get married or for some other reason, they would think, 'I can't do that; Mum will be left on her own.' Nor would she want them to. They had their own lives to lead, just as she did.

There was her teaching career to look forward to, of course. That had been her way of ensuring she had something worthwhile to do in the years that lay ahead, and she did not regret her decision. Nevertheless, no matter how occupied she might be or how fulfilled in her chosen career, there would come a time when she was living alone. It was early days yet, as far as Duncan was concerned – too early, maybe, to be thinking this way, but she liked Duncan, she liked him a lot. She was growing fond of him as she knew he was of her. Moreover, she was not deluding herself this time as she had been with Art Gillespie. This time it could be 'for real', as Sandie might say. And as for Sandie . . . Abbie smiled ruefully. If and when something should come of this, Sandie would just have to get used to the idea.

Abbie was well aware that Greg might be considered to be Sandie's boyfriend now, rather than just someone with whom she played duets. All the signs were there; her daughter's air of excitement, which was hard to disguise, whenever he came round for their piano practice, and her tetchiness with Simon and slight blush when he teased her about Greg. Abbie knew she saw him at other times, too. He had joined her youth club, apparently, and they had been to the cinema together more than once.

Abbie was not unduly concerned, however, about Greg. She felt she could trust him with her daughter. Duncan had told her so, and his parents were a very honest and upright couple who, Abbie felt sure, would have instilled the concept of proper behaviour into their son. Not that sons – or daughters, either – always behaved according to the dictates of their parents. She knew this, but she also knew there was little she could do about it except hope and pray that they behaved themselves; you could not watch over them every minute of every day.

She and Duncan were seeing one another fairly regularly now. At his request she had accompanied him on several of his organ-playing engagements at local hotels, helping him to sort out his music – although he played by ear a lot of the time – and enjoying a drink and a snack supper with him in the interval. On the second occasion, a get-together for the more senior citizens which had finished quite early, she had plucked up courage to invite him in for a nightcap and he had gladly accepted. She had been on tenterhooks because, although Sandie and Simon had both gone to bed, she did not know whether or not they were asleep. She told herself she was being stupid – still one of Sandie's favourite words – to worry about what the children might think. It was her own home and she had the right, therefore, to invite into it anyone she wished. It wasn't as if she and Duncan were behaving improperly in any way; even if they did, then it was still no business of Sandie or Simon.

Duncan had, indeed, been a little more amorous that night. He had kissed her as they sat together on the settee, drinking coffee and listening to a record of Mozart's Clarinet Concerto which, they had discovered, was a favourite of both of them.

'We get on well together, don't we?' he had said. 'I am more and more amazed at the things we have in common. It's good, isn't it? You think so, don't you, Abbie?' She had agreed that she did. 'And I would like, so much, to go on

357

seeing you. This is the first time since Sybil died that I have felt like this. You have helped me to put the past behind me. I feel I can look forward, now, to the future, and I would very much like you to be part of that future. I won't rush you, of course, I think you are feeling as I do, aren't you?'

'Yes,' Abbie replied. 'I enjoy being with you, Duncan. And for me, too, it's the first time since Peter died that I have wanted to . . . to go on seeing someone.' Art Gillespie did not count; she realised now that he never had. 'Let's just see how things go, shall we? I have the children to consider, and my teacher-training course. When I started that I had no thought in my mind of anything like this.' She knew she must choose her words carefully. Duncan had not said he wanted to marry her, just that he would like her to be part of his future. That could mean quite a few different things, but with someone as worthy and honourable as Duncan she felt sure that it would lead, eventually, to marriage. The thought was very pleasing, but she must not take anything for granted.

'I'm very much in favour of your teaching course,' he told her. 'It's one more thing we have in common, isn't it? I'm all for women having their own careers, if that is what they want, in this day and age. Times are changing, Abbie. Sybil didn't go out to work after we married, but her health was never too good. And I guess you stayed at home, didn't you, when you were first married?'

'Yes, until Simon started school, then I took a part-time job as a dental receptionist. Peter didn't entirely agree with it; he was one of the old school who thought he should be the sole breadwinner. But he died the following year, so of course I kept on working then – longer hours, too. It was a question of needs must, but my parents-in-law were very good to me, looking after the children for me when it was necessary. And now – well, the children are old enough to do more for themselves. I worried at first about how my college course might affect them, but they seem to have adjusted to it pretty well. I think it has done Sandie good to assume a bit more responsibility. She can be very difficult at times.' Abbie hesitated. There was something she knew she must say to Duncan before their friendship went any further, but again, she needed to choose her words with care.

'In fact, I'm rather concerned about the way Sandie's reacting just lately,' she went on. 'Since I started seeing you she's been odd – resentful, almost.' Abbie knew she had to warn Duncan that it might not be all plain sailing with Sandie, but it was something that was hard to explain without sounding rude.

'You mean she resents you being friendly with me?' Duncan sounded surprised. 'I can't honestly say I've noticed any difference in her attitude towards me. She's still the same, perfectly polite and well-behaved at her lessons. Rather too polite, maybe. I've told her she can call me Duncan, but she doesn't. She seems a very well-adjusted sort of girl to me. Are you sure you're not imagining it, Abbie?'

'No, I'm sure I'm not.'

'I haven't said anything to her about our friendship, yours and mine, but she's well aware of it; she must be. She's seen me come to call for you, and she hasn't seemed to object.'

'Not to you, maybe.'

'Why? What has she said?'

'Nothing. That's just it; she's not said anything. It's just the way she looks at me, almost as though she hates me at times. Perhaps that's a little strong. But it's as though she's weighing up the situation and . . . and not really approving of it. That's why I hesitated, Duncan, about inviting you to come here, because of Sandie. I wouldn't want her to be rude to you.'

'I can assure you she isn't rude to me, not in the slightest.' Duncan smiled. 'I can't help thinking you're overreacting, my dear. Teenage girls are renowned for their sulks, aren't they? I dare say it's something to do with her age. How is she getting on with Greg? I know their duet playing is coming on nicely. I'll be entering them for the duet class in the next Blackpool Festival, as well as their solo classes. What about their friendship? Do I detect something a little more than piano playing going on?'

Abbie gave a rueful smile. 'I rather think so. Not that Sandie has said anything about it to me. I've told you; she's rather odd just lately, although she was never one to confide in me overmuch. I think she's keen on Greg though. All the signs are there. She can't help giving herself away.'

'And you don't mind?'

'No, I don't mind. I think he's a very nice sort of lad, as you told me he was. So long as their friendship doesn't interfere with her schoolwork – she has her O-levels this summer – or her next music exam. It's Grade Eight next time, isn't it?'

'Yes. She's done very well – she's a talented girl. It wasn't my intention to throw them together, Abbie. I hope you don't think I was matchmaking.'

'Of course not. It would have happened anyway. He had already invited her to one of his concerts. They're very young though. I don't imagine for one moment that Greg will be her one and only boyfriend. They seem to play the field much more now than they did when we were younger.'

'Yes, indeed,' replied Duncan. 'Sybil was only my second girlfriend. I met her when I was twenty and we were courting for more than two years before we got married – that was the year before the war started.' Abbie had learned previously that he had been with the Eighth Army, serving with 'Monty' in the Desert War, and had come through it unscathed. 'I expect it was the same with you and Peter. Didn't you tell me he was your first boyfriend?'

'Yes, the one and only,' said Abbie. There had been Jim Webster, of course. She had been engaged to him, briefly, when she had thought Peter was dead, but it was too complicated a story to tell Duncan now. All he knew was that Peter had been missing, believed killed, and that they had married after the war. Sometime, maybe, she would tell him; no doubt there would be lots of things they would find out about one another. 'I'm afraid my mother kept me very much under her thumb,' she continued. 'I'd never been out with a boy until I met Peter. Goodness knows what my mother would have said about the way youngsters carry on nowadays.'

Duncan laughed. 'That's what parents – and grandparents – have always said about the next generation. "Whatever is the world coming to?"'

'I think we try to be a little more tolerant today about what the younger generation get up to,' Abbie replied. 'I try to understand Sandie, though it's hard at times. Anyway, while she has an interest of her own – namely Greg Matthews – perhaps it will help to take her mind off you and me.'

'That's true.' Duncan smiled. 'But I've told you – she's been perfectly normal with me. I can't help thinking you're being over-sensitive, Abbie.'

But as the weeks went by Abbie knew she was not imagining Sandie's antagonism. It took the form of a studied indifference, rather than out and out hostility. She was not difficult all the time; only on the occasions when she knew her mother and Duncan were seeing one another.

It was towards the end of April when Abbie finally got round to inviting Duncan, and Hazel and Alan Matthews, to have a meal at her home. She chose a Saturday evening when Sandie and Greg were at a Youth Club dance and Simon was staying with his grandparents, Lily and Frank, after going to the football match with his grandad in the afternoon. She wondered how she could ever have imagined she could include the children in a family meal. There would have been too much friction, she had decided; too many people at variance with one another. And yet she knew, deep down, that the only problem was Sandie. She was the only one who would have been likely to create an atmosphere of tension, and that was something Abbie was not prepared to risk. She knew, however, that before long facts would have to be faced. Sandie would have to acknowledge the friendship between her mother and Duncan Hendy. It was a friendship which was steadily growing and which, no matter how much the girl resented it, was not going to go away.

'I wish I could be a fly on the wall tonight,' Greg remarked to Sandie as they sat at the side of the church hall drinking their lemonade. They had just finished an energetic session of the Gay Gordons and were gasping for refreshment. Lemonade was the strongest beverage on offer at the Youth Club dance, not only because the majority of the young people there were under the age of eighteen, but because this was a Methodist organisation.

'Why?' asked Sandie, with that touch of asperity Greg had noticed was always evident whenever there was any mention of her mother and Duncan.

Greg gave an easy laugh, trying to pretend he was not aware of her abrasiveness. 'Because they'll be talking about us, won't they, silly? About you and me. They're sure to be.'

'I don't see why.' Sandie gave a 'couldn't care less' sort of shrug. 'They're far too wrapped up in their own affairs to bother about what I'm up to. I don't mean your mum and dad. I mean my mother and . . . *him*.'

'Duncan, you mean. You could at least use his name, Sandra.'

'Why should I? I don't call him Duncan and I never will. He's Mr Hendy to me and he'll never be anything else.'

Greg glanced anxiously at her, but without letting her see he was worried. She was not looking at him anyway; she was just staring moodily into space. 'OK, OK,' he said. 'There's no need to jump down my throat. I'm just curious about it, that's all, our parents getting together. My mum's really been looking forward to this meal at your house. She's taken quite a shine to your mum. She says what a very nice person she is. They seem to be getting on very well together, the two of them.'

'Do they?' said Sandie. 'How fascinating.' Her tone conveyed that she considered it anything but.

'I expect your mum's spent all afternoon in the kitchen, hasn't she?' Greg persisted. 'I know that's what my mother would have done. What's she cooked for them?'

'Oh, for heaven's sake, Greg, how should I know?' burst out Sandie. She turned her eyes in his direction before quickly looking away again, and Greg noticed, to his dismay, that they were not only blazing with annoyance but were misted with unshed tears. Sandie had lovely, but unusual eyes. They were deep brown, a striking contrast to her blonde hair, with ever so slightly hooded lids – like her father's, she had told him – but it was the first time Greg had ever seen tears in them.

She was a tough sort of girl, or so she had always seemed, with a streak of resilience, almost rebelliousness, about her that he could not help but admire. At the same time, this trait occasionally fazed him and he was relieved, now, to find she might have a softer side. 'I couldn't care less what my mother has cooked for them,' she said. 'Can't you see? I don't know and I don't care. Just shut up about it, can't you?'

'Hey, steady on, steady on.' He took hold of her hand. 'There's no need to carry on like that. I was only trying to show an interest.'

'No, you weren't. You were just trying to stir things. You know how I feel about my mother and . . . *him*. You were just trying to . . . oh, I don't know.' She looked away and Greg could see she was fiercely biting on her lip, trying not to cry.

'OK, love.' He squeezed her hand. 'Forget it. I'm sorry, I didn't mean to upset you, honestly I didn't. You know that, don't you? I'd never want to upset you or hurt you. Come on now. Shall I get you another drink? A lemonade, or do you want something different? A Tizer, perhaps?'

She looked at him then, her eyes still brimming, but he was pleased to see she was smiling a little. She blinked rapidly, then brushed quickly at her eyes with the back of her hand. 'No, nothing else, thanks. They're a bit gassy, aren't they? It'd just fill me up with wind, then I'd be burping all night.' She was nothing if not honest; blunt, sometimes, to the point of rudeness, but he liked her outspokenness.

'I'm OK now,' she said, grinning at him. 'Come on.' She jumped to her feet. 'It's a Paul Jones, so you can get rid of me for a while. Go on, get a move on.' She pushed playfully at him. 'Get in the circle. See you later, alligator.'

What a chameleon sort of creature she is, thought Greg as he joined the outer circle of boys – far outnumbered by the inner circle of girls, several of whom would have to dance with one another – and began to move round to the strains of 'Here we go round the mulberry bush'.

When the music ended he found himself opposite Marcia. She was a friend of Sandie who – so Sandie had told him teasingly – 'rather fancied' him. She smiled at him in a friendly way, though blushing a little and lowering her eyes as they waltzed round to the music of 'I Wonder Who's Kissing Her Now?'. She was a nice pleasant girl, but without the verve and spiritedness he so admired in Sandie.

He danced with Marcia again later in the evening, to her obvious delight, and then with his old friend Paula. Sandie would not mind. She knew that the Last Waltz would be reserved for her and that Greg would walk her home afterwards, to her grandad's where she was staying for the night. He kept a cursory eye on her for the rest of the evening whilst she was chatting with her friends or dancing with some of the other lads who were there and he was glad to see she seemed to have recovered from her bout of ill-temper. He knew that Mike, another member of The Blue Notes – the group that was still thriving – would have shown an interest in Sandie, but Greg had told him, quite unequivocally, that she was spoken for.

Greg knew he was rather young to have what might be termed a steady girlfriend. His mother had told him so, somewhat concernedly, although she admitted to liking Sandie very much. Sandie was always on her very best behaviour, he had noticed, whenever she visited his home. Greg agreed with his mother, assuring her that his friendship with Sandra Horsfall would not detract in any way from his studies, both his musical aspirations and his schoolwork, and that they were, above all, 'just good friends'. Sandie, too, had her O-levels looming and her hopes for a future in the world of music.

He had been out with only a couple of girls previously, a sister of a friend, and then a girl who made up a foursome in a blind date, but he had not sought their company again. Only when he met Sandra – he sometimes called her that, preferring it to the more boyish-sounding 'Sandie' – did he feel any real attraction for a member of the opposite sex. He had been aware of it as soon as he met her at the Festival, when they had been winners in the same class, but he had been somewhat concerned, at first, by the fact that she was only fifteen then, and so he had hung back for a while. Then Duncan, miraculously, had come up with the idea of piano duets and that had given him a second chance. Greg could have hugged him, but he had tried instead to put on a show of nonchalance which, he now knew from the gleam in Duncan's eye, had not fooled him one bit.

Sandra fascinated him. He was becoming very fond of her. He knew he might almost be falling in love with her, although they were both, as the song said, 'too young to really be in love'. He could not help his feelings. She was such a mercurial girl. Her highs and lows of temperament, her sunniness, following quickly upon her moodiness, exasperated and delighted him by turn.

She had told him how, when she was a child, her father

had likened her to the little girl in the nursery rhyme who, 'when she was good she was very very good, but when she was bad she was horrid'. That just about summed her up. There was no one nicer, more charming or friendly when she was in a sunny mood, but when the clouds of gloom and ill-humour descended, then those she was with certainly knew about it. Greg guessed that Sandie's mother – whom he liked very much – must find her very difficult at times. Especially now when Sandie seemed to have taken such an aversion to this friendship between Abbie and Duncan Hendy. Greg himself could only think how great it would be, how very suitable, if his old friend and Sandie's mum were to make a go of it. Sandie had nearly bitten his head off earlier that evening, but Greg was determined to talk to her again about it on their way home; to find out, as tactfully as he could, exactly what it was that was troubling her so much.

She seemed in a more receptive mood when the dance finished and he put his arm round her as they walked through the dark streets towards her grandfather's house. She rested her head against his shoulder – they were practically the same height – and he turned and kissed her, first on the cheek, then on the side of her mouth. Sandra was, in fact, the first girl he had ever kissed properly – a few weeks ago had been the first time – although he had not, of course, admitted that. He guessed that, for her, he was certainly the first. That was as far as it had gone, just kissing. Greg could not envisage anything else, certainly not for a long time yet. He knew that some of his friends and other lads in his form at school might consider him to be sexually immature for his seventeen years, but they were all talk and had nowhere near the experience in such matters that they boasted about. He laughed and joked with them sometimes, not wanting to appear too prudish or standoffish, but at the same time keeping his own counsel. As far as he was concerned, his parents were expecting him to behave himself. He knew, too, that Sandra's mother was entrusting her daughter to his care, although nothing had been said, and this was what he would do. Moreover, he knew he must help Sandie with her problem if he could.

'I'm sorry if I upset you earlier,' he ventured. 'I don't like to see you unhappy. What is it, Sandra? Can't you tell me? What is it about your mother and Duncan that upsets you so much?'

He half-expected her to fly off the handle again, but she did not do so. Nor did she answer at all and when he risked a glance at her he could see her lips were set together in a tight line. In spite of this he knew he must persist.

'Why do you get so distressed, Sandie,' he said, 'whenever there is any mention of your mother and Duncan? I can see you do, but Duncan says you are perfectly all right with him, just the same as you have always been.'

'Oh, so you've been talking about me, have you?' She turned to look at him, but it was more of a curious look than one of annoyance and her voice was not as indignant as he might have expected.

'Not all that much,' he replied easily. 'I'm anxious about you, that's all, you know I am, and so I asked Duncan if you had been any different with him since he started seeing your mum. And he said no, you were just the same as ever; polite and friendly and working very hard at your music. Your mother had asked him the same thing, apparently.'

'So you *have* been talking about me, all of you.' She sounded more heated now, but he continued as though she had not spoken.

'You're giving your mother a hard time, aren't you, love, because she's friendly with Duncan. But with him you're acting as though nothing has happened. It's as though you're pretending it's not there.' The truth suddenly hit Greg. 'Is that what you're doing?' he asked. 'With Duncan, at any rate – trying to pretend that their friendship doesn't exist?'

'I suppose so,' Sandie muttered. Then, 'Yes, that's what

I'm doing,' she almost shouted. 'It's the only way I can cope with it, by pretending it's not happening. I'm OK with Duncan . . . Mr Hendy. But he's my music teacher, that's all he is, and that's all I want him to be . . . *ever*. I like him a lot, but I want him to stay where he is, as my music teacher. There's no need for him and my mother to be so friendly. They're too old, anyway.'

Greg almost laughed. 'What a thing to say! I'm sure you don't really believe that. Of course they're not old. Your mum can't be much more than forty.'

'She's forty-two. But *he's* old.'

'I'm not sure how old Duncan is, but it can't be more than fifty, if that.'

'That's ancient.'

'You're being ridiculous,' he said, exasperated. She could be very childish at times and this argument seemed to Greg to be a particularly silly one. His own parents were still devoted to one another and they were both turned fifty.

'Don't you dare call me ridiculous! I can't help how I feel.' There was anger and defiance in her tone, but a note of dejection there as well, which made him persevere with his gentle probing.

'How do you feel? Try to tell me, love. It might help. What exactly is the matter?'

'I don't know – exactly.' She turned a perplexed face towards him. 'But she doesn't need him. She shouldn't be thinking about another husband. She's been married. She was married to my dad.'

'Nobody has mentioned them getting married, Sandra.'

'You did. Yes, you did – right at the beginning. You said it was high time Duncan started thinking about getting married again.'

'Maybe I did, but I was only speaking generally. Besides, why would it be such a bad idea? You've said you like him, and your mum obviously likes him a lot.'

'I've told you. She's been married once, to my father, and

she said there would never, ever be anybody else for her. She didn't say it to me, but I heard her telling her best friend, my Aunty Doreen, how much she missed Peter – that was my dad – and how she'd never forget him and there'd never be anyone else for her. They were really in love, my mum and dad. You could tell.'

Greg guessed she was romanticising the situation somewhat. No doubt Abbie and Peter Horsfall had been very much in love but how much could she really remember of how her parents had behaved towards one another? She had been only a little girl, eight years old or so, when her father died. Distance, and the passing of time, lent enchantment. Sandie was probably looking back with nostalgia on a very happy time in her life, and there was no doubt that she had idealised her father. That was the problem, Greg decided; she could not bear the thought of anyone ever taking his place, even though her mother was obviously ready to move on.

'Why does she need a man in her life anyway?' Sandie was continuing. 'She's all right as she is. She's got lots of friends. There's Doreen, and Jean at college, and all the women she meets when she's doing her Tupperware thing. And she's got Simon and me,' she added, rather petulantly, Greg thought. 'She should be thinking about us, not gadding about.'

He felt no compunction now in saying to her, 'That's a very selfish attitude, Sandra.' It was time to take off the velvet gloves and make her face reality. 'Your mother gives you the utmost consideration, you and Simon; you know she does.'

'What do you know about it?' she retorted. 'She's always out somewhere or other, at college or doing that Tupperware thing, or with . . . him. We hardly ever see her.'

'Oh, come on, that's just not true. Anyway, your mum has her own life to lead, just like you have. What about all the things you do, eh? Youth Club and choir and your music lessons and dances . . . and going out with me. Your mum

369

hasn't objected to that, has she?'

'That's different.'

'Not so different, love,' he said, more coaxingly. 'Your mum is still quite a young woman and she has every right to have friends – male friends – just as you do. I know she loved your dad, but that doesn't mean to say she can't ever fall in love again. She's ready to move on, and I think you should let her.'

Sandie turned and stared at him for a moment before she spoke. 'She's different,' she said. 'Since she met him, she's not the same with us. We don't spend as much time together, the three of us, like we used to. When we lived in Norfolk we used to go out together, to visit my gran and grandad, and to concerts at the church and . . . and things. We don't do that any more.'

'And that's mainly because you don't really want to, isn't it? Be honest, Sandie. You don't want to be always with your mum, nor does Simon. He's got his football and all his mates and you've got . . . all sorts of things.' He leaned towards her, kissing her fully on the lips, to which she responded eagerly. 'Come on, Sandie, be fair. What your mum is doing is treating you in a more grown-up way, letting you find your own feet. How many times have you told her you don't want to be treated like a little kid? I bet you have, haven't you?'

'S'pose so,' Sandie shrugged.

'Well then. That's what she's doing – letting you grow up. The fact that she's got a new man friend as well is just a coincidence. I reckon you should let her get on with it and stop being so . . . objectionable.'

She did not retaliate. He guessed that the kiss had done it. He kissed her again – by this time they were at her grandfather's gate – with even more fervour. 'Will you try then?' he whispered. 'Try not to mind too much about Duncan?'

She smiled at him then, such a bewitching smile that completely transformed her hitherto sullen face. 'I'll try,' she promised.

Chapter 23

Abbie did not know the reason for it, but Sandie suddenly seemed to be more kindly disposed towards her friendship with Duncan. Neither of them, Abbie nor Sandie, made any direct comment about it – least said, soonest mended, was Abbie's opinion – but there was a definite change in the girl's attitude and for this she was extremely thankful.

Things were going well for Abbie in this late spring of 1963. She had managed to get through her first dreaded teaching practice without too much difficulty. She had been assigned to a school in Blackpool, this being quite usual as there were insufficient schools in the Chelford area to accommodate all the students. The tutors travelled from Chelford on various occasions to supervise lessons, but her report was based largely on the headteacher's assessment of her capabilities. She was pleased to learn that she was considered to be very capable. The report stated that she had a pleasant and easy manner with the children, a good understanding of discipline, and that she would, ultimately, make a very competent teacher.

Putting high-flown educational theories into practice was not easy, nor was it always practical. How were you expected, for instance, to make a class of unruly children shut up, without raising your voice? Abbie felt that it helped to have had children of her own; her mature years, also, might have been something of an advantage.

She regarded it as a two-edged compliment when one of

the more cheeky lads in her class of six to seven year olds asked her, 'Are you a proper teacher, Miss, or are you one of them students?'

Abbie admitted that she was a student at the moment, but that she hoped, one day, to be a proper teacher. 'Why do you ask?' she had enquired with a pleasant smile.

'Well, you're old, aren't you, Miss?' was his unequivocal reply. 'An' you seem to know what you're doing an' all – not like some of them young 'uns we've had.'

They were nice kids on the whole and she had been sorry to say goodbye to them at the end of the month. It had been a relief, also, to be able to drive the short distance to the school near the centre of Blackpool, instead of enduring the lengthy train journey to college every morning. The mornings and evenings were lighter and warmer now, and Abbie's spirits were lighter, too – especially so on hearing the news, spreading round the college like wild fire, that Art Gillespie was leaving at the end of the month.

There were rumours aplenty flying round the college. Whether they were all true, no one was quite sure. There had been no official announcement, not to the students at any rate, but his disappearance seemed to speak for itself.

Nobody could have failed to notice his attraction to the young PE tutor, Gillian Weaver, who had joined the teaching staff in January. They had been seen together on several occasions and his relationship with Carol Pearson was obviously on the wane. Carol put on a good show of indifference, but her overloud laugh and the angry look often to be seen on her face spoke volumes. Not that Gillian, the PE tutor, seemed to be encouraging him. It was Art who was doing all the pursuing. And Art Gillespie, as Abbie knew to her cost, was not one to take no for an answer. The story going around was that he had 'tried it on' with Gillian against her wishes and had turned nasty when she spurned his advances. The upshot of it was that she had reported him to the college authorities and he had been asked to leave.

Whether or not he would get another teaching post no one seemed to know, and the majority did not care. At all events he would not get a reference, that was sure.

His lectures from now to the end of term would be taken by Miss Fairbrother, who was the Drama lecturer. It was she who had interviewed Abbie, with her close friend, Miss Williams, and Abbie already liked her no-nonsense approach to the students. What a difference from Art Gillespie, and what a rotter he had turned out to be. Abbie realised she had been very lucky, considering what had happened to the unfortunate PE tutor. These days, she was happy, almost blissfully so, in her deepening relationship with Duncan. Especially as Sandie no longer seemed to object.

It was because of her daughter's changed attitude that she felt emboldened to invite her along to the Tupperware party at Sylvia's home in Marton; ostensibly to help with the merchandise, but mainly because she was aware of a new feeling of comradeship between them and was anxious to foster this.

It had been a great surprise to Abbie when, in the middle of June, Sylvia Webster had rung to enquire if she was still doing her Tupperware parties. She wanted to hold another one, she said. Her friends had really enjoyed the last one – over a year ago now – and some of them wished to buy several more items. Also, Sylvia said, it would be a good excuse for a girls' get-together. Could Abbie fit her in towards the end of the month?

'Jim will come and collect you and all your stuff, like he did before,' Sylvia told her.

'No need,' replied Abbie, with a certain pride. 'I'm driving myself now. Yes, the end of June will be fine.' They fixed a convenient date. 'Things will be winding down at college by then. I've nearly finished my first year at Chelford, by the way. Yes, I'll look forward to seeing you again, Sylvia.'

She was even more surprised when Sandie agreed to

accompany her. She had made the suggestion tentatively. 'It's always useful to have an extra pair of hands with the loading and unloading, you see, love. And you'll have finished your O-levels, won't you? I wouldn't have asked you if you were still busy with exams.'

'Yes, Mum, why not?' Sandie had replied almost eagerly. 'So long as it's not Youth Club night or the night I practise with Greg. Tuesday? Yes, that's OK. Tuesday nights are free. I'll be able to watch you in action, Mum.'

The mention of Greg reminded Abbie that Sylvia and Jim had a son, Ian. He was a nice lad – she had met him briefly on her last visit there. She wondered if, deep down in her subconscious mind, this might have been another reason for deciding to invite Sandie along; in the hope that she and Ian might meet. Abbie liked Greg Matthews very much, but she feared, sometimes, that Sandie might be seeing rather too much of him. She was, after all, very young, and it could do no harm to have other friendships. It was quite likely, though, that Ian would not be at home that evening.

On the Tuesday night in question, Ian was present. They were all at home; Sylvia and Jim, Ian and his sister Janet, and there were several women already arriving when Abbie, with Sandie's assistance, started to unload the boxes from the large boot of her Ford Anglia. Ian, and Jim, too, came to help.

'Hello there. You must be Abbie's daughter. Didn't know you were coming.' Ian had not waited for an introduction and his ready smile showed how pleased he was to see Sandie. Abbie noted that he was completely unselfconscious, using her own name without embarrassment.

'Yes, this is Sandie,' she said. 'Sandra, to be more correct, but she likes to be called Sandie. Sandie, this is Ian, Jim and Sylvia's son. You met Jim before, didn't you?'

'Yes, hello, Jim. Hello, Ian.' Sandie appeared very relaxed, using Jim's name, and later, Sylvia's, with perfect ease. She had finally started to call Duncan by his Christian name, too, he had reported to Abbie, and they both saw this as a major breakthrough.

'You've come to help your mum, have you, Sandie?' asked Sylvia.

'That's the general idea,' Sandie grinned. 'And I could help you with the supper as well if you like, Sylvia. I did that once before when Mum gave a party for her friend, Doreen, didn't I, Mum?' How exceedingly charming she could be when she set her stall out, Abbie mused.

Ian obviously thought so too. 'Hey, don't have her working all night, Mum,' he protested. 'I'm sure she'd rather come and listen to records with me, wouldn't you, Sandie?' The girl agreed politely that she would like to do so, later in the evening.

Sandie was quite impressed at the way her mother conducted the Tupper party, delivering her spiel about the various items and organising the games with the ease that comes with experience. Mum was coming out of her shell, she realised. She had, in fact, been emerging from it for quite a while now. She remembered her, from the years when they had lived in Norfolk, as a rather shy, retiring sort of person. It was only since they had come to live in Blackpool that she had started to change. Doreen, of course, had always been a livewire. Sandie had wished at times, when she was a little girl, that her mum could be more like her jolly and vivacious Aunty Doreen. They only saw Doreen occasionally in those days, but whenever they met her, her mother seemed to take on a different personality; more animated, talking and laughing in a way that was quite unfamiliar. And Jean Birtles, her friend at college, seemed to have the same effect on her.

There was no doubt about it; her mum had become a much more assertive and positive person since she started the college course. Sandie had wondered at first how Abbie could imagine she would ever become a teacher. She did not possess the self-confidence – or the bossiness – which characterised most of the teachers Sandie knew, but she would never have dared to tell her so. Now it seemed as though she might be wrong. Her mother obviously did have the ability, if her handling of the Tupper party was anything to go by.

Sandie had found herself wishing at times that the old mum was still there; the woman who spent more time in the kitchen, baking and preparing appetising meals and making sure their clothes were always washed and ironed. The mum, in fact, whose life revolved round her children. Since she had embarked on the college course, there had not been as much home-baking and sometimes their meals were rather hit and miss, concocted from a variety of tins and packets. Not all the time, of course, only occasionally, if Sandie were honest with herself. But a little more frequently since Duncan Hendy came on the scene. There had been times when Mum had been out with him and she had left her, Sandie, to make a meal for herself and Simon. Duncan, too, had gone a long way towards making her mother the different person she had now become.

Sandie pulled herself up short now from this rather peevish way of thinking. She had promised Greg she would try not to mind so much. And she really was trying hard. Bur Duncan was not her father; no one could ever take the place of her dad. She had to admit, though, that life was easier and she felt much happier when she was on good terms with her mother. She had only agreed to come here tonight to please her mum, but it was turning out to be not a bad sort of evening, and that boy Ian seemed very nice. He was not like Greg, of course, but all the same . . . not bad.

She joined in a couple of games with a good grace – but honestly! Even Simon would have found these games childish. 'I went to a Tupper party and I bought a tomato cutter, a lemon squeezer, a lunchbox, a tea strainer, a measuring spoon, a cereal bowl,' and so on and so on. Who would think mature women could get so enjoyment from such inanity, but maybe they were approaching their second childhood. Sandie was grinning to herself when Sylvia asked her if she could perhaps help with the supper, as she had suggested.

As they arranged the already prepared sandwiches and cakes on plates and set out the coffee cups, Sylvia told her that she had known her mother for ages; ever since Abbie had worked at this very place as a Land Girl during the war. There was, apparently, a large market garden to the rear which Jim and Sylvia, with a few employees, still ran. Then she, Sylvia, had joined the WAAF, they had both got married after the war and had not seen one another until last year. Sylvia was nice, Sandie decided, and Jim, too. She would ask her mum to tell her a bit more about her time as a Land Girl. It would be another way of cementing their new rapport.

'Our Ian'll be dying to show you his record collection,' said Sylvia, when the kettle had boiled and she was mixing the coffee in a large Perspex jug. 'Off you go now, Sandie love. You've been a great help and I'm sure you don't want to spend any more time with us women. Put some food and coffee on this tray, see, then you and Ian can have it in his room. That's if you would like to, dear?'

'Yes, I would, thank you,' said Sandie. 'Is Janet with him?'

'No; she's watching telly with her dad. They're in the back room, well away from all the hilarity.' Sylvia laughed. 'I'll take them some supper as well. Let's just take this stuff into the lounge, then you can go and have a chat with Ian. His name's on the door, but you might have to knock more than once if he's got his music on.'

Sandie had enquired if Janet was with Ian as it seemed rather odd for Sylvia to suggest she went to Ian's bedroom. She had never, as yet, been invited into Greg's room, nor had she dared to suggest to her mother, when he was at her house, that they should go into her room. Any kissing and cuddling that had gone on between them – and there had been quite a lot – had been in dark corners on the way home from Youth Club, or, somewhat furtively and with one eye on the door, in her mum's or Mrs Matthews's sitting room when they had finished their piano practice. Not that she was expecting Ian Webster to get up to anything; they hardly knew one another, yet. She couldn't imagine her own mum making such a suggestion, though. Maybe she, Sandie, could drop a hint that Greg might be invited to her room . . . to play records. Her Dansette record player and her collection were up there as they were not to her mother's taste. Abbie's records – Bing Crosby, Nat King Cole, Doris Day and the like – were in the lounge with the stereogram.

All was quiet, however, when Sandie knocked, and Ian opened the door with a book in his hand.

'Hi there, I was wondering if you'd come.' His easy smile conveyed his pleasure at seeing her. 'Jolly good, you've brought some grub as well. Come on in. Give me the tray; it looks heavy.' He took it off her, pushing aside a pile of books and papers on his chest of drawers to make room for it.

'I hope I'm not disturbing you. Good book, is it?' asked Sandie, eyeing the Penguin paperback he had tossed on to the bed. *A Passage To India* by E.M. Forster. Hmm . . . he must be a pretty brainy sort of lad if he was reading that for pleasure rather than Agatha Christie, for instance, Sandie's own favourite reading matter. Unless it was a set book for his A-level course.

'Not bad,' he replied. 'My reading has suffered since I started concentrating on just the science subjects – you have to specialise in the sixth form, you see – so I make myself read a book every so often.'

'Make yourself?' Sandie smiled. 'You don't enjoy it then?'

'Mmm . . . sort of.' He grinned. 'Anyway, never mind all that. Sit yourself down. There's only one chair, but I'll sit here.' He plonked down on the bed and Sandie sat on the

Lloyd Loom basket chair. It was quite a small room. She guessed his sister, Janet, would have a rather larger one. That was usually the case with sisters; her own room was larger than Simon's. There was just about room for his bed, a chest of drawers, a small wardrobe and a bookcase which held more records than books. His record player, a Dansette, was similar to her own.

'Tell me about yourself, Sandie,' he said, handing her a cup of coffee and a plate, 'and tuck into this grub. Don't be shy!'

'I'm not,' she grinned. 'What d'you want to know about me? I'm sixteen – sixteen and a half, actually, I'm at the Collegiate School, and I've just finished my O-levels. Will that do?'

'To be going on with.' He smiled slowly. He had thoughtful blue-grey eyes, she noticed, straight hair of a nondescript brown flopping over his brow, and thin features in an intelligent-looking face. He was very much like his father, Jim, in looks, but a couple of inches taller; about the same height as Greg, she estimated.

'What about you?' she countered. 'I know you're in the sixth form, you've just said so. Which school?'

'Arnold,' he replied. 'I've been there since I was eleven. It's fee-paying, mostly – some folk think it's a bit snobby – but I managed to get a scholarship.'

Arnold; of course he would most likely be at Arnold, living at the south end of the town, but she had not realised. He was not wearing his uniform and her mother had not mentioned which school he attended.

'Fancy that,' she said. 'I didn't know you went there. Actually, my boyfriend goes to that school.' There was no harm in letting him know she was spoken for, even though he was very nice. 'Greg Matthews. Do you know him.'

He stared at her for a moment, then he began to laugh. 'Of course – you're Sandra, aren't you? Sandie . . . Sandra – I hadn't realised. Yes, I know Greg, and I've heard about you. He calls you Sandra, doesn't he?'

'Yes, he does, some of the time. What've you heard about me? Nothing bad, I hope.'

'No, you don't need to worry.' He gave a wry grin. 'Greg's not one to shoot his mouth off, not like some of the lads. But he's got it bad, I can tell you that, and who could blame him? Lucky devil!' He looked at her thoughtfully for a moment and Sandie, slightly disconcerted though not displeased, lowered her eyes.

'I don't know him all that well really,' he went on. 'We're not in the same form now. I'm Science and he's Arts, but I like him. He's a good guy. Brilliant pianist, isn't he? And he's in a group as well. Seems as though there's no end to the chap's talents,' he added a trifle ruefully.

'Mmm. That's how I met him,' replied Sandie. 'I play the piano as well, you see – I'm not as good as Greg, though – and we play duets together. We have the same music teacher. But I like pop music as well, like you do. Can I have a look at your records?' It wasn't fair to go on talking about Greg, she decided.

He nodded. ''Course you can. You choose one and I'll put it on.'

She put her cup down on the tray and knelt by his bookcase. Elvis Presley, Cliff Richard, Bob Dylan . . . She had some of these records herself, but nowhere near so many as Ian had. The Rolling Stones, that was a group she hadn't got round to yet. 'Gosh! You've got The Beatles' album.' *Please Please Me* was The Beatles' first LP, which Sandie had not been able to afford, although she had an EP of theirs and their latest single, the chart topper, 'From Me to You'. 'Can we have this on, please?'

'Sure,' he laughed. 'It's a wonder it's not worn out, though, the number of times I've played it. It drives my mother barmy.'

They sang along, sotto voce, to the title track, 'Won't you please, please, please me', nodding their heads and tapping their fingers to the rhythm of the music. Then they listened in a companionable silence, just occasionally breaking into song or chatting easily about the lyrics or the members of this up-and-coming group.

'The Beatles are coming to Blackpool, you know,' said Ian. 'Are you going to any of their concerts?'

'Yeah, sure we are,' replied Sandie. 'Greg's got tickets for one in July.'

'You've a nice voice,' Ian remarked. 'I'm surprised Greg doesn't want you in his group.'

'Oh, that's a strictly male province,' she laughed. 'At least I've always assumed so. It's an idea, though.'

'It's been good meeting you, Sandie,' said Ian, when the Tupper party came to an end and they were loading up the boot of the car again.

Sylvia had come upstairs to tell Sandie her mother was ready to go home. She had knocked and waited before entering the room. Did she think she might be interrupting something? Sandie wondered. Probably not. They were a courteous family, the Websters, all having respect for one another's privacy. Sylvia was treating her son as an adult, just as her own mother had seemed to be treating her, Sandie, of late.

'Yes, it's been good meeting you as well,' replied Sandie. 'Thanks for the music and the chat. See you around, perhaps?'

'Yes, I hope so. See you,' said Ian.

'He's a nice boy, isn't he?' Abbie remarked as they drove home. She turned her head briefly to look at her daughter, but Sandie's face was giving nothing away.

'Mmm, very nice, Mum,' Sandie replied. 'But I've got Greg, haven't I? So it's no use you trying to matchmake, because it won't come off.'

'I'm not, dear, but the two of you seemed to be getting on very well.' Ian had come down from his room with Sandie and had helped to stack the boxes of Tupperware in the boot of the car. Abbie had noticed the smitten expression in the boy's eyes as he said his casual goodbye to her daughter. The lad definitely fancied her. But it is nothing to do with you, Abbie Horsfall, she told herself now, and decided to mind her own business.

'All right, love, I get the message.' Abbie grinned at Sandie, then turned quickly to watch the road ahead. She remembered walking down this very lane on the way back from the pictures or the Cherry Tree Inn during that last winter of the war, when she and Jim Webster, very briefly, had been engaged. Some impulse now prompted her to tell her daughter about it. Neither Sandie nor Simon knew about the episode. It had not seemed necessary to tell them. They thought there had only ever been Peter, their father. But she and Sandie had been more like friends just lately than mother and daughter. It would be good to confide in her. Sandie's next words gave her the opening she needed.

'They're a nice family, aren't they, Mum? Sylvia was telling me she's known you for ages, since you were a Land Girl. You worked there, didn't you? You told me once before, but you didn't tell me much about it.'

'No, maybe I didn't. What else did Sylvia tell you?'

'Nothing much, why?'

'Well, this might come as a surprise to you, Sandie, but there was a time when Jim and I were quite friendly. As a matter of fact, we were engaged to be married.'

'What!' Sandie turned to stare at her mother. 'But I thought . . . you and my dad . . . You were engaged to my dad, weren't you? And then you married him after the war ended. That's what you told us.'

'Yes, that's right, love. But there was all that time, you see, when I thought your father was dead – I told you about that – and then we found out he was still alive although he'd been badly injured.'

'How long?'

382

'What do you mean?'

'How long was my dad missing?'

'Well over a year.'

'That's not long.'

'It was different in wartime, Sandie. Sometimes you had to . . . well, seize the moment. You didn't know what might happen tomorrow.'

'So you decided to forget about my dad and get engaged to Jim?'

'No, it wasn't like that, love. Jim's a very nice person – you've seen that for yourself, haven't you? – and he always knew I didn't love him in the way I loved Peter. But we were good friends, you see, with us working together at the market garden. And so, in the end I said yes, I would marry him. But he knew, as soon as your dad turned up again, that things had changed. He knew I had to go back to Peter.' Abbie glanced warily at her daughter. Her expression was implacable.

'Try to understand, love. There was never anyone like your dad. There still isn't. Even though I'm seeing Duncan, I'll never forget Peter.'

'OK, Mum. Anything you say.' Sandie's tone conveyed that she couldn't care less, but Abbie guessed that that was not so. She wondered if she had only made things worse instead of better. Why on earth couldn't she have kept her big mouth shut?

Chapter 24

They were calling it Beatlemania, this wave of near hysteria which was affecting the young folk of the country. It swept into Blackpool in the summer of 1963 when the enterprising ABC chain booked a package of shows for their Blackpool theatre, formerly known as the Hippodrome. Cliff Richard and The Shadows were starring there for the summer season, and The Beatles had been booked for five Sunday concerts. Their two vacant Sundays had been immediately snapped up by the Queen's Theatre, opposite Central station, which many of the older inhabitants of Blackpool still thought of as 'Feldman's Theatre'.

The ironic thing was that the lads from Liverpool might well have had a much longer season. The Central Pier producer had seen the lads perform at the Marine Hall in Fleetwood in the summer of 1962, and had been offered the band for the summer 1963 season. But he had turned them down, saying, 'I didn't think much of them.'

The tickets that Greg had managed to get hold of were for one of the shows at the Queen's Theatre, on 21 July. There were hundreds of wildly excited teenagers crowding round the entrance when Sandie and Greg arrived there an hour or so before the performance was due to start.

'They're waiting for a glimpse of the lads, no doubt,' Greg remarked, 'but I should imagine they're wasting their time. They'll already be in there, or if they're not then they'll be smuggled in some other way. Just imagine trying to force their way through that mob. They'd be squashed to death. Come on; we've got our tickets. We'd better try and get in.'

Sandie hung back. 'D'you think so? You don't want to wait here a bit, just in case?'

'I've told you, there's no chance. You'll see 'em on the stage anyway. We've got tickets for the stalls. Come on – follow me.'

Somehow they managed to push their way through the crowd. Greg was tall and that helped. The crowd was, on the whole, good-natured anyway. Probably the majority of them had tickets and the rest would know there was no chance of getting in without one. Greg had been right. As they read in the *Evening Gazette* the next day, the four lads had been taken over a wall at the rear of the theatre, up ladders and scaffolding to the roof and then smuggled through a skylight. Police had been called to control the crowd, but Sandie and Greg had seen no sign of them. How the group got out again at the end of the performance, when every avenue of escape appeared to be blocked, would remain a mystery. 'It's my secret!' the Queen's manager told everyone.

Sandie had never experienced anything like it; the atmosphere of barely controlled excitement before the show started, which broke into waves of hysteria, hundreds of teenagers waving, shouting and screaming as their idols appeared on the stage. The four lads presented a much more respectable image now than they had formerly done, when they had sported long hair, black leather jackets and jeans. The most unusual thing about them now was their distinctive mop-head haircuts. Otherwise they could be said to be decorously clad in their neat black suits with velvet collars and slim ties.

They went through their repertoire of songs, several of which were featured on the LP Sandie had heard in Ian's room: 'Love Me Do', the song which had shot them into the charts, 'Please Please Me', 'A Taste of Honey', 'From Me To You'. Some of the songs could scarcely be heard for the screaming, which reached its height when Paul invited the audience to 'sort of clap your hands and sort of stamp your feet'. There was little point in having seats to sit on because most of the youngsters there were standing up, waving and clapping and stamping as Paul had invited them to, then gyrating madly to the strains of 'Twist and Shout'.

'What a night, eh?' said Greg as they walked towards the bus stop outside Central station.

'Yeah, wasn't it fab?' replied Sandie breathlessly. She still felt as though she were in a semi-trance. 'Great, aren't they? Absolutely fab!'

'They sure are.'

'D'you think you might change your act now you've seen them? Have you picked up any ideas?'

'Plenty,' replied Greg. 'Technique, poise, stage presence, how to handle the audience . . .'

'They didn't handle it all that well, though, did they? They couldn't make us shut up.'

'No, I s'pose not. Of course, The Blue Notes could never have a crowd like that.'

'You don't know – you might.'

'No, we're not in the same league. I have the sense to know that. And because we're not in the same league there's no point in trying to imitate them, is there? I know the other lads agree with me.' The other three members of Greg's group had also had tickets for the concert, but Sandie and Greg had not seen them, so great was the crowd. 'No, I think it's best if we just try to do our own thing. Perhaps try one or two innovations. We'll have to see how it goes.'

'Such as?'

Greg shrugged. 'Don't know yet. Why are you so interested all of a sudden?'

'It isn't all of a sudden, Greg,' Sandie retorted. 'You know I've always been interested in your group. I think it's great.'

'As good as The Beatles?' He grinned at her.

'Er, different,' she replied. 'Yes, quite different. I think you're right – you shouldn't copy them. You should think of something really novel.'

It was Greg's turn now to say, 'Such as?'

'Oh, I don't know exactly. It's your group, not mine,' replied Sandie. She was still toying with the idea of The Blue Notes with a female vocalist – herself, of course – but she had a feeling that now was not the time to suggest it. She would have to wait for the right moment. The notion had taken root after Ian's half-joking remark. She hadn't told Greg about her meeting with Ian and the time they had shared playing records and chatting. And she guessed that Ian had not mentioned it either at school, or surely Greg would have said something. At any rate it was no big deal.

Greg waited with her at the bus stop. 'You don't mind if I don't come home with you, do you?' he said. 'It's a long way back to Marton from where you live. It would mean two buses or a long walk.'

'No, that's OK,' said Sandie, although she felt a little deflated. There was always this problem when they went into town at night. At other times, when they were visiting one another's houses, for instance, they used their bicycles.

'Hey, don't look so down in the dumps,' Greg said now. 'It won't be for ever, this riding around on buses. I've got a surprise for you.'

'What?'

'Guess!'

'You mean you're going to learn to drive? Then we can use your dad's car? Is that what you mean?' The idea of driving lessons had been mentioned casually, once or twice, but Greg never seemed to have much time what with school and music lessons and practices with The Blue Notes.

'Better than that,' he replied, his eyes gleaming. 'My mum and dad are buying me my own car for my eighteenth birthday.' That was at the beginning of December.

'Gosh! That's fab! What sort of car, d'you know yet?'

'I thought I might have a mini shooting brake. They're

nice and nippy, but there's bags of room as well. Then I can use it for transporting some of our gear. We have to rely on Dave at the moment – well, Dave's dad, actually – for the loan of his van. And the other two lads borrow their parents' cars occasionally. They can all drive except me. But not for much longer, kid.' He thumped her arm affectionately. 'As a matter of fact, I've got a course of lessons booked with BSM starting next week. School's finished now for six weeks and I've loads of time. So it's all happening, you might say.'

'Gosh!' said Sandie again, quite awestruck. She knew quite a lot of teenagers could drive, but it was usually in their parents' cars. There was one girl in the sixth form who came to school in her own car, parking it in the car park with the teachers' vehicles, but she lived quite a way out of Blackpool, near to St Michael's, and her parents were known to be loaded. Learning to drive herself was not something that had occurred to Sandie. Besides, she was not old enough. You had to be seventeen, she thought. Perhaps, next January. Yes, the idea was quite appealing.

'Your bus is here,' said Greg, as the number 23 bus appeared round the corner. 'See you soon, Sandra.' He kissed her cheek; he was not one to go in for snogging in bus queues in front of other people, as some lads were not afraid to do. 'I'll ring you. Duncan wants us to start on the Dvorak thing before next Saturday. 'Bye, love. Take care.'

Take care. He was such an old-fashioned lad in some ways, thought Sandie. That was more of an older person's remark – an uncle or aunt, for instance. She remembered it was what Jim had said to her mother when they had said their goodbyes after the Tupper party. 'Take care now, Abbie.'

She had been surprised, to say the least, at her mother's revelations about Jim and their brief engagement. Obviously there was a lot more to her mother than met the eye. She, Sandie, had been rather quiet with her for a while after that, a bit offhand, as she thought about what Abbie had told her. Did Jim still fancy her? she wondered. No, probably not. He seemed perfectly contented with Sylvia; they were a nice happy family. Or did her mum look back and wonder what it would have been like if she'd married Jim? After all, it was the second Tupper party she had done there. Just imagine. Jim, not Peter, might have been her dad. And as for Ian . . . Oh, it was all too complicated for words. She had stopped thinking about it in the end and her relations with her mother were improving again.

She switched her thoughts back to The Beatles. They had been fantastic, brilliant. She just wished she could have heard all the words. You'd even had to lipread now and again, the screaming from the audience was so loud, or look carefully to make out which one of them was singing. Greg was right to say they could not be imitated. She didn't think anyone would ever be able to do so. But even The Beatles had sung along occasionally with a female vocalist. In February, in fact, it had been Helen Shapiro who was the big star on their tour, The Beatles being invited along as one of the supporting acts. Then there was Cilla Black who had performed along with them at the Cavern Club in Liverpool. Perhaps not actually singing *with* them, but as part of the same concert. Female vocalists were on the up and up – singers like Brenda Lee, Susan Maugham and Dusty Springfield. She wondered how she could plant the idea in Greg's mind to make it look as though it had come from him.

Abbie was enjoying her long holiday away from college. It gave her time to be a housewife again. No, she corrected herself, that was the wrong term. She was not a wife, not yet, more of a homemaker. She now had time to cook appetising meals without having to make too much use of the tin opener, to bake, to clean and polish and do a bit of gardening – all things which had been put on the back burner whilst she was doing her first year of teacher training. Looking back on it, the year had passed very quickly, and what an eventful year it had been. She smiled to herself sometimes when she thought of her involvement with not one, but two men during the past year. She, Abbie Horsfall, who had been so adamant that she would never marry again, never even fall in love again. She had not been in love with Art Gillespie. She knew that now, possibly she had always known. It was infatuation that had got hold of her. She could think of him now without any feeling of hurt.

There had been a slight reversal in her good rapport with Sandie, following her disclosure about Jim and their engagement. Abbie could have kicked herself for spilling the beans. Why on earth did you do it, you fool? she asked herself. It was because she had thought there was a feeling of 'all girls together' about their improved relations, but now it seemed that they were, after all, just mother and daughter rather than bosom pals, and she would have to try and remember this if she was ever again tempted to confide in Sandie. The girl had come round though. She had come home after the Beatles concert full of the wonderful, 'fab' time they had had there, she and Greg; and full of the talk, also, that Greg was to get his own car for his eighteenth birthday. She asked if she, too, could learn to drive when she was seventeen. Abbie, at one time, might have commented, 'And who is going to pay for the lessons, young lady?' But she held her tongue and made a casual sort of remark. 'Well, yes, it's always useful to be able to drive.' Her daughter was 'sunny side out' again and it paid to keep her that way.

It wasn't until the end of August that the idea was mooted that Sandie might be invited to join The Blue Notes as their female vocalist, and it was Mike, not Greg, who made the suggestion. Not as a lead vocalist, he explained to the others, just as one of the four singers. Tony, who played the drums, did not sing.

'She's got a great voice,' he said. She had been to a few of the band practices lately at Greg's invitation and had not been shy about singing along with them. 'She's a good-looking girl, she's used to an audience, with her playing the piano an' all that, like you do, Greg, and I just think she'd be a crowd puller, that's all.'

The other three members of the group looked at one another and grinned. 'It couldn't be anything to do with the fact that you fancy her, could it?' asked Greg

'No way, no way, man!' Mike held up his hands in protest. 'She's your bird, isn't she? You told me to lay off ages ago and I have, honest. She won't look at me when you're around, or at any other time. Besides, I've got Sharon now, haven't I, and she's keeping me quite busy, for the moment at any rate. So – what do you think, guys?'

'Mmm, not a bad idea at that,' said Dave. 'We're getting a wee bit stale, aren't we? Bookings have dropped off. Could be because it's summertime, but we could do with a bit of a fillip. I say yes, let's give her a try. But it's really up to Greg, of course. Like you say, she's his bird.'

Greg was silent for a moment, deep in thought. Had Sandie suggested this to Mike? She had been behaving rather strangely lately, showing far more interest in the group than she had used to do. That was why he had invited her along to a few practices although he had been in two minds whether or not to do so, wondering if she might be taking a shine to one of the other lads – Mike, for instance. But he had dismissed the thought as unworthy. No, Sandie was definitely his bird, although he would not have used that terminology. Sandie meant far more to him than a casual pick-up. She was crafty, though. Sometimes he thought he was beginning to understand her, then he would come across another facet of her complex personality that had him flummoxed. Yes, he decided, she had probably had the idea all along – hence her involvement in the practice sessions – and had been cunningly waiting for the suggestion to come from one of the group. Greg did not like to feel he was being manipulated.

'I don't know,' he said. 'She's a lot on with her schoolwork and her music lessons.'

'So have you, but you manage all right.'

'Yeah, but she's younger than us. It might be too much for her.'

'Aw, go on – you're just chicken! You're scared one of us'll run off with her.'

'No, I'm not.' Greg was indignant. 'I know Sandie better than that. I know her a lot better than all you lot do.'

'Oooh!' There was a chorus of ribald exclamation and Greg found himself laughing.

'All right then, I'll ask her, but I'm not promising she'll say yes.' He knew only too well that she would, though. 'She's away at the moment. I'll mention it when she gets back.'

Sandie had gone down to Norfolk to stay with an old schoolfriend for the last week of the long summer holiday. Greg and the rest of the group had been camping in the Lake District for a few days the previous week, so he had not seen her for quite a while. He was missing her. They were missing their piano practices, too, and would need to get down to some serious work in September if they were to make any sort of showing at the next Blackpool Festival. He wasn't sure that having her in the group would be such a good idea. It might be too much for her and there was always the possibility her mother might object. Sandie was still little more than a child – young in some ways, though very mature in others – although she didn't like to think so. But he had promised he would ask.

Sandie jumped at the suggestion as he had guessed – and feared – she might. He was still not terribly sold on the idea. 'Just for a trial period,' he told her; he had insisted on that. 'It might not work out or you might not like it. You do have an awful lot on with your exams and everything – and you'll have to ask your mother anyway, won't you?'

'Hey, what is this?' Sandie retorted. 'Do you want me or don't you? You're sounding pretty negative to me. I've told you, I think it's a fabulous idea and I'd love it. I can't believe you've asked me. It never entered my head that you would.' She opened her eyes wide in a guileless stare, but Greg made no comment. 'But if you're going to be so bloomin' half-hearted about it then you can forget it.'

'Hey, calm down, don't get so aerated. It's you I'm thinking about. It'll be extra work. It's damned hard work at times.'

'Oh, really? I thought you said it was only a bit of fun. That's what you used to say.'

'Well, we've been taking it more seriously lately.'

'It'll be great. I'm real chuffed, even if you're not.'

'Yes, I am pleased,' he said guardedly, then, 'Of course I'm pleased.' He forced a little more enthusiasm into his voice and smiled at her. 'What will your mum say? D'you think she'll raise any objections?'

'Why should she? It's nothing to do with her anyway. I can do as I like.' He could see her mouth setting in an obstinate line.

'Sandra, you know what you said – that you'd try. It's best to keep on the right side of her. So it would be better if you asked her permission rather than, well, just going ahead and doing it.'

'I have been trying. I've tried real hard about her and Duncan. I don't mind about them now, honest. OK, OK, I'll tell her – ask her, I mean – when we've finished our practice.'

'Shall I come with you and explain?'

'*No!*' she almost shouted. 'No, I'm better on my own. She won't say no. She never does these days.'

'That's OK then.' Greg sighed. 'Come on, we'd better get on with this Slavonic dance, hadn't we? Duncan wants us note perfect by Saturday.'

★ ★ ★

393

It was true that her mother had raised few objections lately to whatever Sandie wished to do. They were getting on quite well again, but were skirting round one another, each afraid of upsetting the other. Sandie had taken Greg's advice, partially, asking her mother in a loaded question, which would brook no refusal. 'Greg's asked me if I'd like to join his group – y'know, The Blue Notes. So I've said yes . . . That's OK, isn't it, Mum?'

'But you don't play the guitar, dear.'

'No, as a singer, Mum. I expect I'll have a solo spot sometimes. It's great, isn't it?'

'Yes, I suppose so, so long as it doesn't interfere with all your other things. But I know it's only a bit of fun. Hazel says that Greg treats it quite lightly, so that should be all right.'

Sandie knew her mum would not like to say no. She had been rather wary with Sandie ever since she and Duncan had been away for those few days. They had been down to the Cotswolds in Duncan's car, staying away for a couple of nights. Sandie had been in Norfolk with her old schoolfriend, Melanie, at the time, and Simon had gone to stay with his grandparents. Sandie didn't know what Gran and Grandad thought about it. They might well disapprove; she half-hoped they would. At least Mum had been truthful and told her about it and she had tried not to mind, but it was a sign that things were getting more serious with her and Duncan.

Sandie proved to be an asset to The Blue Notes. Even Greg had to admit it. As the autumn session got into its swing they found they were getting more bookings. There was scarcely a week when they did not have a concert, usually on a Saturday night. At first their bookings had been mainly for youth club dances and parties, but now they were being asked to perform at various hotels for twenty-first birthdays or engagement parties. Sandie fitted in well and did not try to hog the limelight. She usually sang the melody line while the lads harmonised below, very occasionally having a solo spot.

Abbie worried in case she would be unable to cope with everything – her schoolwork, her serious musical studies and this pop group. But she appeared to be doing so and as she was at her best at the moment – friendly, happy and quite easy to get on with – she made no comment.

It was said for decades afterwards that everyone remembered where they were and what they were doing on the evening that President Kennedy was assassinated: 22 November, 1963.

Abbie was at her friend Doreen's house. She had received a frantic phone call from her soon after she arrived home from college. 'Abbie, I've got to see you. Something awful has happened.' Doreen's voice shook. 'Our Veronica has taken an overdose.'

'Oh, Doreen, how dreadful!' Abbie felt herself turn cold. 'She's not . . .?' She did not dare to say the word.

'No, she's not . . .' said Doreen, not speaking the dreaded word either. 'Thank God! We found her in time and got her into hospital. That's where she is now. I don't think she really meant to do it. We think it was just a cry for help. Oh, the silly, silly girl!'

'Why did she do it?' asked Abbie, although she thought she could guess. 'Do you know?'

'Yes, we know.' Doreen sighed. 'I can't tell you now. Abbie, come round and see me, please. I can't come to you. I'm in no fit state to go anywhere. I've been at the hospital most of the day and Norman's going again this evening. And the rest of the kids are upset, of course.'

'She will be all right, won't she?'

'Yes, thank God,' said Doreen again. 'She's OK now, but they're keeping her in for a while. She's been such a fool, Abbie. And I never knew about it. If I'd known, then perhaps I could have done something. You don't know what I'm on about, do you? I'll tell you later. Come as soon as you can, love.'

But I do know, thought Abbie as she put the phone down, promising Doreen she would be round as soon as possible. It's all my fault. I should have said something. It would have meant breaking her promise to Sandie, but surely, in this case, that would have been excusable? Just supposing the girl had died. Abbie would have been unable to forgive herself. She decided she would have to make a clean breast of things with Doreen. She must tell her she had known about the young priest for quite a while, but had not wanted to tell tales. There must be no more secrets between the two of them ever again. If that was the reason for Veronica's suicide bid, of course.

It was, and Doreen, understandably, was still very distraught. Mostly about her daughter's overdose, of course, but also about the scandal that the relationship between Veronica and Father Dominic O'Reilly had caused in the parish.

'How far did it go?' asked Abbie. 'Did they ... you know?'

Doreen almost smiled. 'The same old Abbie, aren't you? Can't put it into words. Did they have a sexual relationship, you mean? No, thank God, it didn't get that far. In fact, I don't think it got very far at all except in Veronica's mind. And whatever went on, you can be sure it was her that was doing all the running. Oh, I feel so ashamed.'

It seemed that several people had noticed the blossoming friendship and the word had got round, inevitably, to the parish priest, Father Murdoch. Father Dominic had been questioned and had admitted that yes, he was friendly with Veronica Jarvis, yes, he was attracted to her, but the attraction had not got any further than holding hands. He had been struggling hard against the temptation to break his vow of chastity and obedience, and was only too glad to accept the offer of a transfer to a distant parish as far away as possible, in Wiltshire. All this Father Murdoch had told to Doreen. She was stunned by the revelations, feeling, as was usual in such cases, that everyone had known about it but her.

'He'd already had a talk to Veronica – Father Murdoch, I mean. I think he tried to be quite gentle and understanding with her, but Norman and me – especially me – well, we really had a go at her about letting us down and causing all this trouble for everyone. She was defiant more than anything at first – she can be at times – then, last night, she went and did this! Oh, the silly, silly girl.' Doreen burst into tears again. 'We feel dreadful now that we were so cross with her. We should have tried to be more sympathetic. Oh, if only we'd known sooner.'

Abbie put an arm round her friend as they sat together on the settee. 'Listen, love. I've a confession to make.' She explained how she had known for quite a while about Veronica and the young curate; that Veronica had confided in Sandie, and that Sandie, feeling concerned about it, had told her mother. She was worried as to how Doreen might react. She might have expected her somewhat impetuous friend to be angry and to start blaming her for what had happened. But Doreen only shook her head sadly.

'I know why you didn't tell me,' she said. 'It was because of that business with Ken. I'd accused you of interfering; I said all sorts of awful things and caused all that trouble between us. I'm not surprised you felt you couldn't say anything. I don't blame you at all. It's all my fault. Everything's my fault. It was my affair with Ken that started all the rot, and look where it's led. I nearly lost my daughter . . .'

'You mustn't think like that.' Abbie took hold of her arms and shook her gently. 'Listen to me, Doreen. You didn't lose her. She's getting better, and she's young enough. She'll get over this, but she'll need all your support, yours and Norman's. You mustn't worry about the people at church. They'll soon forget about it. It'll be a nine day wonder. Anyway, this Father O'Reilly didn't actually break his vows, did he?' She knew this was of vital importance to Catholics.

'No, but I bet he would've done if it had been up to her, the naughty girl.'

Doreen sounded a little more composed now. 'But it's often the women who do the leading astray, isn't it? Look at Adam and Eve.'

Abbie nodded. She was thinking more of Sandie and Greg than Adam and Eve, alone together now in the house, except for Simon who would, no doubt, be tucked away in his room with his league tables. She did not think they would get up to anything. She trusted Greg, but she was not quite so sure that she entirely trusted her rapidly maturing daughter. They were very young – Greg was almost eighteen and Sandie would be seventeen in a couple of months – but she could see they were growing very attached to one another. There was nothing she could do about it except hope and pray they were sensible. She felt, however, that Greg was the one with the more common sense and that it would be up to him to put a curb, if needs be, on their relationship.

It was at that moment that Norman came bursting into the room. 'Something awful's happening! On the telly . . . come and watch. It's President Kennedy. He's been shot!'

They dashed into the visitors' lounge where there was a large television set. They saw the President slumped at the back of the open-top car, with his pretty young wife, wearing one of her distinctive pill-box hats, crying in anguish over his motionless body. It was several moments later that the news came through that President Kennedy was dead. He had been driving through Dallas with his wife and the Governor of Texas. Only a few hours earlier he had said in his speech, 'This is a dangerous and uncertain world.' He had been President since 1961, less than three years. During the Kennedy era the White House had been compared to Camelot, an analogy fostered by the President. Now the fairy tale was ended.

'Goodness me, how dreadful,' breathed Doreen, after a few moments of stunned silence. 'It puts your own worries into perspective, doesn't it? Our Veronica's getting better, but that poor fellow and his wife . . . Oh dear, it's just too tragic for words.'

Sandie and Greg were amusing themselves playing a few light-hearted duets when Simon, who had been watching television in the back room, came bursting in with the news. They had been very successful in the recent Festival, winning their duet class hands down. Greg had come first in his piano class and Sandie, now she no longer had to compete with Greg, had also been the winner in one of hers. So they felt they deserved a little light relief.

They watched in silence. American politics did not mean a great deal to any of them, nor to a lot of people outside the USA, but millions had been charmed by the charismatic President. They felt glum after the announcement of his death, not inclined to do any more practice, disinclined to do anything at all.

Sandie was very distressed the following week, as were all the family, on hearing the news that her grandmother, Lily, had to go into hospital again for an emergency operation.

'They've found another lump in the other breast,' Abbie told her daughter, believing she was old enough to know the truth. 'Try not to worry, love. She'll be all right; they'll be able to catch it in time.'

But at heart, Abbie was very worried. She was scared that Lily had left it too late the first time and that now the disease might have got out of control. All they could do was trust in the skill of the surgeon and, as Lily urged, to say their prayers for her.

She was in hospital for ten days, coming home the week before Christmas to a very concerned Frank who could not do enough for her. He had even learned to cook, after a fashion, although he had never attempted to do so before, and to do the washing and ironing. Abbie told him, jokingly, that it was amazing what men could do if they really tried. None of them felt like joking, but they knew they had to put on a brave face in front of Lily; she really did look very weak and poorly.

She had rallied a little by Christmas and was well enough to spend the day with Abbie and her family. Abbie's own feelings were in a state of chaos. She alternated between feeling deliriously happy and then very sad. She was sad about Lily, fearing that her mother-in-law's improvement might only be temporary, but she could not help feeling happy as well, because Duncan had asked her to marry him and she had said she would. He spent Christmas Day at Abbie's home and everyone, including Sandie, made him most welcome. They had not yet made a formal announcement although they had chosen the ring, a ruby and diamond cluster, at Beaverbrook's the previous week. They decided New Year's Eve would be a good time to tell everyone of their engagement. Abbie had thought it best not to make a great show of their friendship in front of Lily and Frank, especially with Lily being so frail. She would prefer to break the news to her in private that she and Duncan were to be married, probably this coming summer, and she saw no reason why her former mother-in-law should object. Duncan had insisted there was no point in waiting too long although they had not yet discussed where they were to live after their marriage. Abbie assumed Duncan would move in with her. It would be less of an upheaval for her children. But then, what about Duncan's pupils? There were so many things to take into consideration.

Abbie still saw Sandie as the greatest stumbling block to their going ahead with their plans, although she was sure

Simon would be amenable to whatever they decided to do. She had not said too much about her doubts to Duncan, however, as he still refused to see that Sandie was a problem at all. He admitted she was a little moody at times, like a lot of teenagers, but he was convinced she would accept their news quite easily. 'It won't be any great surprise to her,' he said, very light-heartedly. 'She must have guessed the way things are heading. Don't worry about her, Abbie my dear. She'll be just fine, you'll see.'

They had decided to tell Sandie and Simon, with as little fuss as possible, on New Year's Eve, and then Abbie would start to wear her ring. Then they would go and break the news to Lily and Frank, and to her father and Faith who had met Duncan and seemed to like and accept him. As a future son-in-law though? Abbie could foresee no objection there. Besides, as she continually tried to tell herself, it was her life and she must live it in the way she chose; it was really nothing to do with anyone else.

Abbie thought it would be better to tell the children on her own, quite casually, instead of making a more formal announcement with Duncan present. Simon accepted the news of their engagement with the words 'Cool, Mum!' and a satisfied grin. Sandie went very quiet, as Abbie had feared she might. She glanced at the ring and said, 'Very nice,' and then, almost inaudibly, 'I hope you'll be very happy.'

She left the room soon afterwards and Abbie thought she could see the glint of tears in her eyes, but when she reappeared a little later there was no sign of them. 'I'm off now, Mum,' she said cheerily, when Greg knocked at the door. He had his own car now and they were going to a New Year's Eve party.

''Bye, love, enjoy yourself,' said Abbie. She decided not to say, 'Don't be late.' It was New Year's Eve after all and she would be safe enough with Greg. Simon was off to a party with some of his mates just around the corner, and she and Duncan had booked a meal at a restaurant as a quiet celebration for the two of them.

Sandie's coming round, Abbie told herself. Give her a week or so and she'll be fine. But her troubles were only just beginning.

Duncan had wondered how Sandie would react at her next music lesson, and how he should behave towards her.

The first quarter-hour of the lesson proceeded normally as this was the time which coincided with Greg's lesson, when the two of them played their duets. They were progressing well and needed little supervision. After Greg had departed there was an uncomfortable silence in which he and Sandie just regarded one another steadily. It was the first time he had seen her since the engagement.

'Sandie, I think you know how much I love your mother, don't you?' he began. 'We are going to be married – this summer, I hope.'

Sandie gave a slight shrug. 'So she said.'

Duncan took a deep breath. 'She loved your father very much – she told me so – but he's been gone a long time now, hasn't he? And your mother is still a young woman. She has her own life to lead, and I want to be a part of that life. She wants it too. I will never take the place of your dad, I know.'

'Don't even try,' muttered Sandie.

Duncan went on as though he had not heard her. 'Your mum deserves a bit of happiness. There has only ever been your father, Peter, she still talks about him, you know. She's never had another friend – a man friend, I mean – and that's why I'm so happy she's fallen in love with me. She has, you know,' he added, as Sandie gave him a strange look.

'That's what you think,' she retorted.

'She does love me, Sandra. I know she does.'

'I didn't mean that. I meant what you said about her not having another man friend. She did, you know.'

'It's the first I've heard of it. I don't think this is true.'

'Then it shows how much you know! She was engaged to a

feller called Jim, Jim Webster, while me dad was missing during the war. She told me. Then it was all off when me dad came back. He lived on the Moss, this Jim, where she lived when she was a Land Girl.' Duncan stared at her. Abbie had not told him about this, if it was true. But then there was no reason why she should have done. 'And I'll tell you something else. He still lives there, and me mum goes to see him. She's done some Tupperware parties there. I know he's married an' all that, but he still likes her, I can tell. And she likes him. I know 'cause I've seen them and the way they look at each other.'

'Sandra, I'm going to forget you've said all this,' said Duncan calmly, although he was feeling far from calm inside. 'You're upset and angry and I can understand why. But it's no use trying to cause trouble between your mother and me. It just won't work. Now, let's get on with our lesson. The Debussy . . . how are you getting on with that?'

Abbie was alarmed and very distressed on hearing what Sandie had said to Duncan. 'But it's not true!' she cried. 'How could she make up a story like that? I haven't the slightest interest in Jim Webster, nor he in me. He's happily married, and that's what we are going to be, Duncan. Oh, the naughty girl! No, this is more than just naughty; it's spiteful. I would never have believed it of Sandie. She's just trying to cause trouble.'

'That much is obvious,' replied Duncan composedly. Abbie had never known him to lose his temper or even to get more than slightly annoyed. 'It is true though, isn't it, that you were engaged to this man?'

'Well, yes, for a short time. But I didn't love Jim in the way I loved Peter, nor as I love you. We were just good friends really, with working together, that's all.'

'Then why didn't you tell me about it? And that you'd met up with him again? I would prefer to have known, rather than to hear it from Sandie.'

403

'Because it wasn't important, Duncan. I would have told you sometime. There must be lots of things we don't know about each other yet. I'd hardly given Jim a thought since I married Peter, until Sylvia happened to turn up at one of my Tupper parties. Please believe me, Duncan.'

'Yes, I do believe you,' said Duncan. 'I wish I'd known about it, that's all. There mustn't be any secrets between us, Abbie. From now on no secrets, mmm?' She saw to her relief that he was smiling. He crossed the room and sat next to her on the settee, putting his arm around her. They were at his home in his comfortable sitting room.

'No, Duncan, no secrets,' she agreed as he kissed her lightly. 'And we mustn't let her spoil things for us. I'm determined she won't. It's not easy though. She's so moody and difficult. Not all the time; she's just up and down, you know?'

'Yes, I'm beginning to realise what you mean, my dear, about the anxiety she causes you. It's the first time I've seen that side of her for myself. But I think we should refuse to get ruffled. We must try not to get upset by anything she does or says. She's certainly not going to come between us, darling. Agreed?'

'Agreed,' replied Abbie. 'She'll get used to the idea of our engagement. Simon has.' But Abbie was far from convinced that this was true.

Greg was also very worried by Sandie's up and down moods which had grown worse since her mother's engagement. At times he was almost tempted to call the whole thing off. He was too young anyway to be committed to a serious relationship with a girl and he had his musical career ahead of him. He had been accepted to start as a student at a prestigious music school in Manchester next September. He was very fond of Sandra and when she was in one of her sunny moods there was no one whose company he enjoyed more. But at other times he despaired of her – her irritability and moodiness and the way she went on about her mother and Duncan, and then, perversely, refused even to mention them.

Sometimes he was convinced he would be better off without her, but what might it do to her, he asked himself, if he ended their friendship? He was aware that she was as fond of him as he was of her, and he knew he was not being conceited in feeling that he gave her some sort of stability in her life. She looked up to him and admired him, and if he could help her in any way to come to terms with her problems then he felt he must try to do so. Besides, she was a great asset to the group. The other lads might well be annoyed with him if he sent her packing. Knowing Sandie, she would quit the group as well if he finished with her.

Anyway, no matter how much he might argue with himself about the pros and cons of their relationship, Greg knew that he loved her. Despite her faults and despite the fact that they were both very young he loved Sandie and hoped that one day – though it could be a long way ahead – they might have a future together.

He knew she was not having an easy time, although many of her troubles were of her own making. One problem over which she had no control, however, and which was upsetting her greatly was the deteriorating health of her beloved grandmother, Lily. He feared the effect on Sandie if the worst was to happen.

Chapter 25

Lily's condition was rapidly worsening. Abbie and Frank both knew, although they did not admit it to one another and certainly not to Lily, that the disease had taken hold of her and that she was not likely to live longer than a few months. Abbie grew more distressed each time she visited her at the way the flesh appeared to be dropping off her body. Her once plump arms and legs were stick-like and her formerly rounded face was almost skeletal. She continued to potter about the house, refusing to go to bed except at the times when she was very tired, until the end of February. She was then forced to take to her bed, but declined the suggestion that she should go into hospital.

'No, I'll stay here,' she told Abbie when she visited her. 'I'm not going to be packed off to any hospital. Frank's very good. He'll look after me, won't you, love?' Her faded blue eyes glowed with love as she smiled weakly at her husband. 'I'll get better much quicker with Frank looking after me.' But Abbie guessed she knew, as they all knew, that she would not do so.

'Yes, Mum, that's the spirit. Get better soon,' said Abbie, kissing her sunken cheek.

'It's the least I can do,' said Frank when Abbie took leave of him. 'I'll look after her as long as it takes. The doctor's very good. He comes every week and gives her something for the pain. It helps, she says. But I don't think it'll be very long, do you, Abbie?' It was the first time he had admitted to what, assuredly, would happen.

'I don't know, Dad,' she said. She had been trying to call him 'Dad' ever since she had started to call Lily 'Mum', and now the word came more easily. 'We can't tell. But, no, I don't think it will be very long. Take care of yourself now, and take care of Mum.' She felt the tears misting her eyes as she kissed his ruddy cheek then hurried down the path to her car.

She knew how upset Sandie would be to see her gran in this state. She visited her at least once a week, Simon rather less frequently, and Abbie knew she then behaved most charmingly, as she could when she tried. She had been very amenable at the time of her seventeenth birthday a few weeks ago, as was only to be expected. Like all girls she loved presents and Abbie had not allowed their somewhat strained relations to make any difference. She bought her the clothes she had requested – the knee-length boots and the short black shift dress to wear when she sang with the group – as well as a couple of records and some make-up, and was gratified to see her face light up with pleasure. But the occasion, this year, had passed with the minimum of fuss, as had Abbie's forty-third birthday the following week.

Her friends had been delighted at the news of her engagement on her return to college after the Christmas break, and she had been equally delighted on hearing that Jean and Eric were now officially engaged.

'A double wedding, eh, kid?' Jean enthused, but Abbie refused to be drawn. She knew Jean was only joking anyway, but she and Duncan had not yet made any definite plans. This was not because of Sandie – they were steadfast in their determination not to let her upset them – but because with Lily so ill Abbie did not want to plan too far ahead. It seemed callous, she said, to be planning a wedding with Lily at death's door.

Duncan reported that Sandie was working well at her music lessons. She was rather sullen at times, certainly not chatty, but the standard of her playing had not deteriorated. Sometimes she seemed, in her almost frenzied rendering of Rachmaninov or Chopin, to be working out her frustrations on the keyboard. Duncan understood this. He, too, found piano playing a relief from stress and anxieties. She never mentioned their engagement or asked about their future plans. It was as though, by refusing to talk about it, she was pretending that the situation did not exist.

Abbie and Duncan both knew this state of affairs could not go on for ever. There must come a day of reckoning, a time when Sandie was forced to face up to the inevitable; the marriage of her mother and the man she refused to see as anything but her music teacher. But for the moment, with no definite plans in mind, they were willing, if not happy, to let things ride.

Lily died towards the end of March. Sandie was inconsolable, as Abbie had anticipated she would be. For a short while their differences seemed to be shelved as Sandie sobbed out her grief, even putting her arms around her mother – a very rare occurrence – as she railed against the unfairness of life and God and everything.

'Why did my gran have to die? It isn't fair. She believed in God, so why didn't He make her better? I don't want to believe in Him any more. I loved my gran. I loved her more than anybody in the world.'

Abbie, despite her own sadness, felt a sharp stab of pain at her daughter's words. More than me? she thought. She had always known Sandie was very fond of her grandmother, but to say she loved her more than anyone? She came to the conclusion that the girl was distraught, not entirely aware of what she was saying or of the effect her words might be having. Greg seemed to be forgotten, too, for a while; she stayed in her room most of the time, refusing to go out except to school.

Abbie decided both her children were old enough to

attend the funeral. Simon would soon be fifteen and was maturing quite quickly now. He was subdued and saddened by his gran's death, but not so grief-stricken as Sandie. Abbie was startled on the morning of the funeral when Sandie appeared wearing her bright red jacket. It was the most colourful garment she had in her wardrobe. Most of the time she preferred, like many teenagers, to wear dark sombre clothes, beatnik-style; black, grey, brown or navy with heavy clumpy shoes. Abbie made no comment now although her surprised glance did not go unnoticed.

'Gran wouldn't've wanted me to be miserable,' Sandie said, a shade too loudly and defiantly. 'She liked me in this jacket and I know she'd want me to wear it. I don't have to dress in black to show how much I miss her.'

'Of course, you're right, dear,' said Abbie, knowing the girl's sentiments were sincere, although she did wish she had been clad more suitably.

There was a short service at the Methodist church that Lily had attended, followed by the burial at the cemetery across the road. Abbie was surprised at the number of people who were there. Lily had made many friends in the short time she had lived here; women from the Guild she belonged to and members of the chapel congregation. Sandie remained dry-eyed and motionless during the service. It was only when the coffin was lowered into the grave and Frank threw the clods of earth into the gaping chasm that she broke down. Abbie put a comforting arm around her and she felt her daughter draw close to her, both physically and, at that moment, mentally and emotionally, too, as they shared their grief for the woman who had been a much loved grandmother and a substitute mother to Abbie.

Duncan, on the other side of Abbie, tightened his hold on her arm. She was glad of his comforting presence. She felt she had not been entirely fair to him, preoccupied as she had been with her own worries and concerns, but he had seemed to understand. Maybe now, though, it was time to look at the future – their future, hers and Duncan's.

They started to make plans. They decided on a Saturday in the middle of August for their wedding. It was to be at the church where Duncan played the organ and they saw the vicar at once to make arrangements. Saturdays in the summer months tended to be booked up well in advance. Abbie had not attended church regularly since moving to Blackpool, although she had occasionally visited Duncan's parish church, mainly, she had to admit, to hear his organ playing.

'It's going to be more difficult finding somewhere for the reception,' said Duncan. 'In the height of the season we'll be lucky to find a hotel or restaurant that isn't already fully booked.'

'It won't be a large reception,' said Abbie. 'Not more than twenty to thirty people.' She did not want a big fuss. All she really wanted was for her and Duncan to be married as unobtrusively as possible. Sometimes she wished it could be much sooner, even at the Register Office as that would cut out much of the pomp and formality. But it was Duncan who had insisted on what he called a 'proper wedding', saying they needed time, too, to go on a real honeymoon. This would not be possible for either of them before the end of the scholastic year.

Doreen came to the rescue, offering to cater for the reception at the Dorabella, especially as it was to be a simple lunchtime meal.

'We don't do lunches for the visitors now,' she said, 'and we never did one on a Saturday anyway, 'cause it's change-over day. No, we've gone on to bed, breakfast and evening meal – much easier all round. Our Vera'll come in and see to the bedrooms and the guests arriving. So long as a cold buffet'll do for you I'll be pleased to oblige. So that's that – no arguments. It's the least I can do for me best pal.'

Abbie was touched. She had already asked Doreen to be her matron-of-honour. Now she wondered if that would be possible with her friend doing the catering as well, but Doreen was determined to take it all in her stride. 'No problem,' she said. 'I can prepare it all the night before and stick it in the fridge. And I've two very reliable women who help out when we're busy. They'll get it all prepared while we're at church. I wouldn't miss your big day for anything. Oh, kid, I'm so happy for you!'

Doreen was much happier herself these days. Veronica had been allowed to leave school at Christmas and was now working at the Marks & Spencer store in Church Street. She had given up any ideas she might have had about A-levels and 'higher education' and decided she wanted a job. Doreen was relieved because she seemed to have recovered from the effects of her abortive love affair and was now on a training course in Manchester. She hoped, eventually, to go into store management.

Abbie called to see her old friend quite regularly now, at least once a fortnight, and they both found it helped tremendously to confide in one another. There were certain things she could not share with Duncan. He had said there were to be no secrets between them, but she did not want to tell him how very concerned she was about Sandie's recent behaviour. She realised he must be sick and tired of hearing about the girl, and at times he even suggested that Abbie might be exaggerating or overreacting to her daughter's conduct. And so, of late, she had said very little to him. Since her outburst in early January Sandie had behaved very well towards Duncan. But he did not have to live with her.

'Sometimes I can't wait for her to go to college,' Abbie said now. 'That sounds dreadful, I know, but maybe we might get on better, like you and Veronica are doing, if we didn't have to see each other every day. But that's eighteen months away, always supposing she does decide to go to college. She's very secretive again now about her ambitions, if she has any. It seems to be all pop music at the moment and singing with this blessed group. Sometimes I'm sorry I said she could join, although whatever Sandie wants Sandie seems to get. I doubt if I could have stopped her.'

'I shouldn't worry too much if I were you,' said Doreen. 'Kids have to have some form of relaxation, especially when they're studying hard like your Sandie is. I thought you'd been getting on better just lately?'

'I thought so too. I felt she was really close to me when Lily died, but it didn't last long. She's worse than ever. I don't know whether it's me and Duncan or her gran's death that's sent her all hay-wire, but she's out nearly every night, and she comes in late. Once or twice I've suspected she's had a drink . . . well, more than one.'

'Mmm, kids do,' replied Doreen, rather too complacently for Abbie's liking. 'Not all landlords are too fussy about 'em being under age.'

'She shouldn't even be in a pub at all. She's only seventeen. But I know this group she's in have had quite a few bookings at hotels recently. I suspect some of them might be rather seedy.'

'Doesn't she tell you where she's going?'

'No, not always. And I don't ask in case I get my head bitten off. I think I might have a word with Greg if I can get him on his own. I never thought I'd say this, but I feel if anyone can stop her from going off the rails it's him. On the other hand, I realise if it hadn't been for him she would never have joined this group. All the same, he's a sensible lad and I trust him.'

'It seems harmless enough,' said Doreen, 'and I agree that Greg's a real nice lad. He'll keep her on the straight and narrow. They're still playing the piano together, aren't they?'

'Yes, but not as much as they used to. And she doesn't practise as much either. I've told you, it's all this pop stuff now. It started when she went to that Beatles concert and since then it's seemed to get a hold of her.'

'She could do a lot worse,' said Doreen. Abbie knew her friend had never really understood about Sandie and her musical studies. In her youth Doreen had much preferred *Worker's Playtime* and *Forces' Favourites* to the more serious music Abbie had sometimes liked to listen to. Now she was a devotee not only of *Housewives' Choice*, but *6-5 Special* and *Juke Box Jury* on the television. She had hinted in the past that Abbie was expecting too much of her daughter; schoolwork and homework and piano lessons and exams on top of it all. 'It's just a harmless bit of fun, isn't it?' she said now. 'You should be proud of her. She might be a pop star, like Cilla Black, before you know where you are.'

Heaven forbid, thought Abbie, although the girl singer from Liverpool seemed a nice enough lass. 'I doubt it,' she replied evenly.

'How's she taken the news of the wedding?'

'As though it's none of her business,' replied Abbie. 'It's as though Duncan doesn't exist, at least, not in relation to me.'

'She'll come round,' said Doreen.

'Yes, I suppose so,' Abbie sighed. But she had little idea of the extent of her daughter's wild behaviour.

Greg was more worried than ever about Sandie. Since her grandmother had died her behaviour had become much more reckless.

The first thing had been when she started smoking. Dave and Mike both smoked, Greg and Tony didn't, although Greg had no objection to others doing so, except, of course, for Sandie. It all began when Dave handed round a packet of cocktail cigarettes, small coloured things in several pretty shades, a novelty one of his friends had brought back from abroad.

'Oh, those are cute,' said Sandie. 'I'll have one of those. Ta very much, Dave.' She grabbed hold of a pink cigarette then looked coyly towards Mike, fluttering her eyelids. 'Could I have a light please, Mike?'

'You don't smoke,' said Greg, more crossly than he would normally have done because he was annoyed, both with

Dave and with Sandie. 'You shouldn't've offered her one, Dave.'

'Who says I don't smoke?' retorted Sandie. 'Just because I never have it doesn't mean I never will. What's it got to do with you anyroad? I can do as I like; I don't have to ask your permission. A light, please, Mike.'

'Oh, let her be,' said Dave easily. 'They're poncy little things anyway. They won't do her any harm. Here, Sandie – you might as well have what's left.' He threw the packet across the table at her. 'They're more suitable for girls anyway.'

Greg tried not to let his irritation show. He would have a quiet word with her later. 'Don't smoke it all,' he said as lightly as he could. He had quite expected her to splutter and choke at the first puff, but she seemed to be handling the new experience quite well. 'You have to sing again later and it'll spoil your voice.'

'OK, OK, Grandad.' Sandie pulled a face at him, but she did stub the cigarette out in the ashtray.

'That goes for all of us,' said Mike reasonably. 'We've all got to sing again, but the odd one just helps you relax, that's all.'

Greg tried to warn her after the concert, when he was driving her home, about the hidden dangers of smoking – they had had a lecture about it at school – but she told him to mind his own business. He decided to do so, for the moment at least. Maybe now was not the time to lecture her. Her grandmother had died only a few weeks ago and he knew she was still very upset.

She had started drinking as well. Only Babycham, to be sure, but she would think nothing of knocking back a couple of bottles in rapid succession and the first time she had been so giggly and legless she could hardly stand. Luckily it was after they had finished their spot or she would have been unable to sing again. He told her off that time in no uncertain terms and made her drink black coffee until she sobered up. Whatever would her mother think if she arrived home in a state like that? They were already out much later than she was supposed to be.

He knew Abbie Horsfall was trusting him to make sure Sandie didn't get into any sort of trouble. He realised she was not all that keen on her daughter being in the group; much more of this sort of behaviour and Sandie might find herself in real bother. He suspected she wasn't practising much either and her piano studies were beginning to suffer as a consequence. Duncan had had a quiet word with him and suggested maybe it was too much for her to cope with the group as well as everything else.

'I'll have a talk to her,' Greg had told him. Really, she was getting to be a nuisance. If this carried on Duncan would be saying that the band was too much for Greg, as well. He did try to talk to her, but to no avail.

'Aw, why can't you shurrup about it?' Sandie had said. Her manner of speaking, too, had worsened since she had got in with a different crowd at school. 'I'm enjoying meself. Why can't you leave me alone. Honestly, sometimes I feel as though I'm going out with me bloody grandad. If it's not smoking or drinking you're on about then it's me flippin' piano practice.'

'You've changed, Sandra. Paula says you have. She says—'

'Paula's a silly stuck-up cow! You've been talking about me behind me back, haven't you? I might've known.'

'Only because she's worried about you, Sandra. And so am I.'

'Then you've no need to be. I'm fine. Everything's just fantabulous.' She had been at the Babycham again and she flung her arms out wide, striking him on the shoulder and causing him to swerve dangerously near an oncoming car. 'At least it would be if you'd give over nattering to me.'

'Look out, you idiot! We nearly had a bump then.'

'No, we didn't. We were miles away from him. And when

415

are you going to let me have a go at driving? You promised, didn't you?'

'When you start behaving yourself.' In spite of feeling so cross with her he found himself smiling. She could still get round him. He was still very fond of her. 'You'd have to get a licence. Listen, Sandra, I'll give you a few lessons, but only if you try and act a bit more reasonably. I don't know what's got into you lately.'

'Neither do I, sometimes,' Sandie replied in a very different kind of voice. Then, 'OK, Grandad,' she said. 'I'll try to be a good girl.' She giggled again and placed her hand on his thigh. He quickly covered her hand with his and gave it a squeeze, then he firmly removed it from his leg and turned back to the wheel.

It was soon afterwards that Abbie confided in him about her daughter. He could tell she was very worried. 'It hasn't been easy for her,' she said, 'with her grandmother dying and everything.' He supposed she meant her engagement to Duncan. 'Does she ever say anything,' she asked tentatively, 'about Duncan and me?' Greg realised how hard it must be for her to ask and he felt sorry for her. 'She knows we've fixed the wedding date, but she just won't talk about it.'

'She doesn't say much,' Greg answered truthfully. 'Maybe she's getting used to the idea. I don't think it's that. Her erratic behaviour seemed to start just after her gran died. I think it must be that. Her way of hitting back, maybe. Try not to worry, Mrs Horsfall. I'm sure she'll calm down.'

'I hope so. You're a good lad, Greg.'

It was at that moment that Sandie appeared in the living room. It sometimes took her ages to get ready and her mother had taken advantage of the fact.

'Talking about me?' she asked brightly, but with a wary expression in her eyes.

'Of course not, dear,' said her mother. 'Off you go now. You've kept Greg waiting long enough. Enjoy yourselves.'

'We sure will,' Sandie replied cheerily.

Greg gave her mother a sympathetic smile which was meant to convey 'Don't worry – I'll look after her.' But he knew that was easier said than done.

'Hey, girls, look what I've got.' Sandie had appeared in the sixth-form common room during the lunch-break waving the half-packet of cocktail cigarettes. 'Who'd like one? Here, Cheryl, Vicky . . . catch.' She tossed a couple of cigarettes, a blue one and a green one, in their direction. 'And one for me. Now there's just one left. What about you, Lindsay? Oh no, you don't smoke, do you?' She pulled her face into a moue at the girl who used to be her best friend.

'No, and neither should you, you silly fool!' hissed Lindsay in a hoarse whisper. 'You'll be for it, I can tell you, if any of the senior prefects catch you smoking again in here. Paula's threatened to tell the Head, you know.'

'Oh, shucks to Paula! She'll not come in. She's at a netball practice – I've just seen her.' Sandie giggled as she threw the last cigarette in the air. It was caught by Hazel, another member of the group that Sandie had once thought of as being rather fast, but who were now becoming her best buddies.

It was not the first time Sandie had had a puff at a cigarette, which was why she had known how to go about it when Dave had offered her one, much to Greg's disgust. The thought amused her. Greg was such an old woman at times, but she was hanging on to him. If she were to let go of him he would soon be snapped up by that simpering Marcia who was always making sheep's eyes at him, or Paula who liked to brag that she and Greg 'went back a long way'. Sandie knew she was the envy of a lot of girls, having Greg Matthews as a boyfriend, and she intended to keep it that way. When he wasn't telling her off he could be quite amorous. Things were progressing very nicely in that direction, especially since he had been given his own car. The way things were heading she might even have something to boast about soon, like Cheryl and Vicky did. On the other hand, maybe she wouldn't tell anyone, if they ever did go the whole way. That would be very disloyal to Greg. She was, after all, very fond of him – in fact, she was in love with him – and what went on between them should be strictly private.

She didn't see Lindsay so much now, nor Paula, out of school hours. She still went to the Youth Club occasionally, but she was beginning to find it rather childish. She had given up on the youth choir, making the excuse that her commitment to The Blue Notes took up most of her time. Which it did, and how that annoyed Paula, who, she knew, had designs on Greg. Her onetime friend was now a senior prefect and had become very bossy, but Sandie didn't care. She was having fun. Cheryl and Vicky and co. sometimes sneaked out to the pub at lunchtime for a quick half, not wearing school uniform, of course. Cheryl lived nearby and they went to her home to change whilst her mother was out at work. So far they hadn't got caught.

'Come with us, Sandie,' they'd said. 'It's a laugh, honestly!' She decided the next time they went she might go with them. She was thinking she might leave school in the summer so it wouldn't matter if she got into trouble, even expelled. Would they be expelled for that? she wondered. What the hell! She had made up her mind she wanted to be a singer, a real singer, like Helen Shapiro, not a pianist, so she wouldn't need to go to college. That would be one in the eye for Duncan, and for her mother.

Duncan had frowned at her once or twice during her Saturday-morning lesson. She knew he was aware that she was not practising so diligently, although she hadn't given up entirely on her practice; she didn't want her mother continually on her back. But this time he was really annoyed.

'Sandra, you haven't practised. I don't believe you've looked at this Haydn since last week. You're still stumbling over the runs on the second page and the rest is too mechanical. You're just not trying. You've an exam coming up and you won't be ready.'

'It's not for ages yet,' she replied sulkily.

'Nevertheless, there's a lot to do. If you don't intend to settle down and work then it's no use, is it? You had better tell your mother there is no point in her wasting her money on lessons if you are not going to practise.'

'Why don't you tell her yourself?' Sandie retorted. 'You see her every night, don't you?' They stared at one another, their animosity revealed in the hostile looks of both of them. It was the first time it had become so obvious.

Duncan felt himself quail a little. He knew now what Abbie meant and he realised that if he didn't try now to alleviate the situation it could be open warfare between him and the girl. He tried to keep the lessons going on a professional level. Abbie had insisted she must keep on paying for them although he had told her this was ridiculous, considering he would soon be Sandra's stepfather. The thought of that now pulled him up short. From the look on her face at that moment it seemed as though she would never accept him.

'Oh, come on, Sandra, let's not be too hasty,' he said quickly. 'Let's try again, shall we? Start at the top of page two.

She stared at him for a few seconds through narrowed eyelids, but when she started to play again it was a good deal more competently. He sighed inwardly. All he could do was try.

Chapter 26

Oh no, not again, Greg thought to himself as he watched Sandie giggling with Mike and Dave. Mike's girlfriend, Sharon, was part of the little crowd as well, and another couple of lads, guests at the party at which the group had been performing. The hotel was one that Greg described to himself as seedy and run-down, in a side street off the promenade, near to the Golden Mile. Not the sort of booking they preferred to take, but they had learned not to turn up their noses at anything. The Beatles had not had to be fussy about some of the dives they had played in at first. From all accounts, the Cavern left a lot to be desired.

Sandy had been at the Babycham again and had had one or two cigarettes. He was keeping an eye on her – not too obtrusively, though, as he knew it annoyed her – whilst he was discussing their forthcoming bookings with Tony. The smoky atmosphere was playing havoc with his throat and he felt he would like to go home soon. They had finished their couple of spots and Greg knew that his singing and playing had not been up to scratch tonight, although none of the others had commented. He set exacting standards for himself, however, and tonight he had fallen short of them.

It was possible the group would be winding up soon, although Greg had told the other members there was no reason why they shouldn't carry on without him. It had been fun while it lasted, but he was off to music college in September. He had the feeling Dave, Mike and Tony would prefer to call it a day as well. They had not made the big time – discovery by a talent scout, TV appearances, recording sessions and all that – which he suspected they had hoped for, but which Greg had felt all along was only a pipe dream. His first love had always been, and still was, for classical music.

What would Sandie do, he wondered, if the group broke up and when he went to college? It might mean the parting of the ways for them for the moment, at least. The thought made him sad, although she was getting to be rather a trial to him, very difficult for him to handle at times. She was firmly convinced she would make it as a pop star and refused to see that her future, like his own, should lie along a different path.

He stole a glance at her now as a shrill peal of laughter – Sandie's; too loud and too high, almost hysterical – rang out across the room. They were passing a cigarette round from one to the other, each of them inhaling deeply and noisily then leaning back with closed eyes.

Greg leapt from his seat, not caring now what Sandie or anyone thought of him. 'What the hell do you think you're doing?' He leaned across the table and snatched the joint from the hand of Dave, who was just about to pass it to Sandie. 'It's a reefer, isn't it? Dave, what d'you think you're playing at? And you too, Mike. You know we've said we'd never do drugs. And you're involving Sandie and Sharon as well. Good God, you're going to get us all locked up.'

'Hey, hey, cool it, man. It's only hash; it's harmless.' One of the other lads, whose name he did not know, placed a hand on his arm. 'We're not popping pills, and they're cool about it here. They don't bother.'

'They may not bother, but I do,' said Greg, a mite self-righteously, but he didn't care if they thought he was a party-pooper. 'Come on, Sandra, we're going.' She pulled away from him when he seized hold of her arm, although he could tell she was already too far gone to put up much resistance. What an idiot he had been not to realise sooner what they were up to.

'Oh, go away, you old spoilsport.' She pushed at him feebly and started giggling again. 'I wanna stay here. I feel as though I've died and gone to heaven.'

'Come along, there's a good girl,' he said coaxingly. He put his arms round her and lifted her to her feet. She did not resist; neither, to his relief, did she stumble and fall. He retrieved her jacket from the back of her chair and put it over his arm. 'We're going,' he said, clinging tightly to Sandie. 'The rest of you can do what the hell you like.'

He managed to steer her out of the room, across the foyer and through the swing doors, out on to the pavement. When the cool air of the early May evening reached her she took a deep breath, then clutched at her mouth. 'I'm going to be sick.' She was very sick indeed, in the gutter behind his mini shooting brake. He held on to her shoulders, then wiped her damp forehead and face with his clean handkerchief.

'Better now? All up?' he asked.

'Yes, I think so. I'm sorry, Greg.' She looked contrite enough, but he was still very angry with her.

'Yes, well,' he began, resisting the impulse to say that it served her right. 'Get into the car and I'll take you home.' Too late he realised he should have been helping Dave with their gear. They usually took half each since he had had the car, but Dave would have to manage on his own tonight – if he was in any fit state to drive. He was furious with Dave anyway.

'How are you feeling now?' he asked, though a little frostily, when they had been driving along the promenade for several minutes. Sandie was slumped at his side; he wondered if she might be asleep.

'All peculiar,' she mumbled. 'All sort of jangly and jittery. I felt great at first, all dreamy and lazy. But now . . . Greg, I don't feel well.'

'You're not going to be sick again?' He looked at her anxiously.

'No, I don't think so. I just want to go to bed.'

'And that's where you're going as soon as I get you home. Let's hope your mother's gone to bed and doesn't see the state you're in. She trusts me to look after you, you know.'

'You needn't bother. I can look after meself,' she replied, but with none of her old spirit.

'That's just what you can't do, Sandra. Didn't you realise what you were doing? I blame Dave, though, and those other lads. A real couple of weirdies, they looked.'

'They said it'd be OK. It doesn't do any harm.'

'That's where they're wrong. You must promise me, Sandra, that you'll never do it again.'

'All right,' she said feebly. 'I promise.'

'And you mean it?'

'Yes, I mean it.'

He helped Sandie out of the car and into the house, hoping and praying her mother would not still be up. Fortunately she was in bed, but still awake, as they heard her call out.

'That you, Sandie?'

'Yes, Mum. Sorry if I'm a bit late.'

'That's all right, dear. Come to bed now.'

'OK, Mum.'

Greg kissed her quickly on the cheek and beat a hasty retreat. He hoped she would have slept it off by morning.

Sandie had gone out like a light and slept soundly until the alarm clock wakened her. She still felt a bit woozy, but her mother didn't seem to notice anything out of the ordinary. She was always in a hurry anyway, dashing off to college.

Sandie felt sorry for herself, down in the dumps and, she realised, a little ashamed, too. It had been a stupid thing to do and she knew that Greg was very angry with her. She mustn't risk losing him.

423

By the next week, however, she had almost forgotten her bad experience and felt ready for a bit of fun. When her new friends at school announced their intention of sneaking out again at lunchtime she decided she would go with them. She crammed her red jacket into her saddlebag and secreted a lipstick in her pocket.

They didn't bother with school lunch. Cheryl, who was the ringleader, decided they would get a sandwich at the pub and this would give them more time. They dashed across to Cheryl's house, giggling hysterically as they changed into their civvy gear, then ran down the road to the nearest pub.

Sandie didn't find it the laugh that the others had said it would be. Neither, she suspected, did the rest of them; Cheryl, Vicky and Hazel. The landlord gave them a funny look, but he did not ask how old they were, nor did he refuse to serve them. Sandie's corned-beef sandwich tasted peculiar and the half of shandy, which she was not used to drinking, made her feel a bit sick. She refused one of Vicky's cigarettes, the memory of the last joint she had had still lingering. This was only an ordinary fag, but she didn't feel she could face it.

She was relieved when they got out into the fresh air. She would be even more relieved when they got safely back to Cheryl's and into their school uniforms again. They stood on the pavement outside the pub grinning sheepishly at one another.

'Fab, wasn't it? What a hoot, eh?' said Vicky, but she did not sound very convincing.

They had just started to walk away up the road when they heard a voice behind them. 'Girls, wait. Cheryl, Vicky, all of you. Stay just where you are.'

They all turned round. An irate figure was hurrying along the street towards them. 'Oh Lord, that's torn it,' breathed Cheryl. 'It's old Midgers. We've had it now. Leave it to me, girls. I'll try and talk us out of it.'

It was Miss Midgeley, who was not only their English

mistress, but had also been their form mistress when they were in the fifth form and knew them all very well. 'This is just great,' hissed Sandie. 'The first time I come out with you and we go and get caught. I might've known . . .'

'Oh, shurrup moaning,' said Vicky. 'We're all in this together.'

'Girls, what on earth do you think you are doing? I would never have believed it if I hadn't seen it with my own eyes.' Miss Midgeley was practically foaming at the mouth; they could see the spittle gathering on her lips. 'Cheryl and Vicky, I suppose I'm not too surprised at anything you do, but as for you, Hazel and Sandra, I'm shocked, really shocked. To be seen coming out of a public house! And dressed like that!'

'We can explain, Miss Midgeley,' Cheryl began. 'It's me uncle, you see. He's the landlord and we've been in to see him. I had to give him a message from me mum, and he gave us some lemonade. That's why we've got these clothes on, 'cause we couldn't go into a pub wearing our school uniforms, could we?' Her voice petered away as the furious teacher stepped nearer to them, sniffing audibly.

'Don't make it worse by lying to me, Cheryl Mason. You've been drinking. I can smell it on your breath. And smoking too. Sixth-form girls! You're a disgrace, all of you. Get back to school now, as quickly as you can. And when you've changed out of those clothes you can all report at the Head's office. Go along now; look sharp!'

They hurried away from her, practically running up the street whilst she following along behind, a bustling angry figure. They knew she would report them, and then what would happen?'

'We might get expelled,' said Vicky.

'No, we won't,' said Cheryl defiantly. 'It's what you might call a first offence.'

'First time we've been caught, you mean.'

'So what? Old Midgers doesn't know we've been out before.'

'My mother'll kill me.' Hazel was tearful. 'You don't know what she's like.'

Sandie was saying very little. Her mother would not be very pleased either. She knew she had been troublesome at home for ages – a damned nuisance, in fact, especially since her mother and Duncan got engaged – but she didn't want to cause Mum any real grief, did she? She had scarcely known what she was doing at times. It had become almost second nature to her now, to behave badly. Perhaps they would let her off lightly at school. She had only just joined up with this crowd and she had a previously good record at school. The Head and Miss Midgeley both knew that. But that wouldn't be fair. As Vicky had said, they were all in it together.

The Head was justifiably angry, but her wrath was more contained than that of the English mistress. 'You are very lucky I don't expel you, all of you,' she said when she had metaphorically wiped the floor with them for bringing disgrace to themselves, to their parents and to the school. She had heard rumours, she said, about smoking in the common room and about certain girls leaving the premises at lunchtime. She could no longer give them the benefit of the doubt.

'I am suspending you all for a week,' she concluded. 'I will be writing to your parents to tell them of this. Please come to my office at the end of the afternoon to collect your letters . . . and *don't* think you can get away with this by not handing them over. I will be asking for a reply from each of your parents, and I know I can contact them by telephone, at home or at work. You may go now.'

They didn't even glance at one another as they sidled away.

'Sandra, this is dreadful!' said Abbie, staring in horrified amazement at the letter. 'I can't believe it of you. Smoking, drinking, going in pubs . . . and in your school lunchtime.

426

And to be suspended for a week. What a disgrace! Whatever has come over you? Why did you do it?'

'I don't know, Mum.' Sandie hung her head, fighting back the tears. At least it was quite an encouraging reaction, thought Abbie. She might have expected defiance; that was the girl's usual way of hitting back, but she seemed almost penitent. 'I was fed up. With Gran dying and everything, I felt like . . . oh, I don't know what I felt like. I'm sorry, Mum.'

'Well, at least that's something if you're sorry,' said Abbie. 'But it doesn't make it all right. I'm very angry with you, Sandra, and ashamed as well. Was Lindsay one of these girls, or Paula?'

'No, it's some other girls. You don't know them.'

'I would have been very surprised if Lindsay or Paula *had* been involved. Obviously they have a good deal more sense. It seems to me you've got in with the wrong crowd and that's nobody's fault but your own. Well, what's done can't be undone, I suppose. You'd better spend this week off school doing some piano practice. I know you haven't done very much lately. And I haven't heard it from Duncan, if that's what you're thinking. I can see for myself that you're falling behind with your music. You'll have to make yourself some lunch each day, and you can make the teas for you and Simon as well. You know I'm busy at the moment with my teaching practice. As if I hadn't enough to worry about without you causing more trouble.'

'I've said I'm sorry, Mum.'

'All right, all right. We'll say no more about it at the moment, but for heaven's sake, Sandra, do think about what you are doing and especially about the friends you are making! It's most important. You haven't fallen out with Lindsay and Paula, have you?'

'No, Mum. Well, not exactly. But they're a bit . . . boring, like.'

'They don't approve of your new friends, you mean?

427

Better to be boring than downright stupid and reckless. Whatever will Greg think about it, I wonder?'

'You said you'd say no more about it, but you're still harping on and on,' said Sandie, with a little more of her old spirit. 'I don't know what Greg'll think. You're always going on about how wonderful he is.'

'He's a very nice boy, Sandra. You've been very fortunate with your first boyfriend. I only wish your girlfriends were half as sensible.' Abbie decided she had done enough lecturing for the moment. She even felt a little sorry for her daughter. She did seem to be contrite and she had listened without a great deal of backchat. Maybe this was what she had needed – a short sharp shock – to bring her to her senses. Was it too much to hope that she might be turning over a new leaf? She smiled at her now.

'Come on, love. It's not the end of the world. Set the table for me, there's a good girl, and I'll get the chip pan on.'

'Really, that daughter of yours is the giddy limit,' said Duncan later that evening. 'How much more of this sort of behaviour are you going to put up with, Abbie, before you do something about it? She needs taking in hand.'

Abbie stared at him in surprise. She had never seen him angry before. She had usually, in the past, evoked quite a different reaction. Duncan would stick up for Sandie as best he could whilst she, Abbie, had a good old moan about her. Now, perversely, when the boot was on the other foot, she found herself springing to her daughter's defence.

'And what do you suggest I do about it?' she asked.

'You're far too soft with her, Abbie. You let her have too much of her own way. If she were my daughter . . .'

'Well, she's *not* your daughter, is she? She's mine, and I've had to bring her up on my own, the best way I could. I didn't think I'd made too bad a job of it until recently. Anyway, what I was going to say – if only you would listen – is that this seems to have done the trick. I've never seen her so penitent. I really think she feels quite ashamed of herself.'

'And so she should. But I'll believe it when I see it. I haven't seen much sign of her being sorry over these last few weeks. You know she's not practising, don't you? And she's quite brazen about it. She gave me such a mouthful the other week when I corrected her. I told her there was no point in her carrying on with lessons if she doesn't intend to practise.'

'Well, I don't think that's entirely fair. She's had a lot on her mind, you know.'

'She's far too involved with that blessed group,' Duncan retorted. 'The Blue Notes, indeed! And it's affecting Greg as well. How can he concentrate on his serious studies when he's a member of a pop group? I blame Sandie for that. He's been far more wrapped up in it all since she joined. I think she's—'

'Well, I like that! How dare you accuse Sandie—' Abbie stopped suddenly and they stared at one another in horror. 'Duncan, we're quarrelling,' she said in astonishment, and in a much softer voice, 'We mustn't. We never quarrel.'

Immediately he was at her side on the settee. He put his arm round her. 'No, we mustn't fall out. Whatever were we thinking about? I'm sorry, my dear. We're both a bit over-wrought. I'm worried about Greg, and then there's my students taking O-level music and end-of-term tests. And you're in the middle of your teaching practice . . . I'm not surprised things are getting us down. And then Sandie misbehaving on top of it all.'

'Now don't start blaming Sandie again,' said Abbie, as calmly as she could.

'I'm not. I'm not. But I sometimes wonder . . .'

'What?'

'Well, I wonder if she'll ever,' he hesitated, 'be able to accept me.'

'What are you trying to say, Duncan?'

'I'm not sure really. I just think it might be as well if I

429

didn't see Sandra for a while. If I didn't have to teach her, it might help to let things cool down for a bit.'

'You mean you want to break off our engagement?'

'No, of course I don't mean that. But Sandie has caused a lot of trouble, hasn't she, one way and another? Perhaps if she doesn't have to see me . . .'

'She'll have to see a lot more of you when – if – we get married, won't she?'

'What do you mean, "if"?' Duncan took hold of her shoulders. 'Listen to me, Abbie. We're going to get married. There's nothing more sure than that.' But Abbie did not feel so sure. She released herself from his grasp and stood up.

'I think I'd better go, Duncan. I've my lesson notes to do for tomorrow. I only came round to tell you about Sandie.' And now I wish I hadn't bothered, she thought. All it has done is cause trouble between us. It was possible that Sandie would always cause trouble; Duncan quite clearly thought so.

'Don't dash away, darling. I'll make some coffee.'

'No, please don't bother. I want an early night.'

'Very well then. If you're sure.' He put his arms round her and kissed her, but she found she was unable to respond with her usual eagerness.

'Goodnight, Duncan. See you soon. Don't bother to come to the car. I'll see myself out.' She hurried away leaving him staring dazedly after her retreating figure.

By the next morning Abbie was already starting to regret her cool parting from Duncan the previous evening. It was the first time they had ever parted on bad terms and she knew she must put things right between them as soon as possible. It had been a misunderstanding, that was all. He had been upset – quite naturally – on hearing of Sandie's bad behaviour at school, and then she, Abbie, had tried to defend her. He had assured her he did not want to break off their engagement, but she had not entirely believed him. Now, in the clear light of day, she realised they had both been hasty. They must not let Sandie come between them, no matter how badly she might behave. They would be able to sort things out; Abbie felt sure of that. Sandie was already beginning to show signs of remorse.

There was no time to phone Duncan now, however. It was always such a rush in a morning. She had to get to her teaching-practice school at the other end of Blackpool, and Sandie and Simon had not yet come down for breakfast. They would have to see to themselves. Of course, she remembered belatedly; Sandie was excluded from school. She would ring Duncan tonight and make things right with him.

The phone rang just as she was putting her coat on. She smiled – that would be him now, but she hadn't much time to speak to him at the moment. It wasn't Duncan, however, but her stepmother, Faith, sounding very agitated.

'Abbie, I'm so glad I've caught you before you go off to college. I've just come back from the hospital. It's your father.'

'Dad? Whatever's the matter? Is it another stroke? He's not—?'

'He's going to be all right,' Faith broke in quickly. 'At least, they think so. He was taken bad during the night so I got him straight into hospital. I've been there since the early hours. He's come round, but he's had two strokes already as you know, and – well, he's a good age, isn't he?'

'He's not all that old,' said Abbie. 'Mid-seventies – it's not terribly old, not nowadays.'

'No, maybe not,' said Faith. 'I was only trying to warn you, just in case. But we must try to look on the bright side, mustn't we? I know he'd like to see you, Abbie, and I'm going back when I've had a few hours' rest, though I doubt I'll be able to sleep. Do you have to go into college today?'

'No, of course not,' said Abbie. 'I'm on teaching practice, actually, in Marton, but I'll ring and tell them what has happened. I'll get to the hospital as soon as I can. When are visiting hours?'

'Oh, afternoon, I think. But they'll let you in to see him whatever the time, under the circumstances. It's Ward Four – he's in a room by himself at the moment. I'll see you later then, Abbie. We'll just have to trust and pray, won't we?'

'Who was that, Mum?' said Simon, coming into the room followed by Sandie, just as Abbie put the phone down.

'It was Faith,' replied Abbie. 'Your grandad's in hospital. He's had another stroke.'

'Oh, no!' Sandie looked quite shocked, as did Simon. 'He won't die, will he?'

'We hope not, dear.' Abbie smiled at her. 'He's come round and they think he'll be all right. Perhaps you could go and see him this afternoon, seeing as you're not at school.'

'Yes, I will,' said Sandie in a small voice. 'Isn't it awful, Mum? First Gran, and now Grandad.'

'We'll just have to hope for the best,' replied Abbie. 'My father's quite strong really. He'll probably pull through. Anyway, it's all part of life, isn't it? Illness and everything. Something we all have to go through at some time or another.'

Sandie nodded glumly.

'Aren't you going to school, Mum?' asked Simon.

'No, not today, not with this happening. And it's Saturday tomorrow. I may be able to go to school on Monday. It'll depend on how your grandad is.'

'We've a concert tomorrow night, Mum,' said Sandie, still sounding very dejected. 'The Blue Notes are playing. It might be the last one, with Greg getting ready to go to college and his A-levels and everything. I shouldn't go really, should I, not with Grandad being ill. Anyway, I won't feel like singing.'

Abbie was touched by Sandie's words and pleased she had told her about the concert. She wasn't always so forthcoming. 'I don't see why not,' she replied. 'You know what they say – "The show must go on". No, you can't let them down, especially as it might be their last performance. Your grandad would want you to carry on as normal, wouldn't he? Now, get your breakfast, Simon; you're up at the last minute, as usual. Sandie doesn't have to go in so she can take her time.'

'Lucky beggar,' muttered Simon. 'Wish I could have a week off school.'

'Not under those circumstances, you don't,' retorted Abbie, rather sharply. 'Anyway, we're not going to say any more about that,' she added, noticing Sandie's slight frown of annoyance. 'I know Sandie's learned her lesson. Now, I'd better ring and tell Duncan about your grandad. I don't think he'll have gone to school yet.' His hours were not regular ones, like those of full-time teachers. 'He might be able to go and see him later today. Duncan gets on very well with my father.'

Sandie nodded, but she made no comment.

'My poor love,' said Duncan on Saturday evening as they sat together on the settee in Abbie's home. He took her in his arms, kissing her tenderly then cradling her head against his shoulder and stroking her hair. They were alone in the house. Sandie had gone to a final rehearsal and then was going on to The Blue Notes' performance with Greg, and Simon was at a friend's house round the corner. Abbie was continually on the alert for another dreaded phone call, although her father appeared to be out of danger. But she was definitely in the mood for comfort and she clung to Duncan now, shedding the tears she had been trying to control since yesterday.

'Cry if you want to,' said Duncan, kissing her wet eyelids and cheeks. 'I don't mind. What a time you're having, my darling. I know you've been very upset since Lily died, and now there's your father's illness. So many problems for you, not to mention Sandra and this school thing.' She gave way to her tears for a few moments at his consoling words. Then, after a gulping sob, she realised she must get a grip on herself. She was indulging in self-pity and that was no good at all.

'I'm sorry,' she said. 'I don't usually give way like this. Thank you, Duncan, for being so understanding.'

'It's nothing, my dear. It's what I'm here for, to take care of you. Have you any idea how much I love you?' His deep affection for her, and ardour, too, such as she had never seen to such a degree before, shone in his eyes as he gazed at her, then brought his mouth down on hers in a kiss that held both passion and tenderness.

'I think so,' she replied when they drew apart. 'Because I love you too, Duncan, so very much.' She did love him, deeply and sincerely. It was not quite the same as the love she had had for Peter; she was not exactly sure how it differed, but that had ceased to matter. Her love for Duncan was, she knew, of the steadfast and lasting sort.

'Do you know what I want to do now, so very much?' he whispered. She shook her head, although she could guess.

'I want to make love to you, my darling. It is time . . . don't you think so?'

'Yes, Duncan,' she replied, though a little timorously; it was such a big step. 'It's what I want as well. It is . . . time.' She had wondered, when they had stayed in the Cotswolds for a couple of nights, if this would happen, but Duncan had booked two single rooms. That was almost a year ago, and since then their embraces and kisses had gradually become more demanding. But this was the first time he had made a definite move towards what they knew they both desired.

'You're sure, aren't you?' he asked. 'You look a little apprehensive. I want you to be very sure. If you are not, then . . .'

'I'm sure, very sure,' she replied quickly. 'I was only thinking about the children, but they're both out.'

'And won't be in for ages. I heard you tell Simon to be in by eleven. And you can be sure Sandie won't be back till late. It's the group's last performance, isn't it? Come along, darling.' He took hold of her hand, looking down at her ruby and diamond engagement ring. 'That shows we belong to one another, doesn't it? And we've waited such a long time, haven't we?'

She smiled a little shyly. 'It would be more private upstairs,' she whispered. She felt it would be wrong, somehow, to make love there on the settee like a sex-mad teenager. Besides, she was a little old-fashioned. Bed was the place for lovemaking.

Duncan was a passionate, though considerate, lover. She felt all her fears and worries and sadness – about her father and Lily's death and Sandie's bad behaviour – melting away in the comfort of his arms, and she experienced, moreover, a great satisfaction and fulfilment in the act of love. She found she was making no comparisons; it was as though it were the first time ever.

They lay at peace afterwards, treasuring the tranquillity and the feeling of harmony, of oneness and belonging to one another. Duncan murmured he would have to get dressed and go home eventually. Certainly before Sandie and Simon arrived home. Much as he wanted to stay the night they both knew it would not be a wise thing to do . . . not yet. Perhaps not ever, before they were married, Abbie thought to herself.

She was almost drowsing, snuggling close to Duncan and wishing she could always feel like this, safe from her cares and concerns, when they were both startled by the sound of a key turning in the lock, then the bang of the front door. Abbie was instantly alert. Which of them was it? Sandie or Simon? Most likely Simon, but it was only . . . she glanced at her bedside clock. It was only a quarter past eight. But it was Sandie's voice they could hear now. She had gone out early, before seven o'clock, saying they were having a final run-through as it was an important performance, then they were going on to their engagement, somewhere over the River Wyre. They weren't on till nine o'clock. So what on earth was she doing here at this time?

'Mum! Mum, where are you?' They heard her going into one of the downstairs rooms. Abbie's heart missed a beat. If she went into the sitting room she would see Duncan's jacket lying on the settee and would realise they were both still at home. His car was parked further down the road so she might not have noticed that.

'It's Sandie,' she whispered, hardly daring to let out a breath. 'Oh Duncan, whatever shall we do?'

'Nothing,' he whispered back. 'There's nothing we can do, is there? Just lie still. She might think we've gone out.'

'But I told her I was staying in. She knows I'm worried about my father.'

'Shhh. She's coming up. But it's not as though we're committing a crime, is it?'

'Mum, are you there? You're not in bed already, are you? I've just come back for my thick sweater. It might be cold by the time we've finished. And I wanted to tell you . . .' She did at least knock at the door before she pushed it open and entered the room. 'Sorry to disturb you, Mum, but . . . oh! Oh . . . no, no!'

Duncan had not even tried to hide beneath the bedcovers. It would have made no difference anyway as his clothes were in a heap on the floor along with Abbie's. Sandie gave a horrified gasp as she stared down at them. They could see the look of shock and revulsion on her face. 'How could you? With my grandad ill in hospital. He might be dying, but you don't care, do you?' She turned and fled out of the room.

'Sandie, wait!' called Abbie. They heard her going into her room and opening a drawer, then there was the sound of her footsteps dashing downstairs and the loud bang of the front door.

'Oh dear, how awful,' said Abbie, almost in tears. 'What shall we do?'

436

'Nothing,' said Duncan. Gently he kissed her forehead. 'You and I are going to be married, my dear, and we have done nothing wrong. It's unfortunate, I know, but Sandie will have to get used to the idea that we love one another. After all, we are engaged. Have a talk to her in the morning. She'll be all right when she's got over the shock. Listen, love, we'd better get up and I'll go before Simon gets back.'

'That's not for ages yet,' said Abbie. 'But you're right. We'll get up and I'll make us some coffee.'

She almost threw on her clothes and rushed downstairs. All the joy and delight they had been sharing but a few minutes ago had vanished. She had been sad and worried, then miraculously freed for a time from her troubles. Now she was more anxious than ever; about Sandie, about everything.

Chapter 27

'Whatever's the matter?' asked Greg when Sandie flung open the door of the shooting brake and plonked down on the seat beside him. He could see she was trying hard not to cry, her breath coming in short gasps.

'My mum . . . my mum and Duncan . . . in bed together,' she wailed, turning an angry, but puzzled face towards him. He might almost have laughed if she had not been viewing it so tragically. Good old Duncan! he thought. About time too. But he had the sense not to voice his thoughts.

'But Sandie, what's so dreadful about that?' he asked, putting an arm round her. 'They're grown-up people and they love one another. They're engaged and they're going to be married, aren't they?'

'I know they are. But it's disgusting! How could she? What would she say if I behaved like that? There's one rule for me and a different one for her. She's always on at me to behave myself.' This was not strictly true. Her mother had given her a lot of freedom lately and had hardly commented on her growing friendship with Greg.

'Oh, come on, love. It's not so bad. I know it's been a shock. The thing is, none of us like to think of our parents doing that. It doesn't seem right somehow. But they must have done or we wouldn't be here, would we? I know my mum and dad still love one another very much.'

'That's different. They're married.'

'And so will your mum and Duncan be. I know Duncan

very well and I know he loves your mother. They're going to get married quite soon.'

'I don't *want* them to get married!' Sandie almost screamed. 'I've told you before – he's my music teacher. He's no business to come along and take the place of my dad. Oh come on, let's get to this concert. We're late now because of them. You'll have to drive fast.'

Their final performance was to be held at a church hall in Preesall, a village in the area that was known locally as 'over Wyre' – across Shard Bridge, the toll bridge which spanned the River Wyre. Dave, Mike and Greg had made their peace over the matter of the drugs. The other two lads, and Sandie as well, had promised never to touch drugs again, and now they were all looking forward to what seemed like being their final concert.

They set off along the road to Poulton and then over Shard Bridge. Sandie was still going on about her mother and Duncan, and after a while Greg said wearily, 'Oh, just leave it, Sandra, for heaven's sake. I'm sick of hearing about it.'

'What's up with you?' she snapped back.

'I'm trying to concentrate on the road, and I can't with you nattering away. And I'm not quite sure where we are. I asked you to mapread for me, didn't I?'

'OK, OK, keep your hair on.' Sandie snatched the map from the shelf under the dashboard and studied it for a moment, then looked at the next road sign. 'Oh heck! I think we've gone the wrong way. You'll have to turn round, Greg.'

'What, here? In the middle of a country lane?'

'Yes – do a three-point turn.'

'I can't. It's not wide enough. I'll have to go to the next turning and then go back. I thought we'd gone the wrong way.'

'Then why didn't you say so?'

'Because you're supposed to be reading the map.'

'Don't start blaming me. It's not my fault.'

'Well, it's certainly not mine.' Greg gave her an exasperated look. 'Just concentrate on the map, for God's sake.' They turned round and started back the way they had come.

The road was veering to the left and the bend was sharper than Greg had anticipated. 'Look out!' shouted Sandie. 'You nearly had us in the ditch. Not much of a driver, are you?'

'I'm doing my best, but you're not helping much, are you?'

'I am! I've got us back on the right road, haven't I? For goodness' sake, drive a bit faster. The road's clear and it's a bit wider here. Get your foot down, Greg. You know we're late.'

'For God's sake, Sandra, will you shut up!' The road turned suddenly to the right and Greg, desperately trying to control the wheel, overshot the bend. The car sped across the road, then there was a sickening thud as it catapulted into the ditch and crashed into an oak tree. There was the sound of splintering glass and Sandie put out her hands to save herself as the car came to rest at a crazy angle. She looked down and saw blood on her hands, then she started to scream. Greg, at her side, was slumped motionless over the wheel. It was his side of the car that had collided with the tree.

'Greg, Greg, speak to me. Greg, come on! We've got to get out of here.' She pushed at him but there was no response. He fell away from her, his head lolling sideways, his hands hanging limply at his sides. She screamed even more loudly. 'Help! Help! Oh please . . . somebody come and help.' Then she, too, felt herself falling.

There was a knock at the door at about half-past ten. Although it was earlier than he usually departed Duncan had decided he would go home soon. He was obviously upset about Sandie finding them in bed together, but he had been trying to make light of it.

'Who can that be?' said Abbie. 'Simon, more than likely. I expect he's forgotten his key. He's early though.' She gave a gasp when she saw the policeman standing on the doorstep.

Her immediate thought was for her father. He must have died. But surely the hospital would have rung, to make sure she got there before anything happened. That was what they usually did.

'Mrs Horsfall?' The policeman took off his helmet, looking at her respectfully and a little sadly.

'Yes, I'm Mrs Horsfall. What is it?'

'I wonder if I could come in for a moment? I'm afraid I have some disturbing news for you.'

'Is it about my father?'

'No, no, it isn't.' He looked at her in some surprise. 'I'm afraid it's to do with your daughter, Sandra Horsfall. She is your daughter, isn't she?'

'Yes, Sandra's my daughter.' Abbie stared at him in confusion. 'Come in, please,' she said automatically. She led the way into the sitting room, hardly aware of what she was doing or saying. 'Duncan, the policeman says he's some bad news about Sandie.'

Duncan had already risen to his feet. Now he took hold of Abbie and gently pushed her into an armchair. 'Sit down, love. Now, officer – what is it?'

'Your daughter, she's not dead,' said the policeman quickly, and Abbie felt herself go limp with relief. She was almost fainting, but she pulled herself round to hear him say, 'There was an accident – a road accident – and your daughter was injured. She's in hospital and they'd like you to go there as soon as possible.'

'What happened? Where was it?' It was Duncan who spoke first.

'It was on a country lane, near Preesall,' said the officer. 'You are Mr Horsfall, I presume?'

'No. My name is Duncan Hendy. I'm a friend of Mrs Horsfall – her fiancé, actually. We're going to be married, very soon. Tell us what happened, officer,' he went on urgently. 'There was someone else in the car, the young lady's friend, Gregory Matthews?'

'Er, yes, sir. That's right. Mr Matthews was driving the car. It appears it crashed into a tree, on a bend in the road. There were no other vehicles involved. A passing motorist rang for an ambulance and they got there very quickly. The young lady, Sandra, she was unconscious, but she's as well as can be expected; that's all they'll say. But I'm afraid it was too late to do anything for the young man, Mr Matthews.'

'Surely you can't mean he's dead?' Duncan had turned white. He had been standing, but now he sank into the nearest chair, grasping on to the arms for support.

'Yes, I'm afraid so, sir. They said it was instantaneous. He wouldn't have known anything about it. It was his side of the car that took the brunt of the accident, I could see that for myself. I was there. But the young lady – we hope she'll be all right. If you could get there as soon as possible, Mrs Horsfall.'

'Yes, of course.' Abbie was so shocked she had scarcely taken in the appalling news about Greg. 'Victoria Hospital, is it?'

'Yes, that's right. Would you like me to run you there now?'

'No . . . no, thank you. It's all right,' she answered weakly. 'I have my own car.' Although she assumed Duncan would take her. 'I'll have to go and tell my son first. He's round the corner at a friend's house.'

'Very well then.' The policeman rose to his feet. 'We never like breaking news like this, but I'm afraid it has to be done. I'm very sorry, Mrs Horsfall . . . sir. I hope you find your daughter is recovering. I'll see myself out.'

Abbie and Duncan stared at one another for several seconds after he had gone, neither of them knowing what to say. It was Duncan who broke the silence.

'I'll have to go to them right now. Alan and Hazel – they'll be in a terrible state. I just can't believe it. Not Greg. Not that talented young man. He had everything to live for.'

'Yes, yes, of course you must,' said Abbie. 'I can't take it in

442

either. It's just too awful for words. And I must go to Sandie right now. He said she was going to be all right, didn't he, that policeman? That was what he said – that they thought she'd be all right?'

'Yes,' answered Duncan curtly. The look he gave Abbie was unfathomable. 'Yes, you'd better go. You'll be able to manage on your own, won't you – driving the car and seeing Simon and everything? I must go now.' He put on his jacket and made for the door. He did not make any move to kiss her or to offer any words of comfort, but she told herself he was stunned, as she was, not fully in control of himself or his feelings. His next words, however, shook her rigid. He stopped at the door and turned round.

'It's our fault, you know. I'll never be able to forgive myself.' There were tears in his eyes as he hurried away.

Abbie could not believe he had gone, like that, without even touching her or saying goodbye or telling her when he would see her again. *It's our fault*. She repeated his words to herself. Yes, she supposed it was. Sandie must have been shocked to find her and Duncan . . . like that. No doubt she had poured it all out to Greg and made him all upset. So upset that he started to drive carelessly . . . and now he was dead. All because of her and Duncan. Abbie, also, knew she would never be able to forgive herself. And what about poor Hazel and Alan? Never, never would she be able to face them. She was hurt at Duncan's treatment of her. She had expected him to stay with her, to drive her to the hospital after they had broken the news to Simon, but she supposed she could understand his reaction. Greg had been almost like a son to Duncan, and his star pupil as well. He had had such hopes and aspirations for him. Now he was dead, at eighteen years of age, with all his life ahead of him.

But Sandie was alive – thank God – and she must go and see her immediately. She flung on a coat, backed the car out of the garage and drove round the corner to the house where Simon's friend lived. The boy was shocked to hear about his sister – she could not tell him about Greg, not yet – but he relaxed a little when she told him Sandie would be all right. When his friend's mother suggested he should stay the night with them, Abbie was relieved; that was the best solution.

Sandie was in a little side room on her own and was still unconscious. As Abbie looked down at her, lying there so pale and still between the clinically white hospital sheets, she felt the tears, which so far had not flowed, streaming down her cheeks. Her dear, dear daughter. She loved her so very much. She had been difficult, rude and downright rebellious, but in spite of everything Abbie loved her deeply and she said a silent prayer of thanks that Sandie was still here, that she had not been taken from her. But was it not a selfish prayer, she asked herself, saying thank you to God when all the prayers in the world would not bring Greg back? The doctor had told her that Sandie would pull through. There were no internal injuries, only cuts and bruises and a broken arm. Abbie supposed she had been very lucky. A gash on her forehead had been stitched and her head was swathed in a bandage, parts of her face were bruised and her left arm, the broken one, was in plaster. She would come round when her body was ready, and when her mind was ready, too, Abbie hoped, to receive the shock that awaited her. All Abbie could do now was to wait. She leaned back in the armchair, and closed her eyes.

Sandie opened her eyes and blinked dazedly. Where was she? Her head felt funny and she could not move it very far, but her eyes flickered around the room and she caught sight of her mother sitting at her side. Abbie got up at once and stooped to kiss her.

'Hello, darling. I've been waiting for you to wake up.'

'Mum, where am I?' She stared at her mother confusedly. 'What's happened?'

'You're in hospital, love,' said her mother. 'You've been

here since last night. But you're going to be all right. A few cuts and bruises and you had concussion.' Sandie frowned at her, uncomprehendingly, then glanced down at her arm. It felt stiff. It was in plaster. 'And you broke your arm as well,' her mother went on. 'But everything's going to be just fine.' But she could tell by the look on her mother's face that everything was not fine at all. It was coming back to her now. Greg . . . the car . . . they had been driving fast . . . then something had happened. She remembered Greg slumped across the wheel.

'Greg,' she said. 'There was an accident, wasn't there? What happened to Greg?'

Abbie sat at the side of the bed and took hold of her right hand. 'Yes, there was an accident. It was a bad accident. Listen, darling, I'm afraid I have something to tell you. You'll have to try and be very brave.' Abbie had wondered about the wisdom of telling her so soon, but the doctor said she would have to know. She would only start asking questions; questions which could not be answered any way but truthfully. Sandie was looking steadily at her mother.

'He's dead, isn't he?' she said. 'Greg's dead. That's what you've got to tell me.'

'Yes, love. I'm sorry. He was killed straight away. He . . . he wouldn't have known anything about it. The policeman said it must have happened . . . very quickly.'

Sandie closed her eyes. It was all starting to come back to her. In her mind's eye she could see Greg slumped at her side. She was shaking him; there had been a lot of blood. But before that, they had fallen out about something. What was it? She opened her eyes and looked at her mother sitting there looking at her so anxiously, so lovingly. Yes, she remembered now. Mum and Duncan; the last time she had seen her mother she had been in bed with Duncan! And she, Sandie, had gone mad. She remembered how angry and upset she had been. It was what she and Greg had fallen out

445

about. They were late and he had been driving too fast. She had made him drive too fast.

'It was my fault,' she cried. 'Mum, it was all my fault! Greg's dead – and it was me who killed him. And what about his mum and dad? They must be angry, and so terribly sad. And it was because of me. They'll never forgive me.' Sandie's voice rose and her tears began to overflow.

Abbie put her arms round her. 'There now, love. We're not going to say very much about it at the moment. Have a good cry. I know you need to.' She held her closely while she sobbed. 'Hazel and Alan will be angry with everyone,' she went on. With Duncan and me especially, she thought, but did not say it. 'But it was an accident. And accidents – well, they just happen. You can't say they're anyone's fault. You didn't *mean* anything dreadful to happen.'

'But it was my fault – I know it was,' cried Sandie. 'I made him drive too fast. We fell out, Mum, me and Greg. We were arguing. And a lot of it was about you and Duncan.'

'Never mind about all that now, love,' said Abbie quickly. The tears were still streaming down the girl's face; she was deeply distressed and sad and Abbie knew she would be so for many days to come.

She stayed there in silence for several moments, kneeling at the side of the bed with her arms round her daughter, a silence only broken by Sandie's occasional sobs. She was becoming calmer though, and Abbie knew that in a little while she must leave her to cope with her sadness in her own way, and to sleep, which was nature's way of healing both mind and body.

'I loved Greg, Mum,' Sandie said, as her sobs gradually lessened. 'I really did love him. I was horrid to him sometimes . . . but I loved him.'

'He knew that, darling,' said Abbie. 'And he loved you, too, I know he did. We are not always as nice to one another as we might be, none of us. But the love is still there underneath it all. Greg was a lovely young man. You'll never forget him, and in a little while you'll only remember the good times.' She kissed her cheek and wiped away her tears again. 'I must go now, Sandie love. The nurse said I mustn't tire you. I'll see you again, very soon. I'm going to see your grandad now.'

Sandie frowned, a little confusedly. 'Oh yes, of course, Grandad. How is he?'

'Getting better, we hope. Perhaps he'll be able to come and see you soon. Or you could go and see him. That would be nice, wouldn't it?'

Sandie nodded. 'Ask Simon to come and see me.'

'Yes, I will. And Aunty Faith and Grandad Horsfall. They'll all come. Goodbye, darling. See you soon.'

'Bye, Mum.' Sandie closed her eyes.

Abbie had not mentioned Duncan. She wasn't sure when she would see him again, or even if she wanted to do so at the moment. She could not have explained how she was feeling about Duncan. She was hurt by the offhand way he had treated her, although she supposed she could understand it. He had been shocked and devastated by the news, as she had been, but his behaviour still hurt. She loved him; she hoped he still loved her, but their future seemed uncertain. They had been so happy together, so blissfully happy for an hour or so as they acknowledged fully, for the first time, their love for one another. And then, in a split second, it had all been shattered when Sandie had come into the room.

That had been the catalyst which had caused the tragedy, Abbie felt sure of it. She could not forget the look of dismay, of shock and horror on Sandie's face and the way she had dashed out of the house. The girl had admitted it had been her fault. She had fallen out with Greg and made him drive too fast . . . to his death. But Abbie knew the real guilt lay with her and Duncan. It was they who had caused it all. It would be wrong now for them to go ahead with their marriage and their future life together when they had been the cause of so much grief.

Abbie walked dazedly along the hospital corridors to the ward where her father was gradually recuperating. 'What are you doing here at this time in the morning?' he asked. His speech was a little slurred, but his eyes were brighter and he seemed more alert. At least he was aware of the time of day and that this was not, strictly, visiting time.

Abbie told him, as calmly as she could, that Sandie was also in hospital. 'She's been in a car accident, Dad. Nothing to worry about; she's coming along fine, but she'll be here for a little while, like you.' She could not tell him about Greg. She did not want him to have a relapse. But he would have to know eventually; he had met Greg a few times and had liked him. Everyone had liked Greg. Abbie could not imagine a greater disaster. But they would all have to pick up the pieces and get on with their lives.

She said goodbye to her father quite soon and drove home. Her head was full of troublesome thoughts, about Sandie and her father, and Greg and Duncan. She felt that she and Duncan would never be happy again, nor had they the right to be. She also realised she was very tired. She had been at the hospital since last night and had hardly slept at all, only dozing fitfully in the chair for a few moments at a time. She tumbled into bed almost fully clothed and slept for several hours.

She was awakened by Simon's voice. 'Mum! Mum, where are you?' She was immediately alert. Simon! She had forgotten all about him. He had stayed at his friend Gary's last night. She should have picked him up on her way home. Oh, what a dreadful mother she was! And whatever would Gary's mother think of her? She jumped out of bed, straightening her clothes and running her fingers through her tousled hair, as Simon cautiously poked his head round the door.

'Mum, are you OK? Did you get my note? How's our Sandie?' He explained that his friend's mum had asked him to stay for Sunday dinner, realising his own mum might have been delayed at the hospital. He had left a note to that effect on the mantelpiece downstairs, but Abbie had not seen it.

'I'm sorry, love. I've neglected you, haven't I?' She put her arms round him and hugged him. 'There's been so much to think about.'

'It's OK, Mum. How's Sandie?' he asked again. She told him that Sandie was getting better, and she knew it was now time to tell him about Greg.

He was visibly shocked. 'Oh, how awful! Poor Sandie. She really liked him, didn't she? And I liked him, too. He was a great guy. And poor Duncan; he must be dreadfully upset.'

'Yes, and there's Greg's mum and dad,' said Abbie.

'Yeah, I know. But Duncan – he thought a lot about Greg, didn't he? As though he was his own son, sort of.'

'Yes, he did.'

'Where's Duncan now, Mum?'

'I expect he's at home.'

'Haven't you seen him?'

'No, love, not today. Not since last night. I've been at the hospital, you see. And then I've been asleep, for far too long.' She tried to smile. 'I'd better get us some tea, hadn't I?' She realised she was hungry. She had eaten a bowl of cornflakes which a thoughtful nurse had brought her in the early hours, but nothing since then.

'It's OK, Mum, I'll make it,' said Simon. 'D'you fancy some toast? I can make that all right. And shall I open a tin of beans?'

'That would be very nice, dear. You're a good lad. And put the kettle on as well, would you?' The routine tasks would bring back a semblance of normality to a world that had been thrown into turmoil.

She took Simon with her when she went to see Sandie again in the early evening. Her daughter was sitting up in bed, but was still subdued and very sad. The three of them found they had little to say to one another, but Abbie was aware of

449

the cords of love and family feeling that were holding them together. She felt, too, that there was a change coming over Sandie. Understandably, she was grieving, but Abbie had the feeling she would come through this tragedy a stronger, and yet a gentler, person.

'I'm really sorry, Mum,' she said, 'about you and Duncan. I shouldn't have gone on like that. You love one another, don't you?' She looked truly concerned and remorseful.

'Yes, we do,' answered Abbie. Or we did, she said to herself. She spoke very quietly, but Simon was taking no notice. A little bored, he was studying the chart at the bottom of the bed.

'Tell Duncan, will you?' Sandie went on. 'Tell him I didn't mean it, and that I'm sorry. I'm glad you've got him now, Mum. He must be terribly upset about Greg. Tell him how sorry I am, won't you?'

'Yes, dear, of course I will.' Abbie did not tell her that she had not yet seen him since the accident, and did not know when she would do so.

Chapter 28

Duncan rang soon after she arrived back from the hospital. His voice was terse. 'Abbie, I must see you. We've got to talk.' There was no note of endearment, and Abbie's voice, too, was devoid of feeling as she replied.

'Yes, I suppose we must. When?'

'Shall I come round now?'

'No, I don't think so. I've just come back from the hospital. I'm rather tired.' He had not asked about Sandie, but she knew she must tell him. 'Sandie's injuries are not serious. Cuts and bruises and a broken arm. She's going to be all right.'

'Oh, I see. That's good.' But he did not sound very concerned. 'Shall I come round in the morning then? Unless you're going in to school?'

'No, I'm not.'

'Very well then. I'll see you in the morning.' He still sounded curt, then, in a quite different voice, he added, 'Goodnight then, Abbie. Sleep well, and take care.'

It was only at Duncan's mention of school that she had remembered her teaching practice. College and her school practice had been the last things on her mind, and now, as she tried to focus on reality, she knew she would be unable to return this term. It was already mid-June and the college year would soon be ending.

She rang the school early next morning – Monday – explaining why she would not be there. The headmaster at the school, a very understanding man, sympathised with her and told her she must not worry about going back at all. It was the final week of the practice and, as far as he was concerned, she had already done very well indeed. However, if the college authorities insisted on it, she could go back and complete it some other time.

Duncan arrived soon afterwards. He looked tense and deeply troubled and seemed to have aged several years since she had last seen him, less than two days ago. He smiled weakly at her, though his eyes were sad, and greeted her with a perfunctory kiss on her cheek. There was nothing in his brief embrace of the warmth and tenderness they had felt for one another.

'Do sit down,' she said. 'How are you?'

'Oh, bearing up, or trying to.' They were like two strangers conversing.

'How are Hazel and Alan?'

'How do you think they are?' There was a touch of anger in his voice. 'Shattered; absolutely devastated. I don't think they've taken it in properly yet. But they will have to try and come to terms with it – we all will. There's so much to do. I said I'd go round again this morning to help them with the arrangements. The funeral and everything.'

'It's very good of you, Duncan.'

'It's the least I can do, isn't it? I haven't told them, you know. About what happened the other night. About you and me, and Sandie finding us together.' His glance was searching, but she could see no affection there, just bewilderment and guilt. 'As far as Hazel and Alan know, Greg must had been driving too fast because they were late, and became rather careless.'

'Yes, I think that's the best thing.' Abbie nodded soberly. 'It's as well they should never know.'

'It lets us off the hook, you mean?' Abbie would not have believed she could ever hear such bitterness in his tone. 'You think we don't need to tell them? That we can forget all about it?'

452

'No, of course not! But there's no point in making things worse for them, is there?'

'Worse for us, you mean. If we told them what really happened they would find it hard to forgive us. And I know I will never be able to forgive myself.'

'Neither will I,' said Abbie. 'I know we were to blame. I keep thinking, if only we hadn't been together like that, if only Sandie and Greg had gone straight to the concert.'

'It's no use saying "if", Abbie. It doesn't alter the facts. This will always be on my conscience, and on yours, too, I guess.'

'I can't face Hazel and Alan. I wouldn't know what to say.'

'You will have to face them, Abbie. They've been asking about you.' Duncan spoke sternly. 'It will be the funeral later this week, and they will expect you to be there . . . with me. No matter how we are feeling, we will have to be there – together. And after that – well, I don't know.' He spread his hands wide in a gesture of uncertainty.

'What do you mean?'

'I mean you and me. I'm not sure, after all this, if we have any future together. It would always be with us, the memory of how we had caused Greg's death.'

'Inadvertently,' replied Abbie. His words sounded so shocking. 'We didn't mean it to happen. It was an accident.'

'Could you carry on as though nothing had happened?'

'No, I couldn't.' It was one of the hardest things she had ever had to say, but she knew she must. 'I think we need some time apart, Duncan, for the moment, at least. And after that, I don't know.' She did not mention Sandie, but she knew her daughter had played a large part in all this trauma. It was doubtful, after what had happened, that Duncan would ever be able to have a good relationship with Sandie. And as for Abbie, she knew her first consideration now must be her daughter. Sandie needed her.

Duncan nodded. 'It would be wrong to go ahead with our

plans now. It would be selfish. Anyway, neither of us are sure, are we?' Sure of what? Abbie wondered. Sure that they loved one another? She had thought that nothing could ever come between them.

'I'll let you know about the funeral arrangements. I'll order some flowers, from the two of us, and we'll go there together.' Duncan sounded so matter-of-fact; it was all unreal, like an awful dream. 'But I think, before that, you should go and see Hazel and Alan. They will think it strange if you don't.'

'I'll try.' They looked at one another in silence for several seconds before Duncan stood up.

'I must go,' he said. 'There's a lot to do.' His eyes softened just a shade and he moved towards her and kissed her cheek. 'I'm sorry about all this, Abbie, but time will tell. We must have time to think.' Again he had not asked about Sandie. She knew, although he had not said so – and no doubt never would – that he must feel bitter that she was the one who had survived.

After he had gone Abbie felt more alone than she had ever felt in her life. No – there were two other times, she recalled. She found herself thinking back to the time when she had received the news of Peter's air crash. That had been a mistake; but ten years later, when Peter *had* died, she had felt devastated again. No more so, though, than she did now.

She knew she must make a supreme effort and go round to see Greg's grieving parents. As Duncan had said, they would think it strange if she did not call and offer her condolences; that was, if they were in any fit state to think clearly at all. Abbie tried to put herself in their position and went cold at the thought. The fact that Sandie was alive and getting better filled her with remorse, but with a deep thankfulness.

She bought a bunch of long-stemmed roses, not as a funeral tribute, but for Hazel. She hoped Duncan would not be there when she called in the afternoon. He was not, as he

454

had a teaching appointment at one of his schools, but Hazel said how much he had helped and what a support he was being. Abbie would never have believed she would feel so relieved at his absence. Hazel appeared reasonably composed, although her eyes were red and strained, showing signs of recent weeping. Alan was out, no doubt dealing with funeral arrangements, and Abbie felt a great relief at this, also. She remembered occasions when he had not entirely approved of his son's friendship with her daughter. He – and Hazel, too – had had such great hopes for their only son.

She did not stay very long. There seemed to be little to say, apart from how sorry she was. Hazel nodded and enquired politely about Sandie. She seemed disinclined to enter into a long conversation. Abbie knew that the recently bereaved often found it a comfort to talk about the loved one they had lost, but maybe Hazel had already done so; to Duncan, perhaps, or to other friends who had called. She said she hoped she would see Abbie at the funeral, and Abbie promised to be there.

She had also promised Duncan they would be there together as a couple; she knew it would possibly be for the last time. She felt it would be wrong, however, to ride with Duncan in the funeral car along with the family mourners; as their closest friend, he had been asked to do so. She drove herself to the church and, later, to the cemetery, although she did stand with Duncan during the simple service and at the graveside.

The church was almost full. The young man had had many friends and Abbie almost broke down when she saw his coffin being carried by the other three members of The Blue Notes – Mike, Dave and Tony – and another young man she did not know. There was a goodly number of boys, too, from Greg's school, and as they came out of church she noticed Ian Webster, Jim and Sylvia's son, amongst them. He smiled at her sadly before coming across to her for a brief word.

'This is dreadful, isn't it?' he whispered. 'We've all been devastated. How is Sandie?'

'Improving,' she told him. 'She might be out of hospital after the weekend. They're keeping a close eye on her. It's the shock of it all, more than anything, that's affecting her.'

Ian nodded. 'I understand.' He hesitated, then, 'Give her my best wishes,' he said, before he rejoined his friends. Abbie wondered if he would go and visit her daughter. Sandie was grieving now, but eventually she would have to pick up the threads of her life again and start making new friends.

Relations and friends of the Matthews family had been invited back to the home after the funeral, but Abbie declined the invitation, saying she must go to the hospital to see her daughter. Duncan did not try to persuade her and they said their goodbyes in a cordial manner; but they were more like casual acquaintances than the loving friends – and lately, lovers – that they had been. Abbie did not know when, if ever, she would see him again. She too, like Sandie, would have to put the pieces of her shattered life together. At the moment it seemed impossible, but for Sandie's sake, she must try to be brave and smile.

Time had ceased to have much meaning for Sandie. She wasn't sure how long she had been in hospital; three days, four days . . . a week? Visitors came and went. Her mother, of course, every day; her Grandad Horsfall and Aunty Faith and Simon. Grandad Winters was now home from hospital and receiving physiotherapy, her mum said, after his stroke. A nurse had wheeled her down to see him in his ward a couple of days ago and that had been very nice, although they had not found much to talk about. Her friend, Lindsay, had visited too, and had acted as though there had never been anything wrong between them. She had been so horrid to Lindsay, she remembered with a pang of remorse. She would tell her so eventually. She had a lot of making up to do to people.

Hazel and Alan Matthews had not been to see her, but she had not really expected them. She knew it was her fault, in spite of what her mother said about it being an accident. One day she would tell them how sorry she was. At the moment, though, no one seemed to be blaming her for anything. They hardly referred to the accident or to Greg and didn't seem to mind that she was grumpy and sad most of the time, and disinclined to talk. Duncan had not been to see her either. She was not too surprised at that, but it was strange that her mother never mentioned him.

Lindsay told her tales of what was happening at school. Sandie had almost forgotten how she had been excluded over that pub episode; such a lot had happened since then. Lindsay did not refer to the incident, but the other miscreants must be back now because her friend told her that Vicky and Cheryl had fallen out. And Constance had actually got a boyfriend! 'You know, Constance, the one whose mother's a Jehovah's Witness? Would you believe it? And I must tell you this; Miss Parker nearly lost her false teeth when she was shouting at Hazel! Honestly, kid, we saw them move. Hey, look out – you nearly smiled then. I thought that'd make you laugh.' Lindsay's humour was infectious and Sandie felt her spirits lighten just a little.

'You're tired, aren't you?' said Lindsay a little while later. 'I'll go and leave you in peace. See you again soon. Paula said she might come with me next time. Tara then.'

Sandie closed her eyes. She wished she didn't feel so weary all the time. But Lindsay had helped to cheer her up. At the thought of Paula, however, her sadness returned. Paula had been fond of Greg; she had known him for ages. She, too, must be very upset.

'I think you might be able to go home tomorrow,' said the nursing sister, one afternoon a few days later. 'We'll have a word with the doctor when he comes round, then we can tell your mother the good news. Keep your fingers crossed, Sandie. It's what you want, isn't it?'

'Yes, I think so,' said Sandie. She felt safe here, cocooned in a comfortable, almost unreal sort of existence where she did not have to worry too much about the future. There was a whole world waiting for her, though, outside the hospital walls, if only she could find the courage and incentive to face it. 'Yes, of course, it'll be good to be home.' But she sounded rather unsure.

She had done a good deal of thinking, lying in her hospital bed. People had been so kind to her, and she knew she didn't deserve it. She had caused such a lot of unhappiness by her stupid churlish attitude towards her mother and Duncan. Sandie knew now that her behaviour – not just on that awful night, but ever since the two of them had become friendly – had been childish in the extreme. And in the end it had led to disaster and to her, Sandie, losing the young man she had come to love – and to depend on – so very much. It could be said that it served her right, but it had brought so much grief to other people as well – to Greg's parents and to Duncan. He had been so very fond of Greg.

She found her thoughts often straying towards Duncan. The strange thing was, she had always liked and admired him, and she knew, deep down, he had never done anything to make her change her opinion of him. He had always been kind to her, courteous and helpful, and there could not be a music teacher to compare with him, not anywhere. And what had he received from her in return? Resentment and moodiness, rudeness at times, all adding up to behaviour that would be more understandable in a twelve or thirteen year old. Sandie, at last, was growing up, and she knew it. She admitted to herself that over the past year she had been nothing more than a selfish, stupid child. It was time now to admit it to others as well.

She had resented Duncan chiefly, she supposed, because he was not her father. And she had resented the idea that her mother could ever fall in love again. She knew now that her mum and Duncan did love one another very much. Greg had told her they did and he had thought it was a good thing that her mother and Duncan should get married. They both deserved a fresh start and to find some happiness in life together.

She realised, now, that she might have idealised her father, Peter, in her mind. She had raised him up on a pedestal, refusing to admit there could be anyone as admirable as him, or that her mother could ever love anyone else as much. It was true enough that her dad had been a great fellow in every way, a loving husband and a wonderful father, but he was gone. He had been dead now for ten years or so, and Sandie knew it was time to move on. Not to forget about him, but to face up to the fact that her mother was ready for a new relationship.

One of her chief worries at the moment was that she, Sandie, might have messed things up completely for them. Not only did her mother not mention Duncan, but she was no longer wearing her engagement ring. Sandie had noticed, but she had not asked her about it. She found herself hoping they had not split up; and yet that was the thing she had wanted – or had thought she had wanted – and which she had tried to bring about by her moody and rebellious behaviour. Sandie knew there were a lot of broken relationships to be mended when she got out of hospital. For the first time in her life she was starting to think more about other people than about herself.

It felt strange to be home again. Sandie had not realised how weak and wobbly she would feel away from the hospital environment. Her various cuts and bruises were healing, she had had the stitches removed from the gash on her forehead, but her arm was still in plaster and she suffered, now and again, from headaches and still gave way to bouts of weeping and self-reproach. Her mother did everything she could to comfort her and help her to return to as normal a life as possible; cooking her the meals she most enjoyed and encouraging her to invite her friends round – Lindsay and Paula, and Veronica Jarvis, who now seemed completely recovered from her trauma. Sandie felt the two of them had a lot in common; they had both lost someone they had loved. Veronica's priest had not died, of course, but Sandie could imagine how she must have felt at losing him. Veronica was looking to the future, though. Maybe, one day, she would be able to do so as well.

Yes, her mum was great, and Sandie was beginning to realise how much she loved her, and how much her mother had always loved and cared for her. But Mum looked sad; in spite of her smiles and cheery chatter her eyes were sad, and Sandie thought she knew the reason.

'You're not wearing your ring, Mum,' she said to her, when she had been home for a few days.

'Oh, you've noticed? No, I'm not, love, not at the moment.'

'Of course I've noticed,' said Sandie. 'Just as I've noticed Duncan doesn't come round any more. I'm not really surprised at that. He won't want to see me. I expect I'd remind him too much of Greg. But you don't go to see him either, do you? You've not split up, have you?'

'I'm not sure, love. For the moment, I suppose we have.'

'But why?' Sandie cried. Her mother did not answer. She just smiled sadly at her and shook her head. 'I know why,' Sandie went on. 'It's because of me, isn't it? Because of the way I've behaved. Not just on that night, but for ages before that. I'm sorry, Mum. I told you to tell Duncan how sorry I was. I don't want you to split up because of me. It isn't fair. You should be happy together. I know you used to be.'

'Sandie, listen. It's nothing to do with you, honestly. Well, maybe just a little, but Duncan and I . . . we feel we are to blame, chiefly, for what happened. When you found us in bed together, it was just as much of a shock to me as it was for you. I'm not surprised you reacted the way you did. I'd always said to you – or if I hadn't actually said it, it was what I'd implied – that you shouldn't do that sort of thing until after you were married. And it's what I really believe, Sandie love. But it just happened. There had been so many awful things, and I was in need of comfort, I suppose. Your Grandma Lily dying, and then my father's stroke.'

'And I was excluded from school,' added Sandie quietly.

'Well, yes, there was that as well, dear. It all added up. And Duncan and I found ourselves making love. I'm so sorry that you had to find us like that.'

'There's no need to apologise, Mum. Why should you? What for? You've not done anything wrong. I was silly and childish to act like that. I told you before that I was sorry, and I've got over it now, honestly I have. I want you and Duncan to be together again, to be happy.'

'Oh, I don't know whether there's much hope of that, love. As I said, we feel we are largely to blame. What we did, it upset you very much, and then Greg got upset too, didn't he, and . . . well, we all know what happened. Duncan feels as though he will never forgive himself. He looked on Greg almost as his own son.'

'But Mum,' cried Sandie, 'you can't look at it like that! Of course it wasn't your fault. It was an accident, wasn't it? That's what you told me when I said it was my fault. You said I didn't mean it to happen – well, neither did you.'

'No, that's true, love. But we can't help the way we feel, can we? Perhaps in time we might be able to stop torturing ourselves. Duncan felt so guilty he even thought he ought to tell Hazel and Alan about our part in it.'

'No, Mum! That's stupid,' said Sandie emphatically. 'What would be the point? It'd only make them feel worse. It would spoil your friendship with them, and it won't bring Greg back, will it?'

'I haven't seen Hazel and Alan since the funeral,' said Abbie musingly. 'It was a good friendship, but I don't know whether it will ever be resumed. I can't face them, not yet.'

'You should try and see Duncan, though. I expect he's

461

missing you just as much as you're missing him. You are, aren't you, Mum?'

'Yes, I dare say I am.' Abbie felt, however, that this was part of her punishment, but she could not say so to Sandie. 'I can't see him yet – we agreed. Perhaps in time, I don't know. You're feeling a little better now, are you, Sandie? In your mind, I mean. You're not still thinking you were the cause of it all?'

Sandie shook her head. 'No, not really. I never told you, Mum – I knew you'd worry when I was out with him – but Greg wasn't a very good driver. He drove fast and he was careless sometimes. It was odd, because he was usually so sensible.'

Abbie smiled wryly. 'Yes, it's amazing how a man's personality can change when he gets behind the wheel of a car. Women as well, I suppose, but mainly men. So . . . he was rather reckless?'

'He could be. We were lucky we hadn't been in an accident before. Anyway, I thought I'd tell you.'

Abbie sighed. 'Yes. Maybe we should try to stop apportioning blame. No matter what we say, we can't change what has happened. We must look forward, Sandie, if we can. You have all your life ahead of you.'

'So have you, Mum,' said Sandie. 'A lot of it anyway.'

Chapter 29

Sandie knew it was up to her to see that her mother did not waste her life, or spend the rest of it in regret. In spite of what Mum might say to the contrary, Sandie knew that what had gone wrong between her and Duncan was largely due to her own awful behaviour. She pondered about the problem for several days, then made up her mind that, however difficult it might be, she had to do something about it.

Her arm was still in plaster, but she was able to get about a little. She had walked to the library and the local shops, and had been to see her Grandad Horsfall. But this would be the first time she had been on a bus. It would mean two buses, in fact, to get to Duncan's house, one into town and then another along Church Street and Whitegate Drive. It was Saturday morning so she guessed he would be at home. It was the time she had used to have her music lesson . . . following Greg's, she reminded herself with a stab of pain. Perhaps Duncan had now got other pupils in the vacant couple of hours; he always had a waiting list. If so she would wait until he was free. Her mother thought she was going to meet Lindsay. A white lie was excusable under the circumstances, she told herself.

It felt strange to be travelling on a bus again. It was awkward coping with a purse and money with only one arm, but the bus conductors were very helpful, assisting her on and off the vehicle and sorting out her coins. She knew she could not let herself in at Duncan's back door as she had used to do when she went for her music lessons, so she rang the front door bell and waited. She almost left when there was, at first, no answer. Her courage was failing, but just as she was half-turning to go away the door opened and there was Duncan.

'Sandra.' To say that he looked surprised was an understatement. He looked as though she was the last person on earth he had expected to see. But his look of shock, almost of trepidation, she thought, was soon replaced by a quiet smile and the words 'Come in. What a surprise.' At least he was smiling a little and he had not shut the door in her face. 'I was upstairs, reading. Do come up and we'll have a chat.' She felt somewhat heartened as she followed him up the stairs and into his comfortable sitting room.

'Well, Sandie.' He looked at her steadily as she stood on the threshold of the room. 'You've not come for a lesson, have you?' There was a slight twinkle in his eyes, not so pronounced as it had used to be, but it was something that it was there at all.

'No.' She gave a nervous laugh, tapping the plaster on her arm. 'I've messed things up, haven't I? But I hope I'll play again, and I hope you'll teach me again, too.'

He did not answer. There was a few seconds' silence before he said, 'Come and sit down, Sandie. We need to talk, don't we? Is that why you've come to see me, because of the music lessons?'

'No, not really.' She shook her head. 'No, it's not that at all. It's my mum. I'm worried about her and—'

'She's not ill, is she?' She could tell by the look of concern on Duncan's face that he still cared, very much. 'There's nothing wrong, is there? I mean, apart from . . .'

'Apart from her still being upset about Greg and everything? No, she's not ill. But she misses seeing you. I know she does. And I want you to be together again. I've told Mum that as well, but she says she feels guilty and she's blaming herself and so are you, and that it's all your fault,

464

both of you, and I've tried to tell her that it isn't.' Her words were falling over one another and her eyes were beginning to fill up with tears, which she hastily blinked away. She was trying to stop all this stupid crying. 'Oh, Mr Hendy, Duncan, I'm really sorry about everything and I want it to be all right again. I know it can't ever be all right, because of Greg, but I don't want you and my mum to fall out because of me. I know it was my fault, no matter what she says. I was horrid to you and I'm really sorry because my mum loves you, I know she does.'

'And I love her too, Sandie,' said Duncan gently. 'We haven't split up because I have stopped loving her, nor was it because of you – at least, not entirely,' he added in an undertone. He crossed the room and came to sit next to her on the settee, taking hold of her hand. 'Yes, we've been blaming ourselves for our part in what happened. But I've been doing a lot of thinking, and I've realised it's time that we stopped apportioning blame, all of us.'

Sandie looked at him in surprise. 'That's what my mum said. Those were her exact words.'

'Yes, great minds think alike. It's a cliché, I know. But your mother and I are really very close. We decided we needed some time apart, and at first – yes – maybe it did seem to us that our love had died, or at least had taken a severe battering. But you say you think she misses me?'

'Of course she does, and I want you to come back. But you said it wasn't entirely because of me, so that means it *was* my fault, a bit of it, anyway? I did cause trouble, I know I did, but I'm sorry and I won't do it again, honestly I won't. I was a silly little girl, but I've grown up now, Duncan.'

'You've had to grow up very quickly, my dear, haven't you?' said Duncan, looking at her kindly. 'And in the worst possible way; losing someone you loved very much. I know you loved Greg and he loved you. You were both very young, but that was not to say you couldn't feel true love. And nothing will ever, ever be able to take that away from you, Sandie. Try and look at it like that, if you can. Your love for Greg will always be young and fresh and that's how you will remember him. It will never grow stale and commonplace, like so many love affairs do.'

'Because he's gone.'

'Yes, I know, and it's hard, isn't it? But there will be someone else for you someday. There's sure to be. You are very young, and you won't always be sad.'

Duncan was being so kind Sandie felt she could hardly bear it, after the way she had behaved. 'But what about me?' she cried. 'I was so awful and caused such a lot of trouble. You won't let it stop you making it up with my mum, will you?'

Duncan shook his head slowly. 'No. I thought at one time that you might come between us, that you might never accept me. Your mother had doubts about it as well, more so than I did at first. But I know differently now. I can see how you have changed, Sandie. You've grown up, like you say.' He smiled at her, but his eyes were still a little sad. 'Listen, my dear. I know I can never take the place of your father, not would I want to. He will always have a special place in your heart, as Greg will. But we have to move on and make new friendships, new relationships. We mustn't keep looking back.'

Sandie nodded. 'I know that now. Losing Greg has made me look at everything differently. I know you're not my dad, and I know you weren't trying to take his place, but I do want you to marry my mum.'

'You're sure?'

'Yes, very sure. But it isn't really anything to do with me, is it? It's up to you and Mum.'

'But we'll all have to live together, and it's important we should get on well, isn't it? Look on me as a very good friend, Sandie, rather than trying to see me as a father figure. And you know, don't you, that I'll always be there to help you and give you advice if you want me to, both you and Simon?'

466

'I know you were always good to me,' said Sandie meekly. 'So you'll come back, will you? You'll come and see my mum?'

'Yes, I will. I was going to come soon anyway, but I didn't know how she would feel. I was very abrupt with her after the . . . accident. I didn't behave very well towards her, because I was so distressed, of course. I want her to understand.'

'I'm sure she will,' said Sandie. 'But you won't keep on thinking it was your fault, will you? I was telling Mum – Greg wasn't a very good driver, you know. I'm not just saying that; he really wasn't.'

'I know, I know.' Duncan looked down at the floor, shaking his head sadly before he looked at Sandie again. 'His mother and father are blaming themselves, too, especially Alan. He wishes now they'd never given Greg that car for his eighteenth birthday. They thought he was so sensible – and so he was in every other way – but rather a madcap driver apparently. They'd seen him zoom down the road, like a bat out of hell, as Alan put it, but they knew they couldn't forbid him to drive. They just kept warning him to be careful.' He shrugged slightly. 'So, you see, we all feel we were to blame, one way or another. But now it's time to stop.' His eyes were a little less sad. There was even a glint of optimism there as he said, 'You'll play the piano again, won't you, Sandie?'

'I hope so,' she replied. 'If this arm mends properly. I'm going back to school soon, to finish the term. And then I'll be having my plaster off. I'll just have to wait and see. I want to play again, if you'll teach me again, Duncan?'

'I don't see why not.' He smiled at her. 'I think you'd better be off home now, hadn't you? No more buses though; I'll run you back.'

'OK, thanks.' Sandie's arm was aching and she didn't feel like coping with two buses again. 'But I didn't want my mum to know I'd been here. She might think I was interfering.'

'Very well then. I'll drop you at the end of your avenue. But I'll be round before very long, Sandie. Maybe tonight. And thank you for coming, my dear. You've helped me a great deal.'

There was a ring at the door bell at about seven o'clock that evening and Sandie felt herself becoming a wee bit nervous. It would be Duncan. Oh, she did hope so much that all would go well for him and Mum. She was very surprised, therefore, when her mother ushered into the sitting room not Duncan, but Ian Webster.

'A visitor for you, Sandie,' she said. 'I'll leave you two to have a chat. Would you like a cup of tea, Ian, or would orange juice or Tizer be more to your liking?'

'Oh, Tizer please, Mrs Horsfall,' he replied with a grin. 'Cycling's thirsty work. I've come on my bike,' he said to Sandie as her mother went off to the kitchen.

'It's . . . nice to see you, Ian,' she said, rather nonplussed. 'Sit down. It's a long way for you to come, on your bike.' Greg had used to make the journey quite regularly until he got his car, she remembered, but it was even further from Marton Moss where Ian lived.

'Not really. I cycle quite a lot.' He shuffled his feet a little embarrassedly. 'And I wanted to come and see you. I've brought you these.' He thrust a box of chocolates at her. They were Black Magic; he had guessed right. She preferred plain chocolates to milk. 'And some books. I hope they're to your taste, and that you haven't already read them. I thought you might be getting a bit bored.' He sat down on the chair opposite her, perching on the edge with his long legs bent at a strange angle, looking not at all relaxed.

'Thank you. It's very kind of you,' said Sandie. There was an Agatha Christie, a Ngaio Marsh and a Margery Allingham, all the sort of detective novels she enjoyed and ones which she had not read. They looked at one another, smiling a little uneasily.

'I wanted to come before,' said Ian, 'but I thought I'd

better wait a bit, that it might be too soon. I know how upset you must have been about Greg, and still are, I expect.'

She nodded. 'Yes, I'm still very sad, of course. Even now I find it hard to believe he's not here, that he won't come walking through the door. But I'm gradually trying to pick up the pieces and get on with my life. You've got to, haven't you?' She gave a quirky little smile.

'We were all shocked to bits at school,' said Ian. 'That's what we felt like – what you've just said – that we couldn't believe he wasn't there any more. Greg was a great guy, one of the best. It seems so unfair.' He glanced at her apologetically. 'Sorry, I don't mean to upset you.'

'It's OK, Ian. I've got to talk about him sometimes. It helps.'

'It's putting a damper on the end of term, I can tell you. Fortunately we were at the end of our A-levels, more or less, or we would have found it hard to concentrate.'

'Oh yes, of course, it's your A-level year, isn't it? Same as Greg. I'd almost forgotten. Mine are next year.' It was the first time since the accident that she had given them a thought. 'So you'll be leaving school in a week or two. What are you going to do then? Are you going to university?'

'Yes. I've got a place at Leeds, providing my A-levels come up to scratch, that is. I'm going to do a science degree.'

'And then what?'

'Oh, I'm not sure. It's a long way ahead. Teaching's an option. My mum says it's a good steady job, but I'm not so sure I really want to teach. My dad wanted me to go into the market-garden business with him at one time, but I think he's given up on that idea. Janet, my sister, is more interested in horticulture than I am.'

'What's your line, then?'

'Oh, chemistry and biology. I did have an idea that I might like to be a pharmacist, have my own business one day – but I'll just have to see how things go. What about you? What do you want to do after A-levels?'

Sandie was silent. School and studying seemed so distant. She knew she would have to go back to school soon and in a way she was looking forward to it; it would be good to see all the girls again. But as for any future plans, they had all been knocked haywire. She had once considered music college, until she had had that wild idea of becoming a pop star. But now, she had no idea of the direction she wanted her life to take. 'I don't really know,' she said, realising it sounded feeble. 'I had thought about music college, but now, with all this happening, I haven't,' she shook her head confusedly, 'I haven't been able to think straight.'

'Of course you haven't.' Ian seemed to understand perfectly. They were interrupted for a moment by Sandie's mother returning with two glasses of Tizer and a plate of biscuits. They smiled at each other and at her a little awkwardly as she put them down on a small table.

'Put the stereogram on, Sandie, if you want to,' she said. 'I know my records are not to your taste, but you could fetch some of yours from upstairs, couldn't you? Make yourself at home, Ian. I'll see you before you go.'

'D'you want to?' asked Sandie when her mother had gone. 'Listen to a record?'

'I'm not bothered.'

'No, neither am I. I've got out of the habit lately. I haven't bought a record for ages. Have you got any new ones?'

Ian leaned back in the chair, more relaxed now, and they chatted about The Beatles and The Rolling Stones, Bob Dylan and Elvis Presley; about the relative merits of Radio Luxembourg and the pirate radio station, Radio Caroline, and about *Ready, Steady Go* and *Juke Box Jury*. He was so easy to chat to, thought Sandie. It was ages since she had felt so relaxed and at ease with someone. Not since Greg. She found her thoughts flying automatically to Greg, but as they did so she tried to push them away. She would not make any comparisons and it was too soon to be thinking about a friendship with anyone else.

470

So when Ian asked her, a little while later, if she would like to go to the pictures with him one night next week, she felt only a teeniest tinge of regret as she shook her head. 'No, I don't think so, Ian. Thanks all the same, but not yet.' She realised that might be it; he might not ask her again. All the same it was too soon . . . too soon.

'That's OK; I understand,' he said cheerily. 'It was just an idea. But I do understand how you feel, about you and Greg. Some other time, perhaps?'

'Yes, perhaps,' she said, smiling at him.

He left a few minutes later after popping into the back room to say goodbye to Abbie. 'Thanks, Mrs Horsfall, for the drink and everything. See you again sometime.'

'Yes, I hope so, Ian. It's nice to see you. Will you show him out, Sandie?' Maybe her mother thought they had something private to say to one another, but they hadn't. Sandie gave a gasp of surprise as she opened the front door to let Ian out, because there was Duncan coming up the path. She should not have felt surprised; she had half-expected him, but she did so hope it would go well for him and Mum. She introduced them. 'This is Ian Webster, and this is Mr Hendy . . . Duncan. He's my music teacher and he's a friend of my mum.'

They shook hands formally, saying, 'How do you do?' then Ian collected his bike from where he had propped it against the fence and wheeled it down the path.

'Cheerio, Sandie. Be seeing you.'

'Yes, see you, Ian.'

Duncan raised his eyebrows. 'A new friend, Sandie?'

'Oh no, nothing like that,' she said hurriedly. 'Well, yes, I suppose he's a friend, sort of. He was in Greg's year actually. You'd better come in, Duncan. I'll tell my mum you're here. I didn't say anything about coming to see you.'

Hearing voices, Abbie appeared at the door. 'Oh. Duncan. What a lovely surprise.' Her voice sounded a little flat, however, as though she was not entirely sure that the surprise was a nice one. 'Come in.' She was ushering him into the sitting room almost as though he were a casual acquaintance, thought Sandie.

'I'll leave you two to have a chat,' she said, just as her mother had said to her and Ian an hour or so ago. 'But before I go, I just want to tell you something, Mum. Ian asked me to go to the pictures with him next week, but I said no. It's too soon after Greg. I just wanted you to know.'

Abbie and Duncan looked at one another a little unsurely after Sandie had gone into the other room. 'He looks a nice sort of lad,' said Duncan. 'She just introduced us. Ian Webster?'

'Yes, he's Jim's son, Jim and Sylvia's,' said Abbie. 'You know, from Marton Moss?'

'Oh yes,' said Duncan. 'I thought the name sounded familiar. Where you worked when you were a Land Girl?'

'Yes, that's right.' Duncan was silent for a second or two. He did not mention her engagement to Jim, but she was sure that was what he was thinking about. Or maybe he was thinking how ironical it would be if Sandie and Ian were to become friendly. Abbie had thought so too. 'Ian knew Greg at school, apparently,' she went on. 'He was at the funeral.'

'Oh yes, of course. I thought I'd seen him before.'

'I knew he liked our Sandie. I could tell when we went round that time. I'm not surprised he's asked her out, but do you know? I'm glad she's said no. It would have done her good, I'm sure, but like she says, it's too soon. I admire her so much for saying that. It shows she really did love Greg and that she's not just thinking about herself. I do believe she's growing up, Duncan.'

'Yes, I know she is,' replied Duncan. 'I noticed a great change in her when—' He stopped abruptly.

'You've seen her then?'

Duncan sighed. 'Yes. I can't lie to you, Abbie. Sandie didn't want me to say anything – she thought you might say she was interfering – but she came to see me this morning.

She was concerned about you . . . and me.' He took a step towards her – they were still standing – and took hold of both her hands in his. 'Yes, she has grown up, Abbie. I'm only sorry it took such an awful tragedy to make it happen. But she's quite a different girl now.'

'So you've come because Sandie asked you to?'

'No. It might seem like that, but I was coming anyway. Please believe me. I was just a little afraid as to how you might receive me. I behaved badly, I know that, Abbie. I was so thoughtless and uncaring. But I've never stopped caring about you, my dear. It was just the shock of it all, and the guilt. I couldn't rid myself of the guilt.'

'No, neither could I, at first,' said Abbie quietly. 'Neither could Sandie.'

'It's something we'll have to live with, all of us,' said Duncan. 'Hazel and Alan as well. They keep saying if only they hadn't bought him the car, if only he hadn't been driving so fast . . . but you can go on and on blaming yourselves, or somebody else. And it's no use. We have to carry on and live our lives, Abbie.' He smiled at her, so very tenderly. 'I love you so much. I've realised just how much in the weeks I've been away from you.'

'I love you too, Duncan,' replied Abbie. 'I was longing for you to come. I've missed you.'

'Yes, Sandie said you were missing me.'

'Did she?' Abbie smiled fondly. 'Yes, she's a good girl. She won't cause any more trouble. That is, if we . . .'

'If we get married? Oh yes, my love; we're going to get married. We're going to carry on with our plans again. What do you say?'

'I say yes,' whispered Abbie before his lips came down on hers. They kissed tenderly, then again, more fervently. They had been apart for only a few weeks, but it seemed much longer.

'It won't always be easy, my darling,' said Duncan as they drew apart. 'Let's not pretend there won't be any problems.

Sandie's still a teenager, and so is Simon. There will be ups and downs, and plenty of them, I dare say, but we love one another, and that's all that really matters, isn't it?'

'Yes,' said Abbie. 'In the end . . . all you need is love.'